my dearest darkest

KAYLA COTTINGHAM

sourcebooks
fire

Published by Sourcebooks Fire, an imprint of Sourcebooks
P.O. Box 4410, Naperville, Illinois 60567-4410
(630) 961-3900
sourcebooks.com

Cataloging-in-Publication data is on file with the Library of Congress.

Printed and bound in Canada.
MBP 10 9 8 7 6 5 4 3 2

To my fifteen-year-old self—
I hope you'd be proud of what your idea became.
And not too surprised by how much gayer it is.

Hell is a teenage girl.

—Diablo Cody, *Jennifer's Body*

one

While all towns have their ghosts, Rainwater's were special. They sank through its submerged sea caves and slithered up its cliffs. They bounced around its caverns and tunnels like electrical pulses in a brain, echoing memories of footsteps and laughter and screams through the ground and into the towering evergreen trees. The peninsula had a habit of keeping things long after they were gone.

And on May 16, when Finch Chamberlin crossed the town line into Rainwater, Maine, it decided to keep her.

"Terrible-looking campus, huh?" her father said, meeting her eyes in the rearview mirror. He nodded up at the soaring spires of Ulalume Academy as they came into view beyond the trees.

"Oh! I...I think it's pretty," Finch defended, looking down at her shoes.

"He's joking, sweetie." Finch's mother shot him a sharp look. "It's lovely."

Ulalume's towering, Gothic campus rose out of the fog-shrouded trees. The peninsula Rainwater rested on was just under forty square miles, vaguely crescent-shaped, with a rocky coastline and the occasional pebble beach. A single causeway led in and out.

The Chamberlins left their car in the guest parking lot. Finch's mother pulled her into a sideways hug, squeezing her upper arm while her father led the way, more interested in getting to the student services office on time for Finch's final audition for Ulalume's renowned music program than the fact that his daughter looked ready to crawl out of her skin.

"You okay?" her mother asked.

Finch chewed her lower lip. "Nervous."

"About?"

"Everything," Finch whispered, barely audible. She might as well tattoo it on her forehead. Or sew it on her jackets as a warning. DO NOT LOOK AT OR APPROACH OR THINK ABOUT, PLEASE. THANK YOU.

Her mom kissed the crown of her head. "You'll do fine, little bird. I'm here."

Finch closed her eyes, took a breath, and nodded. "You're here."

She was trying not to think about the fact that she wouldn't be for long, though. Assuming this audition scored her a spot in the music program, she'd be living here for the foreseeable future. Ulalume was a boarding school that housed three hundred of the most talented prodigies—and trust fund babies—that the administration had handpicked to join their illustrious institution. After two years of rejections, she was hoping this would finally be the year she got in—and procured the scholarship she so desperately needed.

Finch and her family stepped into the student services office a minute later. It was uncomfortably warm, and the persistent humidity from outside seemed to permeate the building's ivy-covered stone walls. Finch dabbed at her forehead with the back of her hand. She was glad she could play off her excessive sweating as weather-related.

"Oh—hey there! You must be Finch," the woman at the front desk said in a faint Maine accent, looking up from a glossy issue of *Cosmo*.

Finch's father confirmed, and an even bigger smile broke across the woman's face.

"Congratulations on the audition." She came around the desk and gestured for them to follow her. "I'll show you to the auditorium."

A twisted smile cut across Kyra Astor's face. "So, you gonna share some of that tequila or do you need the bottle for a couple hundred more selfies?"

Selena St. Clair, phone in hand, paused long enough to pull off a red Louis Vuitton pump and throw it at her. The shoe missed her by centimeters and hit the wall with a loud *thump*.

Kyra broke into hysterical laughter.

The two of them had snuck off to their favorite drinking spot on campus: the orchestra pit beneath the auditorium. The musty space was full of discarded music stands and broken instrument parts, but with most of the year's musical events wrapped up, it was quiet and private.

In fact, the school only had one major event left before

summer: the Founder's Ball, Ulalume's end-of-semester celebration, and Selena had a head start on pregaming. In one hand was a bottle of expensive tequila, and in the other, her phone.

She took a swig from the bottle, then slid her phone back in her purse. "Did you invite the others yet?"

"Amber's still with her tutor working on some paper," Kyra said with an eye roll, "and Risa's pregaming elsewhere."

She held out a hand for the tequila. Selena passed it to her.

Their fingers touched for a beat, a flutter of warmth passing between them. Selena's cheeks flared pink while Kyra swung the bottle up and took a sip. Tequila dribbled down her chin and into the neckline of her silver dress.

Selena tore her eyes away, busying herself with examining her fingernails. She'd had them done yesterday, painted the same shade of ballet slipper–pink that most of the girls in her year would have on for the ball. It was prim, proper—expected. Which made it all the more jarring when Selena remembered how her preened fingers had looked woven through Kyra's red tresses the night before.

Her blush worsened. She was lucky the pit was covered and dark.

"So I'm stuck with you," Selena said, successfully faking an airy, disappointed tone. She steadied her breathing. The mask went back on. "Text them. Risa will cancel if she knows I want her here."

Kyra coughed out a small laugh to cover up her wince. Selena knew exactly where to press her fingers to hit bruises—to hit every girl at Ulalume's bruises.

"Selena, you don't—"

The doors to the auditorium flew open. A tangle of voices flooded the echoing space, instantly drowning out whatever Kyra had been meaning to say.

Selena's heart thundered. Ulalume had strict rules about alcohol—students could get in serious trouble just for having it in their rooms, much less actively drinking on school grounds.

Kyra's eyes bugged and she whispered, "What do we do?"

Selena threw out her hands and furiously mouthed back, "How should I know?"

"Is it okay if we stay and watch?" a woman asked, getting closer to the pit.

"Of course," a voice replied. Selena recognized it—Mr. Rizzio, the head of the music department. "Finch, if you want to head onto the stage, I'll set up the camera so I can record your audition for the admissions committee to review. Then we can get started."

Selena cursed, then reached for the bottle. "Give it to me!"

Kyra shoved the bottle into her hands.

Soft footsteps creaked above them as someone crossed to the grand piano at the edge of the stage. The house lights went down, and Selena lost sight of Kyra in the darkness.

"It's just an audition," Selena whispered. "We can hide until they're done."

"I'm ready when you are," a quiet voice said onstage.

Something about it made Selena pause. Even with the blood pounding in her ears and sweat slicking her hands. The voice was small, barely more than a chirp, but there was a sweetness to it she couldn't describe.

"She's a prodigy, you know," a man in the front row said. "You're going to be amazed at what she can do. All the other girls her age are out there chasing boys, but our Finch—she's got her keys and that's all she needs. Nothing can distract her."

Selena closed her eyes. *Finch.*

"Thank you, Mr. Chamberlin," Mr. Rizzio said. He called to the girl onstage, "We're all set down here. You can get started whenever you're ready, Finch."

Selena pressed her back against the wall of the pit, trying to keep her breathing even. Auditions didn't usually take more than fifteen minutes—they'd be out of there in no time.

Up above, Finch hit the first few notes. They were gentle, like wind chimes in quick succession. But as her fingers glided across the keys, the melody began to swell, growing louder and more intense. It wasn't the sort of song Selena would have expected from such a timid-voiced girl—the energy of it was huge, imposing, growing with a torrent of sound that echoed through the auditorium with a resounding punch that made Selena's heart quicken.

"She's really good," Selena whispered.

Selena could barely make out Kyra throwing her hands in the air. "*Literally* who cares?"

Selena rolled her eyes, then settled in, letting the sound of Finch's song wash over her.

It wasn't particularly long—maybe four minutes—before Finch slammed down on the final notes, a reverberating echo rippling across the auditorium.

"Wonderful," Mr. Rizzio said. "Next, we'll move onto the improvisational part of the aud—"

Without warning, a resonant *bang* burst through the silence as Kyra nudged a music stand at the wrong angle, knocking it into the others and creating a disastrous domino effect. Kyra let out a choked yelp while Selena cursed colorfully under her breath.

The lights flickered on a few moments later and the entrance to the pit opened to reveal Mr. Rizzio standing with his arms crossed, eyebrows up. Selena, out of options, slid the tequila bottle into her dress sleeve and held it behind her back.

"You two," Mr. Rizzio said. "Come up here, please."

Kyra and Selena exchanged a look, Kyra's already pale skin now ghost-white. As they stood from the pile of collapsed music stands, Selena did her best to conceal the bottle-shaped bulge in her sleeve.

The upper part of the auditorium, with its art deco–style, gaudy light fixtures, carved wood accents, and cushy velvet seats, greeted them along with the horrified faces of two people Selena assumed were Finch's parents. Selena glanced over her shoulder—Finch sat at the piano a few feet away, mouth agape.

She was white, small, and waifish with the biggest set of luminous eyes Selena had ever seen, like two searchlights singling her out from across the room. Her hair was elbow-length and chestnut brown, an uncanny contrast to her pale skin.

For a brief second, Selena forgot how far up shit creek she was.

"Do you have a good reason as to why you're in the orchestra pit? During an *audition?*" Mr. Rizzio asked, sounding exhausted.

Selena and Kyra exchanged another look. Selena lied, "Um. We were looking for our friend's violin that she left down there. We didn't mean to interrupt."

"We're super sorry," Kyra agreed, nodding vigorously. "Like, *beyond* sorry, can't even put into words how sor—"

Selena elbowed her, cutting her off.

"Right." Mr. Rizzio pinched the skin between his eyebrows. "Okay. I'm going to give you the benefit of the doubt and assume this is a simple misunderstanding—"

As Mr. Rizzio spoke, Selena gently shifted the tequila bottle in her sleeve, trying to hide it behind her arm so the shape was less visible. As she did, however, it slipped into her hand. She was barely able to catch it before it slid onto the floor, and her breath hitched.

Mr. Rizzio didn't notice.

Selena withheld a sigh of relief. *Thank goodn—*

"Is that…" a voice muttered behind her. "*Alcohol?*"

The second she said it, Finch clapped a hand over her mouth.

She hadn't meant to say that out loud.

The blond girl tensed. She was tall, with a slim, athletic build and natural waves in her golden hair. She was white, but had a natural warm tan to her skin that spoke to days spent lounging in the sun.

As Finch's words met her ear, the girl whipped around and shot her the most poisonous glare she'd ever seen. Even in that moment, though, Finch couldn't help but notice the sharp angle of her cheekbones and the straight slope of her nose—and the way her pretty red lips curled into a scowl.

Finch turned vibrantly red from her throat to her ears.

She stammered, "I—um—sorry—"

Mr. Rizzio let out a pained, world-weary sigh. "All right. Selena, show me your hands please."

Selena winced. After a beat, her tensed shoulders fell and,

averting her gaze to the floor, she let the bottle of tequila slide into her hand. She held it out to Mr. Rizzio.

He took the bottle softly from her hand, reading the label over the rim of his glasses before nodding to himself and letting out a breath.

"Okay. Selena, Kyra, I'm going to have you head to the headmistress's office. I'll meet you there once I finish up Finch's audition so we have a chance to discuss this and call your parents." He turned, meeting Finch and her parents' eyes. "Finch, Mr. and Mrs. Chamberlin—I cannot apologize enough for Miss St. Clair and Miss Astor's behavior. I promise you we don't tolerate this sort of thing at Ulalume."

Selena hung her head while the other girl—a white redhead with a long, sleek ponytail hanging down her back—looked to be on the verge of tears. She, too, turned and glared at Finch, only stopping when Selena waved her hand and summoned her to follow.

Just before they made it to the doors, Selena stopped and turned.

"I'm sorry for interrupting your audition," she told Finch, meeting her gaze with snake-green, kohl-rimmed eyes. "Good luck. Maybe I'll see you around next year."

She turned, heading out the door with her friend.

It swung closed behind her with a *bang*.

Finch tried to swallow, throat dry. *Why did that sound like a threat?*

"Well," Finch's mother said after a pregnant pause. "She seems…spirited."

"That's one word for it," her father said, narrowing his eyes.

But Finch didn't say anything. She was too caught up in the

sensation that radiated from her heart and into her limbs. It was like her skin had been stripped away, leaving her a ball of lightning and exposed nerves.

Selena St. Clair.

—————————

That night, the drive home from Rainwater took the Chamberlin family through the forest. Massive pine trees soared toward the sky, casting their needled branches out like girls twirling their skirts. Raindrops dripped from those needles as the downpour worsened, obscuring the already dark road. Night had fallen and swallowed up what was left of the visibility. Finch's father swore it wouldn't be a big deal.

Her mother turned around in the passenger seat, leaning her head against the headrest as she gave Finch a leisurely smile. "So? What do you think? And be honest—if Ulalume wasn't all it's cracked up to be, there's no pressure for you to go, even if you get in."

Finch was already half asleep. She blinked awake, yawning through her smile. "It was amazing—the brochures don't do it justice. And I think I did pretty good at the audition even with…"

She trailed off, the oily ball of guilt from earlier twisting in her gut. She really hadn't meant to snitch on that girl—she was just so surprised to see someone her age drinking that she'd been taken off guard. After being homeschooled her whole life and only interacting with people her age through music, she'd never known anyone who did that.

"Oh, don't worry about that," her mom said, waving her hand. "Plenty of kids at my high school got caught doing way worse and they were fine. I'm sure it's no big deal."

Finch bit her lip. It felt like a big deal—she certainly hadn't intended to make an enemy at Ulalume before she was even accepted.

"Those girls would be lucky to have a friend like you," her father reassured. "You could teach them a thing or two about focus and goals. Be a good influence."

Finch's mom shook her head at him, then corrected, "He's trying to say we're proud of you. And we'll support you no matter what happens with the admissions process."

Finch nodded to herself, thoughts far away. "I just...I've never wanted something so bad before. I feel like I'd give anything to get in."

"Anything?"

Finch blinked. It was strange—when she heard the word, her mother's mouth hadn't been moving. And her voice sounded a bit...off.

The car lurched as they sped onto a bridge over a pitch-black river Finch didn't know the name of.

Finch shrugged it off, nodding softly. "Yeah. Anything."

Her mother's face pinched, eyebrows pressed together. "What was that, Fi—?"

The words never fully made it out of her mouth, though. Because just then her father let out a strangled cry. He jerked the wheel to the side. In the flashing second before impact, Finch caught sight of a massive stag standing on the bridge.

It met her gaze with eight gleaming eyes.

The next moment, the scene turned toward the edge of the bridge, through the barrier, and into the river.

Finch shrieked.

A sickening crack rang out as metal hit water. Finch's head slammed against glass, dark spots spattering across her vision. Black water rushed through the jammed windows. The violent hiss of it merged with the Chamberlins' screams.

Finch wavered in and out of consciousness. Water poured into her lap, frigid, licking at her skin with a million pinprick tongues. She reached up, dabbing at the wetness in her hair. Red shone on her fingers for a second before the water pouring in through the roof washed it away.

This is a nightmare.

Her head was full of cotton and echoes.

Nightmares aren't supposed to hurt.

Finch's father banged his fist into the driver's-side window over and over until his knuckles bled. Each punch left a new red smear on the glass. Her mother screamed and bawled out nonsense commands. She shook her door handle violently. It was stuck.

Their crying was verging on hysterical. The water rose up to their necks.

It was so, so cold. Even through her fog, Finch felt it. The frigid water snapped her into focus.

Too cold. Death-cold.

Get out.

Get out.

Finch removed one of her heels, slamming it full-force into her window. Small cracks appeared in the glass while she struck it over and over and over. Her pulse went double-time, echoing in her head wound and her ears.

Get out.

The water tickled her chin. Her heart seemed to vibrate, not beat. Her desperation lacked words.

The car hit the bottom of the river with a jolt. Finch gasped in one last breath before she hit the window with all her might. The cracks spread out. There was a sound like ice separating.

The window shattered inward, and the river swallowed the rest of their air.

Water surged against Finch's eardrums, constricting them so they throbbed. She struggled at her seat belt, trying to pry the buckle free. She didn't have long—her panicked breathing had stolen most of the air in her system. She felt the crawling agony of organs starved.

Finally, her seat belt tore free. The current instantly threw her into the opposite window, knocking what little air she had left out of her mouth in a cascade of bubbles. Her lungs burned and spasmed.

Finch fought the current, clawing at the seat backs. Finally, she wrapped her hands around the sides of the window to push herself free. Remaining pieces of glass sliced her palms, sending curls of blood into the water. She'd gone too numb to feel it.

Get out. Or else—

In the front seat, her parents' movements slowed. Their seat belts were stuck. Her mother let out a cry that dwindled to bubbles. The next breath she took let the river flow into her throat.

Finch kicked desperately.

Or else.

Cold. Dark.

Alone.

She was going to die.

The water was thick with debris and silt. Even as she wriggled from the car, she found herself in darkness. Up and down were foreign concepts. Her chest burned like nothing she'd ever felt before. When she finally breathed, it was like a punch to the chest. Her brain short-circuited.

She would be trapped down here in the dark for the rest of eternity.

Help me, she begged no one in particular. *Please don't let me die.*

Sixty seconds passed before she drowned.

———————

Those final heartbeats, frantic like a hummingbird's wings, created an echo. They rippled, a subtle hum for a waiting ear to pick up.

And something did. Something that had been waiting for quite some time.

Its thousand eyes were already turned to the body in the river, with her bluing cheeks and crown of mud and twigs that tangled in her hair. Tiny bubbles still rose from her mouth, the last wriggling symptoms of life peeling away.

It remembered this moment, an echo of an echo, and it smiled.

Miles away from the river, the ground beneath the residents of Rainwater trembled. It was subtle enough that most didn't notice. Some of the girls at Ulalume paused, exchanging looks.

Selena St. Clair asked, "What the hell was that?"

And in the depths of the river, cold, dark and alone, Finch Chamberlin opened her eyes.

two

[three months later]

"I told you I could have taken the ferry," Selena grumbled, leaning her head against the car window as her mother simmered at the traffic. They hadn't so much as crept forward in almost twenty minutes. Outside, gray waves lapped against the causeway that had so rudely stolen Rainwater's status as an island and turned it into a town clinging to the mainland by its fingernails. Selena's eyes blurred, staring at the waves as she imagined how cold they'd be on a dismal day like this.

Roxane St. Clair gritted her teeth and swallowed the heat building in her chest. "I wanted to see you off."

"You wanted to meet Kyra," Selena corrected. "And berate her."

"*Berate?* Selena, I just want to ask her a few questions."

"What, and cross-examine her? This isn't a criminal defense court, she's my friend."

Roxane glanced at her. The sharp state of her eyebrows said otherwise.

"Friend. Pal. Buddy. *What?*"

"It's fine." Roxane looked back at the road. "When your mother and I first started dating, I said the same thing about her."

"I'm not dating Kyra."

"You took the train down to New York City to see her three separate times this summer."

"I'm not dating her! Can you lay off for five minutes?"

"Darling. Listen." Roxane sighed. "I get that part of being a teenager is experimenting with sex. I want to make sure that you're sleeping with a someone who respects you and knows that just because you're cisgender girls doesn't mean there aren't risks for sexually transmitted infe—"

She didn't have time to finish. Selena had already thrown her door open, stepping out onto the road. Her shoes clicked against the blacktop as she rounded the car to the trunk.

Roxane scowled, lips twisting in the particular St. Clair way that she had unwittingly passed on to her daughter. "What are you doing? Get back in the car! Selena Rose, for the love of god—"

Selena popped the trunk and yanked out her suitcase. After slamming the trunk shut, she came around to her mother's window and said, "There's a place to turn around half a mile up the road. Have a safe trip back to Boston."

"Good lord. Get back in the car before someone runs you over!"

Selena locked her jaw and turned, suitcase rolling behind her. She proceeded down the center of the road between the unending line of sports cars and minivans alike. Rainwater residents and Ulalume families alike watched her slack-jawed from inside their cars, whispering her name like a curse back and forth. Selena adjusted her heart-shaped sunglasses and tossed her hair over her shoulder, grinning at each of them as she passed.

She held up her hand and wiggled her fingers, a final goodbye to Roxane.

Her mother furiously laid on the horn, screaming out the open window until the sound faded behind Selena, replaced only by the waves, the wind, and her heels on the asphalt.

"You cannot be serious."

"*So* serious!" Amber Aldridge cheered, clapping her hands together. She threw them out in front of her as if displaying her masterpiece. Freshly back from her parents' McMansion in South Carolina, the mousy-haired, white heiress's accent was thicker than usual. Based on what Selena had seen of her Instagram, she'd spent the majority of her summer drinking spiked seltzer with her sisters while cruising on their father's boat near Hilton Head Island. "Private housing for the four of us right on the Ulalume campus, courtesy of my parents."

"It's…" Kyra began.

"A lighthouse," Risa Kikuchi finished, tucking a lock of shiny black hair behind her ear. She was the most recent addition to their friend group—the daughter of a middle-class family from Japan who'd enrolled at Ulalume her sophomore year. She'd befriended Selena in their AP Psychology class after she let Selena copy off her in exchange for invites to parties.

It turned out Selena was actually pretty good at AP Psych, and

Risa was a great person to lurk in the back of parties with, so their deal was much shorter-lived than their eventual friendship.

"Did your parents buy this?" Risa asked, her tone even. She was very good at sounding nonjudgmental while actively judging someone.

"Yeah!" Amber beamed. "Isn't it cute?"

"Cute would be a seaside cottage." Kyra blew out a breath. "We're gonna look like weird cliff hermits."

The four girls tilted their heads up to get a better view of their new home, a small shoebox building made of gray stone attached to Annalee Lighthouse, a towering giant that overlooked the craggy rocks at the edge of Ulalume's grounds. The waves crashed into the cliffs to their right. Selena was having a hard time hearing the other girls over the sound.

"Come on," Amber whined, "I think it's cool." She pouted, tightening her fingers around the handle of her watermelon-print umbrella. "Right, Selena?"

Selena popped the minty gum she'd been blowing bubbles with for the last hour. "I get the top room."

"Really?" Kyra said, a little too quickly to be subtle. When Risa shot her a look, she added, cheeks reddening, "B-But you won't be anywhere near the rest of us."

"I value my privacy."

The others looked at each other before following Selena toward the lighthouse. She nudged the key into the lock and shoved her shoulder against the front door to force it open.

The last occupants had left their furniture and decorations, a typical Cape Cod aesthetic of interior decorating. Signs about enjoying the beach and living by the sea adorned nearly every wall. Seashells and sea glass took up most surfaces. The whole place smelled like artificial lemon—Amber's family must've had it professionally cleaned before they arrived.

"I wanna show y'all something," Amber said, gesturing for them to follow her up the stairs. The other girls exchanged glances before dropping their stuff in the living room and following her to the spiral staircase on the far wall.

The stairs led them up into the turret of the lighthouse, passing a single room that Selena decided would be hers. The air grew colder as they ascended, the wind blowing in through the stone.

At the top, Amber pushed open a hatch and the girls followed her up into the top of the lighthouse. The light had been removed, instead allowing for an open, glassed-in space that overlooked the entire peninsula. The girls took in the view of the mist over the dark sea, the dripping trees, and the spires of Ulalume Academy rising out of the fog. On a clear day they'd be able to see all the way to downtown Rainwater.

"See?" Amber said, grinning. "It's like gazing down at our little kingdom."

Selena withheld a comment about how deeply cringey that sounded, turning her attention to her buzzing phone.

It was a text from Griffin Sergold, one of two close friends Selena had at Rainwater High, the only public school on the peninsula. He'd been a bit more than a friend at one point, but these days the only sort of hookup he provided was liquor.

> People are meeting up in the tunnels tonight if you'd like to join. I have your favorite rosé.

"Not sure if you all had plans for this evening," Selena said as she texted Griffin back, "But Griffin says there's a party in the tunnels."

"Oh!" Amber lit up, bouncing in place. "I can wear my new dress! My mom got it for me in Hong Kong last weekend—the slit goes all the way to the thigh."

"You want to wear a *dress* to the tunnels." Risa's eyes slid to her, one eyebrow cocked. "The service tunnels under the school. The ones that students aren't supposed to go to because they've been deemed unsafe? And, depending on who you ask, haunted?"

Amber held up her hands. "What?"

Kyra's frown tightened. "Griffin, huh?"

"Oh, come on." Selena gently elbowed her. "It'll be *fun*."

"Yeah!" Amber grinned up at Selena, as if looking for confirmation on her own opinion. Sometimes Selena wondered if it got tiring agreeing with literally everything she said. "So we're going, right?"

"Fine," Kyra mumbled. "But I'm taking some of that rosé he always gets you."

"Fair enough." Selena bit her lip and waggled her eyebrows at Risa. "You want in? People are gonna get sloppy, and you *love* sloppy."

Selena tried not to laugh at the way Risa's mouth shifted from a frown to a faint smile as she considered it. Risa wasn't much of a drinker, and Selena was good at pretending to be sober, so they'd find a dark corner to stand in and act superior while watching everyone else make a scene.

"Okay," she finally said. "But if people are too boring, I'm coming back."

"Deal." Selena clapped her hands together. "That settles it. Put on something nice—we're gonna have fun tonight."

———————

"You have all your clothes? Socks? Underwear?" Finch's aunt, Hannah, lowered her voice. "*Tampons?*"

Finch frowned, pursing her lips. She hadn't gotten her period in three and a half months.

One of the many side effects of surviving the accident that killed her parents.

The doctors had diagnosed her with a lot of things after that night. Anemia, to explain the way the color had leached from her skin, leaving her a nearly translucent shade of white. Bradycardia for her slow, weak heartbeat. Migraines to explain the strange visions of multicolored ripples in the air that made her head throb if she stared at them too long. Issues with hormones, with her thyroid, with her blood and bones and sinew. An amygdala with too much activity, a hippocampus without enough serotonin receptors. They'd even chalked up the way her hair had started to grow in white as either a vitamin deficiency or PTSD.

Sometimes it felt like doctors just threw darts at a board in the break room and whatever it hit was that day's diagnosis.

To their credit, none of Finch's symptoms made any sense.

"Yes," she lied. "I promise I'm going to be okay. You don't have to stick around."

"What if your roommate is terrible?" Hannah nervously ran her hands through her hair—it was dark chestnut brown like Finch's mom, her half-sister. While Finch had relatives elsewhere, Hannah lived the closest to her new school in an artsy corner of

Portland, so she'd wound up with her. Even though Hannah was twenty-six, a stage actress, and hadn't cared for anything larger than a cactus her entire life.

It had made for an interesting, if very depressing, summer. The only glimmer of hope had come in June, when her acceptance letter—and impressive scholarship—to Ulalume arrived.

She finally had her chance. Even if she had nothing else, she had this.

"I-I talked to Sumera online," Finch said. Another lie. She knew nothing about her new roommate except her name—Sumera Nazir. The thought of contacting a stranger through social media made Finch far too anxious to even consider. "She's, um, nice?"

"Are you *positive* you'll be okay?"

"Positive," Finch lied again, "Thank you for dealing with the traffic. I really appreciate it."

Finch leaned over and kissed her aunt's cheek before popping open the passenger-side door of her beat-up Subaru. Hannah reached out and touched her arm, though she quickly tensed upon feeling how cold it was. Another side effect.

"Call me when you get settled, okay?" She bit her lip. "Holly would want me to check in."

Holly would want me to. Finch winced. She'd heard the phrase about a thousand times over the last few months. The painful barb hidden in her late mother's name would probably never go away.

"I will," she promised. "Bye, Hannah."

"Bye, Finch. Good luck out there."

Finch forced a smile and stepped out of the car and into the rain. She stood there long enough to wave goodbye to Hannah before she looked around and realized she had no idea where she was.

"Oh," she whispered to herself. In that instant, the rain seemed to pour down twice as hard, slicking Finch's hair to her skin. "*Shoot.*"

With her suitcase and backpack in hand, Finch rushed over the sodden ground as she tried her best to follow the signs to Pergman Hall, her assigned dorm. While there had been a transfer student orientation, she and her aunt had gotten stuck in traffic for so long they'd missed it. Which was unfortunate, because navigating unfamiliar Gothic architecture and uneven stone paths in a downpour likely would have been easier if Finch had even a single clue what she was doing.

Ulalume's grounds were lush and green, with pine forest surrounding every building. Curved lampposts lined the paths, fat droplets dripping off their bulbs. Mist rose up from the earth, glowing in the yellow light. Everywhere Finch went, she found herself stepping in deeper and deeper puddles. Water soaked through her socks.

When she finally came upon Pergman Hall, she let out a heavy sigh of relief. The walls were dark gray stone, and ivy crept up the side of the building. The doors were heavy wood, which Finch discovered when she had to lean her whole weight into them to make them move. Warm air burst from the opening, and Finch nearly whimpered with relief.

Through a curved wood archway, Finch stepped into a hallway decorated with dark wallpaper and a mix of antique art and school flyers advertising upcoming sporting events, breakfast for dinner in the dining hall, and various clubs. Finch's eyes roved over the walls and down to the common area, a room adorned with heavy curtains, a fireplace, and old-fashioned wood and velvet seating.

Inside were a few parents hugging their daughters goodbye, looking weepy and proud all at once.

Finch paused in the threshold to the common area, a pang reverberating in her chest. She'd always envisioned this day a certain way: her mother helping her make her bed in her new room while her father fussed over how to hang up her posters. The way her mother would cry when they left, and her dad wouldn't be able to stop himself from shedding a tear or two when he hugged her goodbye.

Finch winced. All at once, the images flooded back—the curls of blood rising from the cuts on her palms, the moment her mother's eyes went dark in the rearview mirror. Her memory had gotten hazy after that, as darkness pressed in and cool dread settled into numbness that locked her limbs in place. She'd lost all feeling as the wiring in her brain fizzled out.

Until a strange electric shock had jolted her awake. It had encircled her heart, stabbing inside until it shuddered and started, pumping blood into her deadened limbs and propelling her toward the surface of the river with the sort of desperation that only reared its head when death was closing in. She'd barely been able to drag herself onto the riverbank, slick mud smeared across her forearms and squelching beneath her, before she violently coughed up river water into the reeds.

She remembered reaching up to press a hand to her heart. While everything about that moment had been strange, there was a specific, unsettling sensation in Finch's chest: a pull, like a fist around her heart, pointing her due east.

Toward Rainwater.

Finch tore her gaze from the families, squeezing her eyes shut and shaking her head, as if maybe that would dispel the haze of memories that always crept in during moments like this.

You're okay, she reminded herself. *You're here. You're safe. It's okay.*

Finch took a deep breath. *Okay. Okay.*

She exhaled, shoulders sinking into place. After a few more deep breaths, she opened her eyes and headed down the hall.

No one seemed to notice her. The other girls were too busy exchanging hugs, telling boisterous stories of their summers and running up and down the halls to find their friends' rooms. They all seemed so carefree.

Finch inhaled another steadying breath. This was part of why she was here. Soon, she'd just be another one of these girls. Not a walking tragedy, not a cautionary tale. Just Finch.

After scanning the golden number plates indicating which way to go, she found her room down another musty hallway and to the left. She felt a twinge of excitement at the thought of meeting her roommate. With newfound confidence, Finch pushed open the door to room 124.

Immediately, a wall of sound that had been barely contained by the heavy wood door rushed over Finch, setting the hair on the back of her neck on end. A flamenco-studded, electropop rap song greeted her as she stepped into the two-bedroom suite. Just standing in the doorway, Finch could see a living area, bathroom, and small counter area to account for a kitchen. It wasn't a large space, but it somehow felt even smaller due to the sheer number of people crammed inside. Finch counted almost thirty in the living area, crowded in small circles with red Solo cups in their hands.

And there were boys. Finch hadn't expected *boys.*

Her heartbeat hammered as nearly every eye in the room turned to look at her.

A smiling Arab girl in a floral hijab stood and waved at her. She spoke with an English accent. "Finch Chamberlin?"

Finch stared, dumbstruck. "Um…yes?"

The other girl bounded over and wrapped Finch in an unexpected and enthusiastic hug that left every one of her muscles tense. Finch's next realization was somewhat startling—specifically, the other girl was a solid foot taller than her, probably just over six feet. Finch almost had to tilt her head back to see her face at this angle.

"I'm so glad to meet you! Sorry about all this—word got out I'd already moved in and everyone showed up. I can show you to your room if you like." She held out a hand adorned with a number of gold rings. "I'm Sumera, by the way."

Finch took the hand and shook, trying not to linger on the fact they'd started with a hug and moved to a handshake. "Nice to meet you. I-I'd definitely like to see my room if—if it's not too much trouble." Finch's eyes wandered to the assorted cups in everyone's hands. "Are people drinking?"

Sumera shrugged as she weaved around her party guests, Finch in tow behind her attempting—and failing—not to hit anyone with her suitcase. The smell of alcohol twisted her expression into a scowl. She'd never had more than a few sips of her parents' drinks at family dinners, and the memory of those had kept her away from the stuff.

Sumera said, "I can tell them to stop if you're uncomfortable. I don't drink, but my mum is close friends with our housemother, so everyone knows they can get away with it while I'm here. Sorry again to spring this on you."

"No—it's fine." Finch lifted her suitcase over one last person, a boy who was currently entangled with another boy, their lips just inches apart. She forced herself to look straight ahead, embarrassed they might think she was staring. She wound up clipping one boy with her suitcase wheel, though he didn't seem to notice, despite her repeated, frantic apologies.

Sumera brought her to a bare room with nothing but a plain wooden desk, a bed frame and mattress, and a dresser.

She held one arm akimbo and gestured with the other. "This is you! Are you sure you don't want me to kick everyone out while you get settled in? I'm happy to make them move the reunion festivities."

Finch bit her lip. Sumera added, "I'm also sure they'd be willing to spare a drink or two for the trouble if you're interested. Everyone is really excited to meet you—we've been talking about it all evening."

Finch turned and raised her eyebrows. "They're excited to meet me?"

Sumera nodded, grinning. She had a very genuine smile that crinkled the sides of her dark brown eyes. "Of course! We don't get many transfers."

Finch looked between Sumera and her suitcase. Her first night at Ulalume and people already wanted to hang out with her. Clearly, it was because they didn't know her yet, but this was her first chance at spending time with people who didn't know her as Finch, Who Lost Her Parents or, the earlier version, Finch, Who Is Weird and Homeschooled and Has No Friends.

Finch sucked on her lip for a moment before setting the suitcase and her backpack down on the floor. "I think I'd like to try a drink, if that's okay."

Sumera nodded as if she were withholding a laugh. "Sure. Come on, let me introduce you."

"So…are you from England?"

Their gathering had grown over the past hour, with people spilling into Sumera's room. Sumera had introduced Finch to what felt like a hundred people, all while Finch forced down a drink one of the boys from Rainwater High had made for her. He had said it was mostly orange juice, but Finch was pretty sure it was at least 75 percent vodka.

"London, born and raised," Sumera said. "Accent gave me away?"

Finch nodded. Talking felt easier than it had earlier. Maybe even a little too easy. "You sound like my favorite contestant on *Great British Bake Off.*"

Sumera nearly snorted as she attempted to withhold a laugh. "High praise."

A finger tapped Finch's shoulder, and she looked up to find the boy who'd made the drink for her earlier. He'd introduced himself as Griffin Sergold, and he had some of the most symmetrical features Finch had ever seen.

She popped up. Sumera's smile faded and she rolled her eyes.

Griffin was white, with thick blond curls that he ran his hand through as he grinned. "Hey—Finch, right? How was your drink?"

"Terrible," she blurted out.

Sumera and a few of her friends did a poor job stifling their laughter.

Griffin laughed, an open, friendly sound. "Well, shit. Sorry about that. I've, uh, got some rosé if you'd prefer that—I'm meeting some friends down in the tunnels soon if you'd like to come and try some."

"What tunnels?" Finch asked. She gravitated closer to him.

Before she could take another step, she felt a tug on her pant leg. When she turned around, she found Sumera and two of her friends—identical twin sisters named Ira and Zara who'd explained they'd just flown in from their hometown of Kolkata—gesturing for her to join them for a moment.

Finch bent down. Sumera cupped her hands around her mouth to whisper, "Stay here, trust me. Griffin's nice, but you're better off leaving that be."

Zara's head bobbed in a slightly feverish nod. "He's been hooking up with Selena St. Clair since first year. You don't want to get on her bad side."

Finch's heartbeat sped up so quickly it startled her. "Selena St. Clair? I met her when I toured! She's—she's so pretty."

"Among other things," Sumera grumbled, crossing her arms.

"Are you talking about Selena?"

The girls looked up to find Griffin had joined them. He grinned, clearly oblivious to the tone of the conversation.

"Selena's the best." He turned his gaze to Finch. "If you want to meet her, she might be coming to this tunnel party."

"Don't pressure her, Griffin," Sumera said, standing up. At her height, she looked Griffin straight in the eye. Finch thought it was the coolest thing she'd ever seen. She'd always had a bit of a preoccupation with tall women, for whatever reason.

Griffin's brows furrowed. Before he could respond, Finch said, "I, um, do want to see the tunnels. If that's okay."

Sumera's eyebrows shot up. "Are you sure?"

"It'll be fun!" Seeing Sumera's expression, Griffin rolled his eyes. "Come on, Sumera. It's not a big deal. You can come too if you like. That is, if you're not too afraid of ghosts."

"Ghosts?" Finch asked.

Sumera's jaw locked. "There's this stupid urban legend around here about a local band that went missing. Apparently, they did something evil down in the tunnels and now they haunt it and target students. But everyone knows it's just something the older girls use to scare the younger ones away from the tunnels."

"I heard they kidnapped a girl from the dorms and ate her," Ira said in a monotone as she typed something on her phone.

"Ew, no, that's not it," Zara snapped. "I heard they sacrificed a boy from Rainwater High to the devil down there."

"Oh, wow." Finch's pale eyes widened. "Something like that happened here?"

With a heavy sigh, Sumera started, "No, it didn't—"

"I can tell you about it on the way," Griffin said.

Finch's face brightened. "That would be amazing."

Ira cleared her throat. "I think we need to adjust the playlist anyway. Come on, Sumera."

Sumera's eyes lingered on Finch for a long moment before she finally shook her head and stepped away, following the twins toward the speaker system.

Griffin put a warm hand on Finch's shoulder. "You're gonna love this."

———

Tunneling was a tradition at Ulalume Academy.

The underbelly of the school was home to a network of

maintenance tunnels and rooms that ranged in size from cavern-ous passageways to tiny spaces only some of the first-year girls could fit in. While students technically weren't allowed inside, that didn't stop groups of adventurous girls—and often their friends from Rainwater High—from descending into the tunnels through certain accessible routes only some knew about. It had become a common late-night pastime to explore the miles of concrete and the secrets held in their passages.

That night, the air beneath Ulalume Academy was stifling from the combination of late-summer heat and rain. Selena had brought the girls first to the halls beneath the school and then to a trapdoor hidden in a side room. They'd descended the rusted ladder and headed in the direction of where Griffin texted Selena he was meeting the others.

Or, he had. Half an hour ago.

"Where are we even going?" Amber moaned. She wrapped her bare arms around herself. She'd committed to wearing the glittery new dress with the slit in the side from Hong Kong and, in a twist that was shocking to no one but her, it wasn't working out in her favor. "It's so creepy down here."

"Can you be quiet for a second?" Selena held her phone up toward the web of pipes on the ceiling, hoping to catch a signal. "This is why I hate the tunnels. No reception."

"We could head toward the Tunger entrance," Kyra suggested. Tunger was a recently closed dorm on campus. Before it had been deemed unsafe for student habitation due to its crumbling infrastructure and its community of weirdly robust rats, Kyra and Amber had lived there together their first year at Ulalume. The next year, Selena moved in with them, and they'd been friends ever since. "That's where the party was last year."

Selena didn't know the tunnels well. Admittedly, she hated coming down here. She'd heard way too many ghost stories about the tunnels to want to hang out for more than a brief period of time.

Finally, she said, "Let's try…this way?"

Selena led them down a cramped, dark hallway. Dust motes danced in the air, lit up by weak, flickering light overhead.

Amber's nose wrinkled and she sneezed. "*Selena—*"

Selena stopped, holding up a hand. Up ahead, she spotted a white-haired girl turning the corner.

"She must know where the party is." Selena gestured to the others. "Come on. Let's follow her."

———

Griffin had just been telling Finch about his top five favorite sports plays of the last year when something overtook her.

She stopped dead in her tracks. Griffin kept talking, kept walking, not stopping long enough to discover Finch frozen in place, a statue in the center of the concrete.

The feeling of it—it was the same sensation that had clung to her ever since she'd woken up in the river. The hair on the back of her neck rose, and her skin prickled. The sound of her slow heartbeat drowned out everything else, and her vision narrowed while blood filled her ears. The air seemed to crackle and hiss.

The grip around her heart tightened.

Something stirred in the corner of her eye and she spun, her breath little more than sputtered gasps.

The tunnel was empty.

"Hello?" Finch whispered. She took a single step toward the hallway. "Griffin?"

Her eyes wandered back and forth, scanning the hall for signs of life. Griffin was nowhere to be found. Instead, a strange, rippling aura hung in the air around the far tunnel wall. It had the iridescence and color of an abalone shell, wavering softly like a curtain in the wind.

Finch realized with a jolt that the ripples framed a piece of graffiti on the wall. The design of it made her heart shudder and the hair on the back of her neck stand to attention.

It was a life-size image of a stag that looked to be drawn in charcoal. She reached out, brushing it with the tips of her fingers, and they came back stained a chalky black. Her chin tilted up to take in the full size of it—the shading made the creature appear to be protruding out of the wall. It glared down at Finch with eight unblinking eyes.

Just like how it had stared down the Chamberlins' car before it swerved into the river.

Finch took a shaking breath as she blinked.

When she opened her eyes, the image was gone.

She stumbled back with a gasp. A pang of dull, aching pain began to emanate from the front of Finch's skull—the beginning of another migraine. The kind that only seemed to appear when Finch saw those strange iridescent ripples.

Just as soon as Finch thought she was safe to make her retreat, another one of those ripples appeared farther down the hall. She took a hesitant step forward only to discover they were once again surrounding the same image of the eight-eyed stag.

This time, however, it was craning its neck, staring directly at her from its new place down the corridor.

The gripping sensation in Finch's chest tugged at her. Without meaning to, Finch let her legs carry her deeper into the corridor. Every couple of steps she would blink, and the stag would be gone, only to reappear farther down the hall. Each time it was framed by that shifting, distorted curtain in the air. Goose bumps rose across her skin.

Her mind seemed to disconnect from her body, slowly at first. Then, a single blink blocked out six seconds, then ten—it felt like sleepwalking. She couldn't hear the soft patter of her sneakers on the floor anymore. The bulbs above her flickered, the moths clouded around them wavering in and out of view.

The image of the tunnel flickered before her. Where concrete had been moments before, the walls turned to soil and gnarled roots, writhing as if it were full of worms. The air danced with glimmering, distorted shimmers.

Finch winced, shutting her eyes against a sudden spike of pain at the front of her skull. When she opened them again, it was the same as before: concrete, pipes, graffiti on the walls.

Then the light flickered out above her and plunged her into darkness.

She froze, holding out her arms, searching for the walls. The breath between her teeth sharpened to a desperate whisper. Her crawling fingers fumbled in the dark for something solid.

They brushed something soft. Finch pressed into it.

Flesh.

Finch shrieked, reeling back. Just then, a burst of light flooded the space around her, blinding her. Finch pressed the heels of her palms into her eyes and rubbed until red speckled the backs of her lids.

"Margo?" a boy asked. "Don't be scared, okay?"

"Scared?" a girl replied. "Me? Come on, Victor. What's there to be afraid of?"

Finch's hands fell.

She was alone. As she blinked back into focus, she found herself in a rounded room with soil walls and a ceiling coated in thick, pale roots. Small bioluminescent lights brightened and dimmed inside the roots, casting a blue-green glow across the room. The packed-dirt floor was littered with strange objects. Circles of different sizes were drawn in pale ash on the ground and the walls, lines bisecting them. On the ground, the lines formed a pentagram. Half-burned candles were tipped over in the corners and stippled dark brown stains marked each tip of the star.

Up against the wall was an altar made of antlers, though they were unlike the kind Finch had seen on deer. These branched off in twin patterns, shaped like blood vessels. Loose velvet peeled off in sections, hanging in wet chords.

All around the altar were those aura-like ripples, larger and brighter than Finch had ever seen.

Finch's heartbeat sped up. Adrenaline shot through her—how had she even gotten here? Was this place a hallucination? Had those voices been the ghosts the others had mentioned?

She spun, looking for a door, but found only an impossibly long, dark tunnel behind her. She was about to turn back and run when she heard another voice.

"*Help,*" it whispered, cold against her neck. "*Please—please help me.*"

She whipped back around to the altar. The colorful ripples had shifted. Now, there was a long rift through the middle of them. Inside was an inky abyss, like a deep-sea trench completely devoid of life.

Except for one thing.

Finch gasped as she realized there was a hand reaching for her from inside.

It was attached to a feminine figure—through the distortion, Finch couldn't make out her features. But she could see that she looked almost human—and very, very desperate.

"Please," the voice repeated, choked with sobs. "Get me out of here, please! You have to help me!"

The voice sounded vaguely familiar. It could have been anyone in Finch's life—a friend, a family member.

It had been long enough since she heard it that she could almost imagine it was her mother's voice.

"Please," she begged.

I can't leave her there, Finch thought. *She's in trouble.*

She plunged her hand into the darkness. The second she did, the pain in her head shifted from a throbbing ache to a shooting agony that penetrated every fold of her brain.

She let out a cry, barely registering the events happening behind and in front of her.

At the same time the woman's hand wrapped around hers, four pairs of footsteps came to a halt behind her.

Someone said, "Um. I'm gonna guess this isn't the party."

Then, the room exploded.

Fire licked up from the fallen candlewicks in blue-green columns of flame. The ash star in the middle of the room rose into the air, trembling, while Finch stood in the middle of it. Her white hair floated around her face and her eyes began to glow as light from the void-woman's hand shot up through Finch's veins, illuminating them beneath her skin. Finch's mouth curled into a grimace as she screamed, using all of her power to wrench her hand free from the darkness.

When she finally did, she tumbled back, nearly falling into the cluster of lost girls behind her.

Before them, the void-woman hovered a foot off the ground, features indistinguishable as the light blinded them.

Searing, stabbing pain jolted through Finch's skull, paralyzing her. Her knees weakened and she swayed, the air in front of her swimming with visions of shifting colors.

The creature reached out, and Finch's vision split into fragments. Or, it seemed to, because all at once the being appeared to outstretch five hands, one gently touching the center of Finch's forehead.

"Thank you," the creature said, "for this."

It was the last thing Finch saw before she fell unconscious.

three

"Selena? What are you doing here?"

Selena let out a faint groan in response. Her skull felt as if it were full of cotton balls. As feeling rushed back to her, she became aware of the fact that she was lying on the damp ground in the fetal position. A jagged rock dug into her hip and cracked, and dried mud was caked across her exposed skin. When she forced her eyes open, she discovered her fingers knotted in forest undergrowth, sunlight dappled through the leaves.

She bolted upright, jerking her head left and right. Turns out it looked like she was lying in the undergrowth because she was.

In front of the Pergman Hall entrance to the tunnels.

Where groups of girls were now leaving to go to their first classes of the semester.

"Oh," Selena said. "Shit."

The speaker—Zara, from her dance class—tilted her head to the side. "Do you need me to get someone? What happened?"

Selena ran her fingers through her hair, knocking loose some leaves. She pulled herself up, dusting plant matter and dirt from her bare arms. "It's, ah, a meditative practice. It's called *earthing*. Google it."

"Oh—really?" Zara drew back, eyes wide. "And you just... sleep on the ground?"

"Well, that's once you get to *advanced* earthing. It's a multi-step process." Selena brushed a fern aside and plucked her bag off the ground, securing it over her shoulder. "How long do we have until first period?"

Zara glanced at her phone, "Fifteen minutes. You want me to stall Miss Stein for you?"

Miss Stein was their dance teacher—and not someone who appreciated tardiness. It didn't help that Selena was, at the moment, not in her good graces. At best, she'd be forced to run a lap around the building for each minute she was late. She didn't want to think about what might happen in the worst-case scenario.

"Absolutely yes—thank you." Selena glanced around once more and added, "Don't...tell anyone about this, okay?"

Zara nodded somewhat frantically. "Oh, of course not! No worries. Secret's safe with me!"

Selena pursed her lips—she knew when she was being lied to. "Great. See you in class."

She took off briskly toward Annalee Lighthouse.

———————————

All across Ulalume, the sun shone down on the campus, the smell of rain evaporating from the ground and leaving the grass and foliage the brilliant emerald of late summer.

Girls donned their uniforms: blue and green plaid skirts, knee-high socks, blouses, ties, and blazers with the Ulalume emblem—a raven with twin arrows through its neck in an X—stitched to the chest. First years drowned in their oversized clothes, lovingly chosen by the ladies in the front office who always sized up. Meanwhile, the seniors' skirts from first year hit the mid-thigh, and their blouses looked tailored.

In her bare room, Finch changed into fresh black socks and tried to hike her skirt up—sadly, it barely stayed in place around her slim hips. Still, it was certainly better than the torn, dirt-stained clothing she'd woken up in.

She didn't remember how she'd made it back. Everything after that last image of the glowing woman was fuzzy at best—her body seemed to have gone into autopilot, dragging itself back to Pergman Hall. She'd come to on the floor of her new room, bags still packed in the corner and raincoat thrown across her bare mattress. The terrible pain in her head had faded, replaced with an unsteady feeling that left her reeling every time she began to picture last night.

What, exactly, had she done?

And what was that thing she'd pulled through the rift?

Finch swallowed thickly as she buttoned the collar of her blouse. She was going to have to go back down to the tunnels and investigate. But for now, answers would have to wait—she had to get to class.

As she exited her room, she was surprised to find that the common area of her and Sumera's suite was spotless. A little card with her name on it sat next to a bottle of water, a clementine, a granola bar, and a couple of ibuprofen tablets on the counter. She unfolded the card and read:

Finch,

I heard you come in late last night and figured you might want something quick for breakfast. If you want to get lunch with Ira and Zara and me, we typically eat in the Waite Garden on the south side of campus. My number is below—text me and I'll send you a map of Ulalume with instructions on how to get there ☺

Have a good first class!

Sumera

"That's so nice of her," Finch whispered to herself. She took the ibuprofen for the lingering ache in her head and pocketed the food for later. Before she headed out the door, she checked her half-dead phone.

She had to be in class in three minutes.

Finch squeaked and ran out the door.

She nearly got lost on her way to the classroom, wandering through oak-paneled hallways adorned with paintings of former headmasters. Their long, thin faces watched Finch as she rushed toward the music room, panting from running.

Inside, the classroom had raised levels in the floor so the musicians could see the teacher as they played. Most of the other students were already seated in front of music stands, chatting idly with instruments over their knees. Finch recognized the teacher, Mr. Rizzio, from her audition.

While Ulalume wasn't specifically an arts school—really, it was just a picky prep school when it got down to it—it did fervently seek out artists. Finch had been set on attending ever since she'd seen the school's statistics. Ulalume was a feeder school for both the Ivies and every elite arts program in the country. Her chances of getting into a strong music program for college were significantly higher with an Ulalume education.

Finch found a spot near the piano and took a seat, trying to catch her breath. The bell rang soon after, and Mr. Rizzio launched into a speech about all the great things he had planned for the class. He was middle-aged with a scraggly beard and big glasses, and Finch found his dad vibes comforting.

"I recently spoke with Miss Stein, our dance teacher," he explained, after going into some of the larger projects for the semester, "and I've invited her students to join us for the day. Let's give them a round of applause."

Finch glanced over her shoulder to see another teacher—this one younger, with a big Afro and smile—leading her students inside. The dance girls all looked similarly sleek, with lithe limbs and their hair tied back in manicured buns. They took seats along the wall, whispering to each other despite Miss Stein's sharp glare.

"This semester, we're doing something special for Homecoming," Mr. Rizzio explained. "As you know, Ulalume has a nontraditional Homecoming—instead of a dance or football game, our Homecoming provides a chance for alumni to visit the campus and see a performance featuring all of our most talented students. This year, we've decided to pair up dancers and musicians to create collaborative pieces."

The music girls sized up the dance girls and vice versa. On the whole, the musicians looked terrified, clutching their instruments while the dancers rolled their eyes.

Finch stopped part way down the line, freezing on a familiar face. Her hair still wet from showering and face clean of makeup, Selena St. Clair sat there, jaw clenched and tense. She was, of course, as beautiful as when Finch had seen her in May, though she looked much more her age without makeup. When she caught Finch looking at her, recognition passed over her face for a brief moment before her mouth fell into a scowl.

Finch waved.

Selena stuck out her tongue, blew a big green bubble with her gum, and popped it with her teeth. They never broke eye contact.

"We've paired you up based on previous performances and who we think would work well together," Miss Stein explained. "In that sense, we'll have some larger groups and some pairs. For example, Selena," she glanced back at her, "with your ballet skills, we were thinking of pairing you up with a more classically inclined musician—"

Selena's eyes darted to Finch before she blurted out, "I'd actually rather do a jazz piece, if possible. I'm looking to expand my horizons."

Miss Stein's manicured eyebrows rose before she shrugged. "I see. Well, Greg, you were saying one of your new students is quite adept with jazz piano, correct?"

Mr. Rizzio gestured to Finch, nodding. "Finch did some spectacular improvisational jazz for her audition."

Finch felt like she was going to puke.

Miss Stein nodded her approval. "Perfect—then Finch and Selena will work together. Now, let's sort out the rest of you. Once you have a partner or group, meet with them and discuss your ideas."

Finch's heartbeat turned frantic, sweat prickling across her brow and the back of her neck. Her thoughts raced as images of her and Selena's unfortunate first meeting trapped her in an anxiety-induced fog while other groups were paired up. Selena gritted her teeth across the room.

Finally, Selena stood up, closing the distance between them. The second she was in range, Finch said, "Well, um, good to see you again. It was nice meeting you back in May—"

Selena held her hand out. "Give me your phone."

"What?"

"Your *phone*." Selena narrowed her eyes. "So I can give you my number. Since apparently, despite that charming classical piece you played at the start of your audition, it turns out you're a *spectacular* jazz pianist."

Finch chewed her lower lip. "Oh. Um. I just—prefer jazz. It's more fun."

"Of course. Because you, Milquetoast Chamberlin, really look like someone who likes to cut loose and have *fun*."

"Are you…mad at me?"

Selena's brows furrowed while she scowled, voice dripping with poison. "Oh, did you forget how you narked on me back in May? I guess that must not have seemed like a huge deal, seeing as you weren't there for Headmistress Waite screaming my ear off about the 'Ulalume image' and 'tarnishing its spotless reputation to a prospective student.' Thanks to you, I got put on probation from the dance company for the rest of last year and probably majorly screwed up my chances of getting into my dream college."

"I-I-I," Finch stammered, hands slick with sweat. "I'm so sorry—I definitely didn't mean for you to get in trouble—"

"Please stop talking." Selena stuck out her hand. "And give me your phone so we can…"

As Selena's lips moved, however, the sound coming out of them faded out. Ever so faintly, the air around her seemed to ripple, as if she were emanating a faint ribbon-like glow. Finch stammered while trying to put the words together, but she realized at that moment it wasn't just Selena that had gone silent.

Everything had.

They'll come back to me, a distant voice echoed in her mind. *I won't be alone much longer. And the hunger—the hunger will finally be over.*

Before Finch could process what she was hearing, however, sound flooded back. She winced, closing her eyes for a moment.

When she opened them, Selena was glaring at her like Finch had spat in her food.

"Uh, hello?" Selena asked. "Are you going to give me your phone or just stare at me for a couple more hours?"

"S-Sorry. I thought I heard—" Finch shook her head. "Never mind. It's nothing."

Finch fumbled for her phone in her skirt pocket and barely got it into Selena's hands without dropping it.

"Great. Thanks," Selena said flatly.

While she typed her number in, Finch glanced down at her

hands, trying to keep her breathing even. First there was whatever had happened last night in the tunnels and now she was hearing things? This did not bode well for her.

Selena passed the phone back. "Well, I'd love to stay and prolong this waking nightmare, but I feel like hot garbage, so I'm going back to my room. If Miss Stein asks, tell her I've got endometriosis pain again. Find us some not-shitty music and text me later so we can get this over with."

That was enough to snap Finch out of her thoughts. "Oh. Sure. Are you oka—?"

"Like you'd actually care." Selena shouldered her bag, wincing as she rubbed her temple. "I'll talk to you later, Milquetoast."

And just like that, Selena left Finch sitting there alone.

————————

After her unpleasant reunion with Finch Chamberlin, Selena returned to Annalee Lighthouse only to be greeted by a messy scene in the living room. Amber sat on the couch, sobbing into her hands, dark dirt smeared up and down her arms. Risa paced nearby, her expression hardened. Her typically silky black hair was tangled in knots on one side, leaves sticking out.

"Ah, damn." Selena's shoulders fell. "You too?"

Amber looked up, tear tracks carving out pale spots on her dirty face. "What *happened* to us last night?" Her voice rose to a screech. "Why did I wake up in the *woods*?"

"Maybe there was something that disturbed our sleep cycles and caused us all to sleepwalk," Risa posited, pacing back and forth faster than before. At this rate, she'd wear a path in the hardwood. "Or we were drugged somehow. Could be something in the water—"

"Risa." Selena stepped into her path, and the other girl paused, looking up at her. Selena touched her arm. "I don't think we were drugged. Or that we were all somehow sleepwalking at once."

"Oh? Then what explanation is there?" She reached up and pulled a twig from her hair, frowning. "There has to be something I'm missing. It doesn't make sense that we'd all share the same... hallucination."

"Speaking of all of us," Selena said, "have either of you seen Kyra? Did she go to class?"

Risa shook her head. She'd begun picking at her cuticles, expression distant. "No. She hasn't come out of her room."

Selena blew out a breath. "Damn. Okay."

"What are we gonna *do*?" Amber whimpered. "What if the woman we saw down there is in trouble? Or—what if she was a ghost! Like in those stories we heard first year about that band that cut out girls' hearts down there—"

"Don't be ridiculous, Amber," Risa said.

"I'm not!" She pouted, shaking her head. "It could be anything. Considering we saw—we saw—"

"We don't know what we saw," Selena quickly cut in. She cleared her throat, and Risa and Amber both looked at her as if she were a general leading them out of a war zone. "But we're going to find out."

"How do you propose we do that?" Risa asked, narrowing her dark eyes. "Go back to the tunnels?"

"No—look, I know who to ask." Selena took out her phone, hurriedly sending out a text. "Just trust me, okay? Focus on getting cleaned up and going to class."

Risa nodded. "You're right. We need to keep it together."

Amber sniffled, dabbing at her teary eyes with the sleeve of her uniform blazer. "What about Kyra?"

"I'll deal with her." Selena let out a breath and squared her shoulders. "Listen, we've got half an hour before second period, and we can show up just like normal. Once we're done with class, I'm going to figure out what we saw down there."

Risa and Amber exchanged a look. Amber, at least, said, "Okay."

And while the other girls got up to piece themselves together, Selena pulled her phone out of her pocket and started typing.

TODAY, 9:02 AM

> I need you to come to campus asap

> something happened

Simon
> Fine

> Be there at 4

> Maybe to distract yourself you could attend some classes at that fancy boarding school your moms pay out the ass for

> youre such a nightmare

> youre lucky I love you

Simon

Wait, you're capable of love?? Hold on

> get fucked

Simon

"You got paired up with Selena?" Sumera inhaled a hissing breath through her teeth. "Ugh. Bad luck."

Finch sighed. She and Sumera had the same final class of the day—calculus, her secret love—which made it easier for them to walk back to their dorm room together once the school day finished. The two of them walked side by side, a somewhat comical sight considering the impressive height difference.

The summer heat and humidity clung to them as they headed down the cobblestone path. Done for the day, other girls had shucked off their blazers and tied together the bottoms of their blouses to create crop tops. A surprising number of them were barefoot, walking through the grass with their shoes and socks in hand. Finch had heard some of them whispering about something called *earthing* but didn't bother to ask.

Sumera went on, "Maybe you could ask for a new partner. Zara has said Miss Stein is pretty understanding."

Finch shrugged. "I dunno. Maybe I can convince Selena I didn't mean to get her in trouble if I put in the effort with this collaboration."

Sumera furrowed her eyebrows, dabbing sweat from her forehead. "That's a losing battle."

"You, um, seem a little...uh..."

"Bitter? Maybe a bit." Sumera shrugged. "Sorry—that makes it sound like I'm some jaded ex. It's not like that. Selena and I just have some...history. And it annoys me the way she treats other people sometimes. She didn't used to be like that."

"Used to?" Finch began.

But Sumera had stopped in her tracks. Something up ahead caught her eye. Her face lit up and she cupped her hands around her mouth, shouting, "Simon! Hey, Simon!"

A boy up ahead shielded his eyes from the sun and waved. Sumera gestured for Finch to follow and they met him at the edge of a forking path, one end headed toward Pergman and the other toward the sea cliffs on the far end of campus. Once they were close enough, the boy said, "Sumera! Hey."

"Simon." Sumera grinned—maybe the biggest smile Finch had seen since they'd met yesterday. "I'm so glad I ran into you—this is Finch. She's my new roommate."

"Hi." Finch waved. "I-I'm Finch. Nice to meet you, Simon."

He smiled. Simon was Black, with a bleached buzz cut, round wire-rimmed glasses, and thick eyebrows. Finch couldn't imagine pulling that style off, and yet, he did it well. The only thing she didn't understand was his shirt, which was a deep shade of purple and said HAIL AND WELL MET, MY DUDE across the chest.

"Nice to meet you, Finch. Sumera was freaking out last night after you left—I'm glad you turned up."

Sumera blushed—not subtly, either. "Well—she disappeared

with Griffin, of all people. He's perfectly nice and everything, but he also…"

"Gets around?" Simon finished.

Sumera giggled. "Yeah. That."

Simon hooked a thumb toward her. "Not sure if you've noticed yet, but you basically have a new mom. She's a worrier, this one. Gonna need to start sending check-in texts if you're gone past ten."

"I'm not that bad," Sumera protested.

"You're exactly that bad," Simon argued good-naturedly. He looked back at Finch and paused, his eyes falling on the white binder that sat in the crook of her arm. She'd spent most of her earlier classes doodling on it to try and keep her mind off things, which meant the whole thing was a mess of geometric shapes and animals.

"I like your drawings," Simon said. He pointed to one at the top corner of the binder. "This deer—does it have eight eyes?"

"Oh! Yeah." Finch had almost forgotten she'd drawn it. After last night, she hadn't been able to get the image of it—or the strange void creature—out of her head. She'd spent most of her classes, all discussion of plans for the semester, doodling on her school supplies.

"Do you know much about cryptids?" Simon asked. "Because there's one that's been seen around Rainwater a bunch of times that looks just like that."

Seeing the way Finch tensed, Sumera quickly explained, "Simon is a bit of a…documentarian. He makes videos about unexplained phenomena and urban legends. It's all just for fun, though."

Simon's eyebrows shot up. "Speak for yourself—I didn't spend eight hours in the Berkshires this summer with my Bigfoot call for the laughs."

"Other people have seen this thing?" Finch cut in, pointing to the stag. Sumera and Simon both stopped smiling. She swallowed thickly and said, "I-I saw it last May. What is it?"

Simon's entire being seemed to light up. "You *saw* it? Like, in person? Wait—can I have your number? I have to interview you."

Sumera put her hands on her hips. "Simon, you can't spring that on someone—"

"No, no—it's okay. I want to know more about it as well." Finch swung her backpack to her front and withdrew her phone, handing it to Simon. "Go ahead."

"This is incredible," Simon said as he hurriedly sent himself a text via Finch's phone. "God, I wish I didn't have to meet up with Selena or I'd pick your brain right now."

Sumera furrowed her brows. "You're meeting with Selena?"

"What? She invited me."

Sumera opened her mouth, seemingly ready to offer a biting comment, but closed it at the last second. She adjusted her bag over her shoulder and said, "We'll have to talk later, then."

"Definitely." Simon turned a smile to Finch. "It was great meeting you! I'll text later, okay?"

"Sure," Finch waved. "Nice to meet you too, Simon."

———

When Simon finally texted that he'd arrived, Selena was standing in front of her bedroom mirror, examining the scrapes on her knees and trying to remember where they came from. There was a hazy, half-formed memory of semiconsciously slogging through the tunnels buried deep in her brain, and she could have sworn she'd tripped before wandering out of the tunnels and into the night.

She pulled up her knee socks, concealing the bruises and newly formed scabs. She rushed down the spiral staircase and met Simon at the door.

Simon grinned at her. "I dig the spooky lighthouse vibe. When you said Amber's parents bought it, I was expecting something more…pretentious."

Selena exhaled, stepping to the side and holding her arm out. "If only. Come in."

Simon stepped inside, kicking his purple Jordans off in the entryway. His eyes swept the walls, taking in the white wooden paneling and the beach house décor with a bit too much satisfaction on his face. He gestured to the flat screen in the living room and said, "So, is that where you're gonna replay all your dating sims for the hundredth time, or do you keep it in your room?"

"Shut up." Selena gestured for him to follow her. "My friends don't need to know about that."

"You know, if you keep inviting me over like this, they're gonna figure out that you're just as bad as me sooner or later."

Selena whipped around, holding out a finger in his direction. "You're a menace."

"Only on my father's side. I'm mixed rapscallion and hooligan on my mother's."

"Oh my god, Simon."

He chuckled, self-satisfied, and followed her the rest of the way up the stairs to her room. The walls inside were blank, most of her things still packed away. The back wall was the same slate stone as the outside, with a window looking out at the spitting sea and the jagged cliffs below.

"Nice view," Simon started. "So, what is it you wanted to—"

"I think I saw a monster last night in the tunnels."

Simon whipped around. "Hold up. What?"

"Keep your pants on." Selena nudged down one of her socks to reveal her scraped knee. "I got this last night while I was leaving and I barely even remember it happening. I saw... Well, I'm honestly not even sure what I saw."

Simon blinked a few times before, seeming to realize the weight of what Selena had just said, a huge smile broke across his face.

"This is, unequivocally, the best day of my life." He held his hands out like he was about to grasp her face and kiss her. "Tell me everything."

Selena did, to the best of her memory. She recounted how they'd followed the figure and then found themselves walking through a strange, dirt part of the tunnels. And then—the darkness, the girl reaching into something Selena couldn't see and pulling free that strange, humanoid figure. And blacking out only to wake up outside Pergman.

Selena finished, shoulders relaxing. "So. I know it sounds impossible, but—"

Simon shook his head. "No, I think I have an idea of what to look for. Give me a few days to research, okay? Come to my house this weekend and we'll figure it out."

"You don't think I'm crazy?"

"Do you know who you're talking to? Of course not."

Selena fought back a little smile and paused for a moment

before stepping forward and throwing her arms around him, pulling him into a tight hug. She pressed her face into his shoulder, hoping the pressure would stanch the tears threatening to push past her eyes.

"You're the best, Sy," she whispered into his T-shirt.

He patted her back. "I know. Just…let me know if anything else weird happens in the meantime, all right?" He pulled away, pursing his lips. "*Especially* if you run into any more random glowing women. Maybe take pictures. It'd be great for my Instagram."

Selena stared at him for a moment.

"I'm joking. Mostly." He held out his hand. "But we'll figure this out together. Deal?"

She took it. "Deal."

four

That night, after chatting with Sumera about their hometowns over tea, Finch put on her coziest pajamas and tucked herself into her new bed. The mattress was extremely stiff, and Finch became acutely aware of every spot where it pressed up against a bone. She'd have to buy a mattress pad.

These days, she could afford that sort of luxury. Her parents had left her a fair amount of life insurance money—enough to get Finch through her junior and senior year at Ulalume and most if not all of college, depending on whether or not she could get a scholarship. In a strange way, it made Finch feel guilty, as if she were benefiting from her parents' deaths.

Of course, she'd spent a pretty significant amount of her time over the summer speaking to various therapists about her guilt. All of them reminded her of the same thing: what had happened wasn't her fault.

Her brain, of course, refused to believe that.

She turned over, letting out a heavy sigh as she stared across the room at her window on the far wall. Her room was at the very edge of Pergman Hall and looked out at the dense woods that surrounded the school. Tall pines loomed over the dormitory, standing like sentinels in the misty dark.

Even though she was dead tired, Finch could tell this was going to be another bad night for her insomnia. That was another thing therapists loved to ask her: *Have you been sleeping enough? Have you had multiple days without sleep in a row?* The answer to the latter was a resounding yes, but she didn't like to mention it. The less sleep she had, the more it compounded the inherent anxiety she got from every social interaction. And unfortunately, she had plenty of awkward moments from the day to obsess over—namely, speaking to Selena St. Clair.

She truly hadn't meant to get her in trouble last May. She could be a little naïve, sure, but she wasn't the sort of person who ran her mouth in an attempt to win approval from teachers or whatever reason Selena had cooked up to explain her blunder. She'd never want to put someone's future at risk.

And yet, she had.

Feeling restless, Finch stood, crossing her room and bracing her hands against the windowsill, staring out into the darkness. The chipping paint dug into her palms, leaving dusty residue.

Outside, a full moon lit the trees in silver. In the distance, the light from the curved lampposts along the cobblestone paths between buildings burned through the fog. No one was out this late—Sumera had told her at dinner that getting caught outside after 10 p.m. without permission was a great way to get detention or lose off-campus privileges.

Between Selena, the strange figure in the tunnels, and the eight-eyed stag, all Finch wanted was for her mind to be quiet.

At least with one of those, she thought, *I know where to look.*

Finch pushed open her window, swung her legs through, and slid out onto the soft earth below.

It was easier to find the strange underground room than Finch had thought it would be. Thankfully, she still had a strange pull leading the way, telling her where to turn, which pipes to duck under, which tight spaces to shimmy through with her back pressed against the wall.

She came upon the dirt hallway once again and felt her heartbeat quicken. Just like the night before, the bioluminescent roots lit the passage in eerie blue light, and now hanging panes of distortion rippled through most of the hall.

How can this be real?

Her head began to throb. She gritted her teeth and rubbed her temple before pressing on.

"Hello?" she called, voice barely loud enough to carry. "Is anyone here?"

Instead of a response, the grip around her heart fluttered.

Finch closed the distance between her and the room, checking over her shoulder. Every one of her senses was on high alert. She had halfway convinced herself that maybe the room from last night didn't really exist, and it had all been a strange nightmare. But as she came upon it at the end of the hall, she was quickly proven wrong.

It was definitely real. But it was empty.

Finch took a hesitant step inside. The candles remained scattered around the room, the lines drawn in ash as stark as before. The altar stood against the wall, the antlers massive and sweeping, almost looking like open hands waiting for someone to place an object inside.

Finch's mouth had gone dry, so it took her a moment to ask, "H-Hello?"

One of the ripples in the air suddenly glowed bright. Finch leaped back. In a flashing second, a figure stood before her, hovering above the ground.

"It's you," the shadow said, cocking her head softly to the side. "You're back."

Finch's breath caught as she tried to make sense of what she was seeing. From the sound of her voice, Finch knew this was the same being she'd pulled out of the darkness last night. But, just like before, the sight of her felt impossible.

She wasn't human—at least, not quite. While she had the general shape of a young woman, her body lacked the detail of a human being, making her look almost like a doll cloaked in a black shroud. Her skin was snow-white, as was her hair, which hung all the way to her hips. Strange scars cut across all of her exposed skin, creating a crisscross pattern. When Finch studied her face, she found herself confronted by entirely black eyes framed by long, white lashes.

The moment Finch stared into those eyes, her thoughts began to swim. Her vision closed in at the corners, and she felt a strange sensation as if her consciousness were losing its grip on her body.

She finally tore her eyes away with a gasp, bracing herself against the wall.

"I wasn't sure if you were coming back," the creature said. She had a black tongue barely visible behind her pearlescent teeth. "You seem overwhelmed."

"That's a good word for it." Finch shook her head in disbelief. "What exactly are you?"

The creature raised her pale eyebrows. "That's…a fair question." She reached up and tucked a lock of hair behind her ear. "If I'm being honest, I don't quite remember. But you can call me Nerosi."

"Nerosi," Finch repeated. She'd never heard a name like that before. "What do you mean you can't remember?"

"I suppose it is strange, isn't it?" Nerosi mused. She took a step toward Finch, following one of the lines drawn on the floor as if she were walking a tightrope. She was impossibly graceful, light on her feet like a creature from a fairy tale. "All I remember is darkness. Being trapped in that void for a long, long time. And then…" she trailed off before casting a look Finch's way. "You."

"Why me?" Finch breathed. Her hand found its way over her heart. "Why did it feel like something was leading me here? Was that you?"

Nerosi bit her lip. "No idea. It does seem like there's a connection between the two of us, doesn't it? Perhaps it's because you're the one who set me free." She frowned. "Or—got me out of the darkness, anyway. I'm still trapped."

"In here?" Finch clarified.

Nerosi nodded. She pointed to the lines on the floor. "I can't fully explain it, but it feels as if I'm not entirely here. Like this part of me," she gestured to herself, "is just a fragment. And I don't know where the rest is."

Finch's eyebrows shot up. "That makes it sound like you're a ghost."

Nerosi blinked. "A—ghost?"

Finch nodded. "I mean, I can't be sure. But last night a bunch of the girls were telling me that these tunnels are haunted. If you can't remember your past, or how you got here, maybe it's because there's some truth to the stories."

"A ghost," Nerosi repeated, staring at her hands. This close, her scars looked fresh, barely healed enough to keep from bleeding. "Maybe that's it." she trailed off. "That reminds me. I haven't even asked your name."

"It's okay—I'm Finch," she said, holding out a hand. "Nice to meet you, Nerosi."

Nerosi reached out to shake it, but her hand went straight through Finch's. The sensation immediately left her chilled to the bone.

"Oh!" Nerosi exclaimed. "I'm so sorry."

Finch stared down at her open palm. Standing next to Nerosi almost made her chalky skin tone seem half normal. "Well. That supports the ghost theory."

Nerosi smiled sheepishly. "I suppose so. Does that make you a medium?"

Finch didn't think she was. She'd certainly never been able to speak to a ghost before.

But things had changed since May. Something had stolen the color from her features, the strong beat of her heart, and the warmth in her skin. Could it have also given her the ability to speak to the dead? Was that what the strange iridescent ripples in the air were? Signs of ghosts?

"Finch?" Nerosi asked. "Are you okay?"

She nodded. "Just…thinking. If I am a medium, I'm not a very good one." She coughed out a weak laugh. "You're the only ghost I've spoken to. Assuming that's what you are. Other than you, it's just…these weird ripples in the air. And staring at those for too long makes my head spin."

Nerosi pointed to one. "You mean these?"

Finch nodded. "Yeah. You can see them too?"

"Yes." Nerosi reached out as if to touch Finch again, but hesitated, remembering what had happened last time. She opened her mouth to say something else, but a shadow passed over her expression.

"Nerosi?"

"I have to go," the figure breathed. "I can't—I can't maintain this form for long. I'm too w—"

She couldn't get the word out, however, because the image of her floating in the center of the room began to flicker. Her mouth moved, but no sound came out.

"Shoot," Finch breathed. She quickly said, "I—I'm going to look for answers, okay? I'll come back as soon as I know something."

Nerosi tried to say something, but Finch never got a chance to hear what it was.

Just as suddenly as Nerosi had appeared, she winked out of existence.

five

Things seemed to hang in a precarious calm for the next few days at Ulalume. While Selena was plagued by nightmares of glowing figures in the tunnels, her waking moments were relatively normal. She went to class, hung out with her housemates, and watched the sea roil from her bedroom in the lighthouse. It was almost easy to pretend that night in the tunnels had never happened.

Except when Simon sent her messages about it, of course. He had a ton of theories, ranging from aliens to ghosts to government conspiracies as his research went deeper. He asked Selena about her nightmares and whether or not she'd developed some sort of supernatural abilities. She reminded him that was ridiculous, and he quickly shot back that a strange *something* living in the tunnels under Ulalume was just as absurd.

Saturday morning, Selena threw her bag over her shoulder and headed for the road to Rainwater. The sky was overcast, but the humidity was high enough to immediately make Selena regret wearing a beanie and an oversized flannel over a black crop top.

"Where are you going, St. Clair?"

Selena jolted at the sound of Kyra's voice. The redhead appeared from around the corner of the lighthouse. Based on the Lululemon leggings and sports bra she had on, she must have just come back from a run. She reached up and tried to flatten some of the flyaway baby hairs around her forehead—she was still dealing with the result of a bad bleach job last semester that had wrecked her hair and turned it an unfortunate shade of carrot-orange. Its current auburn had taken a significant chunk of her parents' money to achieve, but it did little to hide the breakage.

"Out," Selena responded. "I'll be back later."

"Ooh, how cryptic." Kyra came to Selena's side, touching her arm gently. "Cute outfit. Strong bisexual energy."

Selena bristled. The path between Ulalume and Rainwater was right in front of the lighthouse, which meant on a day like this, it was full of both Ulalume girls and townies who liked to walk their dogs around campus. Most of them didn't offer the girls a second glance, but Selena could feel their eyes on them.

Without thinking, Selena snapped, "Yeah, well. I guess everybody knows that about me already, huh?"

Kyra frowned. "Wait, wait, wait. I'm sorry, are you saying you're still mad about *that*? I thought we'd agreed to put it in the past."

Selena pursed her lips. Technically, she was supposed to be past *that* incident. She and Kyra both had a nice cry about it over a bottle of champagne in the Astors' Upper East Side apartment over the summer. They'd kissed and made up, plus a bit more than that in the haze of too much sparkling wine. Selena had woken up the next morning in Kyra's bed wondering if the hollowness in her chest came from the absence of the anger that had lived there for so long or if it had simply morphed into something else.

"Right. Well…I guess being back here makes it hard not to dredge up the past." Selena waved her hand to dispel the idea. "Sorry to bring it up."

She took a step to leave, but Kyra caught her wrist. As Selena turned to ask her what else she wanted, Kyra rose onto the toes and kissed her.

Selena's cheeks flared pink.

Kyra laughed, pointing to her face. "That never gets old. See you later, St. Clair."

She turned and went inside, smirking.

Selena scowled, muttering *asshole* under her breath. Adjusting her bag, she shook her head and turned toward Rainwater.

The cobblestone path ended once it hit Rainwater Road, the town's main street. There was no sidewalk, so Selena skirted the edge of the asphalt, her boots crunching against withered pine needles and twigs. The soil smelled of petrichor from the last rain, which had stopped earlier in the morning.

Before long, Simon's house came into view around the bend. Simon lived at the exact middle point between Ulalume Academy and downtown Rainwater. He and his mother had a small cottage with colorful planter boxes hanging out the front windows. The sides were the typical gray shingles Rainwater shared with other New England sea towns, weathered and peeling from years in the rain.

She found the door unlocked and dropped her bag on the couch before heading to Simon's room. She stopped short, though, when she heard voices inside. Carefully, she pushed the door open to discover that Simon wasn't alone—Finch Chamberlin was sprawled out on his bed.

"Hello." Selena's eyes slid from Finch to Simon. While Finch was seated on his bed, Simon sat in his office chair in front of the half of his room he used to record videos. Various microphones and cameras hung over and around the desk, some being used as drying racks for his clothes. Simon was nothing if not chronically disorganized.

"Hey!" Simon stood up and grinned at her. "I forgot to mention—I invited my new friend Finch over. I figured since you're both interested in the unexplained phenomena of Rainwater, we could all meet up."

Selena narrowed her eyes at him. "Did you?"

"Yeah—Finch has seen weird stuff too!" Simon trailed off, seeing their expressions. Finch looked like a deer caught in the lights of a semitruck while Selena looked like, well, the human personification of that semitruck. "I...take it you've met?"

"You haven't sent me any music yet," Selena said, meeting Finch's eyes.

Finch quickly looked away. "Oh. I've—I've just been really busy."

"Of course. I'm sure bleaching your roots must be quite a chore—the white is, ah, truly a statement." Selena stepped to Simon's side and whispered in his ear, "If you wanted me to wing woman you, you should have told me *before* I came here with need-to-know information."

Simon tensed, eyes widening, before Finch chimed in, "Um, Simon—you were about to show me your research."

"Right." Simon stepped away from Selena, undeterred. Mostly to her, he added, "I thought you'd *both* be interested in hearing this."

Simon went to the closet and, before they could ask what he was doing, he opened the door to reveal the inside pasted with pictures, red string, and rainbow Post-it Notes—a classic crime show murder theory board.

Simon held a hand out toward the title. "Impressive, right?"

"*The Mysterious Disappearance of Killing Howard*?" Finch read aloud.

Selena narrowed her eyes. "Simon, what does this have to do with—" she caught herself, sensing Finch's eyes on her "—what I told you about?"

"Everything! Or—I think everything, at least. Listen, these dots?" He gestured to the board. "I think I've connected them."

Selena crossed her arms and quirked an eyebrow. "Do tell."

"Okay—so." Simon pointed to a few of the pictures. They were of teenagers, though the photo quality and outfits made it obvious that they were likely taken sometime in the early aughts. It was hard to make out their faces, because in most of the shots they were on stage, playing instruments energetically enough that the shots had come out blurry.

"The year is 2004," Simon said, using his foot to keep the door open while he gestured to various images and news clippings he'd taped up. "Rainwater is wildly boring as usual. Except for," he tapped the board door, "these five people, the members of a local pop-punk band called Killing Howard. They had a reputation for frequenting the Ulalume campus, especially the tunnels, since two of their members were students. After becoming a local sensation with a record deal seemingly on the horizon…they vanished. And were never heard from again."

Selena wrinkled her nose. "If these kids up and vanished, wouldn't people in Rainwater still talk about it?"

"Well—that's the thing. I'm pretty sure they're the source of all those urban legends about the band that did human sacrifices or cult rituals or Satan worship or whatever the rumor du jour says about the tunnels under Ulalume. And because I think there was a cover-up." Simon gestured to the images. "These pictures? I had to dig *everywhere* for them. It's like they were scrubbed from any sort of public record. I couldn't even find the members' names anywhere."

"Then how did you get these?" Finch asked.

"Oh—um." He smiled a little sheepishly. "There are some interesting digital archives if you know where to look."

"What, the dark web?" Selena guessed, cocking an eyebrow.

"You don't have to say it like that." Simon restarted, "Anyway, aside from the fact that it's weird how little information exists about Killing Howard, there's also this." He pointed to a blurry scan of a flyer advertising a Killing Howard concert at a bar in downtown Rainwater. Above the text was a sketched image of a stag.

When Selena squinted at it, she realized it had eight eyes.

"What is that?" she asked.

"They used this on all of their promotional materials," Simon explained. "Which is odd, because right after they started to get more popular, there were more sightings of the eight-eyed stag around Rainwater. And—"

"Hold on. You lost me," Selena said, cutting in before Simon could switch topics again. Selena had known Simon long enough to be accustomed to how quickly his brain jumped around when he was talking about a hyperfixation—normal ADHD stuff. She had to stop him if she wanted to keep up.

Finch nodded in agreement. "Yeah—what do you think the stag has to do with their disappearance?"

"Well—" Simon paused. "Well. Actually, that I'm not sure about. But there's this weird history of that creature appearing around Rainwater right before terrible things happened. Like how Mothman appeared before the Silver Bridge collapse in West Virginia. Last May, there were sightings of it right before a whole family drowned in a nearby river."

Finch seemed to grow even paler. Selena had heard about that accident in passing, but she'd been a little distracted having her life upended by getting caught with booze on campus to pay much attention to some randos driving off a bridge. Not to mention that was also the night of the Founders' Ball, and all the Ulalume girls had been much more focused on the fact that a student caught two teachers hooking up in an empty classroom when they were supposed to be chaperoning that night.

Simon looked to Finch. "Did you hear about that accident? Must have been around the time you saw the stag."

"Um. Yeah." Finch nodded. "It was…around that time."

"I still don't see how this ties together," Selena pointed out.

Simon rolled his eyes. "Listen, I'm positive it's all connected somehow. I just need to figure out how and why."

Finch bit her lip, pointing to the stag. "You don't want to… find that thing, do you?"

Simon pressed his palms together and touched his fingers to

his nose. "My entire goal in life is to see a live cryptid, and I'm not even a little bit joking."

Selena rolled her eyes. "You always know how to charm 'em, huh, Simon?"

"Wow," Finch echoed. "That's...huh."

"Anyway, my plan is to try and interview the owners of some of the venues where I know Killing Howard played in case they might remember anything about them," Simon said, unfazed. He looked between Selena and Finch. "Once I get ahold of their names, I bet we can get a lot more information about them and what they might have done in the tunnels. If you two are interested, anyway."

Selena studied the scan of the stag. Something about it didn't sit right with her.

Simon might actually be onto something.

Selena nodded. "I'm in."

"*You are?*" Finch countered in horror. When Simon and Selena stared at her, she stammered, "I-I mean, it might be dangerous to look into something like this."

"I think I can handle it," Selena said, narrowing her eyes.

"I—" Finch pursed her lips. "You know what? Yeah. I'm in too."

Selena's brain fumbled for a reason to uninvite her from whatever this strange investigation was shaping up to be. There was no way she was spending more than one awkward afternoon watching Simon indulge in his two main interests: unexplained phenomena and girls. Especially not when the girl in question was Finch Chamberlin, and the unexplained phenomena was what had been making Selena feel like she was losing her mind for the last week.

Simon grinned. "Great. I'll make us a group chat and send you both any information I find."

Finch gave an awkward arm swing. "Sounds good to me!"

Both sets of eyes fell on Selena and she let out a sigh. "Yeah, sure," she grumbled. "We'll be in touch."

Finch hadn't had much time to overthink her decision about agreeing to spend even more time with Selena in the future, because soon after, Simon's mother arrived home and whisked him away to some event at a family friend's place. Finch and Selena excused themselves, setting out on the path back to Ulalume together, staring in opposite directions as their feet scraped through the undergrowth.

"So," Finch finally said. "What made you interested in learning about all this weird stuff around Rainwater? I didn't take you for the type to get into ghost stories—or whatever this is."

Selena's lips twitched into a small frown. Finch instantly regretted the question.

"I was bored," she finally said. "And I think it makes Simon happy to talk to someone about this kind of thing."

Finch waited for Selena to ask her what had drawn her there, but instead, she kept walking.

Finch gulped. *Come on, Finch. You can keep a conversation going for fifteen minutes. It's not that far to Ulalume.*

"H-How do you know Simon?" Finch finally managed.

Based on the way Selena's eyes fluttered and briefly rolled into the back of her head, Finch wondered if maybe she should have stayed quiet. But after a second, she sighed, seeming to admit to herself that she couldn't just ignore Finch when she spoke to her.

"His parents are divorced. Mom lives here, dad lives in Boston. My parents are his dad's neighbors. Simon's been spending summers there since we were kids, and we naturally became friends. Now that I go to Ulalume, I get to bug him all year round."

"Oh." Finch smiled. "Boston. That's cool. I always wanted to live in the big city."

Selena shot her a sideways look. "It's not that big of a city."

"I grew up in a town of under two thousand people. It's big to me."

"Rainwater must be a real bustling metropolis to you then."

Finch laughed, but a moment later, the silence returned. Selena took out her phone to text, and Finch worried at a loose string on the hem of her skirt.

"You know," Finch said after a minute, "I'm sorry if I made a bad impression the first time we met—I really didn't mean to get you in trouble. I feel terrible about it."

Selena scoffed, though it wasn't a wholly unfriendly sound. "You've really got to stop apologizing so much. You sound like a total suck-up."

"You think I'm a suck-up?"

Selena bit back a laugh. "One of the worst I've ever met."

Finch laughed at that, too, even if it was probably meant to be an insult. She snuck a glance at Selena to find her biting her lip and looking at the pavement and the plant debris under their feet. This close, Finch could see a few zits on her jawline carefully hidden under her makeup. The breeze tousled the ends of her hair.

"Um." Finch pursed her lips and took a breath. She suddenly felt quite warm—it must be the humidity. "There's, um, something I should tell you."

Selena wrinkled her nose and bunched her mouth up in a small smile. "You like Simon, right? I think half the goal of that meetup was to woo you with his awkward allure. I'd say it was the whole point if I didn't know how obsessed with all of that stuff he actually is."

"What? No." Finch shook her head. "I just met him."

Selena bit the tip of her tongue and chuckled. "Fair enough. Is that a taste thing or a gay thing?"

"A gay thi—um, no. Not so much." Not thinking, Finch blurted out, "But I saw you and your girlfriend earlier."

Selena froze. Her steps stopped and an empty look passed over her face.

"I saw you kissing that redhead this morning when I was walking to Simon's," Finch admitted. Not entirely knowing why, she added, "I'm sorry."

Out of nowhere, Selena was grabbing Finch by the wrist and pulling her into the forest. Finch yelped and tried desperately not to trip on roots as Selena dragged her along. Finally, once they were hidden from the road, Selena let go and whipped around, golden blond hair spinning with her.

Finch pressed her back into a tree. The bark bit at her skin through her dress. Selena got up close to her face, looming over her. One arm pressed into the tree, trapping her, while the other pointed a finger between her eyes.

"If you breathe a word of that to anyone," she snarled, "I will end you. I'll—"

Finch threw up her hands. "Selena, I'm not going to tell anyone. I would never do that."

Selena drew back a bit, eyebrows pinched. "What?"

"If you're not comfortable with people knowing you're with a girl, I won't tell anyone." Finch slowly lowered her hand. "Promise."

Selena blinked, furrowing her eyebrows. Her stare was piercing, made more so by the way the fog rolling in made her green eyes seem to glow. She slowly moved away, running her hands through her hair and pinching the bridge of her nose. She gazed out at the pines, jaw working. Finch eased away from the tree, wrapping her arms around herself.

Almost a minute passed of Finch waiting for Selena to snap at her again. Instead, the other girl hardened her expression—maybe, to stop herself from crying. Finch hadn't considered how tender of an issue this would be.

"You want to go back to school?" Finch finally asked.

Selena shook her head as if it would dislodge a thought. "Yeah. Right, yeah."

Slowly, they made their way out of the woods, and once they were by the road again, a silence fell over them. Cars sped around the bends to their left and looked as if they were about to go up on two wheels and flip. The sky grew darker with clouds overhead, and mist blew in thicker from the sea.

"It's not that I'm afraid of people knowing I'm bi," Selena finally said, looking straight ahead. Her shoulders relaxed. "It's... Kyra. The girl you saw. I don't want people to think we're together. Because we're not, and we have a...messy history."

"Oh." Finch nodded. "I see."

"That's it? You don't want to know why?"

"Do you want to talk about it?" Finch asked.

Selena hesitated. "I—no. Not really."

"Then no, I don't. But...thank you for trusting me with that."

Selena tilted her face toward the sky, taking a breath and exhaling it as a sigh.

"Don't make me regret it."

six

The next night, Finch was almost out the door when Sumera said, "Hey, are you headed somewhere?"

She turned. Sumera paused the true crime documentary she'd been watching—she seemed to have quite a thing for them, Finch had discovered, which was nice seeing as they had that in common. She had her dark brown hair up in a bun and a white sheet mask over her face.

"Oh—yeah." Finch rubbed the back of her neck. "Going to the tunnels."

"By yourself?" Sumera frowned.

"I, um, forgot something down there the other day. Going to find it." Finch opened the door. "Anyway—"

"Let me send you a map." Sumera pulled out her phone and AirDropped a picture to Finch. "That way you won't get lost. It can get confusing down there."

"Thanks, Sumera." Finch saved the picture, a hand-drawn map of the tunnels that looked fairly weathered, like maybe it had been passed around a fair amount, shoved in Ulalume girls' pockets and backpacks as they navigated beneath the school. "That's super nice of you."

She shrugged. "Any time. I used to go down to the tunnels a lot last year—mapped out most of them. If you ever need a guide, let me know."

Finch shook her head. "I-I'm okay. Thank you, though."

Sumera studied her for a second, fingers twisting a blanket thread around her finger over and over. Finally, she said, "Are you all right? You seem…tense."

"Me? Tense? Never," Finch lied, voice cracking. She held up a hand and waved. "Anyway, I'll just be a minute. Maybe I can catch the end of that documentary."

"Sounds like a plan. See you later, Finch."

"See ya!"

Finch closed the door behind her, her pale eyes a little brighter than before. She wasn't exactly the most popular person back home, so it was still a little surprising to have someone who wanted to spend time with her. She definitely liked the idea of being friends with someone as cool as Sumera, though.

After making her way down to the tunnels, Finch was drawn to Nerosi's room the same way as before. Concrete walls soon shifted into dirt, the thick, white roots with their flickering lights knotted in the ceiling above her, casting their strange light down onto her.

When she reached the end of the passageway, Nerosi appeared from a shimmering ripple in the air. She was in the middle of braiding her hair, her lithe fingers taking their time weaving the strands together.

"You're back!" She grinned. "It feels like it's been so long."

Finch tried not to wince at that—being trapped in this room with no one to talk to for days on end must be absolute torture. Maybe she should start making a point of coming down here more, if only to preserve Nerosi's sanity.

"Sorry it took so long—I wanted to wait until I'd actually found something."

Nerosi's face brightened. "Oh? Any luck?"

Finch nodded. She took out her phone, which she'd used to take a few pictures of Simon's closet door, and held the screen up for Nerosi to see.

She cocked her head to the side. "That's…a lot of string."

"Oh, yes. My friend's methods are a little eccentric."

Finch almost stumbled over the word. Could she call him that? They'd only spoken a few times over the week Finch had been in Rainwater. At what point did she get to call someone a friend?

She restarted, "Anyway, he found evidence that, maybe, something happened to a group of teenagers down here. Does the name Killing Howard ring any bells?"

Nerosi's eyes widened. She was quiet for a moment before she began to bob her head, slow at first, then quicker as she said, "I—yes. I think I remember…that they were like you. Humans who came down here and spoke to me sometimes the last time I was here." She blinked, looking around the room. "I forgot I was here before. But that can't have been too long ago. Do you know when they might have been here last? A couple months?"

Finch bit her lip. "Um. Not exactly. Think more in the ballpark of…two decades. Give or take."

"*What?*" Nerosi's mouth hung open. "Two decades? That can't be true. How could I have been in the void for…" she trailed off, mouth curving into a frown. She wrapped her arms around herself. "Almost twenty years."

Not knowing what else to say, Finch whispered, "I'm so sorry."

"Time moves in strange ways when you're alone." Nerosi righted herself, straightening her shoulders. "I suppose that explains why my memories are so foggy. But Killing Howard—I definitely remember them. They came down here to see me and play their music. Honestly, they were pretty bad at first."

"You don't know what happened to them, would you?" Finch asked. "Or any information about them? Like their names?"

"Names…no, not right now. I'm sorry." Nerosi blinked, as if just realizing what Finch had said before that. "Something happened to them?"

Finch inhaled sharply. Maybe she needed to stop asking Nerosi these kinds of questions. "They vanished. Nobody has seen them since 2004."

"That's awful." Nerosi sank down, sitting back and crossing her legs. She still floated a few inches off the ground, weightless as always. "They were my friends, I think. I used to…help them. With little favors."

Finch paused. "Favors? What do you mean?"

"Oh, yes! I meant to tell you." Nerosi hopped back up. She held out her hand, and the air around it began to distort, rippling and turning shades of blue and pink and green. "It seems I'm not totally powerless after all."

Finch drew back. While entering the room hadn't given her a headache like it had the last few times, staring into the distortion in Nerosi's hand did. "What is that?"

"I'm not exactly sure, but when I control it, I can…change things." She pointed to one of the candles. "Watch this."

Her hands shimmered as she spun them around each other slowly as if through water. A colorful ripple appeared around some of the fallen candles, blurring them from view. Nerosi focused, pursing her lips, before throwing her hands out.

When the distortion vanished, the candles had doubled in size, the white wax now starkly black.

While Finch's jaw fell open, Nerosi shot her a grin. "See?"

"That's impossible," Finch breathed. She reached down and picked up one of the candles. She rubbed the wax with her thumb, expecting a fine layer of black to come off, but it didn't. It was solid in her hand.

Nerosi shrugged. "Maybe not. When you mentioned Killing Howard, I remembered how I used to do things like that for them. Little favors—polishing their guitars, fixing their amps, turning one-dollar bills into twenties…"

Finch's mouth hung open. "So you can…change reality? Manipulate it to your will?"

"Yes—that seems like a good way to describe it." Nerosi stared down at her hands, eyes tracing the scars along her arms. "I couldn't tell you how, and I don't think I could do more than change little things, but I know that when Killing Howard used to come down here, helping them made me feel more…grounded. Like there was more of me in this world than just this little fragment. And I didn't fade away like I did the other night."

While Finch was listening, she still couldn't tear her eyes away from the candle in her hand. Ghosts, she could understand. She could maybe even wrap her head around strange deer with too many eyes lurking in the woods. But this? It seemed too much like—well, magic.

Nerosi went on, "Maybe, we could make a sort of...trade. If I'm lucky, helping you will be the key to getting myself out of this room."

"Trade what, exactly?" Finch asked.

Nerosi shrugged. "That depends. What do you want, Finch?"

Finch paused. She hadn't thought about that in some time. For so long, her goal had been getting into Ulalume. Now that she had it, it was hard to imagine what else she could want.

Aside from the obvious. But Finch doubted that Nerosi could use her ability to bring back the dead.

"I...I'm not sure." Finch bit her lip. "Let me think about it. Maybe I can find a little more information about Killing Howard and come back in a day or two."

Nerosi nodded, smiling. "I'd like that. It's always nice to see you, Finch. And really—think about it. I'd like to use these powers to help you if I can."

"That's very kind of you." Finch set the candle down with the others, brushing the wax off on her pants. "I should probably get going, but I'll be back soon."

Nerosi grinned. "I'll be waiting."

Finch said her goodbyes and left the room, waving to Nerosi as she turned the corner into the dirt corridor. As she made her way back to the tunnels, she wondered how anything of what she'd seen could be possible. Could a ghost really do something like alter reality on a whim? Sure, it had been something small, but Finch had never heard of anything like that before.

Of course, it wasn't like all the stories were true, per se. She certainly hadn't ever heard anything about a creature even close to Nerosi.

She was exhaling a breath when the sound of footsteps halted her in her tracks. Sumera's warning about being out after dark flashed through her mind again—if lurking outside of Ulalume at night was bad, Finch couldn't even imagine how much trouble she'd be in getting caught in the tunnels, seeing as they were technically off-limits to students.

She barely had time to slip into a small passageway and tuck herself around the corner before someone stepped into view. Finch silently reached into her pocket and withdrew her phone, sticking it around the corner so the only the very top of it poked out.

The screen showed nothing but darkness.

But then, the footsteps grew louder, and Finch quickly snapped a picture before ducking back around the wall, heart slamming in her chest. The person walked past, shoes clicking on the concrete with each step. It sounded distinctly like the echo of high heels.

As the sound of them slowly grew quiet, Finch exhaled the breath she had been holding. What was someone else doing down here at this hour?

Her phone clicked as she went to her photos, opening up the one she'd snapped before hiding. The hallway was just bright enough for her to make out the color of the girl's hair and the color painted across her lips. Both were red.

Finch's heart shuddered. She recognized this girl from yesterday morning—the one who'd been kissing Selena outside the lighthouse.

Kyra.

———————

The next morning, Selena woke up to find Kyra, Risa, and Amber finishing up breakfast in the living room. Selena barely had time to say good morning before Kyra shot up out of her chair, bounding toward Selena with uncharacteristic enthusiasm.

"You're awake," Kyra said, flashing a smile. "I was hoping you'd be up soon."

Selena studied her, taken aback. "You...look nice."

Kyra beamed, revealing a mouth full of brilliant white teeth. Selena could have sworn that weren't that white yesterday. She also could have sworn that Kyra had at least a little bit of acne on her forehead. And breakage from the bad bleach job.

But now those tiny flaws were gone. This version of Kyra had the most flawless skin Selena had ever seen, along with flowing, fiery red hair no longer muddied by the auburn dye and completely devoid of broken baby hairs. The smattering of freckles across her nose stood out like she'd been in the sun recently—it was maddeningly cute. Selena couldn't explain it, but she looked as if someone had used a photo editor on her actual face.

Selena's cheeks felt hot. It was downright unfair for Kyra to look this good at 8 a.m.

The redhead finger-fluffed her sleek hair. "Good news, St. Clair—the thing we saw in the tunnels wasn't a monster."

Selena's eyebrows shot up. "What?"

"Sorry—your little investigation was taking too long." Kyra shrugged. "So I decided to go down there by myself last night. You wouldn't believe what's down there. She's—well, I honestly don't know what she is. But," she gestured to her hair, "she did this."

"*She?*" Selena asked.

Kyra offered a somewhat smug close-lipped smile. "For the record, her name is Nerosi." She reached up and wound a lock of hair around her finger. "And she wants to help us. As a thank-you for freeing her."

"Help us?" Selena blinked, slowly beginning to shake her head. "You understand how wild that sounds, right? A strange glowing woman in the tunnels wants to grant our wishes?"

"I didn't think you'd be so closed-minded." Kyra shrugged and pulled her backpack over her shoulder. "I'm headed to class. If you change your mind, I'm going to see Nerosi again tonight."

"There's no way in hell," Selena said pleasantly.

"Your funeral." Kyra wiggled her fingers. "See ya."

As soon as the door shut with Kyra's departure, Amber curled a lock of mousy hair around her finger. "So, like. I don't want to sound mean but—what is the likelihood that Kyra was like…on mushrooms or something last night?"

Selena shook her head. "She's the one always saying her body is a temple. She doesn't mess with stuff like that."

Risa looked unconvinced. "One time I watched her drink vodka mixed with milk because we didn't have any other mixer. I believe she called it a *Whiter Russian.*"

"Okay, so there are exceptions." Selena let out a breath. "Look, let's not jump to conclusions. We need to know more before we do anything."

"Are you implying we should go back down there?" Risa asked.

Selena shook her head. "Definitely not. Remember last time when we all woke up outside afterward with no memory of how we got there?"

Amber shrugged. "I mean, maybe it's worth it. Whatever happened to Kyra made her look amazing." She stared off into the middle distance dreamily. "If there is actually a weird magic lady under the school, do you think she'd dye my hair blond? I think that'd be nice."

"You're unbelievable." Selena took her to-go cup of coffee and slung her bag over her shoulder. "Whatever, I'm leaving. Please don't go poking around the tunnels for weird women who might bleach your hair for free."

Amber sang out, "No promises!"

Selena let out one more disgruntled noise before stealing an apple off the counter and heading for the door.

seven

The night after her chat with Nerosi, Finch turned the heat up in the shower so the small room filled with steam. Finch was grateful she'd been put into one of the nicer rooms on campus—most girls had to use the showers in the communal bathrooms in each hall.

As Finch leaned back to wash the conditioner out of her hair, however, she had the sudden, distinct feeling that she was being watched.

She quickly rubbed water out of her eyes, heart racing. How could someone have gotten in? She'd locked the door behind her, and the door to the suite was locked. Gingerly, she caught the edge of the shower curtain in her fingers.

Finch peered out. She held the curtain in a vise grip. A cloud of steam hovered in the air, but otherwise, the bathroom was empty.

You're imagining things, Finch gently reminded herself.

She did her best to keep her breathing even, regardless of how her heart still slammed against her ribs.

She stepped out a few minutes later, wrapping a towel around herself. The steam was still thick as she made her way to the mirror, gently wringing her hair out. The mirror was clouded over, and her reflection was nothing but a faceless blur.

Finch squinted. It was strange—in the steamed-up glass it almost looked like there was a second pale-skinned person right behi—

She whipped around.

The room was empty.

Finch's breath was ragged as her hand went to her chest. She hugged the towel tighter around herself before using her hand to wipe away the condensation on the mirror.

Her face stared back at her, gray eyes rounded. Finch squinted—maybe it was just the droplets of water sticking to the glass like tiny constellations on the mirror, but it seemed almost as if there were strange colors rippling in the air around her.

Just as Finch was leaning forward to get a better look at them, something swallowed up the sound around her.

How easily they walk into a trap, a voice whispered softly within her mind. *Humans are but animals, I suppose. And all animals can be lured with the right bait.*

A chuckle. *I've missed this.*

Before Finch could process the words, however, she heard a distant knock. She yelped as sound came back, washing away whatever trance had fallen over her.

"Finch?" a London accent called.

"S-Sumera!" Finch opened the bathroom door, starting to sputter, "I-I'm so sorry, I—"

"You okay?" Sumera asked. She was dressed in her volleyball uniform, which had been modified so she didn't have to show as much skin as some of the other girls on the team. "I thought I heard you scream."

"I'm so sorry—I guess I listened to too many creepy podcasts recently and convinced myself..." she shook her head. "Doesn't matter, really. I-I'm okay."

"You sure?" Sumera thick eyebrows pressed together.

Finch nodded. "Yeah. Totally. Um..." She glanced back at the bathroom. "You probably want to shower since you're back from practice, right? I'll get out of your way."

While Sumera still had her eyebrows drawn and lips pursed, she didn't say anything as Finch stepped out of the bathroom to let her inside. She whispered her thanks and went around her.

Finch had only taken a few steps from the door when Sumera called, "Did you draw this?"

Finch frowned and turned back. She poked her head into the bathroom to find Sumera pointing to the mirror.

"It's cool," she said, shrugging. "Maybe a bit creepy."

But Finch couldn't respond—her mouth had gone dry.

Drawn in the condensation in thick lines was the crooked head of the eight-eyed stag.

———

"I know it's a little bit much, but I've reserved it for us until the performance to practice. I want to make sure we're used to the stage before Homecoming."

The lights flickered on to illuminate the space. Ulalume Academy's auditorium was decorated like a vintage theater, with all the careful art deco details. Although Finch had seen it before, her eyes still got wide as if it were the first time.

It had been a few days since Finch's strange experience with the voice in her bathroom. With the collaborations beginning to rehearse outside of class, Selena had approached Finch to compare notes. After they'd set their stuff down, Selena sat on the stage, in the process of untying her boots.

She spotted Finch staring at her and said, "Go get my phone out of my bag. I want to show you something."

Finch did just that, then lowered herself to sit beside Selena while she finished up removing the other shoe. She flicked her hair out of her eyes. Her face was in shadow, jaw tight.

"Are you all right?" Finch asked, expression softening.

"It's nothing. Roommate drama." Selena paused for a moment, then corrected, "Well—whatever, you saw us. Kyra drama."

Finch thought of Kyra down in the tunnels a few nights ago. What would drive her to go down there? Was it possible she knew something?

Finch decided not to overthink that. Instead, she snuck a glance at Selena. "Do you want to talk about it?"

"Maybe? It's just that there was this…thing that happened last year, and we both apologized and agreed to move on, but I guess I'm bad at letting go of things. And now she's acting like such a selfish asshole…" Selena shook her head. "I'm sure you don't actually care about this."

Finch sat down, crossing her legs in front of her. "It's okay. I like to listen."

"Well, that makes one of us."

Finch laughed, running her fingers through her hair. She

blushed, a subtle but noticeable thing. It used to be much more prominent before May, when she still had the ability to blush like a normal person.

Selena's brows furrowed. "What? It wasn't that good of a joke."

"I—sorry." Finch turned her burning face the other way and nudged her toe against the floor. "It's just... You're being so nice."

Selena's eyebrows shot up. "If it's too weird, I can go back to being a dick. I've got some insults lined up about this whole haunted doll aesthetic you have going on."

"I think I prefer nice."

"Noted." Selena looked down at her phone. "Anyway, enough about Kyra. I was listening to music while I jogged last night and I thought *Hey, this song makes me think of Finch*, so I went looking for a piano cover and I found one. Maybe we could use it for the performance."

She passed Finch one of her AirPods. Once they'd both put one bud in, Selena hit play. Finch tapped her foot with the notes, subconsciously keeping time. She covered her empty ear with her hand to drown out other sounds, focusing entirely on the music.

"Is this from a movie?" Finch asked, still bobbing her head so her short, white hair bounced with the movement. "This song sounds familiar."

Selena looked down at her tapping finger, trying and failing to hold in a sheepish smile. "Don't make fun of me, okay?"

"Why would I make fun of you?"

Selena lifted a hand and rolled her eyes. "I don't know. I guess my other friends would. It's from *Spirited Away*."

Finch's eyebrows shot up. "What? No way! I love that movie." The ghost of a smile threatened to overtake the edge of

Selena's mouth. "Oh, cool. If you like it, I can show you the sheet music I printed out."

"Definitely. I can memorize this pretty quickly." Finch pulled the AirPod out as the song ended. "Do you have any ideas for the dance portion?"

Selena nodded and hopped up, stretching her arms up and back and making circles with her ankles. "A couple. Can I show you?"

Finch nodded, pulling her knees up to her chest and resting her chin atop them. Selena hopped up and ran backstage to where the speaker hookups were. A moment later, the same song filled the auditorium, and dust motes in the spotlights seemed to sway to it.

Selena reappeared, pulling her tank top over her head to reveal the sports bra underneath. The fabric was thin, and Finch quickly pulled her attention away from that section of the outfit. Selena dropped the top by her bag and went to the corner of the stage. The loose hairs in her ponytail shone gold in the spotlight.

"I've mostly got the middle done," she explained, stepping into fifth position. "I know we went into this meaning to do jazz, but I changed my mind back to ballet. Constructive criticism only, okay?"

Finch grinned. "Can do."

A few beats passed before Selena lifted herself onto her toes and glided across the stage, her arms floating weightlessly in the air. Each movement flowed into the next like water over stones, fully calculated but graceful. Finch took in each flex and pull of the other girl's muscles, tracking the way they extended and contracted with each movement. Her exposed skin lit up under the lights.

Finch's breath hitched for a second as Selena launched into a leap. She hung in the air, as if suspended from the ceiling.

She landed, effortlessly, on the other side. Finch stood and clapped, bouncing on the tips of her toes. A little surprised, Selena let out a small laugh and bowed.

"That was amazing! You're so good." Finch crossed the distance to her, grinning. "I've never seen anyone move like that. That leap was incredible."

Selena waved her away. "Oh, come on. It's a double stag leap—they're not hard."

"Maybe for you, but that would kill me."

"Oh, bullshit." Selena held out her hand. "Here, I'll show you."

Finch started to protest, but Selena took her hand and pulled her to the center of the stage. Finch wobbled for a moment, but then Selena's hands were on her, lifting up her arms and nudging open her stance. Finch stood like a statue, the warmth of Selena's hands sinking into her skin until it seemed as if her entire body were flaring with pink. She laughed nervously, unsure of what else to do.

Once she was satisfied, Selena stood in front of her, taking a much more graceful version of the pose she'd put Finch in. "Okay, copy me."

Selena pointed her toe, stepped, then pivoted on it, managing a quick sliding step before flinging herself into the air with power Finch had no chance of matching. In fact, when she tried, it was more like a duck dragging its feet through sludge than a leaping deer. She hopped a good six inches into the air and landed with a *thud*.

She held out her hands. "See? I told you."

"No, no, no." Selena came to stand behind Finch, hands pressing into her hips. "You gotta contain these. Pelvis tucked under."

"Tucked under *where*?"

"Just trust me!" Now Selena was laughing too. She held on and said, "I'll guide you. Now, point your toe—oh, good, yes, just like that. You have meat-hook feet! God, your feet are beautiful, and entirely wasted on you."

Finch laughed, losing her position again. Selena's warm, minty breath tickled her cheek. Finch's skin was typically so cold, but now she was on the verge of breaking a sweat.

"Really quickly now, same movement." Selena stuck her foot out. "We'll do it together. Ready? One, two, *three!*"

Finch fumbled through the steps, then jumped. This time, though, instead of slamming to the ground, she was in the air, legs bent and arms out. She almost didn't realize Selena was lifting her until she spun her around. Finch shrieked, half in terror, before dissolving into giggles. Selena held her for a full other turn before spinning her back to the ground, shaking with laughter herself.

Finch took hold of Selena's arm to steady herself, still laughing. "How did you do that? You're so strong!"

"Ballet is cutthroat," Selena explained. She held up her free arm and flexed, revealing surprisingly defined muscles.

Finch's eyes widened.

Selena added, "And I weight train."

Finch breathed, "Wow."

For a moment, they just looked at each other, still grinning and warm, studying each other's faces. Finch's gaze involuntarily fell on Selena's lips, faintly parted and painted berry-red.

Warmth blossomed in her chest.

Selena's eyes, typically so sharp, softened. Finch realized too late that she was still cradling Selena's arm and pulled away, heat flaring from her ears to her throat.

"Sorry!" Finch took a few steps back. "Y-Y'know, I actually made, um, *plans* with Sumera—I just remembered, oops! So sorry, I—I need to go."

"Right now?" Selena's face fell. "We've barely started."

"I um—need to practice the music on my own for a little. We pianists typically work alone, you know. Very important to get that...alone time." Finch moved away, frantically gathering up her things before she could be caught staring once again. Her thoughts were disjointed and wild, and the sooner she could escape, the better. "Well, great seeing you. Here—around—everywhere." *Shoot.* "Bye!"

She hurried to leave. Behind her, Selena called, "Finch? Where—?"

Too stressed to think of anything else, Finch blurted, "I'll see you later, okay?"

She sprinted back to Pergman, heartbeat slamming in her chest.

Selena spent the rest of her free period practicing in the auditorium by herself. It was a good excuse to try and stop the way she was second-guessing everything that had just happened.

Why would Finch up and leave like that? Was she one of those straight girls who got uncomfortable when a queer girl touched her? Did she think Selena was some kind of creep who was trying to take advantage of her?

Selena's stomach clenched. Sometimes, moments like this made her wish that people didn't know she was bi. Most of the time, people would say to her face that it was fine, that they weren't bothered by it, but then she'd smile at them too much or nudge them or *something* and suddenly they acted like completely platonic actions were flirting. Like maybe her identity inherently made her a threat.

She'd made a point of never even getting physically close platonically with other girls these days. It had been dumb of her to let her guard down around Finch. One seemingly nice girl saying one seemingly nice thing to her clearly didn't mean she was any different from other straight girls.

Red in the face, Selena swiped her bag up from the floor and headed out.

She thought about the interaction over and over again for the rest of the day, cringing every time she considered how it had felt to boost Finch into the air and spin her around. She walked through her classes in silence, not attempting conversation in the way she usually would. It felt as if there was fog around her that was simply too thick for her to see through, and the rest of the world was outside of it.

What finally snapped her out of it as she was leaving her final class was a girl whispering to her friend, "Did you see Kyra and her friends earlier? I wonder if they all use the same skincare routine or something. I'm so jealous."

Kyra and her friends? Since when was Kyra the de facto leader of their friend group?

Selena kept walking, heading in the direction of the lighthouse. The farther she went, though, the more whispers she managed to catch from girls passing by. Whispering Kyra's name, complimenting her in hushed tones. Not just her, though—she heard them mention Risa and Amber as well.

Each time one of them noticed her, they'd shoot her a very specific look. Selena couldn't quite place it at first, but they'd narrow their eyes, grimacing faintly.

Was this…pity?

Just as Selena was going to pull one of them aside and ask them what the hell was going on, her phone buzzed.

Risa

> If you're done with class, we're in the Waite Garden. We have bubble tea.

Selena pursed her lips before pocketing her phone and making a sharp turn toward the gardens.

The Waite Garden had been designed by Ulalume's headmistress back when she first got the job back in the early nineties. What had once been yet another wooded grove at the southeastern side of campus had been cleared out to make room for a luxurious, verdant garden. It was framed by tall, neatly pruned hedges and wrought-iron gates adorned with creeping moonflower vines. As Selena pushed through the gate, the smell of fragrant daylilies, aster, and pale pink Japanese anemones hit her. They swayed gently in the breeze.

The garden was large, with a stone path leading through. It was common for girls to come here to study, or simply hang out after class on Rainwater's rare sunny days. Despite the cloud cover that day, the garden path was lined with girls studying beneath the magnolia trees, shoes abandoned in the grass beside their backpacks.

However, Selena immediately noticed a small crowd a bit farther into the garden. While they were all seated in their own groups, they seemed to be orbiting the same central spot at the center of the garden. Selena walked past them, once again catching the same couple words in their hushed conversations: *Did you see Kyra's hair? Amber's skin looks amazing! Do you think Risa did something new with her nails?*

Selena finally spotted them as she came around a corner. Kyra, Amber, and Risa were all seated beneath a bubbling fountain carved in the shape of a mermaid spitting water into the pool below her. Kyra was lying back with sunglasses on her face, joined by Amber, cross-legged and texting, and Risa, straight-backed with a psychology textbook spread across her plaid skirt.

It was then that Selena knew exactly what everyone had been talking about.

All three of them looked amazing, hair smooth and shining, skin clear, nails immaculate. Posed beneath the fountain, they look like nymphs from a Greek myth somehow transported onto the Ulalume campus.

Selena's stomach flipped.

A voice at her side said, "Weird to not be the center of attention, hmm?"

Selena spun to find none other than Sumera Nazir leaning against a tree, eyebrows raised. Selena scowled, shooting a poison glare at her.

"Can I help you?" Selena growled.

Sumera shrugged. "Sorry, did I say that out loud? My mistake."

Selena's face reddened. "Bite me, Mer."

Sumera flinched briefly at her old nickname. Still, she immediately shook it off, going back to looking at her phone and pointedly ignoring Selena.

Selena rolled her eyes and closed the distance between herself and the other girls.

Risa's eyes rose first. "Good, you're here." She held out a brown sugar bubble tea for Selena. "The ice was melting."

Selena hesitantly took it, sitting down on the lip of the fountain on Risa's other side.

For the first time in her life, she felt out of place sitting with them. It wasn't like their features had changed at all; they were just so…polished. Like they'd sat through hours of hair and makeup before going onto a set. It was the kind of perfection that was nearly impossible for the average person to achieve.

Selena was suddenly very aware of her humidity fizz and stress acne.

She took a sip of her bubble tea, waiting for one of them to say something.

Amber, of course, was the first to crack. She fluffed her hair. The day before, it had been mousy, but was now a rich shade of golden brown. "So? What do you think?"

Selena chewed and swallowed a few pieces of boba. "Did you have to sacrifice a virgin or what?"

Amber looked fully scandalized while Kyra glared at her. Risa failed to withhold a chuckle.

"No," Kyra said, removing her sunglasses so Selena could get the full impact of her glare. "We went to see Nerosi last night. I figured you wouldn't want to come after your little tantrum."

That set Selena on edge for two reasons. First, purposefully not inviting one member of the friend group to an event was the kind of mind game bullshit Selena typically prided herself in doing whenever someone annoyed her—not something Kyra was supposed to level at her. And second, the much more important point, which was that they hadn't listened to her about going to the tunnels.

"She's really nice," Amber said, a bright smile appearing on her face. "And she's trapped down there. She told us that if she helps us, it might strengthen her connection to this world so she won't be trapped anymore."

"She was quite polite," Risa agreed. "And it seems that assisting us benefits her as much as it benefits us."

"And look," Kyra agreed, twisting hair around her fingers. "Everybody is talking about it. They're jealous."

Selena followed Kyra's gaze to the other girls seated around them. They were all sneaking glances at them, quickly looking away as if they were staring into the sun.

Something panged in Selena's chest as she realized none of them were looking at her.

"You don't even know what Nerosi is," Selena whispered, just loud enough for them to hear. "How do you know she's not just using you?"

"You're the one judging without even meeting her," Kyra pointed out.

Amber's head bobbed, a little frantic. "Exactly! You'd change your mind if you had a chance to talk to her."

Seeing how Selena's face pinched, Risa added, "You don't need to ask her for anything. But I suspect you'd feel better if you had a chance to talk with her."

"But you could ask, if you wanted," Kyra said with a little shrug. Her hazel eyes fell on Selena's hand wrapped around her bubble tea. "She could probably fix all those hangnails. Looks like you must've been pretty anxious today."

Selena flinched, pulling her hands in closer. She had done a number on them after her awkward moment with Finch. She'd picked at a few so much that they'd bled.

"You don't need to worry," Amber said, reaching out to touch Selena's knee. "We'll introduce you."

Selena looked at each of them. She felt so wildly out of her comfort zone. She was used to being the one who called the shots, the one who everyone else revolved around. And somehow, in less than two weeks, she'd gone from the core of their friend group to someone standing on the fringes looking in.

Like all the other girls, sneaking glances at them from under the magnolia trees.

Selena bit her lip. Then, carefully, she said, "I…I guess it wouldn't hurt. Speaking to her, I mean."

Kyra's mouth curved into a wolfish grin while Amber cheered, throwing her arms around Selena and nearly knocking both of them back into the fountain. Risa hid her small smile as she took another sip of her bubble tea.

"You're gonna love her!" Amber exclaimed, beaming. "She's so cool, Selena. She's got this, like, glowing skin…"

Selena tuned Amber out. Instead, she met Kyra's eyes.

Kyra took a sip of her strawberry bubble tea, leaning back on one hand. Her hair fell in soft waves over her shoulder, like a stream of fire glittering in the sun.

Selena's heart skipped a beat.

"Atta girl, St. Clair." Kyra slid her sunglasses back on, grinning. "You won't regret it."

eight

That afternoon, after she'd sat in bed anxiously chewing on the end of a pen for an hour, Finch turned the brightness on her laptop down low and tilted the screen toward her. She opened an incognito window. Her fingers hesitated on the keys for a moment before she typed out her search.

How to tell if you are attracted to someone?

She quickly deleted it. That wasn't quite right.

Can being around gay people make you gay?

No, that wasn't it either.

How to tell if you aren't straight?

Better.

The search results popped up, yielding a number of think pieces and women's magazines that advertised how to spot the "signs." Finch dabbed sweat from her brow. This was silly. She was wasting time.

She clicked on an article.

You love when your favorite actresses wear suits.

Finch *did* love when her favorite actresses wore suits.

Someone knocked on her door and Finch nearly vaulted through the ceiling. She closed the tabs and slammed her laptop shut.

"Come in!"

Sumera poked her head in. "Did I startle you?"

Finch ran a hand through her hair to settle it and pushed her laptop a little farther away. "N-No."

"You're not a very good liar, you know." Sumera leaned against her doorframe, raising her eyebrows. "You want to talk about it?"

"No," Finch blurted, too fast. She quickly held up her hands, amending, "Shoot—sorry, that sounded harsh. I just—it's—"

"Hey—it's okay. You don't have to tell me." Sumera slid her hands into the pockets of her loose canvas pants. "Anyway, I came to invite you to come hang out with Ira and Zara and me this evening. I'm worried about you, and I think it might be a nice change of pace."

Finch was a little startled. "You're—worried about me?"

Sumera shrugged. "Well, sure. Your first night you disappeared from my party and didn't show up until three a.m., then you start going down to the tunnels by yourself and acting like something is following you around."

Finch wasn't sure how to take that. On one hand, it was sweet that she cared enough to be worried. On the other hand, Finch felt somehow…judged.

"I…guess." Finch ran a hand back through her hair. "I'm busy tonight, though. But thank you—maybe we could invite them over tomorrow."

A smile broke across Sumera's face. "I'm sure they'd appreciate that. Maybe we could show them that Netflix documentary you were talking about."

"Oh! The one about the Mormon forgeries?" For a moment, the idea of a movie night was enough to distract Finch into smiling for the first time since that morning in the auditorium. "Definitely. Say hi to them for me tonight."

"Will do." Sumera's expression softened. "Take care of yourself, Finch."

Sumera closed Finch's door behind her, leaving her in silence.

Soon after Sumera left, Finch immediately regretted not taking her up on her offer. The moment she was alone again, Finch's mind began to offer up the same couple of thoughts over and over again: the way her heart had raced when Selena lifted her into the air and the way her mind had gone blank staring at her lips.

It was definitely just because Selena was attractive, objectively speaking. Could have happened to anyone.

Right?

Finch grabbed her things and threw them into her backpack. She needed a distraction ASAP.

The sun hadn't quite set when Finch left Pergman Hall. She wandered down the stone paths toward the center of campus, unsure of exactly where she was headed. Anywhere, perhaps, where she could focus on something other than Selena St. Clair.

Finch put in earbuds to block out the sound of the other girls chatting on their walks back to their dorms from dinner. She learned recently that most of the student body seemed to treat

Selena and her friends like on-campus celebrities, especially today, for whatever reason. If she wanted to get away from the thought of her, she needed somewhere quiet.

Which was how Finch eventually found herself climbing the stairs to the Ulalume library. It was made of the same gray stone as the rest of Ulalume, with its own set of soaring spires and slim windows, rectangular at the bottom with pointed tops.

Inside, the scent of old ink and crinkled pages warped by time hung in the air. Other girls sat at long, mahogany tables lit by small green lamps. They were surrounded by papers, coffee cups perched precariously atop stacks of books. Behind them were rows and rows of bookshelves below a soaring ceiling.

Finch hadn't realized she'd paused beside the circulation desk until the librarian behind it asked her, "Can I help you find something?"

Finch froze. The librarian had dyed-black hair, winged eyeliner, and dark red lipstick. If she hadn't known better, Finch would have assumed this person was a student but, looking at her closer, she appeared to be in her thirties.

"O-Oh—um." Finch swallowed the anxiety that had begun to bubble up in her throat and asked, "You wouldn't happen to have any yearbooks from 2004, would you? I-I'm doing a project on some students from that era."

The librarian smiled. "Are you looking for Ulalume's yearbook or Rainwater High's? The public high school doesn't have space in their library for local history, so we keep things like yearbooks for them."

"Oh, really? I guess both, then."

The librarian went back to her computer and gestured for

Finch to follow. As she reoriented herself in front of the desk, the librarian clacked away at the keys, her screen reflected in the lens of her rounded glasses.

"Huh. Strange—we're actually missing the 2004 yearbooks from both schools. Never had a chance to digitize them. Would 2003 or 2005 work?"

Finch nodded. "Maybe 2003?"

"Of course." The librarian stood. "Follow me."

Finch did. The librarian—whose name tag read HELENA—led her down a floor into a separate section in the basement, some of the shelves cordoned off with glass. They passed a sign that read: RAINWATER LOCAL HISTORY.

"The yearbooks are through here," Helena said, gesturing for Finch to follow. The librarian barely had to pause in front of the shelf before grabbing two books and holding them out for Finch.

"That's 2003. Feel free to check out any of the earlier ones as well—they're all right here."

Finch thanked her and took the yearbooks—plus a couple others she snagged from the shelf—and sat down at a table to examine them. The second floor of the library was empty, so she had the entire area to herself.

For the next hour, she pored over the yearbooks, studying the names and images, looking for any clues that might point her toward the identities of the members of Killing Howard. She found some pictures of the school band and checked to see if any of them looked like the images she'd seen at Simon's, but it was hard to tell considering how poor the photo quality had been.

Another hour passed, and the sky outside darkened. As the clock ticked toward 9:00, Finch sat back in her chair, sighing.

She wasn't getting anywhere. She currently had the 2003 Rainwater High yearbook open to the juniors, and nothing about any of their faces caught her attention. It wasn't like she'd expected someone to be wearing an I ♥ NEROSI shirt or anything, but she'd hoped for at least something that might distinguish them.

Finch closed her eyes, debating if there was anything else she could ask the librarian to get more information, when the sound of voices caught her attention. She cracked open an eye to see a group of students seated a few tables away laughing and shoving each other. The only reason they caught her attention—aside from how loud they were being—was the fact that some of them were boys. They must be Rainwater High students.

"I just think we should ask her to get us a spot at Octavia's," one of the boys said, his arm around one of the others. There were three boys in total and two girls. "What's the worst she can do? Say no?"

"Maybe we should stick to open mics," one of the other boys said.

Finch paused, staring at the one who had just spoken. He was pale—unnaturally so—with white hair and gray eyes that looked startling similar to her own. He chewed his lower lip as he made eye contact with one of the girls—a Latina with a cloud of dark, curly hair around her head—for support.

The girl waved a hand to dismiss the idea. "Victor, we're done with open mics. We should be playing shows, not random one-offs at coffee shops! What's wrong with asking Nerosi for help? Like Theo said—the worst she can do is say no."

The white-haired boy shrugged. "I-I dunno. I don't want her to feel like we're using her."

Finch stood up without thinking. Were they talking about the same Nerosi? Was it possible she wasn't the only one who knew about her?

She closed the space between them. None of them looked up at her as she approached, but she cleared her throat all the same when she got there.

Still, none of them looked up.

"Excuse me?" Finch asked, feeling self-conscious about the fact none of them seemed to even register her presence. "C-Could I talk to you guys? I overheard you saying…"

She trailed off. None of them were looking at her. In fact, it was like she'd never spoken, because they immediately continued with their conversation about playing Octavia's, their enthusiasm unchanged.

"I…" Finch's face fell. "Oh. Okay. Sorry."

That was the moment, however, that Finch became aware of the faint, multicolored aura around them. It had been subtle enough that she hadn't seen it at first, but now that she was closer, it was clear as day, rippling over the scene in shades of pink and blue and green, a curtain hanging between them.

She reached out to touch it, but wrenched back when one of them looked up.

It was the white-haired boy. He stared directly at her with his eyes wide, mouth faintly agape. He choked on whatever he was about to say.

The curly-haired girl looked at him. "Vic?"

"Do you…do you see a girl?" he asked her. The others' heads all whipped around as he pointed to her and added, "Right there?"

The other girl, who had dyed-orange hair, raised her eyebrows. "What are you talking about? There's n—"

Finch felt a hand on her shoulder and jumped, letting out a choked yelp.

"We're closing soon." It was Helena, her eyebrows arched. She cocked her head to the side and asked, "Are you all right? I didn't mean to startle you."

"O-Oh, no! Of course not. I just…"

Finch glanced back at the table.

It was empty.

Ice crept up her spine as the librarian added, "If you wouldn't mind packing up your things, I can re-shelve any books you borrowed."

So now I'm seeing things too? What's wrong with me?

Shaking her head, Finch quickly said, "T-That would be great, thank you!" She rushed back to her table, quickly stacking the yearbooks. "S-Sorry, I—"

She paused just as she was going to close the final yearbook. There, at the bottom of the page, was a familiar picture. This one, however, had brown hair and eyes and perfectly normal, rosy skin. Not alabaster white, as she'd seen it a second before.

It was him. The boy from the table.

"You all right?" Helena asked.

"Y-Yes—absolutely." Finch took out her phone. "Can I just take a picture of this real quick?"

Helena nodded, clearly giving up on rushing her. "Be my guest."

Finch quickly snapped a picture of the boy, then passed the yearbook back to her. "Thank you! I really appreciate your help."

As she left the library, Finch sent the image to her group chat with Simon and Selena.

> I think this is one of the members of Killing Howard.

The name beneath the picture read, in stark, black letters: VICTOR DELUCA.

nine

Simon

Finch, you were right about Victor

His mom still lives in Rainwater

I found her in the phone book and she confirmed he was in Killing Howard

She gave me the other members names too

Selena

I'm sure she was stoked to get a call from a stranger out of the blue about her dead son

Simon

missing, not dead!

Do you think she'd be willing to answer some questions for us?

Simon

Yeah! I asked about that too and she said tonight or Saturday works

Selena

sry, busy tonight

sat works

Same with me!

Simon

Saturday it is

Just before midnight on Friday night, Selena, Kyra, Amber, and Risa all donned black outfits and snuck out the front door of Annalee Lighthouse. There was a light rain, and mist rose from the sodden earth, pulling a ghostly veil over the campus. The curved lampposts flickered, illuminating brief glimpses of the girls as they hushed each other, creeping as quickly as they could across Ulalume until they came to the tunnels.

They went in through the entrance near Pergman Hall, Kyra

leading the way. She'd told Selena that she'd used this entrance almost every night last week.

Selena's heart beat double-time, sweat dampening her clammy forehead and palms. She'd been convinced that every rustle in the trees was an Ulalume campus safety officer walking the grounds. If she got in trouble again after the tequila incident, she doubted the Boston Conservatory, her dream college, would forgive two marks on her permanent record.

But thankfully, their descent into the tunnels was uneventful.

"You good, St. Clair?" Kyra asked, biting back a laugh. "You look pale."

Selena squared her shoulders and glared. Sarcastically, she said, "Ugh, you're so right. If only they'd installed more flattering lighting down here. Where are our tuition dollars even going?"

Kyra rolled her eyes. She muttered, "Charming as always."

It took them another ten minutes or so to reach the dirt passage that Selena remembered from her first night at Ulalume. The bioluminescent plants pulsated ghostly light down upon them. Selena's stomach clenched and she hung back a bit while Kyra proceeded at a brisk pace, gliding toward the room at the end of the hall like she owned it.

Selena felt a gentle touch on her arm and whipped around to find Amber looking at her with a little smile on her face.

"It's okay," she said. "I was afraid at first too."

Selena wrenched her arm away. "I'm not afraid of anything."

Arms wrapped around herself, Selena quickened her pace to catch up with Kyra.

However, she came to a screeching halt the second she

stepped into the room. Kyra stood in front of a creature that stole the breath from Selena's lungs and left her cold.

Nerosi's black eyes fell on Selena. When Selena tried to meet them, a painful stabbing sensation cut through her. It was like nails on a chalkboard or metal grinding against metal but worse, as if it could wrench Selena's consciousness out of her like the pit of a fruit.

"Oh! I'm so sorry." Nerosi looked away, only looking at Selena sidelong. "I forget that happens to you humans when you look at me."

Her voice was soft and lilting, with an unplaceable but musical accent. It reminded Selena of something a fairy might have in a children's movie, sweet and inviting.

"Nerosi, this is Selena," Kyra explained, holding out a hand to her. "The one I told you about."

Nerosi nodded before approaching Selena, her feet delicately following the lines drawn on the floor with perfect balance. She moved on the balls of her feet like a dancer.

"You're just as beautiful as Kyra said."

Selena was paralyzed as the creature reached out as if to touch her. Nerosi froze when Selena's shoulders tightened. Nerosi took a step back.

"Ah," the creature said, face falling. "You're afraid of me."

"What even are you?" Selena snapped, shaking her head. "A ghost? A demon? There's no way you're real."

"You can look at something standing directly in front of you and be unsure whether or not it's real?" Nerosi asked, not with any amount of judgment—it was purely curiosity.

Selena paused, praying that no one could see how her hands

had begun to shake. "I don't mean *physically* real." Selena gestured to her. "I mean whatever is underneath this. Whatever you actually are, appearances aside."

"Selena," Kyra started.

Nerosi held out a hand to stop her. "No—I understand. There's nothing wrong with being slow to trust. Why would you? We've only known each other for a few minutes. I need to earn it."

Selena nodded. "Exactly. So, tell me why you're doing this." She gestured to the others. "Granting wishes for a couple of random kids. What do you get out of it?"

For a flickering second, Selena thought she saw Nerosi's mouth twitch toward a frown. But if it had, the expression was instantly caught and re-formed into another soft smile.

"Well, I'm sure Kyra has explained that I'm trapped here," Nerosi said, gesturing to the room. "And I'd like to get out. Trouble is, I don't have a strong enough connection to this world." She gestured to them. "Except through you. Whenever I use my abilities to assist you, I feel myself become more…solid, if you will. Less like a ghost and more like a person. I suspect that if I continue to strengthen my connection to you, then I'll be able to leave."

"And what would you do then?" Selena asked. "Assuming we help you leave? Where would you go?"

Nerosi eyes wandered to the hallway, the blue light from the roots reflecting like stars in the black void of her eyes. "Home, I suppose. Wherever that is. I can't yet remember where I came from."

"You can't remember," Selena repeated, crossing her arms. "That's convenient."

"She's just trying to help, Selena," Amber defended, eyes wide.

Before Selena could snap at her, Nerosi said, "No, she's right. I know I don't have a better explanation. I wish I did. But the time I spent trapped in the void—it stole my identity from me. Only now am I beginning to pick up the pieces. The darkness…" she averted her eyes, wincing. "It takes everything from you. Your thoughts, your voice, everything that makes you *you*." She looked at the scars cutting across her snow-white arms. "I don't even know where I got these."

Selena's eyes widened as tears began to drip down Nerosi's cheeks. Kyra quickly went to her side, putting a hand on her shoulder, and Amber quickly followed. Risa stayed back, shooting a scowl at Selena, who could do nothing but stand in place as Nerosi embraced Kyra and Amber.

For a figure who seemed so ethereal, it was startlingly human.

"I'm sorry," she apologized, catching her breath. "It's hard for me to remember that."

"It's okay." Kyra's narrowed eyes slid to Selena. "Selena's never been the best at delicacy."

Selena's mind reeled. She hadn't expected anything like that. Her stomach tightened.

"I-I," Selena started. "I'm sorry, I didn't realize—"

Nerosi shook her head. She let go of the other girls before she dabbed at her eyes. "No, that was unfair of me. You were just asking a question."

Kyra glared at Selena over her shoulder and mouthed, *You're such an asshole.*

Selena winced. It wasn't the first time someone had accused her of such. But usually, when that happened, it was in response to something Selena had done intentionally. Hearing it about something like this made her feel strangely, painfully guilty.

"Sorry," Selena muttered.

"It's all right." Nerosi dabbed away the rest of her tears. She came a step closer to Selena. "I understand. You want to protect yourself and your friends. But I truly do want to help you, if you'll let me."

Selena swallowed thickly. She almost felt like she couldn't say no after that—not with the way her friends were all looking at her in varying degrees of admonishment.

Nerosi added, "What do you want, Selena?"

Selena bit her lip. Her gaze fell on each of her friends, thinking of the way everyone had stared at them in the gardens like they were something exceptional, more than human.

She nodded to herself. "The same thing you gave them."

Nerosi smiled. "Ah. Easy enough. I may not have most of my abilities, but that I can do."

Nerosi approached her, and Selena braced herself, closing her eyes. When the creature's hand touched her cheek, Selena opened them again and saw herself reflected in those black eyes.

This time, she didn't look into them—only at herself. A feeling of euphoria washed over her as she watched her hair smooth out, her skin clear, a brightness seeming to illuminate her from the inside. The feeling of guilt from before faded, replaced by wonder that brought a blush to her cheeks and a shine to her eyes.

Nerosi pulled away and smiled. "There you are."

"Yay!" Amber cheered, coming over to hug her. As she threw her arms around her, she said, "See? Nothing to worry about."

Selena looked down at her hands. All the torn skin along her fingernails was healed. Same with the dance bruises on her calves.

Every surface-level flaw was gone.

"I know it's not much," Nerosi said. "But I hope this means you'll come back and see me."

Oddly enough, Selena barely remembered why she'd felt so mistrustful before. Why would she doubt someone offering gifts out of the kindness of her own heart? Especially someone who seemed so intent on helping.

"Thank you," Selena said, smiling up at Nerosi and meeting her mirror-like eyes once more. As she did, she noticed her teeth had become even whiter.

Nerosi nodded. "Of course. You're always welcome to come back down here and see me. While I can't promise I'm powerful enough for every request, I'm sure I can find ways to make them happen."

"I wish there was a way for us to communicate with you without coming down here," Amber said. "Sometimes it's scary sneaking across campus."

Nerosi nodded. "I understand. Can I let you in on a little secret?"

All of the girls seemed to perk up, leaning in closer.

Nerosi grinned. "I have an emissary here on the island. If you tell him things, I'll hear them."

"An emissary?" Risa repeated, unsure.

Nerosi nodded. "A sort of…messenger. I've only just recently remembered I had a connection to him, as he's begun sharing messages with me again. Perhaps you've seen him—he appears as a stag."

Selena's eyebrows shot up. "The eight-eyed stag? It works for you?"

Even with the warmth buzzing in Selena's veins, something about that left an unsettling taste in her mouth.

Nerosi nodded. "Yes. Sometimes he allows me to see through his eyes. I'd been unsure of what sort of visions I was seeing until now, but I realized this whole time, it was him. So if you need me, look for him. He'll keep an eye out for you."

"That's amazing," Kyra breathed. "You're amazing."

"Kind of you to say." Nerosi's eyes fell on Selena once more. "Lovely to meet you, Selena. I hope I'll see you again."

Selena nodded. "Absolutely."

After that, the girls said goodbye to Nerosi, thanking her again before heading out through the tunnels. Nerosi's gift left Selena with a smile on her face and a lightness in her step. The sort of giddiness that came with feeling invincible.

As they emerged onto the Ulalume campus, Kyra turned around, walking backward as she spoke to them.

"I have one more piece of good news," she said, swinging around the backpack she'd brought and unzipping it. She withdrew a bottle, grinning. "A deliveryman *accidentally* dropped this off today after I asked Nerosi for it last night."

Amber's eyes brightened. "Is that sparkling pink Moscato?"

Kyra nodded. "To celebrate Selena finally coming to her senses." Kyra nodded sideways. "Wanna go split this on the beach?"

Amber cheered, throwing her hands in the air and doing a little spin. Risa nodded while Selena couldn't help but smile.

For a second, anyway. Until they heard the sound of footsteps behind them.

Selena was the first to duck out of sight behind a tree, quickly followed by Risa, who yanked Amber along with her. Kyra, however, stayed put.

Not far away on the cobblestone path between dorms was a

campus security guard doing a late-night sweep of the campus. He swung his flashlight left and right, not looking in their direction. All he had to do, though, was turn around and they'd be caught red-handed.

With alcohol.

Again.

Selena's throat tightened. *This time they'll do a lot worse than suspend me from the dance program.*

She hissed, barely audible, "Kyra, get over here!"

But Kyra just chuckled under her breath, shaking her head. She slowly brought a finger to her glossy lips, then nodded to the woods.

From the trees came a bellowing scream, echoing and drawn out. It made the hair on the back of Selena's neck stand pin-straight. There was a rustle in the bushes, and the security guard called out, asking who was there.

For a second, the glow of eight eyes and a pair of massive antlers adorned with torn velvet came into view. The eight-eyed stag let out another scream, lips drawing back from a set of jagged teeth. It was almost the tone of an elk's bugle but just a bit too… human.

Which is probably why it fooled the guard into running into the woods.

The stag turned and darted away, leading the guard with it.

"See?" Kyra laughed. "Nerosi is looking out for us. Nothing to be afraid of."

Risa shivered. "Let's get out of here before he comes back."

Amber nodded in agreement and they all rushed toward the beach, keeping an eye over their shoulders. As they did, though, and they realized they weren't being followed, the smiles reappeared on their faces. Soon, they were giggling, their laughter only growing louder as they reached the beach on the southern tip of Rainwater. The sound usually would have been enough to draw attention, but now? It felt like nothing could touch them.

Even if, just faintly in the back of Selena's mind, a voice whispered, *It's too good to be true.*

She chose to ignore it.

ten

Do you know much about ghosts?

Simon

Too much, arguably

Great!

Perfect!

Awesome!

Do ghosts typically respond
when you talk to them?

Hypothetically

Simon

Sometimes? I'd expect it to be the same with people. They might ignore you if they don't want to talk.

Why?

Just curious! Nothing weird hahaha

But if I had seen a ghost, would it be normal for them to sort of…repeat an event?

Almost like reenacting a scene from when they were alive?

Simon

That sounds more like an Echo

Echo? Capital E?

Simon

Yep. It's exactly what you described—something that appears to be ghosts reliving something that happened in the past. Some people think it's not actually ghosts, but instead actual moments that happened in the past being reflected into the present. Very spooky

What would cause something like that?

Simon

Dunno. They're uncommon, except in a couple specific hotspots around the world. There are a few out west, one in Japan, a few in Russia. And one more I can think of off the top of my head

Here?

Simon

Ding, ding, ding

Are you serious?

Simon

Uh-huh. Tons of people around Rainwater have reported seeing their dead relatives around, going about their lives as normal. Never strangers, weirdly enough.

Have you?

Simon

Nah. No one I want to see. Or no one who wants to see me, I guess.

You think the Echoes are…sentient?

Simon

That's what people typically say

Or that the living control it

The Echoes show us what we need to see, whatever that may be

Huh.

Simon

Still sure you didn't see anything?

Whaaaaaaaaaat?

Me?

Of course not

Hahahahaha

Simon

(¬_¬)

Anyway, see you tomorrow!
Excited to talk to Mrs. DeLuca!

Simon

Yeah. See you tomorrow, Finch

Saturday morning came with a faint touch of sunlight peeking through the gray sky. While Finch got dressed, she thought about her conversation with Simon yesterday. Was it possible her desire to figure out more about Killing Howard had caused that Echo?

Or had Killing Howard wanted to contact her?

And how, if it was an Echo, had Victor been able to see her?

She let out a breath, picking up her backpack and swinging it onto her shoulders. Maybe this meeting with Victor's mom would help to answer her questions.

Twenty minutes later, Finch had made her way to Rainwater Road where it connected to campus. Simon and Selena were already waiting in Ms. Hemming's Jeep.

"You made it!" Simon cried as she climbed into the back seat.

Selena turned around in her seat to look at her. She pointed to Finch's chest and said, "Nice sweater. We love a commitment to uniform even on a Saturday."

Finch's cheeks warmed. She couldn't explain what it was about Selena that made her heart palpitate even faster than it had the last time she'd seen her, but she looked absolutely incredible. Like an airbrushed model who had stumbled off the cover of a magazine and landed in this Jeep.

A beat passed before Finch realized they were waiting for her to say something. *Right, right—uniform. What was she saying?*

Finch looked down at herself. She'd thrown on the sweater she'd bought back in May that read ULALUME ACADEMY across the chest. It did, technically, meet dress code standards, but it had felt too casual to pair with her usual plaid skirt and white tights.

"Um," Finch managed. Her voice cracked as she said, "School pride?"

Selena flashed her a stunning smile before mouthing, *Suck-up*. Finch's heart felt like it was going to punch straight out of her chest.

Luckily, Simon started the Jeep and took off before Finch could respond. Selena turned around and messed with the radio until she found some bubblegum pop to blast while Simon rolled his eyes.

When the three of them pulled up to the house, they found Mrs. DeLuca sitting on the porch, smoking a cigarette. Based on the tinfoil in her hair, she was in the middle of dyeing her gray hair to match the rest of her auburn locks. She didn't move when Simon and the girls exited the car.

"Mrs. DeLuca?" Simon asked as they approached. "I'm Simon. The one who called you?"

She pulled the cigarette out of her mouth, put it out in a chipped teacup at her side, and tucked what was left behind her ear. She studied the three of them, her eyes lingering longer on Finch. A glint of something like recognition flashed across her watery blue eyes. Before Finch could ask, Mrs. DeLuca pointed to the Ulalume sweater she had on.

"Shouldn't mess with that school," she said. "If your parents had any sense, they'd send you somewhere without a track record of killing their students."

A cold chill ran up Finch's spine. "W-What?"

"That's what we wanted to talk to you about," Selena said, unfazed.

"Right." Mrs. DeLuca stood, waving her hand. "Come inside. You want coffee? Tea?"

All three asked for coffee. They sat down at the creaky kitchen table while Mrs. DeLuca went to get mugs. Finch marveled at the sheer number of photos Mrs. DeLuca had managed to hang up.

She quickly recognized Victor as the woman's only child. He was cute, with a big, gap-toothed smile and olive skin. In nearly all the photos, he had the same dark hair and tan complexion. Except one that Finch couldn't stop staring at.

In one photo of him posing with his mother in front of a sea cliff, his hair had gone chalky white, as had his skin.

Exactly like in the Echo.

Subtly, Finch took out her phone and snapped a picture.

Mrs. DeLuca returned with coffee, cream, and sugar. Finch sprung at the chance to dilute the taste and quickly filled most of the cup with cream. Meanwhile, Simon went on about how thankful he was that Mrs. DeLuca had agreed to meet with them, and how sorry he was to dredge up bad memories.

"He meant everything to me," she said, glancing at the photos on the wall. "Sometimes I think, maybe, he'll walk right back in like nothing's happened. I think I see him around town, still wearing the same clothes and everything. It's strange, y'know?"

Finch nodded softly. After her parents died, she'd spent the first few weeks thinking she saw her parents everywhere she went. A woman in the grocery store with the same hair color and build was her mother for just a few seconds, and a man raking his lawn in a thick flannel shirt was her father. For a moment, she'd convince herself she'd been lied to, and her parents had made it out of the car all along, and they'd been here the whole time.

And then they'd turn around, prove to be someone else, and Finch's chest would ache with the weight of a tiny second—or third, or fourth, or fifth—death all over again.

"I understand," Finch whispered.

Mrs. DeLuca shot her a look, one eyebrow raised—less in judgment, more in question—but didn't ask. Instead, she went on, "But I'm sure you didn't come here to listen to me talk about grief. I can't imagine what you want to know about some disappearance from well over a decade ago."

Simon took out his phone and started recording. "Well—okay. So. A few things. Can you tell me a little about Killing Howard? How they started, maybe how Victor got involved?"

Mrs. DeLuca rolled her eyes at the mention of Killing Howard. "Vic always wanted to be in one of those whiny bands back in the day—especially after the accident."

"What accident?" Simon asked.

Mrs. DeLuca chewed her lip. "A little more than a year before he disappeared, Vic drove off the road and hit a tree. They pronounced him dead at the hospital, but somehow, he pulled through out of nowhere. He was different after that."

She pointed to the photo on the wall of them in front of the sea cliff. "Pale like that. His hair started growing in a different color, like yours, dear. It was the damnedest thing."

Finch's skin went cold, eyes wide. "He—he *died*?"

Mrs. DeLuca nodded. "For a bit, yes. No pulse, no breathing. And then…boom. Wide awake and asking for me. They'd already pulled the sheet over him."

"Sounds like a miracle," Simon said.

"Guess so. If you believe in that sort of thing." She took a big sip of coffee, exhaling as she set the mug down. "Wasn't long after that he met his girlfriend, Margo, at one of those little Ulalume parties. She was the one who decided to get their band together."

"Sounds like you didn't like her much," Selena scoffed.

Mrs. DeLuca rolled her eyes. "She was…well, she was real *driven*, I'll give her that. I think Vic liked that about her. It's probably why he stuck around even when the band kept getting kicked out of practice spaces."

"Kicked out?" Finch asked. "Why? Were they disruptive?"

"You could say that," Mrs. DeLuca chuckled. "They were terrible. No one would let them play at any venues around town. They got booed off the stage at an open mic in Portland once."

Finch couldn't even imagine how she'd react if someone did that when she was first learning to play the piano. "But—I heard they improved a lot, right?"

"I guess—if you like that sort of music," Mrs. DeLuca said. She tapped her fingers against the table. "But yes. They got much better. Little Theo—their singer—seemed to stop being tone-deaf overnight. They got an anonymous donation from someone at Ulalume for new instruments. They were leaving town to play shows in Portland every other night—even got invited to go down to Boston and New York. People started showing up out of nowhere. Like magic.

"I suspect that's why so many people in Rainwater think they left to pursue their music." Mrs. DeLuca narrowed her eyes and scowled—the deeply etched frown lines framing her chin told Finch she did a lot of scowling. "But I know that's not true. Vic would never leave without saying goodbye."

"It does sound like quite a success story," Simon said. He

tapped his phone to make sure it was still recording, then asked, "If you don't mind me asking…what do you think changed things for them? Dumb luck? More practice?"

Without missing a beat, Mrs. DeLuca said, "A deal with the devil."

Simon's eyebrows shot up while Finch's mouth fell open softly. Selena, who had been examining her nails for the last couple minutes, jerked her gaze up to meet Mrs. DeLuca's, wide-eyed.

"That's what Vic used to tell me," Mrs. DeLuca said, not so much as cracking a smile. "Strange joke, huh?"

The three of them exchanged glances.

Finally, Simon broke the silence. "You…don't think he was serious, do you?"

"Wouldn't that be something?" She took a breath, locking eyes with Simon's still-illuminated phone at the center of the table.

She reached out and paused the recording.

"This might be better off the record," she said.

"Of course." Simon slid his phone into his pocket.

Mrs. DeLuca stood, holding up a finger to tell them to wait. Finch mouthed a question to Simon, but he just shrugged, clearly no more informed than her. Meanwhile, Selena took the opportunity to refill her coffee, despite the look Simon shot her.

"What?" she asked. "This is the first decent coffee I've had in three weeks."

Mrs. DeLuca returned with a few sheets of paper that she spread across the table. Finch, Simon, and Selena all leaned forward to take in the images, squinting and furrowing their brows.

They were all incredibly skillful renditions of the eight-eyed stag from different angles, drawn in thick, blocky lines with bold shadowing. The velvet Finch had seen on its horns before was drawn even bloodier here—as if the stag had gored something with them.

"Some of the folks around town used to say the kids were devil worshippers," Mrs. DeLuca explained. "I didn't believe it until I overheard Victor telling Margo about some…*Horned Queen*, I think he said. And then I found these in his room—Margo drew them. I thought he might mean some Wiccan thing, but he acted all confused when I asked him about it later, so I guess not."

"Do you think that Victor and the other members of Killing Howard were worshipping this stag?" Simon asked, a bit more point blank than Finch would have expected.

Mrs. DeLuca was quiet for a beat, her finger still holding the corner of one of the drawings.

"I don't know if it was exactly this," she admitted. "But I do think they were up to something."

Finch couldn't help but notice the color drain from Selena's skin.

Simon raised his eyebrows. "So you think they were a…?"

"I want you to know, before I tell you this, that Victor was a good boy. He'd never hurt a fly. He had a soft heart—too soft for a world like this, if you ask me." Mrs. DeLuca took a long breath, staring at his picture on the walls. "But those kids… It may have started out as a band. That I believe. But it didn't stay that way."

Her eyes flashed up to meet Finch's.

"Killing Howard was a cult."

eleven

The drive back to Ulalume was deathly silent.

Simon tried his best to wade through the dour cloud hanging over the girls by suggesting this was a huge break for them. He mused that this could mean Killing Howard had some kind of supernatural cause to their disappearance, but neither Selena nor Finch seemed prepared to discuss it.

Selena snuck a look at the rearview mirror. Finch was somehow even paler than normal, hands pulled into the sleeves of her sweater. While she always looked somewhat frail and sick, the shadows under her eyes seemed heavier now, and her expression was dark, eyes barely blinking.

Selena pursed her lips and exhaled a heavy breath, leaning back in her seat with her eyes closed.

A cult. Killing Howard was a cult.

And if they knew about the eight-eyed stag, that had to mean they knew about Nerosi. It stood to reason that she used her abilities to help them garner fame and success—didn't it? Of course, things like fame and fortune seemed like much bigger requests than smoothing out some split ends and whitening teeth.

Nerosi's voice echoed in her head: *While I can't promise I'm powerful enough for every request, I'm sure I can find ways to make them happen.*

What way had she found to make that happen?

Selena's stomach churned. Was it possible that Mrs. DeLuca was wrong and they had just left town to play music? Started new lives away from Rainwater?

Somehow, Selena doubted it.

Simon pulled the Jeep to a stop at the edge of Ulalume's campus. "Here we are." He looked between Finch and Selena. "I'm going to see if I can find any more information about the other members based on what Mrs. DeLuca told us. I'll be in touch?"

Selena patted his shoulder. "Thanks for the ride, Sy. See ya later."

Finch muttered her thanks as well and opened the door, sliding out onto the pavement.

Simon threw the Jeep into reverse and took off into the trees. As it faded from view, Selena found Finch staring at her shoes, eyes shining. Without thinking, Selena reached out and touched her arm.

"You okay?"

"I-I need to get back," Finch said, jerking away from Selena's touch and nodding toward Pergman Hall. "I…feel pretty sick."

Selena's face burned as she pulled her hand away. *Right. Shit. I forgot about not touching her.*

"I just need to be alone," Finch whispered, shaking her head. "I-I'm sorry. I'll...talk to you later."

She hurried off without another word, leaving Selena to open and close her mouth in silence.

———————

That night, as the sun set on Rainwater, Selena curled up on the couch with a pint of mint chip ice cream, opting for that over an actual dinner. She had the TV blaring, a newscaster droning on about the bad weather for the next couple days. It seemed there were nothing but storms in their future.

Elsewhere in the lighthouse were a mix of sounds. Amber was blasting her typical annoying playlist—it was jam-packed with female-led Top 40 songs and she'd named it some infuriating shit like *Girlbosses Only* unironically—while Risa's usual indie folk competed with it across the hall. Kyra had a hairdryer on in her room.

The other girls had texted her earlier to invite her to a party with them, but Selena wasn't in the mood. She was too busy worrying about Finch.

Which was absolutely not a thing she wanted to be doing, but here she was. Finch had looked like a kicked puppy, and somehow, the same sad face that had made Selena want to scream at her a month ago was now pulling Selena's heartstrings and plucking them like harp chords. As she'd watched Finch shuffle off toward Pergman Hall earlier, she'd felt an actual ache in her chest, quickly followed by the desire to pull Finch into her arms and hold her.

Which—*hold her*? What kind of sentimental bullshit was that?

Selena calmly set down her pint of ice cream before grabbing a pillow and screaming into it.

She definitely did not have a crush on Finch Chamberlin, of all people.

She refused to have a crush on Finch Chamberlin.

"What's going on with you, St. Clair?"

Selena nearly jumped. She hadn't even heard Kyra turn off the blow-dryer, much less leave her room and appear behind her. Selena turned, ready to make a sharp comment, but it died in her throat at the sight of Kyra.

She was dressed in a low-cut black dress that hugged her curvy frame. She had on dark lipstick and eyeshadow, going for an uncharacteristically vampy aesthetic. But that part of it only really caught Selena's attention for a moment.

Instead, her eyes widened at the sight of Kyra's new haircut. It was a sharp bob that scraped her jawline, her red hair shining in the light.

Selena's eyebrows shot up. "Never took you for a bob girl."

Kyra reached up and fluffed it a bit. "Cute, right?"

"Who cut it for you?" Selena asked, narrowing her eyes. "I thought you didn't trust, and I'm quoting exactly here, *any of those small-town hicks to do it?*"

For a moment, she looked a bit pale, but she quickly brushed it off with a shrug. "I don't think I ever said that. It was just a girl in town."

"Yeah? What was her name?"

"Like I'd remember a hairdresser's name," Kyra scoffed, rolling her eyes. "Why are you wound so tight?"

"Because I can tell when you're lying to me, Kyra." Selena's nose wrinkled. "Especially about something this mundane. What are you hiding?"

"*Nothing*, jeez." Kyra crossed her pale arms, frowning at her. "Such a killjoy. I came out here to invite you to the party one more time in case you changed your mind."

On cue, Amber's door flew open, and she stepped out in jeans and a crop top. "You should definitely come to the party! It'll be so much more fun if you come."

At the sound of conversation, Risa also emerged from her room. She had a gossamer, collared shirt tucked into a skirt, her black hair back in a ponytail. Selena could smell she'd put on warm, powdery perfume.

"We can always leave early," Risa offered. "If it's bad."

Selena shook her head. "Nah." She gestured to the TV. "Thanks though. I actually have a date planned for tonight."

All three girls' eyes widened.

Selena held up her ice cream. "With Ben & Jerry."

While Kyra rolled her eyes, Amber blinked, clearly not understanding the joke, and Risa stifled a chuckle.

"You tell jokes as badly as my dad," Kyra groaned.

"We should go," Risa said, putting her hands on Amber and Kyra's shoulders. "Enjoy your ice cream, Selena."

Selena waved at them as they left. "Bye! I'll miss you dearly!"

Kyra shot her one more narrow-eyed glare as she shut the door behind them.

Selena sat back, left with nothing but the drone of the newscaster. She lay down, balancing her ice cream spoon on her nose as she stared at the ceiling. Without prompting, her thoughts immediately went back to Finch.

Fuck it, she thought, pulling out her phone.

TODAY, 9:32 PM

you up?

Finch

9:30's a pretty early bedtime, don't you think?

listen I don't judge. you feeling any better?

you seemed kinda sad earlier

I hope it wasn't something I did

Finch

You didn't do anything!

I just have a lot of personal stuff going on

ooh gotcha

sorry you're still not feeling great

Finch

Eh. C'est la vie

what do you usually do to feel better?

Finch

Oh. I'm not sure. Listening to music maybe?

what kind?

Finch

I dunno. Happy? That's pretty vague

that's perfect, actually

please stand by

Finch set her phone down, waiting for Selena to send whatever it was she had in mind.

She was curled up on her bed in a nest of blankets, a mug of tea she'd made over an hour ago sitting untouched on her desk. She'd told herself she was going to get a head start on homework, but considering how high her anxiety had decided to crank up, that felt borderline impossible.

It was what Mrs. DeLuca had said about Victor's accident that had stuck with her, the words playing on a loop in her head like a broken record: Drove off the road and hit a tree. He was pronounced dead at the hospital.

In the way it sometimes did, the memory of Finch's own accident rushed back to her.

She remembered how the chill in the water had bit into her nerves, shooting through her like an electric shock. How her lungs had burned, begging for air as she unsuccessfully fought the current. How the world had gone blurry, then dark. How she'd lost the feeling in her body.

Then nothing.

Nothing at all.

She shook her head. She couldn't have *died*. That was impossible. How would she have been able to open her eyes and claw her way to the surface if she were dead? She wouldn't have been able to drag herself through the mud and collapse in the reeds, vomiting up river water. Nor would she have been able to pull herself onto her feet and shamble to the road, standing at the edge of it in shock until another car pulled past, the headlights illuminating her fish belly–white skin and her wide, gray eyes. Her bare arms and clothes were slick with mud and blood.

The driver of that car had hardly been able to slam his brakes before he flew past her. When he got out of the car to ask her if she needed help, she'd collapsed into his arms.

The next time she'd woken up, she was wrapped in a shock blanket, surrounded by police and paramedics. One of them had asked her for her name as she shone a flashlight in her eyes. She'd barely been able to respond as reality set in and she'd realized it wasn't a bad dream.

"My parents are still down there," she'd sobbed, tears cutting through the mud on her cheeks. "They're still in the car! You have to help them—or they—or they'll—"

"We're going to take care of everything, okay?" the paramedic had said. "You just focus on staying awake while we get you to a hospital."

"I can't leave them," she'd cried. She'd tried to stand, but her legs had failed her. The paramedic had barely been able to catch her as her voice cracked and she shakily begged, "Or I'll be alone. Please—I don't want to be alone. I need them."

"We need to take care of you right now, Finch," the paramedic said. "Focus on me, okay? We're going to get you help."

Finch had broken down after that, unable to speak as they loaded her into the back of an ambulance. Everything had slowed as if time itself were halting, trying to stop Finch from entering the After that came when this terrible thing put an end to her Before. The thing the cops would later tell her was just an accident when they interviewed her about it in her cold, sanitized hospital room. The thing that shouldn't have happened, but despite all reason, had.

Tears pricked in Finch's eyes.

Her phone buzzed.

Wiping away tears and sniffling, Finch unlocked her phone to find Selena had texted her again. This time, it was with a link to a Spotify playlist.

It was titled Happy Songs for Sad Finch.

TODAY, 9:55 PM

Selena

give this is a listen

might help get your mind off whatever is making you sad

Oh

Wow

This is really sweet Selena 🖤

Selena

me? sweet? imagine

but seriously, if you ever want
someone to talk to, I'm here

sorry I know that sounds cheesy as hell

Hahahaha

It's okay

I appreciate the thought

Selena

any time 🖤

Finch felt a disarming warmth in her chest.

Doing her best to shove down the memories, she grabbed her headphones off her bedside table and turned on Selena's playlist. The first song began with a soft piano melody before shifting to lyrics of an unexpected love. Finch lay in a fetal position, curling around the shape of her phone against the covers, closing her eyes as she listened.

For a moment, she didn't feel alone.

As the clock ticked later into the night, however, Finch couldn't sleep.

Not when she had a very specific question on her mind.

Rising out of bed, Finch left her headphones on the pillow before slipping on a pair of shoes and sneaking through her window.

When she reached Nerosi's room, she was standing in front of the antler altar. Her form seemed opaquer than the last time Finch had seen her. A bit less ghostly.

She spun the second Finch stepped inside. "Oh—hello, Finch. I haven't seen you for a bit. I've missed you."

She had a warm smile on her face as she closed the distance between them. "It's a bit late to be down here, don't you think?"

"I'm okay," Finch lied. She sniffled, still a bit stuffed up from crying. "I um. I came down here because I had kind of a...strange question."

Nerosi blinked. "Of course. How can I help? Did you need a favor?"

"I-It's not that, really," Finch corrected quickly. "It's a question about you."

Nerosi seemed tense, but it might have been a trick of the light. "I haven't remembered much more than I already told you, unfortunately."

Finch shook her head. "I understand. But I remember when we first met, you said you felt as if there was a connection between us. And I was wondering... Is it possible we were connected somehow before I pulled you out of the void?" While Nerosi's eyes widened, Finch added, "Because a couple months before I met you, something really terrible happened to me, and after that... well, I felt drawn here. Like there was something guiding me down here to you."

Nerosi froze for a moment. Her fingers twitched at her sides, and her eyes were even wider than normal—Finch had to remind herself not to look directly into them. Her mouth pressed into a line.

Finally, she said, "Perhaps there's...something."

"Also," Finch asked, "what exactly is the eight-eyed stag, and why does it seem to be associated with you? Because it was there that night." Finch didn't realize that she'd started to breathe faster, and that her heart rate had picked up when, louder, she added, "The night that my parents died."

Nerosi jerked back, putting a foot behind her like she might run the other way. "I-I don't know anything about a stag."

"Then why does it seem to know where you are?" Finch demanded. "It led me here the first time."

"I can't remember anything about a stag," Nerosi said quietly, shaking her head. She glanced up at Finch, frowning, eyebrows bent in sympathy. "Finch, I'm so sorry. Maybe it does know me, but I don't know anything about it, I swear."

"Are you lying to me?" Finch demanded. She wasn't sure why she felt so emboldened, but the pieces just weren't lining up. Not with her parents' death, not with Victor's disappearance—none of it made sense.

Nerosi's face crumpled. It was such a human reaction that Finch flinched. She was quiet for a long beat.

"I suppose there is one thing I've been keeping from you." She reached up to rub her eyes. "I didn't want to hurt you, Finch. But it seems like you've figured it out."

Finch's eyebrows rose.

Nerosi took a shaky breath. "You're right. There was a connection between us before you came down here for the first time. It's because I heard you calling out the night that..." she swallowed. "The night of the accident in the river."

Those words felt like a punch to the gut. "You were there?"

Nerosi shook her head. "Not exactly. The void I was trapped in—it was in a reality parallel to this one, and sometimes I could hear things from this world where the barrier between us was thin. And that night I heard you begging for help, asking not to die, so I...I used what little power I had to connect our life forces. The connection allowed you to take some of my power and stay alive. Think of it like a conduit. I suspect that's why you've come to... look a bit like me."

Finch glanced down at herself. It was true—her white hair and skin looked nearly identical to Nerosi's.

Finch's mind reeled. "Is that why I can see the weird ripples in the air as well?"

Nerosi nodded. "Yes. Our connection seems to have made you sensitive to things beyond this world. You have an inherent sense for the supernatural."

Finch was stunned silent.

"I'm sorry I didn't tell you," Nerosi said. "I only wanted to protect you."

"But..." Finch let out a shaking breath. "If you saved me, why couldn't you save my parents?"

Nerosi winced. Silence spread thickly between them, Finch on the verge of tears. Nerosi's onyx eyes glittered as she shook her head, biting her lip.

"I'm sorry," she managed. "I only heard you. I wish I could have helped them—I really do. I know that's no excuse, but it's all I have."

Finch stared at the ground, watching as two tears dripped onto the ash circle that Nerosi was trapped within.

"Finch—" Nerosi started to say.

But Finch had already started for the tunnels, leaving Nerosi with nothing but the echoes of her footfalls as she left.

twelve

The next week passed in a blur for Finch. During the day, she went to class, practiced with Selena, and then spent the evenings with Sumera and her friends. All the while, she zoned out, unable to pull herself out of her own memories. She struggled to sleep, instead opting to stay up and write down notes about what she knew in a spiral-bound notebook late into the night when she was finished with her homework. Somehow, getting her thoughts down on paper seemed to be the only way to get them to stop repeating over and over in her head. Each night she was comforted by the sound of a thunderstorm outside—it had been raining nonstop for nearly a week.

Finch considered this as she popped open her umbrella to walk back to Pergman from her calculus class on Friday afternoon. The clouds were heavy in the sky, blotting out the sun in a gray blanket. Just as she drifted off into her thoughts again, her phone buzzed in her pocket with a new text from Simon.

TODAY, 3:21 PM

Simon

Hey! My mom's out of town this weekend so I'm throwing a party tonight if you want to come

That sounds so fun! What time?

Simon

9:30ish. You're welcome to come over whenever though

9:30 sounds great!

Simon

Amazing

Can't wait to see you ♥

She shoved her phone in her pocket, eyes rounded. Since when did he write texts like that? Why was he now using *hearts*?

"So you're going to Simon's tonight?"

Finch nearly jumped out of her skin, but she turned to find Sumera had fallen into step beside her, in the process of typing out a message on her phone.

"How did you know?"

Sumera turned her phone around to reveal her own text conversation with Simon. "He told me. You didn't hear it from me, but he's planning on asking you out tonight."

Finch stopped cold. She'd obviously spent time with Simon with Selena for their Killing Howard investigation, and once or twice when Sumera had invited him over to watch movies with them and her friends, but they've never been...*alone*. Much less on a *date*.

Her first date.

Sumera furrowed her eyebrows. "You all right?"

Finch nodded and resumed her sad attempt to keep up with Sumera—the height difference put Finch at a strong disadvantage. "Sorry, I—I haven't thought about Simon like...that."

Now it was Sumera's turn to go wide-eyed. "That's a joke, right?"

Finch's forehead wrinkled.

Sumera held up her hands. "You talk about him all the time! You've hung out with him almost every weekend since school started! That sounds like something you'd do with a boy you fancy."

Finch bit her lip. She did genuinely enjoy spending time with him, but it wasn't like she got butterflies in her stomach when they talked or that she daydreamed about him. Maybe it could turn into something like that someday, but to her, they were still just becoming friends. Going on a date was ten steps ahead of her current train of thought.

Her mind conjured an image of him holding her waist and leaning in for a kiss. She cringed, nose wrinkling.

Sumera saw and furrowed her brows. "Do you want me to

hint that he should back off? I don't want both of you getting all awkward—"

Finch shook her head sharply. "No! No, it's okay. I'm fine with him asking me out."

"Are you *sure*?"

Am I sure? Well, Finch knew that Simon had a good sense of humor. He was kind. Generally speaking, he was also pretty cute—Finch was always a little envious of his collection of button-downs. That meant he was everything she could possibly ask for in a potential first boyfriend, right? He checked every single box.

I'm just nervous because I've never been on a date before, she told herself.

She nodded again. "I'm sure. I just..." she trailed off. "What do you wear to a party where a guy is going to ask you out?"

Sumera grinned. "I'll text the twins."

While Sumera shot off a message to Ira and Zara, Finch felt an iron ball settle in her stomach.

That afternoon, Selena shoved through the theater's side doors and discovered that Finch was already seated at the piano, playing the most pissed off–sounding rendition of Beethoven's "Piano Sonata No. 8" that she'd ever heard. She took a seat in the first row, realizing after a moment that Finch didn't know she was there.

Finch slammed her fingers down on the keys to play the final notes, biting her lip as she concentrated on every tiny sound. When she finally completed the song, she let out a huge breath, a whimper, and then punctuated it by letting her head fall against the keys, striking them at once in a cacophony.

As the sound from the random notes dissipated, Selena stood and applauded, much to Finch's horror. Finch jumped and threw a hand over her heart.

Selena burst out laughing. "Brava! Well done."

Finch let out a low groan, and—still giggling—Selena climbed onto the stage and offered her a hand. Finch rubbed her forehead as she accepted Selena's help and stood.

In a huffy, almost childlike tone, Finch grumbled, "You surprised me."

Selena grinned. "Would you rather I announce my presence every time I enter a room?"

"Maybe." Finch crossed her arms.

Goddamn, she's so cute, Selena thought. She pinched herself. *Jesus—can I not be gay for, like, ten minutes?*

"I'll be sure to make myself known next time." Selena shrugged off her jacket and stretched. "On the bright side, I think I've figured out that one turn and leap I was struggling with—"

Out of nowhere, Finch blurted out, "Why aren't you dating Simon?"

Selena let her arms fall. "W…What?"

Finch put her face in her hands. "I'm so sorry, that was totally invasive—"

"No—it's…fine." Selena put her hands on her hips and shrugged. "I guess I've never been attracted to him. He's like a brother to me." She narrowed her eyes at Finch. "Why do you ask?"

She stared the other direction, one of her legs bouncing frantically. "Sumera told me that he's planning to ask me out tonight at his party."

Selena froze, feeling as if the floor had bottomed out under her. Finch just sat there, leg still jumping, not looking at her. Finch, with her literal doll face and her hair in a tiny ponytail and her soft voice that made it feel Selena was floating every time she heard it.

Shit.

"I guess I just wanted to make sure it's…okay with you," Finch finally said. She met Selena's eyes. "Since he's your best friend and all."

Selena's mind conjured an image of Simon Hemming, of all people, pulling Finch close and kissing her. Heat filled her cheeks, and a scowl painted itself across her mouth. She inhaled and felt her composure fall away.

Finch couldn't date Simon.

Selena tossed her hair out of her face. "I guess if you're okay with everyone knowing your standards are low."

Now it was Finch's turn to look surprised. "What is that supposed to mean?"

"It's not like I go around talking about being friends with the cryptid kid—nobody gives a shit about whether he's nice or not when they know he's such a weirdo."

Finch furrowed her eyebrows. "Well, it matters to me."

Selena let out a dry laugh. "Are you even attracted to him? Or are you just saying yes because he's paying attention to you?"

Finch crossed her arms and shook her head. "I don't understand why you're being so…mean."

"Because I am mean!" Selena threw out her arms. "Hasn't Perfect Sumera told you? Hasn't everyone told you? It's not like this is news."

"You're being ridiculous." Finch gathered up her things,

swinging her backpack over her shoulder. "We can practice on Monday."

"That's it?" Selena stood at the edge of the stage while Finch hurried for the door. "Nothing? You're just going to run away?"

Finch stopped with her hand on the door handle and looked Selena in the eye. "I'm going to say yes to Simon tonight. If you have a problem with that, say something, but I'm not going to stand around letting you step on me and him just because everybody else does."

She yanked the door open. "Goodbye, Selena."

thirteen

Zara let Finch borrow one of her dresses for the night—which would have been fine if Zara weren't five inches taller than Finch, who barely scraped five-foot-one. What typically would have been a dress that dusted her ankles trailed behind her, and she had to hike it up as she walked up the steps to Simon's house.

On the bright side, the red in the dress might fool someone into thinking there was some color in Finch's complexion. Maybe that was why so many people stared at her as she entered the party, flanked by Sumera and the twins.

Or maybe it was because the rumors were already spreading that she'd told off Selena St. Clair.

She really hoped that wasn't it.

Inside, the party was teeming with other Ulalume girls and Rainwater townies, crowded in tight circles and around tables where beer pong and flip cup were set up. Music pounded out of the speaker system, vibrating the floor when the bassline hit. Multicolored lights bounced around the living room in shifting patterns like a kaleidoscope. Solo cups waved in the air, which felt heavy with sweat and lingering humidity.

The twins quickly peeled away from Finch and Sumera to talk to some of the other Ulalume girls, leaving Finch to wring her hands beside her roommate. Sumera reached out and touched Finch's shoulder.

"You okay?" she asked, eyebrows raised. She'd put on some golden eyeshadow that accented her amber eyes well.

She sighed. "Just…nervous. Jumpy. Kind of sick."

"Ah," Sumera marveled, "young love."

"Hey, guys! Over here!"

Simon ran up to them, dressed in a button-down shirt with a pattern featuring tons of tiny sasquatches. He waved to Sumera, then instantly went in for a hug with Finch. Try as she might, her body went board-stiff in his arms. The amount of cologne he had on made her eyes water.

"Can I get you something to drink?" he asked, offering her a huge smile. He had to practically scream to be heard over the music.

"Yes!" Finch nearly smacked herself for sounding so eager. "Um—yeah I could, um, go for something."

"Beer?" Simon offered.

Finch considered this, then remembered all over again: *he's planning on asking you out tonight.*

"You know what?" she said, putting a hand on her hip in an attempt to look casual, despite how deeply anxiety had settled into her bones and made her feel like every single person in the room could tell how nervous she was. "We should do shots."

The word "shots" sent a ripple through the crowd, and Finch blushed. She'd never actually taken a shot before—she'd just heard people talk about it on TV. For a second, she wondered if that was the wrong word to use.

Simon raised his eyebrows for a second but shrugged, grinning. "I'm down."

———

To make up for her lack of experience with shots, Finch decided the best course of action was to take three in quick succession.

The first was vodka, with Simon. If death had a taste, Finch thought, this was it. She gagged and nearly threw it back up as it burned its way down her throat. Laughing, Simon offered her some of his beer to chase it down with, but that just made it worse. When Simon wasn't looking, she turned and spit the beer out into his mom's spider plant, mentally begging for Ms. Hemming's forgiveness.

"You look beautiful tonight!" he shouted over the music, which kept changing every thirty seconds because no one could agree on what to listen to. "I—I like your dress."

"Thank you. It's very long."

Simon chuckled. "Um—yeah. I guess."

Finch hooked a thumb down the hallway. "Where's your bathroom?"

"First door on the left?"

"Great."

She zipped away.

The second shot came after her time in the bathroom, when she ran into two girls from her music class who told her she was one of the best pianists they'd ever heard at Ulalume. With the threat of impostor syndrome breathing down her neck, Finch asked, "Do you guys want to do shots?"

This time, it was pink lemonade vodka. It did not taste like lemonade.

This was the point at which Finch should have stopped drinking. At her size, two shots were enough to make her laughter obnoxiously loud and her balance a little off. She barely noticed that half an hour had passed as she went around the room, introducing herself to everyone.

She got her third shot, tequila this time, from a group of Rainwater High boys. They cheered like she'd scored a touchdown when she finished swallowing it and bit into the slice of lime they'd shoved in her face.

"Finch? Are you okay? I've been looking for you."

Finch turned from the Rainwater boys to find Sumera standing behind her, her arms crossed and one eyebrow raised.

Finch gave a thumbs up, wiping a dribble of tequila from her chin. "I'm peachy."

"Don't like the way that sounds." Sumera huffed. "Look, I think we should go home. It's getting late, and I'm worried—"

There was a creaking sound, and then Selena St. Clair and her friends walked through the front door.

Finch's entire world screeched to a halt.

Selena had on cuffed ripped jeans, Chelsea boots, and a cropped black T-shirt that left her stomach exposed. Her blond tresses cascaded around her face, and when she ran her fingers through it, Finch could see that she'd gotten clawlike black acrylics. Her green eyes had their usual swooping eyeliner, but with more of a smoky look that made them all the more piercing. And her lips—

Glossy, crimson red.

That was the moment that Finch knew for sure that she was irrefutably, unquestionably attracted to Selena St. Clair.

"Finch? Can I talk to you?"

Finch spun to find Simon, holding a red cup with white knuckles. Sweat beaded on his forehead. He swallowed and his Adam's apple bobbed.

Finch pointed to his cup. "What is that?"

"Uh—rum and coke. But honestly it's about ninety percent rum—"

Finch plucked it from his hand, drained the rest, and passed it back to him.

"Sure. Let's talk."

Selena's heart dropped as Finch disappeared around the corner with Simon.

She stood there, unmoving, while Amber and Kyra on either side of her both stepped into the crowd, greeting a number of girls who shouted their names in high-pitched voices. They had drinks in their hands within seconds, people hanging on their every word.

Risa reached out and touched Selena's shoulder before nodding toward the far wall. Selena nodded, following her out of the way of the door.

They found an open corner, each taking a drink as some girls passed it to them. Risa quickly dumped hers out in a spider plant while Selena took a sip of hers. Lemonade and vodka—passable.

They surveyed the crowd, particularly Amber and Kyra soaking up the attention.

"It was like this last weekend as well," Risa said, pretending to take a sip from her Solo cup so no one would come around and try to fill up her drink. "No one would leave them alone."

"Do you think it's Nerosi's gift?" Selena asked, happy to be talking about something other than the fact that she'd seen Finch disappear to, presumably, make out with her best friend. She'd considered following them, but she knew, ultimately, that it was a terrible idea. It was sure to only make Finch madder at her.

Risa sighed. "Part of it, certainly."

"Can I ask you something?"

Risa lifted her gaze from her cup. "Hmm?"

"Has Kyra been acting...weird the last few days?" Selena's fingers drummed on the side of her cup. "I think I caught her lying to me about the haircut, of all things."

Risa's eyebrows shot up. "She didn't tell you? Nerosi asked for it. She said she needed something physical from this world to harness the kind of power needed to do what Kyra wanted."

A cold shiver rushed up Selena's spine. Her eyes widened as she demanded, "She gave Nerosi *her hair*?"

Risa nodded. "Kyra wanted the ability to make people do as she says. A sort of...boosted charisma." Her dark-brown eyes fell on Kyra in the crowd, who was in the middle of receiving kisses on the cheek from two different girls. "It appears it's working."

"Whoa, whoa, whoa—what?" Selena shook her head. "No, she definitely didn't tell me that! How could she do something like that?"

Risa shrugged. "Hair seems a small price to pay for a gift like that. I know people who would give much more to be heard."

"You don't mean…" Selena's mouth fell open. "You're not considering…"

Risa shook her head, hair falling in inky waves around her heart-shaped face. Selena had always thought she looked the most regal out of them. Selena's looks had been compared to different Instagram influencers, Amber had that girl-next-door quality, and Kyra liked to pretend she was some sort of femme fatale. But Risa looked like she could be sitting on a throne, ruling over a kingdom. It was something about the way she carried herself, shoulders back and chin held high, that made her small frame seem ten feet tall.

"I don't care what people think of me," she said plainly. "Not these people, anyway. But…" her expression fell. "I've been having some…trouble, recently. Academically."

"You?" Selena blinked. "I thought you were in the running to be valedictorian."

"I was. Before we started dealing with all of this," she said, gesturing to Kyra and Amber in the crowd. "I can't focus like I used to. It's like the only thing I can think about is all this stuff with Nerosi. I've been so distracted my grades have started to fall."

Selena scoffed. "Knowing you, that means you got a B on a pop quiz."

Risa glared at her sharply. "No, it doesn't. It means I'm failing math, actually. And I'm at risk of losing my scholarship."

Selena's eyes widened. "Risa—"

She exhaled through her nose. "Not that you'd think of that, because white people look at me and assume that I'm good at certain things. I know what you people are thinking about me, and it's not very flattering."

Selena drew back. Suddenly, it made all the more sense that Risa had wormed her way into Selena's friend group by offering to help her cheat. She had to win the other students over somehow, and that was exactly how they'd expect her to.

"Risa, I'm so sorry." Selena ran a hand back through her hair and held it there. "That was really insensitive of me."

"I'm used to it," she said, grinding her teeth. Without meeting Selena's eyes, she said, "I'll be with Amber and Kyra if you need me."

She waded into the crowd.

Finch smoothed down her dress for what felt like the millionth time. She sat on the end of Simon's bed, her knees nearly touching his. The world spun, and she wasn't sure whether it was her nerves or the shots.

Her stomach lurched. Definitely the shots.

"So, um." Simon patted his hands on his pants. Finch's eyes fixated on his lips, willing herself to see them the same way she'd seen Selena's. "There's something I wanted to ask you. Since we started hanging out…"

She zoned out, staring at his lips. They were, admittedly, not the worst lips she'd ever seen. They were full for a boy's and looked fairly soft. Better than average, for sure. A solid six out of ten.

"…Now might be a good time to ask you how you feel. Because I think you're absolutely incredible, Finch."

Finch opened her mouth to talk, then closed it again, heart racing.

She kissed him.

He tensed at first, but after a second, he kissed her back. Finch squeezed her eyes closed, focusing on the sensation of his hand reaching into her hair and the pull of his teeth on her lower lip. At first, nothing in her stirred.

But then she thought about those glossy, red lips she'd seen in the living room. If she could just pretend—pretend that she was feeling Selena's hands on her waist, and her tongue sliding into her mouth. She kissed back harder, balling Simon's shirt in her fist. She imagined his breaths coming from between Selena's pearly teeth, and the soft skin at the back of his neck as hers.

She could do this. So long as—

Simon pulled away from her, gasping for breath. "Wow. I-I wasn't even sure if you liked me."

The illusion shattered.

He leaned in for another kiss, but Finch wrenched away. Her stomach churned. Looking at Simon's face now, she felt as if she'd pulled away from making out with a wax figure. Tears welled in her eyes.

"Finch?" Simon reached out to touch her but pulled away when she flinched. His eyes were wide. "Did I—? Was it something I—?"

"No, no—you—" Fat tears slid down Finch's face. She shook her head, trembling with nascent sobs. "I'm so sorry, Simon. I can't...I can't..."

"Finch—"

She stood, arms wrapped tightly around herself. "I'm so sorry. I need to go home."

He tried to touch her hand, but she jerked away and ran, trying to ignore the sound of his voice echoing her name behind her.

Selena was downing her second vodka lemonade when a familiar figure approached her.

"Haven't seen you in a minute, beautiful."

Selena glanced up to find Griffin Sergold, with his angelic curls and beautiful baby face, smiling down at her. He leaned against the wall at her side, taking a drink from his cup.

"Oh, hey, Griffo." Selena hadn't spoken to him since that first night at Ulalume when—from his perspective, anyway—she'd basically ghosted him. He'd been her go-to for her first two years at Ulalume, even if "go-to" at that point had just meant kissing with their shirts off. He'd never tried to push her any further, which is half of what made her like him so much.

"You look a little sad," Griffin said, raising his eyebrows. "Some guy got you down?"

Selena managed a small laugh. Griffin was dumb as rocks and definitely played the field, but he had a good heart. For all his flirting, he'd spent some long evenings listening to her stress about her future plans to go to the Boston Conservatory and her past drama with Sumera. Listened, and then helped give her a distraction.

Selena shrugged, looking off in the direction Finch and Simon had disappeared not long before. "You could say that."

"You want me to beat someone up?"

"Nah." She patted his shoulder. "I'll figure it out. You here with anyone?"

He shook his head. "No. Tried to hit on that new girl, Finch, at Ulalume the first night but she ghosted me."

Selena sputtered a laugh. "*You* hit on *Finch*? That's hysterical."

"Why?"

"You're not her type at all."

He put a hand over his heart, a little theatrically. "Not her type? I'm everyone's type! Have you seen these dimples?"

Selena chuckled. "Touché."

Just as Selena went for another sip of her drink, movement caught her eye. Finch darted out from the hallway, tears streaming down her face. She sprinted through the door before anyone could stop her. Simon appeared after her, his mouth stained with Finch's lipstick.

"Oh, shit," Griffin muttered. "Speak of the devil."

Selena straightened up at the same time Sumera did across the room. Sumera looked toward the door, then to Simon, and made a beeline for him. Selena caught just enough of what she was saying to know she was asking what the hell he'd done to Finch. Selena's eyes flickered between them and the door.

She shoved her drink into Griffin's hand. "I gotta go."

She was out the door the next second.

———

Finch didn't even feel the chill of the night as she started down Rainwater Road toward Ulalume. Her legs wobbled with each step, and her head felt like it had been stuffed with cotton. A cold sweat broke out on her forehead as her stomach lurched, nausea reaching its tendrils up from her stomach and into her throat.

She barely had time to stumble into the woods and brace herself against a tree before she vomited.

She coughed, tears welling in her eyes. The tree bark bit into her hand as she spit Coke-flavored bile into the undergrowth. She wiped her mouth with the back of her fist, smearing her lipstick across her cheek. Mascara-stained tears rolled down her cheeks in tiny black rivers.

She straightened up, shoulders quivering as she cried. Her arms wrapped tightly around her torso, she shuffled back to the road, dress dragging behind in the dirt.

She made it about ten feet before the ache in her head became too intense to ignore.

Finch hissed, rubbing her forehead. She caught a rippling in the air in the corner of her eye.

There, on the other side of the road framed in undulating color, was a white pickup truck. The front of it was bent around a tree, smoke rising from the misshapen hood. The front window was obscured by spiderweb cracks in the glass, and one headlight hung by its wires on the right side like an eye pulled out of its socket.

Finch stepped onto the asphalt. Gingerly, she crept forward. As she got closer, she realized there was a figure in the front seat, slumped forward so his hair hung in his face, hiding his eyes.

His blood was splattered all over the dashboard.

"Oh my god," Finch breathed, clapping a hand over her mouth.

She ran to the passenger side door, shouting, "Sir? Sir, can you hear me?"

She reached out to grab the handle only to watch in horror as her hand passed right through it.

The figure stirred. He whispered, "I don't…I don't wanna die."

"Come on," Finch begged, desperately trying to grab hold of the handle. Each time she tried, it slid out between her fingers like smoke. She tried to bang her hand against the window, but just the same, it sunk right through.

The figure turned his neck to look at her, blood streaming

down his face from a gash in his forehead. What little of his skin Finch could see was deathly pale. Voice weak, he looked her in the eye and begged, "Please...please..."

Finch's heart skipped a beat—she recognized him. She'd seen his face at every age staring down at her in his mother's kitchen, a thousand tiny ghosts of a son lost too soon.

Victor DeLuca.

The cold night air blew against Selena's skin as she stumbled outside, scanning the road for Finch. The trees swayed in the sharp breeze, looking like nothing but shadow in the dark. There weren't many streetlights between here and town, so there was nothing but the half-moon to light up the black asphalt that slashed through the undergrowth.

It didn't take long for Selena to spot Finch at the edge of the road, staring intently at the other side. Selena took off after her, cursing herself for wearing shoes she couldn't easily run in.

Finch veered onto the blacktop. She reached out and grabbed at something Selena couldn't see. She was still crying, her shoulders shivering as she frantically spoke to something into the darkness.

Light touched the corner of Selena's eye as a car coasted around the bend. It was one of those electric ones—almost totally silent aside from the gravel under the tires. It had to be going at least ninety.

Finch didn't seem to notice the headlights speeding toward her.

The driver hit the gas. They didn't see her.

"*Finch!*" Selena screamed, sprinting for her.

Finch looked up just as the headlights illuminated her in full, her massive, tear-filled eyes reflecting it back to them.

Selena took a running leap and threw herself at Finch.

Time slowed to a crawl. The car coming around the bend didn't slow. Selena flew toward Finch, arms outstretched.

And then something else came into view over Finch's shoulder. A truck, crumpled around a tree—and a boy inside, staring directly into Selena's eyes.

Selena collided with Finch and sent both of them sprawling onto the shoulder of the road, directly through the vision of the truck.

The car sped down the empty road, oblivious.

Selena gasped for breath, shuddering as she blinked and the world around her came back into focus. Finch was beneath her, back to the pavement. Selena's hands framed her face on either side. She was moon-pale, eyes huge and makeup smeared all over her face from crying. Her chest heaved, arms shaking.

Selena reached out, touching her cheek. "You okay?"

Finch shook her head, slowly at first, then very fast. "No."

"Okay, you know what, that's fair." Selena twisted around to look over her shoulder at the road.

No more truck.

No more boy.

Selena began to ask, "D-Did you see—?"

"Victor DeLuca," Finch murmured. "Victor DeLuca was in that truck."

"Yeah, he was," Selena agreed. She straightened up, then held a hand out to Finch. "Let's get the hell out of here. We can talk at the lighthouse."

Finch took it without hesitation. Selena pulled her up, gripping her shoulder as she swayed to steady her. Finch sniffled, blubbering out an apology as she leaned against Selena for support. Selena wasn't listening, though.

Instead, while she began to guide Finch down the road, she tossed another look over her shoulder.

This time, standing half-obscured by the foliage, was the menacing form of the eight-eyed stag. Its glowing gaze pierced Selena's. She couldn't tell for sure, but it almost felt like the creature was glaring at her.

It let out a puff of air through its nostrils before disappearing into the forest.

fourteen

Back at the lighthouse, Selena brought Finch up to her room and offered her a blanket to wrap around herself before running downstairs to grab her water and saltines. When she got back upstairs, Finch was sitting on Selena's bed, using a tissue she'd stolen off the bedside table to dab at her eyes.

Selena passed her the water and pulled herself onto the bed next to her. Finch took a tiny sip.

"You're gonna want to finish that," Selena said.

Finch frowned. On the walk back, it had become quite apparent that she'd had too much to drink, and her words were a bit slurred. "I don't…I don't need this."

"You do, actually. You really, really do." She passed her a cracker. "This too. You'll thank me tomorrow."

"You sound like Sumera," Finch muttered under her breath, biting off the corner of the cracker.

Selena withheld a wince. She realized she had, in fact, been on the other side of this very situation with Sumera once upon a time—Sumera offering her crackers and water and telling her she'd call their housemother if she didn't finish them. At the time, Selena had found it wildly annoying, but now she got it.

Finch finished the water and sniffled. "Sorry. You're just trying to help."

Selena nodded. She grabbed a pack of makeup remover wipes and passed them to Finch. "These might help too. You look like you busted out of clown college."

Finch got a little laugh out of that and went about wiping the mascara tracks and smeared lipstick from her cheeks. It was nice to see her smile, even if it was fleeting.

Selena tried desperately not to pay attention to how close their hands and legs were to touching, but it was like the nerves had taken on a life of their own. Everyone one of Finch's tiny movements sent shock waves through them, the signals reaching her heart and making it race.

Once she'd finished, Selena asked, "Is there anything else I can bring you? Tea? More blankets? Aspirin—?"

Finch giggled, shoving Selena's arm lightly. "Look at you. Fussing over me."

Selena turned brilliantly red. "F—no! I'm helping you because I'm your friend. Get that stupid grin off your face."

Finch did not get that stupid grin off her face. In fact, it only grew larger. "We're friends?"

Selena frowned, cheeks continuing to burn. "Yes, obviously. I wouldn't exactly jump in front of a moving car for you unless I gave a fraction of a fuck."

"A fraction of a fu—" Finch bit back a smile. "High praise."

"I'm going to kick you out if you keep this up."

Outside, thunder rumbled—a prelude to the downpour that began seconds later. Rain pelted against the windowpane, blurring the mist outside that obscured the roiling slate-gray sea. Lightning cut across the sky like a jagged grin, lighting up the room for a flashing moment before crackling into darkness.

Finch looked at her expectantly.

Selena rolled her eyes. "Point taken. You can stay here—I'll crash on the couch tonight. But not until you explain what happened."

Finch's smile vanished.

"Simon told me they're called Echoes," Finch explained. The question seemed to have sobered her up a bit. "He said they're like…visions of something that happened in the past being repeated in front of you. I've seen a few."

"A few?" Selena's eyes widened. "Is that how you figured out Victor's name before?"

Finch nodded. "Yeah. I saw an Echo of him in the library with the other band members. I had overheard them talking about Nerosi—"

Finch clamped her mouth shut, hand flying over it.

Selena felt cold. She repeated, "Nerosi?"

Sweat prickled on Finch's forehead. "Did I say Nerosi? S-Slip of the tongue, I meant, um…uh…"

"You know about her too?"

A beat of silence passed as Finch's eyes rounded. Even if she didn't say it, the answer to Selena's question was written all over her face.

"We found her the day before school started—in that room in the tunnels. There was another girl there. With white hair." Selena shook her head as the pieces clicked together and she wished she could go back and scream it in her own ear—it was so obvious. "That was you."

"You were there?" Finch breathed.

Selena nodded. "Why don't you tell me what you remember, and then I'll do the same?"

So she did. Finch recounted that first night, how she'd felt a pull in her chest that led her to the tunnels and into the room. How she'd pulled Nerosi free and passed out soon after. In turn, Selena explained how they'd followed her thinking she was heading to the same party as them and woke up outside the next morning disoriented and terrified. As they did, Selena felt some of the tension leave her shoulders—it felt almost like she was in some kind of confessional, and it was strangely comforting to get all of this off her chest.

"Kyra's been speaking to her the most since then," Selena clarified. "I…I haven't been down as much."

"Why not?" Finch asked.

Selena bit her lip. She worried she was saying exactly the wrong thing, but admitted, "Because I don't trust Nerosi."

Selena winced, waiting to get the same kind of admonishment that she'd gotten from Kyra when she'd expressed her suspicions.

Instead, Finch began to nod.

"I don't trust her, either. Something isn't right about all of it."

"Shit, yeah. Tonight, Risa told me that she asked for some of Kyra's hair."

Finch's eyes widened. "To do *what*?"

"To make her stronger, I guess." Selena bit the inside of her cheek, letting her eyes wander to the window once more. The sound of the rain was loud against the lighthouse, and the wind was enough to leave a dank chill in the air. "Which is wildly sus, if you ask me."

Finch nodded. "I think I caught her in a lie the other night. About the eight-eyed stag—she said she didn't know anything about it, but I think she does."

Selena inhaled sharply. "Yeah, that was a lie."

Finch's eyes widened.

"It's her emissary," Selena explained. "She can see through its eyes or something. And *that* I do believe. Just now? On the road? It was watching us."

"Why would she—" Finch shivered. Her expression wavered, and she took a sharp breath. "Oh."

"What?" Selena asked.

"Nothing," Finch said. "Just a…bad memory. Before it happened, I saw the eight-eyed stag. It never felt like a coincidence and if Nerosi doesn't want me to know…"

"Then she's hiding it for a reason," Selena agreed. "Just like I'm sure she hid things from the last people who summoned her right before they vanished off the face of the earth. She must have been playing the same sort of game with them as she is with us."

"So if we find out what happened to them…" Finch bit her lip. "Then maybe we can stop it from happening to us."

"Exactly."

Selena noticed, then, that Finch's hand had scooted even closer than before, their pinkies nearly touching. For a moment, she considered reaching out, but remembered how Finch had wrenched away from her before. So she folded her hands in her lap, exhaling a breath.

"Maybe we could tell Simon," Selena breathed. "If he knew, he could probably…"

She stopped speaking when she saw the way Finch's face fell.

"Or—we don't have to." Selena tilted her head to the side, taking in the way Finch's cupid's-bow mouth curved into a frown. "Did something happen tonight? Between the two of you?"

A tiny sob escaped Finch's mouth, despite the way she clenched her jaw to try to keep it in. Her eyes began to shine—they were exactly the same color as the stormy sea outside.

Selena started to reach out again but paused. "I-If you don't want to tell me, you don't h—"

But the next moment, whatever unspoken boundary had been up between them for the last couple of weeks shattered. Selena was frozen as Finch leaned against her, pressing her face into her shoulder to stanch the flow of tears. Selena sat, dumbstruck, for a moment. Then, she gathered Finch against her and rested her chin on top of her head.

"It's okay," Selena promised. "I've got you."

Finch shook her head, squeezing her eyes shut to stop tears from escaping. "It's like I'm…missing something, y'know? My whole life I've been waiting to feel the way other girls do about boys, all giddy or excited or anything like that but I just *don't*. When I was younger, I thought maybe it was because I was still a kid but now…" her face crumpled as she tried and failed to stop herself from crying. "I was sure things would change tonight. B-But I kissed Simon and I felt…nothing."

Her shoulders shook, and Selena untangled herself enough to

fetch her a tissue from her nightstand, which she gratefully took to dab her eyes and blow her nose.

Selena wiped a stray tear from Finch's chin and said, "Hey, listen—there's no rule that says you have to be attracted to boys. Or anyone, for that matter. And frankly, boys aren't nearly what they're cracked up to be. At our age they've barely committed to wearing deodorant and we're supposed to be impressed like that's some huge fuckin' victory."

That managed to get a tiny laugh out of her. Finch sniffled and lifted her head to meet Selena's eyes. Their faces were only a few inches apart, noses nearly touching. A blush rushed through Selena's cheeks—this close, she felt strangely vulnerable, like Finch might be able to see inside her and know what she was hiding under the surface. Her heart thrummed, echoing a warm ache through her chest.

Finch blurted out, "I think I like girls."

"Oh. Huh." Selena was so stunned the synapses in her brain all seemed to misfire at once, unable to process the information in front of her. Which is probably why she wound up saying, "Welcome to the club. We can make T-shirts."

Finch's mouth twitched for a moment before she burst out laughing, once again burying her face in Selena's shoulder. Selena mentally cursed herself—*make T-shirts? Christ, St. Clair*—while Finch wrapped her arms tighter around her. She sat like that for some time, giggling into Selena's shirt and intermittently sniffling.

"You're still super drunk, huh?" Selena guessed as her mirth began to taper off.

"I don't know what you're talking about," Finch yawned into her shoulder. She nestled in closer. "I'm fine."

"Cool—cool, cool." She leaned back against her headboard, arm still around Finch's shoulder. "Why don't I just leave you here and I'll go pass out on the—"

Finch snored softly against Selena's side.

"Of course," she sighed. She took a breath and did her best to try and unwind herself from Finch, but the other girl tightened her grasp when she tried. Selena let out another breath, leaning her head against Finch's and closing her eyes.

I'll just stay awake until she moves, she told herself. *And then go downstairs.*

But, despite her best efforts, it was only another couple minutes before she fell asleep as well.

———————

Selena and Finch woke the next morning to Selena's old oak door flying open and Kyra starting, "Hey St. Clair, Amber's making pancake—"

She trailed off when she saw Finch tangled in a mess of sheets and blankets. At the sound of the door opening, Finch opened her eyes a sliver, groaning as the sunshine streamed in and highlighted the pounding headache that had taken refuge in the front of her skull.

She hadn't realized there was someone else in bed with her until Selena sat up and, running a hand through her tangled hair, asked Kyra, "Would it kill you to knock?"

Finch's cheeks warmed as reality set in on her.

She was in Selena St. Clair's bed. She'd spent the *entire night* in Selena St. Clair's bed after their conversation about...

She froze.

She'd told Selena she liked girls last night.

And now Kyra, who got on her tiptoes to plant kisses on Selena's cheek, was glaring at Finch like she was a rat in their pantry.

"What the hell is she doing here?" Kyra snapped, pointing to the blanket pile that Finch was currently sliding deeper into.

"Kyra, it's eight in the morning," Selena said. "Please chill out. Finch slept over because of the storm last night."

"*In* your *bed*?" Kyra shrilled.

Finch winced—*how is it her voice is so loud this early?* "I'm sorry—I-I drank too much at the party and fell asleep without meaning to."

"You don't need to apologize," Selena told her. She turned her glare toward Kyra. She'd fallen asleep with her makeup on last night, but somehow the way it had morphed into a smoky eye made the electric quality of them more vivid. Like lightning in a volcanic plume. "Kyra, get the hell out of my room."

"This is my house too, thanks." Kyra turned her livewire stare on Finch. "You're the one who needs to go."

Kyra's words had a strange quality to them—while it wasn't exactly a command, it felt like one. The weight of it sunk into Finch's thoughts, then duplicated over and over so the only thing she could think was *go, go, go.* She'd never wanted to listen to Kyra before, but suddenly it felt like the most important thing in the world. She felt her face go slack and her body begin to move of its own volition.

She heard herself say, "Okay. I'll go."

"What?" Selena reached out and grabbed her wrist. "Finch, you don't have to listen to her."

"Actually, she does," Kyra said, a lopsided grin cutting across her face. "Hurry up, Finch."

Hurry up, hurry up, hurry up, Kyra's voice echoed in her head.

Finch slid the rest of the way out of Selena's bed, a passenger being driven by a body she could no longer control. She pulled out of Selena's grasp, her stare glassy and distant. She picked up her bag from the floor and started for the door.

"Kyra!" Selena snapped. "What the hell are you doing? Stop!"

"Stop what?" Kyra asked, tilting her head to the side and widening her eyes.

"You know what," Selena growled. "Using the powers Nerosi gave you."

At the sound of Nerosi's name, Kyra froze. Finch felt herself step toward the door, but Selena caught her arm again. The feeling of her hand on her wrist was enough to bring Finch's mind back into focus. She took a sharp breath, putting a hand to her chest as she regained control over her movements.

Kyra's eyes rounded. "Y-You know about…?"

"That you cut off your hair for her? Yeah, I do." Selena let go of Finch and added, "You're a bad liar, Kyra. Always have been."

Kyra's eyes shifted from Selena to Finch again and she said, "Don't you think we should have this conversation some other time?"

"Well, the good news is that Finch already knows about Nerosi." While the color drained from Kyra's face, Selena added, "Because she's the one who summoned her in the first place."

Kyra met Finch's gaze, her nose wrinkling. "*You* summoned Nerosi? She's never mentioned you."

For a moment, Finch couldn't exactly place Kyra's tone. She

was still glaring at her, but the tone of her voice had a bruised quality to it, like somehow Selena had struck a nerve by implying someone other than Kyra had a relationship with the creature. It only took a second, though, for it to become chillingly obvious what Kyra was feeling.

"You're...jealous," Finch realized aloud, almost awestruck at the concept.

Kyra's face flared red. "*Jealous?* Of someone who Nerosi doesn't even bother to mention? You must not be that important if she didn't care enough to say anything to me about it."

"To be fair, she never mentioned you to me, either," Finch offered.

As Kyra's mouth curled into a scowl, Selena wheeled around to look at Finch. A small smile crept across her face as she nodded, impressed.

Before Kyra could start again, Finch—feeling strangely bold at the sight of Selena's smile—added, "Maybe it would be good for us all to talk to each other. Because I think Nerosi is hiding something from us, and clearly she wants to keep us all apart for a reason."

"She's right," Selena said. "Everyone should hear what Finch told me last night. There's definitely something about it that doesn't add up."

"Do we all get to crawl in your bed and spoon while we do it too?" Kyra shot back.

"Come on. Stop being ridiculous," Selena said, rolling her eyes. She nodded to the bed and added, "There's no way all five of us could fit in there, even if we did spoon."

Finch stifled a laugh with her hand while Kyra's face fell into an even tighter scowl.

"I'll be downstairs," Kyra said flatly.

She slammed the door behind her.

Amber's eyes widened. "So *you* summoned Nerosi?"

Finch shrugged. "Well—yes. I'm not particularly proud of it."

"Oh." Amber leaned back, resting her chin in her hand. "Bummer."

The girls—Finch, Selena, Kyra, Amber, and Risa—had gathered in the living room, tensely eating pancakes, an event Finch hadn't thought possible until that very moment. The sun faded in and out of brightness as fat clouds meandered by, the possibility of rain hanging in the air.

Finch went on, "I was…drawn down there. I think she lured me into that room so I could summon her."

"What makes you so special?" Kyra asked. Selena shot her a sharp look, and Kyra added, "What? It seems like a reasonable question. Why would Nerosi want *you* of all people to bring her back?"

Finch had begun to wonder the exact same thing. If Nerosi had been telling the truth about connecting the two of them to save Finch's life, how did that benefit Nerosi? On the surface, it seemed like a selfless act, but Finch was beginning to realize more and more that Nerosi had other motivations. If it was their connection that had led Finch to the tunnels to summon her in the first place, was that the whole reason Nerosi had done it? Just to get Finch to pull her out of the void?

And if the eight-eyed stag really was her emissary, it seemed unlikely it would be standing in the center of that bridge randomly.

Was it possible that it had been waiting for the Chamberlins to cross? Just like, she realized, it might have been for Victor DeLuca the night that he crashed his car into a tree?

That couldn't be a coincidence.

Finch bit her lip. "I'm not entirely sure. Maybe I'm an easy target. Maybe we're all easy targets to her. She thinks we're easy to manipulate into helping her achieve…whatever it is she's trying to achieve."

"Wow," Kyra said in a monotone. "How dare Nerosi want to get out of that room she's trapped in? Sounds pretty evil to me."

"Haven't you wondered why she's trapped in there in the first place?" Finch pointed out. While Kyra and Amber didn't react, Risa's eyebrows went up, driving Finch to add, "And what she'll do if she gets out?"

"Finch is right," Selena said beside her. "We all have to admit that there are a lot of gaps in her story. Even assuming she has been truthful with us, isn't it strange that she never told us about Finch? Or that she suddenly needs things from us in exchange for favors? Those seem like big red flags."

Risa argued, "She hasn't done anything to hurt us. If she had bad intentions, why would she take the time to do things like chat with us and do us small favors?"

"Because that's how you manipulate people to do things for you," Selena pointed out. Eyebrows shot up around the room and Selena gestured to Risa. "You understand what I'm saying, right? She's getting in our heads."

Risa pursed her lips. "I…I suppose you're right."

Kyra, meanwhile, rolled her eyes. "You're just saying that because you don't know her like I do. I talk to Nerosi almost every night, and all she wants is to be free like any of us are. She only asked for my hair because she didn't have enough of a physical connection to our world to help me. Why would she ask my permission first if she had some evil scheme?"

Selena blinked. "You talk to her *every night?*"

Kyra's cheeks burned. "Yeah? Is something wrong with that? Am I not allowed to talk to someone who actually gives a shit about me for once?"

"*Kyra,*" Selena started.

"I understand why you don't want to believe she'd lie to you," Finch offered. "I just...I'm worried about all of this escalating. Because I think this happened before, and the kids involved disappeared."

"Disappeared?" Amber repeated, paling. She glanced frantically between Kyra and Selena, eyes wide. "Why would Nerosi do that?"

"You know what I think?" Kyra said, leering at Finch. "I think you're the one being manipulative here. We barely know you at all—why should we trust some random new girl butting into our lives and making us doubt the one good thing that's happened to us in *years?* You show up here with no proof, baseless accusations, and an *obvious* crush on Selena. I think you're just trying to isolate her from us so you can have her to yourself."

Finch winced and drew back like she'd been hit. She felt Selena looking at her and warmth flooded her face. Finch's heart began to pound—after what she'd admitted to Selena last night about liking girls, was she going to believe that Kyra was right? That this was all a ploy to win her over?

She started to stammer, "I-I would never—"

"Piss off, Kyra," Selena snapped. "Finch wouldn't know how to manipulate her way out of a wet paper bag. You're just scared she's right."

Kyra's face drew into a scowl. She shot up from her chair. "You know what? Screw this."

Selena stood. "Kyra—"

"I'm done with your judgment for today, St. Clair." Kyra gestured to Finch. "And considering what I saw in your room, I'm guessing you have other *things* to do anyway."

She stormed out, slamming the door behind her.

———————

Not long after, Finch excused herself and headed back to Pergman Hall. Selena offered to walk with her, but Finch refused. Her mind was still a matted net of thoughts that would take a while to untangle.

When she opened the door to her dorm, however, it quickly became clear she wasn't going to have much time for that.

Sitting in the common room were Sumera and Simon, sharing mugs of tea. Simon had a blanket around his shoulders and dark rings under his eyes. They both looked up at her as she walked in, and Finch halted in her steps.

Simon quickly put his cup of tea down and stood. "I should go. I'll text you later, Sumera."

"Simon—" Finch reached out as he went for the door. "I—can I talk to you? Please?"

He studied her like something wriggling under a microscope. "What is there to say? I get it, Finch. You're not interested. I'll leave you alone now."

"No! Simon, that's not it—"

"So you are interested?" Simon shook his head, squeezing his eyes shut. "I don't understand you. One minute you're kissing me and the next you're running away like I make you sick."

"I—there's a reason, okay?" Finch's shoulders slumped and she pinched the bridge of her nose. "I...just don't know if I can...say it."

He threw up his hands. "Great. In that case, I'm going to head out. Give you some time to choke it out."

He pushed past her, opened the door, and slammed it behind him.

Behind her, Sumera's eyebrows shot up.

"You have some explaining to do."

fifteen

Selena didn't hear from Finch for the rest of the weekend. She tried to send a few texts, but they all went unanswered. After their unsuccessful plea to Kyra and the other girls about Nerosi, along with everything that had happened at the party, Selena figured she just needed some space.

She did, however, hear from Simon, who was wondering how much she knew about Tunger Hall.

"Where I lived for two years? The quarantined dorm? Of course I know Tunger." Selena said as they sat in her bedroom. Technically, boys weren't allowed in rooms at Ulalume, but Selena and her friends had a bit of leeway with the lighthouse, seeing as they didn't exactly have a housemother to enforce the rules.

Simon nodded. "Do you remember how Victor's mom talked about his girlfriend, Margo, and showed us some of her drawings? I dug through some old Ulalume room records and found out she lived there. You've said Tunger has lots of places to hide stuff, so maybe we can find something."

This was true—Selena, Amber, and Kyra used to keep their booze stashed in the drop ceiling tiles above their beds. One time, they'd decided to explore their ceiling and found a bunch of weird stuff with labels from the 1990s. The girls across the hall from them even mentioned that they'd found old marionettes in their ceiling, and everyone in Tunger kept joking they had a puppet curse. Still, it was tradition to hide stuff up there, and it was entirely possible Margo could have left something.

"Do you know which room she lived in?" Selena asked.

He shook his head. "No, but the records mentioned it was a single, and based on the dorm blueprints, singles only fit up against the elevators. So we can try the rooms on either side of those on each floor."

"You do know that Tunger is entirely off-limits to students, right?" Selena said, but she was already smiling.

"Not if you go through the tunnels," Simon corrected.

He jokingly elbowed Selena in the ribs, flexing his eyebrows, and saying, "Eh? Eh?" She did the same until they were smacking each other's arms like they had when they were kids, giggling. Simon whipped around and tickled her, and she involuntarily smacked him in the face so hard it stung her palm. They both just stared at each other for another minute before Simon cussed Selena out, and she laughed out a halting apology as she gasped for breath.

"Can I say something?" Simon eyed her sideways. "Sometimes I feel like I…miss you. It sounds kinda stupid, but I miss talking to you and not…Ulalume Selena."

"What, like I'm two different people?"

Simon shook his head. "No. But you act so different around your Ulalume friends. You're all mean and shitty like they are, and it sucks because you're not actually like that. Every time we come back from Boston after the summer you change again."

Selena wanted to snap and correct him, but she paused. He was right. She was different back home—every summer when the two of them went back to Boston they were the sort of friends who goofed off and played video games and stole their parents' beer to drink in the basement. They didn't go to parties or even go *out* much at all beyond Red Sox games and movies by the Common. Hell, sometimes Simon even convinced her to watch anime, and she liked it.

Selena bit her lip. "Maybe it's a coping mechanism."

"Coping? With what? Being friends with assholes?"

Selena managed a laugh and then reached out to shove him. "Yeah, you got it. Assholes beget assholes."

"Too bad Finch turned out to be just as bad," Simon mumbled. "I really had my hopes up."

Selena opened and closed her mouth. She knew Simon had been moping the last few days, and clearly Finch hadn't reached out with an explanation. As much as she liked Finch, Simon was her best friend, and she wished Finch could at least pluck up the courage for an *it's not you, it's me* explanation if nothing else. It sucked seeing him suffer, but as much as she'd like to just say *Hey, Finch doesn't like boys*, that wasn't her secret to tell.

Finally, she said, "If it makes you feel better, I really don't think it's personal. She's got a lot going on."

Simon's eyebrows shot up. "Is she seeing someone else? Does she have a boyfriend back home or something?"

Selena sputtered out a laugh. "Oh, no, not like that. She told me a little about it this weekend and it's…complicated. But not about you."

He pursed his lips. "It would just be nice to hear *anything*, y'know? When people leave you hanging like that you assume the worst. I thought maybe I did something that made her uncomfortable. I'd never want her to think I was trying to take advantage of her—"

"Generally speaking, great intention, but it's nothing like that." Selena reached out and gave him a one-armed hug. "Listen, I'm sure there's some other weirdo out there who would love to hear you drone on about the supernatural. Other fish in the sea and all that."

Simon withheld a laugh. "Delicate as always, huh?"

"Just being honest." Selena stood, grabbing a hair tie from her desk and began to pull her hair into a bun, adding, "But enough about Finch—let's head to Tunger. We've got cults to find."

Simon led the way through the tunnels, following the map that Selena remembered Sumera making their first year at Ulalume. It didn't take long for them to pop up from the Tunger basement.

They found themselves in a dining hall, the chairs scattered haphazardly around the room. Dust floated through the musty air, coating every surface. Most of the windows were covered by paper so only tiny slivers of the waning sunlight peeked through. There was graffiti all over the paper and carved into the tables.

"Let's look for the elevators," Simon said as they headed toward the stairs. The halls were covered in plastic tarps, empty paint cans and power tools scattered across the hardwood. The Ulalume administration had promised to reopen Tunger sometime in the next year, but that seemed unlikely based on the current state of it.

"There's only three floors. We can work our way up."

Selena paused for a moment, staring at a window. It was nearly sunset. The last thing she wanted was to be in a spooky abandoned building after dark. They had to be smart about this.

The two of them split up on the first floor, each shoving open the door to the respective rooms and finding the usual Ulalume starter setup of a pale brown desk, a chair, a dresser, and a mattress without a sheet. They pushed up and slid away the ceiling tiles while balancing on chairs to examine the crawl space above the rooms. Selena came up empty on the first floor while Simon let out a shrill scream. When Selena rushed to help him, he ducked down from the ceiling, cursing about a rat.

"Rainwater's made you soft," Selena said, shaking her head. "The Allston rats could swallow these rats alive."

They failed to find much on the second floor as well, aside from a few boxes of various latex barrier methods that had to be a decade old. Simon tossed a box of condoms to Selena as a joke, and she launched it back at him. It struck him in the shoulder, scattering ancient condoms everywhere while Simon cracked up.

"You sure you don't need those?" Simon asked, mock-concern in his voice.

Selena mirrored his tone. "You sure your mom didn't need them?"

Simon flipped her off as she withheld a chuckle.

They carried on to the third floor, where the air felt mustier. Selena sneezed into her elbow while Simon's nose wrinkled— clearly no one had been there to get rid of the dust in a while. It was also darker up here—whoever had put the paper on the windows had done a much better job here. Simon withdrew his phone from his pocket, turning on the flashlight.

"Creepy," Selena muttered.

"Maybe we should stay together," Simon offered. When Selena shot him a raised eyebrow, he clarified, "S-So we have more light. From both of our phones."

Selena's lips twitched into a smile. "Simon, are you *scared*?"

"What? No! I just..." Simon looked to his left and then his right and lowered his voice. "Listen, I've seen plenty of horror movies. Characters who look like me die a whole lot faster than characters who look like you."

"Fair enough," Selena mused. She nodded to the room on the right. "Shall we?"

Inside was the usual setup, though the walls were more scuffed up. Someone in the past seemed to have covered the entire room in hung-up decorations considering the number of holes in the walls. Selena grabbed the desk chair and stepped onto it, trying not to think about the creaking sound it let out. She held up the phone flashlight with one hand and used her other to press up on the ceiling tile. She pressed softly at first, only to discover it was jammed. She twisted up her face and pushed harder.

"So you're positive that Finch didn't run away because of something I did?" Simon asked.

Selena rolled her eyes. "One hundred percent positive. Think of it like…she just realized you're not her type."

"Ouch," Simon muttered.

"Sorry, man. It's nothing personal." Selena gritted her teeth, pushing harder on the ceiling title. "Christ, did they glue this shit or something?"

Simon rubbed the back of his neck. "By *not her type*… Do you mean she's a lesbian or something?"

Selena choked on what she was about to say. "Uh—"

At exactly that moment, Selena finally dislodged the ceiling tile, only to have something spring free from the crawl space. She leaped off the chair just as a book tumbled down from inside.

"Jesus Christ," Selena breathed, hand over her racing heart. "What is that?"

Simon reached out and picked it up, gently blowing on the cover to get rid of the dust. He squinted, shining his phone light on it and read aloud, "Property of Margo Velázquez-White. Do not fuck with." His eyes rounded. "Dude, this is totally hers."

"Seriously?" Selena took a step closer to him, peering at the cover. It was a haphazard collage of various political stickers, all anti-government, pro-queer, and strongly feminist. There was also a custom-made one of the eight-eyed stag beneath the piece of duct tape she'd written her name and the warning on. The sight of it made Selena's skin crawl.

Simon flipped open to the first page. He took a step back, sitting down on the bare mattress. "I can't believe it. We hit the jackpot."

Meanwhile, Selena wrapped her arms around herself, chilled. Even the tiniest slivers of sunlight were gone now, and with the sun having dropped into the ocean, the heat of the day was immediately beginning to fade along with the light. She wished she could flip on a light, but the power had been shut off in Tunger for nearly a year.

The floor creaked in the hallway and Selena tensed.

She shone her light at the closed door and whispered, "Did you hear that?"

Simon didn't look up from the book. "Hear what?"

There wasn't supposed to be anyone in Tunger, but if someone found them, they'd be in massive trouble.

Selena lowered her voice to a whisper. Her heart began to pound. "Simon, there's something outside."

"Hold on," he said, squinting down at the book. "This is—Selena, you're not gonna believe this. Come look."

Selena was frozen.

"It's an old building, Selena, it's gonna make weird sounds." Simon gestured for her to come over. "Come on."

Selena stared at the door for another moment.

The halls were silent.

She took a shaky breath before joining him, still keeping an ear out for more noise.

Selena's light met Simon's, illuminating a number of Polaroids taped into what Selena realized was a sketchbook. The first was a pair of girls hanging out together: one was Latina and wore Doc Martens and a chain wallet while the other was white, with pixie-cut orange hair that screamed Manic Panic. Someone had lovingly drawn cat whiskers and ears on the girl with orange hair, and someone with a less deft hand had added devil horns and a tail to the girl with Doc Martens. Under it were the words: *I'll see you into hell.* The next one was a selfie of the two girls with three boys standing behind them making silly faces. In the next were just the boys, two of them were draped over one another lazily while one kissed the other's cheek and the third boy smiled nervously a few feet away. Selena squinted at them.

She pointed at the palest boy. "That's Victor, right? And these two—what did Mrs. DeLuca say the other boys were named?"

Simon nodded. "Theo and Xavier. Theo was Killing Howard's singer, Xavier was on drums. I think they were together." He picked up another picture, which was of Victor and the Doc Martens girl. She wore a cropped Coca-Cola T-shirt and black jeans, the picture of an all-American girl. Victor was kissing her cheek, and she was grinning.

"And that's definitely Margo," Simon said. "Victor's girlfriend."

"They don't look like a cult," Selena murmured.

"Right. No matching T-shirts that say 'join our sick cult.'" Selena shot Simon a glare and he chuckled. "What? Of course they don't look like a cult—anyone can be in a cult."

Electing to keep it mature, Selena presented her middle finger to the front of his nose.

Still laughing softly to himself, Simon flipped the page.

"Looks like a diary entry," he said after a moment. He held it out to Selena. "Look."

She read:

September 24, 2004
I've never really kept a journal before—not really into that

kind of touchy shit, honestly. But everything's started to feel so much like a dream recently. I want to keep a record of what's going on, even if we're the only ones who believe it.

Victor found something under the school. I can't explain what she is—maybe a witch? An angel? A spirit? I can't seem to find the right words. But she offered to help us with the band, and it seems like this might be our big break.

When Victor and I went down to talk to her, I mentioned how bad our equipment sucks. All of it's hand-me-down stuff—I got my bass at Goodwill, for god's sake. It's total shit. Xavier's punched holes in his drum kit, and Sloan's keyboard won't turn on for more than ten minutes at a time.

So lo and behold when I get a message from the Ulalume mail room saying I've got all these new packages and they start bringing out all these boxes. I get Sloan to help me take them back to our room and we're taking them apart, throwing packing peanuts all over the floor, and it's all new equipment from an anonymous benefactor. Bass, guitar, keyboard, drums, mics, amps—everything. And it all sounds incredible.

I don't know how she did it, but Nerosi sure did deliver.

Margo

Simon asked, "Who's Nerosi?"

A cold shiver went up Selena's spine. She lied, "I-I don't know. Mrs. DeLuca never mentioned her."

"Her?" Simon asked.

Selena stammered, "I-It sounds like a woman's name."

"Does it?" Simon flipped the page. "Here's another one."

October 22, 2004

Nerosi's asking for human sacrifices now.

Just kidding. Got you there for a second, right?

No, it's just little things, not whole humans. Honestly, considering what she's offering it's totally worth it. Sloan shaved her head and gave the pieces to Nerosi in exchange for magically convincing the owner of Octavia's to give us another chance after we fucked it up so bad last time. Xavier's was a little more painful, but he got us money. Like, actual money! Money that can buy us stuff to promote our music, money we can use to rent a van to go play some shows in Portland or Boston. It wasn't a lot, but it's definitely more than nothing.

Only problem is, even with bitchin' new equipment and opportunities the real problem comes down to the fact that... some of us still kinda suck at this.

I'm not trying to be the bad guy, but Theo's voice cracks all the time, and Xavier gets so distracted listening to his boyfriend beef it that he gets off-beat and messes us all up. We're never gonna make it anywhere if we don't get our shit together soon, shows or no shows.

Margo

Simon pursed his lips. "What do you think she meant by painful?"

"No idea." Selena reached over and flipped the page for him.

November 9, 2004

We totally bombed at Octavia's.

*It was a nightmare. Theo sounded like a cat being stran-
gled and everyone else pretty much followed suit.*

Tempted to just crawl in a hole and give up.

They flipped the page.

November 14, 2004
Maybe not all is lost.

*Theo called everyone and told them to come to practice,
which we haven't done since we messed up our show. When
we met up, he sang us a few bars and…wow. I have to assume
this is Nerosi's doing, but the kid's got pipes all of a sudden.*

*Only problem is, it seems like there's something a little…
off about Theo. When he was singing, I noticed he kept needing
to wipe away blood from his mouth. When I asked him what
he gave up to Nerosi, he wouldn't tell me.*

*But whatever it is, it's probably worth it. For the band.
Maybe there's hope for us yet.*

Margo

When Simon skipped ahead a few pages, they found drawings
instead of words. Some of it looked similar to what they'd seen
at the DeLuca's house—the sharp contrast of black and white
with images of a stag in the woods, of a guitar, of a keyboard that
appeared to be wet with some kind of dark liquid.

But the more Simon flipped the pages, the darker in tone
the art became. It went from everyday objects to strange, abstract
images. Fractals with mouths hidden inside, teeth emerging from
the darkness. Another showed what appeared to be eyelids with

dark tendrils in place of eyeballs. Still, the style was distinctly Margo's.

"Do you think she saw something like this?" Simon whispered. "In the tunnels?"

Selena was white as a sheet. "I—I don't know."

The next page was another diary entry.

December 2, 2004
It's worth it. It's all worth it, right? The crowd, the energy—
I'll give anything to keep this.
   Anything.
   Right?

They flipped another few pages ahead, past violent images of a deer with a human head at the tip of each of its antlers and a sharp-toothed woman laughing, eyes rolled back in her head. The next entry was written in jagged scrawl, like it had been done with Margo's nondominant hand. There were faint reddish-brown fingerprints on the corner of the page.

   I didn't need them
   I don't need them
   She'll see for me
   And they'll all see me

Once more, Simon turned the page. The scrawl made Selena's gut clench. With a shaking hand, she ran her fingers over the pages, only to realize that the marks in the background weren't mindless scribbles—they were words.

she's in my

                              head hooks in my brain inside
        my hair fingers clenching fingers tight suck inside
        like a burr on a

                                        shoe

                spines she has spines her spines teeth chewing me
                up chewing my guts
        she's gonna

                        eat me you
                        alive

Selena heard someone giggle.

She looked at Simon, horrified. "What was *that*?"

"I didn't say anything."

Out in the hallway, footsteps creaked.

Selena and Simon froze. Their flashlights hung on the door, illuminating the chipping paint and shadow where a poster had been. Selena moved forward, even as Simon opened his mouth to stop her. She held up a hand and shushed him.

Carefully, she went to her knees, eye-level with the brass keyhole. She placed a hand on the door and leaned forward. Her nails scraped the paint as she bent her fingers.

Darkness.

"It's gotta be those rats," Selena muttered. Her heart still hammered in her chest. "Because I don't see—"

At exactly that moment, two things happened.

Simon screamed bloody murder.

And on the other side of the keyhole, an eye popped open.

She flung herself back.

The laughing behind them became hysterical, screaming.

Selena flipped around. Simon clutched Margo's sketchbook, white-knuckled. A figure had appeared behind them, sitting on the bare mattress, curled up with her knees pressed to her forehead and her face hidden. Her shoulders shook as she laughed, dirty fingernails digging into her legs.

Her fingers loosened as she looked up at Selena. At first, Selena thought she had tears running down her face, until she saw where they were coming from. The girl had no eyes, only torn sockets that dripped blood down her cheeks and off her chin onto the mattress. She clawed at her legs with bloody hands, coughing on her laughter as blood dripped into her mouth. Her movements were slow, out of sync, like a glitch in a video game. Selena recognized her from the pictures—she had tan skin, curly hair, Doc Martens, ripped black jeans.

Margo.

"It's worth it," she laughed, teeth blinding white against the blood caked around her lips. "It's worth it! Right? Isn't it?"

Selena grabbed Simon by the arm. "Come on!"

He hugged the sketchbook tighter to his chest as he and Selena fled the building, never once looking back.

sixteen

Selena

I think simon and I saw an echo

or a really fucked up ghost I'm not sure

Finch stared at the message, unsure of how to respond. Unsure if she *could* respond, consider how executive dysfunction had sunk its talons into her brain the last couple of days and stolen her ability to do much more than exist.

She was on her bed, a textbook laid flat on the blanket in front of her. She'd opened it and uncapped a highlighter just to reread the same sentence four times before realizing she wasn't absorbing any of the information.

She put her phone down. As much as she knew she should respond, she couldn't.

Instead, she told herself this time was for real and tried, once again, to read the first sentence on the page. It was about then that the pages began to shimmer.

Just as she tried to blink it away, the darkness pressed in. It was just like before when she'd been looking in the bathroom mirror.

Shouldn't be long now, A voice whispered. *Can't be long now.*

Finch's hand went to her stomach as hunger suddenly gripped at her. It was a hollowness like she'd never felt, scraping at her insides, making her feel like her body was collapsing in on itself. It hurt, made her feel like her brain was short-circuiting. Which was strange, because she'd just eaten dinner.

It was almost as if it wasn't her hunger. It just felt like it was.

The more I consume, the voice murmured, *the more the hunger grows.*

Finch looked around frantically. The aura was everywhere, but she was alone.

"Hello?" called out a voice from nowhere. There was something familiar about it, but Finch couldn't quite put a finger on it.

There was a soft rumble in her chest, not quite a laugh. Somewhere between a purr and a growl.

There she is, it thought. *Right on time.*

The aura vanished then, and Finch gasped for breath, rubbing her hands through her hair.

She'd been so sure at first that she was just hearing things, but now that she knew what those auras meant, there had to be something else to it. That, paired with the fact it wasn't just hearing things anymore—it almost felt as if she were in someone else's mind *and* body. But what could it possibly be? More Echoes?

Or something worse?

> I know you're kinda of In It rn
> but this was some wild shit

> just text me when you can ok

"Shit," Selena breathed, dropping her phone down on the couch beside her and closing her eyes. She sank down sideways, lying down and covering her eyes. "When did I start sounding desperate?"

There was a soft crumpling sound as she laid down her head on a pillow, and after a moment, Selena reached underneath to retrieve what she realized was a sheet of paper. It was balled up—considering what she'd seen earlier, she half expected to find another twisted journal entry.

Instead, it was a pop quiz from AP Statistics with Risa's name on it. The score, 12/30, was circled in red at the top.

Selena pursed her lips. *I guess she wasn't kidding.*

Just then, the front door handle turned as someone jammed their key inside. Selena tensed, half expecting that eyeless version of Margo to bust in.

Instead, she found Risa standing by the door in her posh trench coat, trying to hang her keys on the hooks in the entryway.

They slipped out of her grasp and hit the floor. She cursed. Even in the low lamplight, Selena could see that her hands were slick with blood.

"Oh my god." Selena stood from the couch. "Risa?"

Risa glanced up from her blood-soaked hands, dark eyes stirring with unshed tears. She looked pale, long black hair sticking to her sweaty cheeks. "Selena. H-Hello."

Selena took a shaky breath. "What happened to you?"

Risa quickly rubbed away the tears on the edge of her vision, leaving a streak of blood on her cheek. She hesitated for a moment but, seeing that she'd been caught, she took a deep breath.

"I made a deal," Risa admitted in a whisper. "With Nerosi. I *had* to."

Selena felt like she's been smacked. "You...what?"

"I'm sorry," she muttered. She dragged herself past Selena into the kitchen, slumping over the sink. After a few pained breaths, she pumped far too much soap onto her hands before running them under steaming hot water. She hissed through her teeth, barely cutting off a whimper. Selena was too stunned to speak.

Risa clenched her teeth. "Can you get me some bandages?"

"You *had* to?" Selena had to raise her voice to be heard over the water, closing the distance between them until she also hovered over the sink. "What did she do?"

Risa turned off the water. She leaned against the counter, looking up at Selena with pursed lips.

"I'm fine," she said. Selena could practically see her counting in her head to calm down, steadying her breaths. "I got what I wanted. That's what matters."

That was when Selena noticed new blood bubbling up from her fingers where her fingernails were supposed to be.

"Holy *shit*."

"Bandages," she repeated. "Please."

Selena rushed to the bathroom and grabbed their first aid kit. She started taking out bandages and pulling them from the wrapping, handing them one by one to Risa, who shakily applied them to her hands.

As she did, Selena softly asked, "Why? Even after…"

Risa sniffled, trying to hold back tears. They'd been friends for a year now, but never once had Selena seen her cry. "I…I know that what you and Finch said about Nerosi might be true. You're right that there are holes in her story, and you're right that maybe she doesn't have good intentions." She let out a shaky breath. "But she was the only one who could help me."

"Help me understand," Selena said. "Is this about your scholarship?"

Risa nodded. "I got my official warning today that if I don't pull my grades up, I'll lose it." She finished bandaging her final finger, wincing as she flexed them. "I asked Nerosi for a photographic memory. Fingernails grow back—a scholarship doesn't."

Selena felt a pang in her chest. She came from a wealthy family, and she'd never had to worry about paying for Ulalume. Her moms were two and a half hours away in Boston. If she ever wanted to go home, it was barely a discussion.

She'd never stopped to think about how isolating it would be to be so far from home and have to work night and day just to stay there.

"My family gave up a lot for me to be here," Risa said. "I…I can't disappoint them. That's why I had to do it. The rewards outweigh the risks."

Part of Selena wanted desperately to admonish her, to say that she was the last one she'd expect to be making deals with devils, and that she couldn't believe it. But thinking of it now, if she were in Risa's place, she probably would have done the same thing.

"I get it," Selena finally said. She looked up, meeting Risa's eyes. "And I don't blame you."

"Thanks, Selena." Risa nodded to herself, reaching up to dab her eyes. "Can you get my keys for me? So I can wash the blood off?"

"Of course." Selena took a step, but paused, asking, "Risa?"

The other girl raised her eyebrows.

"I don't mean to sound like I'm telling you what to do, but I don't think we should go down there anymore," Selena said. "To see Nerosi. It's just—I care about you, all right? Sometimes I feel like you're my only real friend in this house, and I'm scared of what's going to happen if we keep giving her what she wants."

Risa paused for a moment, staring down at her fingers with tear-bright eyes, and nodded. "So long as you don't either, yes."

Selena nodded. "Deal."

She went to fetch Risa's keys, worry knotting deep within her chest.

When Monday came, Finch realized she'd spent the weekend in one of the worst depressive episodes she'd had since her parents died. She hadn't left her room for two days and spent her waking hours switching between binge-watching Netflix series and ignoring her texts. The thought of replying to anyone felt like a feat.

Sumera knocked on her door a couple times, but Finch pretended to be asleep. Sumera was still frustrated about the party, but Finch didn't have the energy to explain it to her. She didn't have the energy to explain anything to anyone.

She didn't want to be this way. Like someone who couldn't handle the motions of a normal life. But on days like that—when she awoke in a pile of still-crusty Lean Cuisines and couldn't fathom washing her hair—that was how she felt. All she could do was curl up and wait for the dark storm cloud of her emotions to pass over.

On Monday, Finch slept through her first class. She managed to pull on a semi-clean blouse and drag herself to the next one, doing her best don't-look-at-me face to stop anyone from speaking to her. Thankfully, it seemed to be working through most of her classes, including AP English Lit, where they finished the lesson early and started on their next assignment at the end of class. Finch stared at her laptop screen blankly, debating whether or not she had the energy to critically analyze *As I Lay Dying* without crying.

Kyra and Amber sat in the row ahead of her, whispering over the din of fingers on keyboards.

"Just look up the SparkNotes. It's all there," Kyra grumbled. "Now leave me alone. You should be able to figure this out on your own."

"Kyra," Amber whimpered. "Come on. There's got to be something about this stupid barn scene I'm missing!"

"It's not my fault you're an idiot," she snapped, rolling her eyes. She stood up. "I'm going to fix my eyeliner. Get yourself together in the meantime."

Kyra left the room and Amber's face fell. She pursed her lips and squeezed her eyes shut. When she inhaled, she choked on it, barely catching the tears before they slid out of her eyes.

Quietly, she whispered, "*Damn it.*"

Finch bit her lip. English wasn't her strongest subject, but she had a decent handle on Faulkner. After a moment of debating, she took her book and hopped up a row, sitting down in Kyra's seat.

Amber furrowed her eyebrows. "Finch?"

"You're talking about the barn scene with Dewey Dell, right?" Finch opened her book, showing Amber the passages she'd annotated. "Look at this line. She's talking about her…guts, right? And then she says 'I know it is there because God gave women a sign.' What do you think she's talking about?"

"Something wrong with her stomach?" Amber guessed.

Finch shook her head. "Close. Remember Dewey Dell's thing with Lafe? So…if they're getting together, and Dewey Dell got a sign from God about something in her guts…"

"Oh!" Amber's eyes lit up. "She's pregnant!"

"Yes!" Finch pointed to the page again. "She talks about it later with the cow too. That's what she's so worried about."

"Oh, that makes so much sense!" Amber smacked her hand to her forehead. "God, I'm so stupid. Kyra's right."

"No—Amber, no she's not." Finch set her book down, doing her best to keep her voice low as to not disturb her classmates working on their assignments. She looked up at Amber again. She had her mousy hair back in a ponytail, and fairly heavy makeup. She'd gone too heavy on blush, and her eyeliner was uneven.

"Give yourself more credit," Finch said. "You figured it out.

And this is hard—it's supposed to be hard. Everyone needs help sometimes."

"But I need help *all* the time." Amber cupped her cheek with her palm, sticking out her lips. "I'm not smart enough to go to this school. I'm not an artist or a scientist or a writer—I'm just a legacy student."

Finch bit the inside of her cheek, trying not to let her face show the bitter note that reverberated through her clenched muscles. A legacy student—someone whose family had gone to Ulalume for generations and earned the favor of the administration through impressive donations that earned them buildings named after them. People with money who didn't *have* to be good at anything to get in.

People who didn't have to spend years toiling away just to get a scholarship.

Finch's jaw tightened.

"It's just, like…a lot," Amber said, her eyes falling on her book once more. She had long eyelashes—enough she didn't need mascara. "Everyone here has something special. I wish I could be pretty like Kyra o-or have Risa's grades or dance like Selena, y'know? Something to make me…memorable."

Finch forced herself not to let the bitter note reverberating through her head echo in her voice. "Everyone has different talents, Amber. You shouldn't count yourself out because you aren't a perfect artist or valedictorian. There are tons of talented, passionate people who had a hard time in high school."

"Average people," Amber muttered, twirling a lock of hair around her finger and frowning. "Who become, like, secretaries."

"The world probably needs secretaries more than people who can analyze Faulkner," Finch argued.

The corners of Amber's mouth pulled up. "Faulkner's a bad writer anyway. This book totally sucks."

"It really does, doesn't it?"

Now, she'd broken into a small smile. "You know what? Even if Kyra thinks you're an annoying, shrill friend-stealer, I think you're really nice, Finch."

Finch wrinkled her forehead. "Shrill?"

Amber nodded. "That's what she said. She thinks your voice is annoying."

"Oh." Finch nodded to herself. "Great."

"She's just—"

"So, do I get my seat back, or are you keeping that too?"

Kyra glowering down at them, hazel eyes freshly lined with swooping wings. Finch was taken again with just how beautiful she was—even with a scowl on her face. She felt small under her stare.

"Get up," Kyra told her. "Go."

Finch didn't have a chance to fight it as the words started to echo in her head like they had before in the lighthouse. She was on her feet in a second, scooping her book to her chest and retreating to her desk.

"Kyra," Amber started, eyes flitting to Finch for a moment. "She was just helping me with—"

"As if she knows what she's talking about." Kyra shot Finch a look. "You're better off on your own, Amber. Trust me."

They were quiet for a moment, and Finch put her head down, wishing she could turn invisible. It felt like everyone in the room was staring at her. The dark thoughts pressed back in. *Leave it to you to just mess things up more. No wonder you're so depressed.*

"Finch is a good person, Kyra," Amber finally whispered. "Just because Selena likes her more than you doesn't mean she deserves to be treated like that."

Finch had to stop her mouth from falling open.

Kyra's pencil snapped. Her hand shook and her shoulders tightened. After a long beat of silence, though, it seemed Kyra wasn't going to dignify the statement with a response.

Finch could practically hear as Kyra's veneer of perfection cracked.

That afternoon, Finch stood Selena up for rehearsal. Homecoming was on Friday, but she didn't care. After being beaten down by both her dysfunctional brain chemistry and Kyra, the thought of sitting in front of the school and performing made her insides prickle.

Instead, she scrolled through TikTok for four hours and fell asleep at 9 p.m.

The next day, she got up and did mostly the same. That is, until around four, when wild knocking woke her from one of her multiple naps that day.

Finch made no move to get up, so Sumera finally cracked and answered. The walls were too thick for Finch to hear much, but whenever Sumera and the other person were discussing, it seemed heated.

Without warning, Finch's door flew open and slammed against the wall.

"What the hell—?" Selena took in the scene of Finch's room. To add to the crusty food packaging scattered around the room, her clothes littered the floor, and trash sat in piles around the edge of the bed. Finch, not even wearing her usual makeup to cover up the dark circles around her eyes or bronzer to fake a tiny bit of color, looked at her through a gaze befitting of a zombie.

"Go away," she moaned, unable to manage much more than that. Selena had seen her in a number of compromising situations, but this somehow felt worse. Finch hid her face in the blankets, unable to look at her.

"Two things. One, Simon and I saw a very scary Echo in Tunger that you're lucky you missed. Second, we have four days before we're supposed to get on stage and perform for the entire student body. Which is to say: how do I get you out of bed so we don't make fools of ourselves?"

Finch peeked at her from beneath the blankets. "Try again tomorrow?"

"Wrong answer." Selena cracked her knuckles. "Last chance, or I'm picking you up and carrying you to the auditorium myself."

Finch squinted at her, frowning. "You wouldn't."

Selena held out an arm and flexed it, once again revealing her surprisingly defined arms. "I can and I will. Gladly."

For a brief second, Finch considered how it might feel to be literally swept off her feet and thrown over Selena's shoulder. Unfortunately, her traitorous brain welcomed the idea with great enthusiasm. That was enough to finally get her to stand up, if only out of fear that she'd make a fool of herself by turning vibrantly red while being carried across campus like a swooning maiden in a fairy tale.

Selena grinned. "Great choice. Let's go then."

Finch let out a whimper of protest, but Selena wouldn't hear it. Fifteen minutes of shuffling her feet later, Finch collapsed onto the piano bench in the auditorium. She looked at the keys and groaned, rubbing her face with her hands, desperately wishing she'd at least had the chance to shower before this. It felt somehow dehumanizing to be sitting in front of such an expensive instrument looking like she'd been chewed up and spit out by the world's most depressing loungewear store.

"You," Finch muttered as Selena set down her bag, "are not a nice person."

"No, but I am charmingly persistent." Selena came and sat on the other half of the piano bench, straddling it so she faced Finch. "Look, I know this isn't the ideal situation, but I really want this performance to go well. It's gonna be recorded for part of my application to the Boston Conservatory, and it would mean a lot to me if it went smoothly."

Finch bit her lip, but didn't say anything.

Selena sighed. "Is this about the party?"

Finch went quiet. She stared hard at her hands, which were folded in her lap. She was still wearing sweatpants from two days ago, dotted with food stains. Her hair was a greasy curtain around her face. Her body ached from lying in the same place. Her fists tightened.

"Yeah," she finally muttered.

"Do you think talking about it would help?" Selena asked.

Finch dully said, "No."

Selena's jaw tightened, and she took a deep breath that turned into an impressive sigh.

"Okay. Fair enough. There are no magic words that are going to make you feel miraculously better," Selena said, splaying her fingers out across the chestnut wood in front of her. "That's not how this works. I know that. But what I do know is that I get it."

Finch shook her head. "I doubt it."

"Give me some credit." Selena leaned closer, trying to catch Finch's eyes. "I might be one of the only people on this whole planet who understands what it's like to be in this bizarre Nerosi situation *and* what it's like to realize you're not straight."

Finch froze at the second half, and that's when it seemed to click for Selena.

"Oh. It's the not-straight thing?"

Finch ground her teeth. "I wish I hadn't said anything. I was drunk and stupid and—"

Selena held out a hand to stop her. "Hey, it's okay. You said you didn't want to talk about it. So allow me."

Finch lifted her eyes.

Selena ran her hand through her hair, settling back. "I know it's not quite the same for you and me. I knew I liked boys from the time I was a little kid. I never really questioned that because it felt so obvious. Everyone around me validated me being straight. It made sense to people.

"But when I got older, I had all these issues whenever I met girls I perceived as being pretty or attractive or whatever. I got so angry with myself because I just obsessed over them, and I got nervous when I talked to them and I didn't get *why*. So I wound up being a total ass because I didn't know how to handle how I was feeling.

"Last year, I got especially obsessed with one girl in particular. She was gorgeous, and she stood up to me, and I hated how jealous I was of her. And one night, when we were shitfaced at a party, I started touching her hair and couldn't stop thinking about how beautiful she was until I finally gave in and kissed her. And we kept kissing, and we wound up going back to my room and—"

She cut off, taking a moment to bite her lip and breathe. "I lost my virginity to her. When I woke up the next morning, I felt sick. I was supposed to be the perfect popular girl, and girls like that don't lose their virginity to other girls, y'know? They're straight and they're mean and they certainly don't let themselves be vulnerable like that with *other girls*. I didn't like the idea of feeling like I was suddenly somehow different than the person I saw myself as, and all I wanted was to have time to figure it out myself.

"Problem was, I never got that time. The girl I hooked up with—"

"Kyra?" Finch guessed.

Selena nodded. "Correct. Kyra took me sleeping with her as evidence that I wanted to be in a relationship with her. At that point, I had barely figured out I liked girls and definitely hadn't had a chance to come to terms with it. So I told her that I wasn't ready and she took it very poorly.

"Kyra outed me to the whole school and started this rumor that I was trying to sleep with as many people as I could before graduation, like it was some kind of game and I'd somehow lured Kyra in just to check her off some kind of list. So whenever I talked with other girls at school, they assumed I was trying to sleep with them. I got called all kinds of nasty stuff."

"That's horrible," Finch breathed. "Why would you ever stay friends with someone who did something like that to you?"

Selena's face fell and she bit her lip. "Because…I guess when it comes down to it, I still like the way Kyra makes me feel. When we're together, it feels like we can do anything. Whether it was going to clubs in the city this summer or sneaking around campus to get drunk or going to parties—there's something about her that's so fun and alive. It makes me feel…important. Special. And I…I like the attention that comes from it. So when she actually owned up to it and apologized for everything, I forgave her. I didn't want to give up that feeling."

Finch nodded to herself. "I guess if that's the sort of friendship you have, it's a whole lot less vulnerable than being together romantically."

"I—yeah. Exactly." Selena shrugged. "Being Kyra's friend is easy. But I could never be her girlfriend. She hurt me too much for that kind of vulnerability, I think. Maybe not forgiving her fully makes me a bad person, but…"

"That's not the sort of thing you just forgive," Finch said. She felt a spark in her chest that grew hotter the more Selena spoke—it was about to build into something destructive. "She hurt you in a way that crosses a lot of boundaries. That's—that's *bullshit*."

Finch immediately felt heat in her cheeks but Selena's eyes scintillated as she said, "You swore."

She looked away. "S-Sorry—"

"Oh, no, please never apologize for that again, it was amazing." Selena chuckled. "But yeah, you're right. My relationship with Kyra sucks, and it's part of what made it so hard for me to accept I'm bi. But after some time, it's gotten a lot easier. Now it's part of who I am, and it doesn't feel like trying to reconcile it with the rest of my identity, y'know? All the pieces fit together."

"How…how did you do that?" Finch asked. "Make it feel like it fit?"

Selena shrugged. "I started saying it out loud more. I brought it up when I met new people. The more I said it, the more it felt normal."

"That's it? Just saying it?"

"Well, that and getting positive responses. Hearing people I cared about saying it didn't change anything. That helped convince me I was still…me, if that makes sense."

Finch nodded. That was a lot of her fear, ultimately. That if anyone found out, she wouldn't just be Finch anymore. That people would assume they knew her because of this, that they wouldn't like her or would treat her differently. That they'd perceive her as something other than herself, whoever that was.

Finch hadn't noticed when she'd started crying. She quickly wiped away the tears and sniffled to keep her nose from running. She apologized, but Selena shook her head.

"Crying is healthy." Finch let out another hearty sob as Selena wondered aloud, "Are you a water sign? You strike me as a water sign."

That made Finch laugh, a choked little thing. "What does that have to do with anything?"

"Y'know. Identity stuff. I'm a Scorpio, I'm bi—it's all little stuff when you really think about it. You get to a point where they're equally easy to say, and that's when you realize everything sucks a lot less than it seems."

"O-Okay." Finch rubbed her eyes. "I-I guess then…I'm a Pisces. And," she took a deep, shaking breath, "a lesbian."

"I should have known you'd be Pisces. You're such a Pisces."

Finch raised her eyebrows. "That's what you're stuck on?"

Selena bit back a laugh. "Look, if we're being honest, I'm a lot more judgmental about astrology than sexual orientation. Like, I'm not saying I'd stop being your friend if I found out you were a Libra, but it would definitely be your first strike."

Finch sniffled and managed a giggle. "You're ridiculous."

"But I made you smile, right?" Selena grinned, all dimples and white teeth. "So maybe if you can say you're a lesbian with a smile on your face, then maybe it's not that big of a deal."

A tiny quarter-smile quirked up the corner of Finch's mouth as she dabbed at her still-teary eyes. "Yeah. You're right."

"Exactly." Selena reached out and touched Finch's knee. "Congratulations, you're out of the closet. If I had confetti, I'd shoot it at you." She leaned in close to Finch's face and wiped away a tear with her thumb. "I told you I could help."

Finch shook her head, somewhere between laughing and crying. "I'm a mess."

"Who isn't these days?" Selena peeled her hoodie off to reveal the tank top underneath. She shook out her leg muscles, stretching her arms up. "Just don't lose it too much to play my music. This performance has gotta be perfect."

Finch rolled her eyes. "Way to make it about you."

"Please, I'm an Olympic gold medalist in making it about me." She cracked her knuckles, bouncing from foot to foot so her hair swung back and forth in its ponytail. "So? Will you give me a dress rehearsal?"

Finch sniffled and rubbed her eyes, but nodded.

"Fine. But you'll have to tell me about this Echo you saw after."

Selena responded with a jubilant leap across the stage.

seventeen

For the next few days, Selena practiced long into the night, even after Finch went home. She set her phone on the stage and repeated the same *relevé-pas de bourrée-leap* combo over and over, each time ending on the floor swiping her finger across the screen to get the music where she wanted it. Sweat soaked her back, and her legs and feet ached, but she had to get it right.

She swept a cloud of baby hairs out of her face, thankful for the sweat that stuck them in place when she did. She put her arms in position, chest still heaving from the last hundred times she'd repeated this move. *It has to look perfect*, Selena reminded herself. *Boston Conservatory perfect.*

Selena had been vying for a spot in their dance program since she was a child, repeating the same pointed-toe moves on the barre every afternoon at the studio in Fenway, famed Red Sox epicenter and Selena's childhood neighborhood. Her middle school had been close enough to the conservatory that she'd occasionally see groups of girls, still in their activewear, chatting and walking to grab coffee after practice. They were all talented and beautiful and Selena wanted nothing more than to be them.

Selena pursed her lips and took off once more, putting careful focus into each movement until the leap, when she used all the power in her legs and core to fling herself in the air.

For a moment, time slowed. Those seconds in the middle of a leap felt like being suspended from the ceiling, like she could float off the stage. But this time, that feeling lasted a second longer than it usually did for Selena.

And it startled her. She couldn't be in the air this long—she'd made a mistake. And so she corrected herself.

Overcorrected herself.

When she landed, it was directly on her ankle.

She shrieked, hands flying to her injured leg. She cursed in quick succession, sinking her fingers into her skin. Her ankle began to swell. She tried to move it and quickly wrenched back as it twinged hot pain up her leg.

"Shit!" Selena tried rubbing it, repeating the same word over and over again. The harder she rubbed, the more tears threatened behind her eyes, burning at the back of her throat. She cried out in rage and punched the floor.

Desperate, she tried to stand. While she could manage it, when she tried to put more than a tiny bit of weight on her toe, the whole leg collapsed. She fell to the floor once more, rolling onto her back. She pulled her knee to her chest and cradled the leg, breaking down in sobs. The stage light burned red blotches into the darkness behind her eyes.

I messed up. I messed up. I messed up.

Tears ran down Selena's face as she gritted her teeth. What options did she have? Hobble to the school infirmary? Call someone for help?

This was the kind of injury that could end her dance career before it even started. This was every athlete's worst nightmare.

But—

But.

She could ask for help. Even if it meant going back on her promise to Risa, and the unspoken agreement she had with Finch.

This isn't going to heal overnight, Selena realized. *I don't have a choice.*

In the corner of her vision, Selena saw a shadow move in the stage light. When she looked up, the shadow shifted into the shape of a stag.

Exhaling a shaking breath, Selena stood. She took a limping step toward the stag, whispering, "Fine. *Fine.*"

On weeknights, the tunnels were almost completely abandoned. Without the laughter of friends to cut through the tunnels' inherent creepiness, it was easy for them to go from an adventure to a nightmare, with the cold walls, the flickering lights, and the sounds that were just a bit too eerie to be groaning pipes.

Selena let the stag-shaped shadow guide her back to Nerosi's room. The lights in the vines flared brighter as soon as she walked through the dirt passage, shadows bouncing around the room like spirits with their own autonomy. The ground beneath her hummed like it was electric.

She found Nerosi waiting for her, cross-legged, on the ground.

The second she stepped inside, whatever had been supporting Selena's ankle this long gave out, and with a shout, she collapsed. Her hair splayed out across the strange markings on the floor. Her arms shook as she pulled herself up. The pale figure floated before her, head tilted to the side and lips slightly parted.

"What happened?" Nerosi asked. "That looks…painful."

No shit, Selena wanted to say, but the pain choked her throat. Her body shook—she wished desperately that she could pull it together, look this creature in the eye and make a cool demand, but she couldn't. Not with tears soaking her sob-reddened cheeks and panic eating at her insides.

"I fell," Selena whimpered.

"I'm so sorry," Nerosi said, bending down to look at her ankle closer. "Oh, my. That looks serious."

"What do I have to give you to make it stop?" Selena forced herself to say. She rubbed a trembling hand across her cheeks, ash from the floor leaving a dark streak across her skin.

Nerosi considered her, pursing her lips. For a brief second, Selena looked into her jet-black eyes and saw her own reflection, teeth clenched and mascara lines down her cheeks. Her head began to pound, and she looked away as her thoughts began to blur.

"This is going to take more power than I currently have," Nerosi said grimly, looking down at her hands. "I'll…need to take something of yours. Something physical."

"You can have my hair—all of it. Or all of my fingernails. I don't need those to perform," Selena begged. "Please. It's all yours."

Nerosi tilted her head the other way, studying Selena's face while frowning faintly. She shook her head, and said, "I don't think something that small will do it. I can't manipulate the human body beyond tiny tweaks. Healing an injury this severe…I'll need something more solid."

"Like what?" Selena demanded.

Nerosi nodded to herself. "I suspect your teeth will do."

Selena froze. "Teeth?"

"I don't need all of them. Maybe just…four. Yes, that should be enough." Nerosi's mouth bent with sympathy. "I'm so sorry to make such a demand, but it's the only way."

Selena looked down at her ankle, which was bruising now, a swatch of purple throbbing under the skin. It could hardly bear weight, much less get her through the performance tomorrow. Who knew how long it would take to heal on its own? Would it even heal correctly? In time for her to salvage her place at the conservatory?

Teeth can be replaced, Selena thought. *This can't.*

"Fine." Selena took a shaking breath. "The molars. In the back. They're yours. Just make me better."

Nerosi nodded. "Understood. Will you close your eyes when I take them? I don't want you to have to see this."

Selena didn't need to hear it twice. She closed her eyes. "Go ahead."

The next moment, Selena felt a tug in the back of her jaw, then a wrench, and then she was screaming, wailing, as something unseen gripped her teeth and tore. Blood spilled from her lips, spattering across the floor. She tried to clamp her mouth shut but it kept pulling, wiggling the molars free. The nerves fired hot pain through her jawbone and into her skull. It was stabbing and aching and throbbing all at once, and her screams turned to gurgles as the blood filled her mouth and she choked on it.

With a final tug, her four back molars tore free of her jaw. Selena sputtered up blood that stained the floor, mixing with the ash.

Without meaning to, her eyes flew open.

For less than a second, she caught sight of four writhing, black shapes protruding from Nerosi. They seemed to have slid free from four of the scars on her arms, and each one of them was wrapped around one bloody tooth. They each engulfed their tooth before slithering back into Nerosi's arms, the scars healing into place instantly.

"I told you to shut your eyes," Nerosi whispered.

She reached out, and Selena flinched as her hands brushed her cheeks. Instantly, the pain ebbed away. Selena crouched on her hands and knees as the holes in her mouth closed, the blood slowing to a trickle until her spit was only pink instead of red.

"I don't mean to hurt you," Nerosi said, her face inches from Selena's. This close, Selena's skin began to crawl as she tried desperately not to look directly into her eyes. "I know I scare you, but I don't mean any harm. In fact, I had enough power to make you a little…better. I think you'll be pleasantly surprised."

She released Selena's face and stepped back before vanishing into thin air.

She left Selena alone in the dark with a twinge in her jaw and tears dripping down her cheeks.

eighteen

Homecoming at Ulalume Academy was unlike most American high schools. Instead of centering around a football game or a dance, Homecoming invited alumni back to Rainwater for an evening of performances, competition and, most importantly, fundraising. When Finch woke up, the campus was flooded with alumni from all over the world returning to visit their alma mater. Headmistress Waite called an assembly where she talked about the importance of giving back to your community while all the students giggled about how uptight she looked. After that, some of the alums sat in on classes taking notes as girls specializing in math or science showed off their skills.

It made Finch all the more nervous for her performance.

"Close your eyes," Selena said as she swept a fluffy white brush over the eyeshadow palette she balanced on her knee. The two girls sat facing each other on folding chairs backstage, in a bright corner away from the dressing rooms where the choir kids were making bizarre noises in preparation for their performance. The walls were all white paint over cinder blocks, the floor industrial concrete. If it weren't for the piles of costumes, it would have looked like a prison.

Finch did so, keeping her breathing even as Selena swept the terracotta shadow across her lids. She'd already taken the time to darken Finch's eyebrows—which was to say, for once, they were actually visible against her skin. She'd even applied enough blush to hide Finch's trademark pallor.

Selena was silent as she worked—uncharacteristically so. Usually, even if Finch was quiet, Selena found a way to fill silence with whatever happened to be on her mind. Sometimes it felt like Finch didn't even need to be there for Selena to carry out an entire conversation.

As Selena's finger found Finch's chin to tilt it up, Finch asked, "Are you okay? You seem quiet."

Selena paused. Her expression had been somewhat distant up until that second, as if her hands were on autopilot while her mind was somewhere else. She cleared her throat and shook her head, focusing back on Finch's makeup.

"I had a…rough evening last night. I'd rather not talk about it."

Finch's mouth tugged into a frown. "If there's anything I can do…"

Selena shook her head. "Nah. It's over now."

She leaned back as she shifted things around in her makeup bag. She'd already applied her own makeup, going for red lipstick and blush that would look cartoonish in another context, but Finch understood that was the nature of stage makeup. The stuff Selena was putting on her likely wouldn't be noticeable to the audience, but then again, she was behind the piano.

For a moment, Finch thought Selena's lipstick was smeared, but then she realized it was a trickle of blood escaping Selena's mouth.

She pointed to it. "Y-You've got—"

Selena quickly wiped it away with her fist. "Sorry. Got a…cut on my lip last night. Keeps opening up and bleeding."

Finch squinted. She didn't see any cuts, but maybe it was hidden under her lipstick.

"Hope it doesn't hurt too bad," Finch muttered. It was strange for Selena to be this reserved, but she didn't want to pry.

"I'm fine," she said as she came back with a pale mauve shade of lipstick and leaned closer to Finch to swipe it over her lips. "And with luck, you won't look like you have the world's worst circulation here in a second."

A few minutes later, a curly-haired stage manager in all black cleared her throat, and the girls turned to find her giving them the five-minute signal. Finch stood from the chair, doing her best to flatten out her dress. Selena had put her in a dark blue outfit with a puffy skirt and a sweetheart neckline—not something she would have chosen for herself, but it was pretty.

Selena had gone for a classic ballet dress with a flared tutu and corset top that was a little more revealing than Finch would have thought was acceptable for a performance like this. Not that she was complaining, other than the fact that she had to keep reminding herself to stare directly into Selena's eyes when they were talking so she didn't get distracted. It really did look amazing on her.

The two of them picked their way up the stairs, Selena making light of how stupid her feet looked in pointe shoes and how her tutu was a health hazard. Finch didn't hear much, aside from the pounding of her heart, and the unending soundtrack of *you're going to ruin this, you're going to make a fool of yourself, you'll regret this* looping through her head. She'd barely gotten any sleep last night thanks to that.

Once they were in the wings, it felt like an eternity before the first year onstage finished the third rendition of "Landslide" so far that night. When she hit the last note and the crowd burst into applause, Finch's breathing sped all the way to hyperventilating. Her vision blurred.

The first year walked off stage and the stage crew rolled the piano out. Finch's mouth dried.

I can't do this.

Selena touched her arm. Just as the announcer was reading off their names, Selena ran her fingers through Finch's hair before planting a kiss on her cheek.

"It's going to be okay," she promised. "You've got me."

She pulled away and walked on stage.

———

Selena, at her core, was a modest person who craved one thing: undivided attention.

As she walked onto the stage, she tested her ankle again. It was as steady as it had been when she'd finally stood from the bloodstained floor in the tunnels last night. Nerosi really had fixed it—and seemed to take away the rest of her physical grievances as well. Her weak knee felt stronger, and her muscles didn't ache like they usually did after such a long night of practice. When she rehearsed this morning, she'd spent an hour throwing herself across the stage and had barely broken a sweat.

She'd also nearly torn her bedroom door off its hinges this morning. It seemed Nerosi's definition of making her "better" meant increasing her strength to almost supernatural levels.

She was down four molars, but even if Selena hated to admit it, so far it seemed worth it.

Her heart raced as Finch hit the first notes. Every eye in the audience traced the angles of her arabesque. She stepped into the slow, fluid movements of the first section of her choreography. The stage lights bathed her in a pale pink.

As she went into her first turn, her eyes fell on Finch, sitting behind the piano. She used her as her spot, staring at her lips, pursed in concentration. Still, her face was relaxed, fingers as graceful on the keys as Selena was on stage.

They made eye contact. Finch smiled.

Selena went out of the spin and into a leap across the floor that felt perfectly seamless. After all the evenings the two of them had spent together, Selena knew the notes that tripped Finch up, and Finch knew the moves that Selena had to repeat over and over to land.

But this time, it paid off. Selena landed every jump, roll, and leap while Finch didn't so much as hesitate on a single note. Periodically, as Selena's body flowed into a new spin or leap, they'd catch each other's eyes.

By the time Finch softly struck the final keys and Selena's movements slowed to just the flow of her arms, they were grinning, eyes alight and hearts racing.

Just like that, it was over. Nearly two months of work condensed into five minutes.

The audience burst into applause. Selena heard her name, and warmth filled her cheeks. She held out a hand, and Finch came to her side, practically leaping across the stage herself. Before they could shake hands, Selena pulled her into a hug, not caring about the fact that she was sweaty and radiating heat.

"You did amazing," Selena whispered.

"I couldn't see that much," Finch said, "but I know you did too."

They pulled apart and joined hands for a bow that earned them another round of applause before they exited into the wings.

Backstage, they ducked out of the way to avoid the next act as they replaced them on stage. While their music started, Selena turned to Finch, bouncing on her toes.

"That was so good! God, I'm so happy someone from the conservatory will get to see it—that was perfect!" she said, spinning in a circle. She hadn't felt this effervescent in months. It made her grin widen and a laugh bubble up from her chest.

She threw her arms around Finch and pulled her into a tight hug. Into Finch's neck, Selena said, "I'm proud of us."

Finch slowly wound her arms around Selena. "I'm proud of us too."

"You want to watch the rest of the show and then go downtown for milkshakes later?" Selena asked. "I heard a bunch of the music and dance girls are going after. We could tag along."

Finch considered, biting her lip. Finally, she said, "Actually... I'd rather...hang out with you. I-If that's okay."

"Me?" Selena almost laughed.

"Yeah." Finch shrugged. "We've had this a-and all the stuff

with Nerosi but we've never hung out for fun. If you're interested, of course."

"Oh." Selena tried and failed not to let the surprise register on her face. Plenty of people invited her to things, or asked if she would show up somewhere, but she couldn't remember the last time someone had wanted to just hang out with her.

A huge smile broke across her face. "Yeah. Let's go back to my place."

———————

"Wait, wait! How do I use my sword?"

"R2—the top trigger."

Finch looked down at the controller in her hand, letting out a distressed peep. "The what?"

The path that led to Annalee Lighthouse had been totally empty, the grounds quiet with everyone either at the performance or tucked away in their rooms studying for their looming midterms. Selena had bounded home, high on adrenaline, as Finch trailed behind.

Now, they were holed up in Selena's room, and Finch was attempting to play Selena's favorite video game. Selena had a small TV and a PlayStation set up on her desk, and since she usually kept a large pot of succulents in front of it, Finch hadn't noticed it at first.

As soon as she'd said something about it, Selena had turned bright red. "You can't tell anyone."

"Why? I always wanted to play video games, but my parents never let me. They said they were too violent." Finch had picked up the controller, turning it over. It had fingerprints all over it, and the handles looked a little worn down. "Do you use this a lot?"

"Well—let's just say I've sunk triple-digit hours into some of those games."

"*Really?*" Finch tilted her head to the side. "Is it that fun?"

Which led them to Finch sitting on Selena's bed, facing the TV and attempting to make her elf warrior fight a horde of demons on screen. Two warm mugs of hot cocoa sat nearby, which Selena had made while Finch spent far too long in the character creation menu debating between two different nose shapes.

"What is R2?" Finch cried, hitting random buttons. She opened and closed the menu, then swung her sword at one of her companions. As much as her ineptitude stressed her out, it seemed like Selena thought it was funny. Somehow, that made Finch *want* to keep looking like a fool.

Selena reached down and moved Finch's finger on top of the button. Finch instantly tensed as Selena's hair tickled her cheek and her body pressed into hers.

"Hold this down to keep attacking," she instructed, pushing Finch's finger down gently. "Like this. Or—well, walk up to the demon first. You're not gonna get very far standing in the back slashing at snowdrifts."

"Can you do it?" Finch finally asked, after hitting the wrong button again and downing a needless health potion.

Selena chuckled. "Sure."

She took the controller and wiped out the entire group of enemies at once. Still laughing, she handed the controller back to Finch and said, "You're still in the tutorial level. You've got time to practice."

"How are you so good at this?" Finch asked, tucking a lock of white hair behind her ear. Their legs were touching now, Finch still in her dress from the show while Selena had changed into a tank top and sweatpants.

"I've played through it eight times." Selena shrugged. "Combat's super easy once you get the hang of it. You'll breeze through this stuff soon. Plus, it's the romance that makes this game good."

"Romance?"

Selena smiled, waggling her eyebrows. "That's the best part."

"I didn't take you for the romantic type."

"Oh, I'm hopeless."

"I guess we have that in common."

"Do we?"

Selena snuck a sidelong glance at the same moment Finch did, and they both quickly looked away from each other. Slowly, Finch scooted closer to Selena. She hit a few buttons and managed to pause the game.

"I really like spending time with you, Selena," Finch said. "Like this. I wish we could do this more often."

Selena turned herself to face Finch, their faces inches apart. She said, "I think we could work something out."

Finch felt frozen, but Selena slowly leaned in, her eyes falling closed. The tip of her nose brushed Finch's.

But suddenly, sound vanished from the room. Finch immediately drew back from Selena, causing the other girl to mouth her name. No—she was definitely saying it. Finch just couldn't hear it.

She thinks she can do this so easily? a voice hissed in her mind. *Deny me? When I've been nothing but kind? I'll tear her apart.*

Perhaps then they'll know not to reject me.

Hot rage simmered in Finch's chest. Her teeth clenched, and

her shoulders tensed. Her eyes had gone glassy, and she couldn't see Selena in front of her anymore. In fact, she wasn't seeing her bedroom now. She saw darkness, with only tiny pinpricks of light from something growing along the walls.

It was…roots. Glowing with bioluminescent light.

"Finch?" called a voice. "Finch!"

Her eyes focused once more, and the light rushed back in. Finch had to brace herself against Selena's shoulder before she toppled sideways, head spinning.

"What's going on?" Selena asked, cupping the side of her face in her palm. "Are you okay?"

"It's her," Finch whispered, the realization sending a shiver through her. "Nerosi. This whole time, I've been hearing her thoughts—I just didn't realize it was her. Something must've happened. Something that made her mad."

And then, out of nowhere, a scream cut through their silence.

"Amber?" Selena said. She met Finch's eyes. "*Shit.*"

The next moments passed in a flurry of running feet and more wailing cries. Finch nearly tripped on the stairs rushing down. Selena led her to Amber's room at the end of the hall from the kitchen. She'd decorated the inside with fairy lights and taped up everything from doodles to movie ticket stubs to photographs of herself and the girls like a room-wide collage.

When they stepped inside, Finch stopped, a scream of her own catching in her throat.

Collapsed in front of a mirror on the wall was Amber, tears streaking her face. She was in fetal position, cradling her arm. A trail of black, viscous droplets marked the path behind her. She was shaking, biting back a scream.

At the sound of Finch and Selena stepping inside, Amber wailed, "Don't—don't look!"

Selena dropped to her side. "What happened? Amber, tell me so I can help."

"It hurts," she moaned. Shaking, she lifted the arm she was holding, and Selena cradled it in her hand. The color drained from her face. Finch took a hesitant step closer and immediately saw why.

There was a bite mark on Amber's forearm. The teeth that had done it must have been jagged, maybe canine based on the way her skin had torn like tissue paper. The mark itself wasn't as bad, however, as the strange thornlike black growths that poked up around it. The veins around the injury were blackened, standing out against her pale skin. Fluid leaked from the bite wound, beginning to pool under Amber like ink.

Cold crept up Finch's spine and settled in the vertebrae. She whispered, "What did this to you?"

Amber only sobbed harder.

"Please, Amber," Selena pushed. "You can tell us."

Amber clutched the wound. The thorns pressed into her delicate fingertips, drawing beads of crimson to the surface.

"It was the stag," Amber wailed. "*Nerosi's* stag."

nineteen

Amber cried, a quiet, muffled sound, for the next hour as Selena used a pair of tweezers to remove the thorn growths from her skin, peeling them free like fresh scabs. When she was done, she did her best to wash the strange black fluid from the bite with wet paper towels that wound up crumpled in a pile on the coffee table. Finch hovered nearby, only leaving when Selena told her to grab something from the kitchen or first aid kit.

Kyra and Risa returned from the Homecoming performance right around when Selena had finally managed to wash the wound out. There was still a strange discoloration to the veins around it, but it wasn't nearly as dark as it had been when Amber arrived.

At the sight of the black-stained paper towels and the bowl full of thorn growths, Kyra let out a sharp curse. Risa froze, eyes wide, unable to formulate words. Finch quickly hushed them while Selena tenderly applied an antiseptic to the torn skin. It had started to bleed red now, which seemed like an improvement.

"What the hell did you do?" Kyra finally asked, breaking the silence as Selena removed a roll of gauze from the first aid kit to bandage the wound.

Amber wiped her eyes, almost out of tears now. She shook—from cold or fear Selena wasn't sure.

"A little delicacy would be nice," Selena warned, shooting Kyra a glare.

"I went to Nerosi just like any other night." Amber looked between the girls, lower lip quivering. "I wanted to ask her a favor."

"What kind of favor?" Risa pushed.

Amber's cheeks pinkened. "I...I wanted to be like you." Her eyes passed between the girls as she explained, sniffling, "All of you have something that makes you special. I...don't. I'm not pretty like you guys o-or talented or smart—I'm just...me."

"Amber," Finch said softly, reaching out to touch her hand. "That's not true. We all know that's not true."

"Speak for yourself, Chamberlin," Kyra snapped, crossing her arms. "You didn't answer Risa's question."

Amber flinched. "I asked for what you all have. To be smart and beautiful and talented. And Nerosi—" she paused to catch her breath, her voice tightening and rising, "—she asked for eyes. *Human* eyes. She said I could give her mine if I was in such a pinch, but I wasn't gonna give up my sight! So I said...no."

Silence fell over the room.

Selena's heart raced. Was it her fault that Nerosi had upped the price of her favors after last night? Did Amber know about her teeth? Selena hadn't told anyone, and she desperately didn't want to admit that she'd made a deal with a monster.

And Nerosi was most certainly a monster if she'd done something this horrible to her friend.

Selena thought back to Tunger Hall, where she'd seen Margo with her eyes torn out as she sat curled on her bed.

This was exactly what had happened before.

Kyra pointed to Amber's arm. "So you're saying *Nerosi* bit you? I find that hard to believe."

Amber shook her. "No, it wasn't her. When I told her I changed my mind, she got all…short with me. I panicked. She started saying she wouldn't be able to protect me if I didn't bring her what she wanted, and it felt like I could hear her in my head! So I ran.

"When I got out of the tunnels, the stag was waiting for me. It had these teeth like a wolf. It bit me and I thought it was…" She winced, holding back tears. "I thought it was going to kill me. I only got away because I threw dirt in its eyes and ran. But when I got back here…" she pointed to the end table with the pile of thorn growths, "Those started growing around the bite."

Amber doubled over, sobbing louder. The remaining girls all stared at each other, dread creeping in. Risa covered her mouth with her hand while Selena and Kyra gaped. Finch let out a tiny wisp of a breath.

Kyra's jaw clenched. Finally, she grumbled, "Well, crying's not going to help, is it? And like you said—it was the stag, not Nerosi. You can't blame her for this."

"Kyra," Selena snapped, narrowing her eyes in warning. "The

stag is Nerosi's emissary. It was obviously acting on her behalf. Plus, you heard what Amber said—Nerosi threatened her."

Kyra held up her hands. "It's Amber's fault for asking for such a massive request."

"You can't be serious," Finch said. When Kyra didn't immediately respond, she added, "Listen, I know this is going to sound strange, but recently I've been hearing this voice in my head. And right before Amber showed up here, I heard it again saying how angry it was that someone told it no. And I think…I think I might be hearing Nerosi."

"Do you hear yourself right now?" Kyra spat. "You're obviously full of shit."

Selena snarled, "Don't talk to her like that."

Finch, however, held out a hand to stop Selena before she and Kyra could go for each other's jugulars. "I know how it sounds, but you have to believe me. Nerosi and I have a…connection. I think maybe it's a little deeper than I realized at first."

"Oh, please." Kyra rolled her eyes. "You think you're so goddamn special, don't you?"

"Kyra, please," Risa said, shaking her head. "Think for a minute, won't you? We've known for a while that Nerosi might not have our best interests in mind, and this is very clear proof of that. What more do you want? A signed confession?" She narrowed her eyes and went to Amber's side, hand on her shoulder. "Even if what Finch is saying sounds a little…fantastical, I believe her. After all, Nerosi hurt Amber. And if you're not careful, she'll hurt you too."

"Nerosi is the only one who's ever given me any kind of power—the only one who's ever given a shit about me at this stupid school," Kyra said, voice cold as stone. "If you all can't handle that, fine. Cry and scream and whine about it. But I don't want to hear it just because you don't understand what a fair deal is."

Kyra stormed down the hall to her room, slamming the door behind her.

Over the next couple of days, Finch began to notice something strange.

It started with a group chat that Selena made the next day that included herself, Finch, Amber, and Risa. Then, the requests started coming in. Finch kept all of her social media cleverly hidden under privacy settings, but suddenly she got requests from Risa and Amber on nearly everything at once. On Sunday, she woke up to a link to a dress that Amber had sent her and said would look cute with her "aesthetic" (Finch wasn't sure what she meant by that—the dress in question looked like something out of a *Jane Eyre* adaptation) while Risa sent her images of a breakfast spread and captioned it Selena once again attempts to murder us by undercooking meat.

On Monday morning, Selena texted her and invited her to grab lunch with them. Finch was torn—she almost always ate with Sumera and her friends, and it felt weird to change her plans. But she still went, meeting them in the Waite Garden to eat under the magnolia trees.

Immediately, people around campus noticed. A few strangers in class asked Finch if she was friends with Selena's clique, and how she'd managed to get in with them. Other girls went for flattery, praising her hair or her clothes despite her putting nearly no effort into her appearance beyond brushing her hair.

Finch wasn't used to the feeling of being stared at and, frankly, she hated it.

Wednesday night, she curled up on the couch in her dorm room with Sumera, who was typing up a paper on her laptop.

Her roommate's eyebrows rose. "Haven't seen you in a bit."

It was true—Sumera had been gone with the rest of the volleyball team at an away game over the last weekend. After a few solid weeks of only hanging out in their dorm room together, it was a little strange to have the change of pace.

Finch shrugged. "Busy weekend. How did the game go?"

Sumera rolled her eyes. "Those girls from Portland were terrified of me—don't know whether it was the height or the hijab or both, but they couldn't take their eyes off me. I think it worked to our advantage though—I just kept being a decoy while our opposite hitters did fast attacks." She chuckled. "Didn't help that I had four inches on their middle blocker."

Finch's nose wrinkled. "Sorry you had to deal with that."

Sumera shrugged. "We absolutely trounced them, so that helped quite a bit. What about Homecoming? I know you were nervous about that."

Finch shivered at the thought. "The performance went well but afterward was…weird. I know Selena's happy to have it off her plate so she can focus on college applications. We've been hanging out with her friends a lot more the past few days."

Sumera scoffed. "I was wondering why everyone kept talking about *Selena's new friend*. You're a regular Ulalume celebrity."

"Oof. No thanks." Finch sipped her tea—it was lavender-flavored and apparently supposed to help with stress relief. So far, it wasn't doing much. "I don't understand why everyone acts like they're so cool. Like, I get that they're rich and pretty or whatever, but the way girls talk about them makes it seem like they're famous."

"Weird, right?" Sumera closed her laptop and tucked her dark hair behind her ears. "My best guess is it's the social connections. They always seem to be the first ones to hear about parties and things like that. But specifically, in Selena's case…as much as it pains me to admit, she's got a lot of natural charisma."

Finch nodded. She was more than aware of that fact.

Seeing how Finch had gone quiet, Sumera asked, "I don't mean to pry but…is there a reason you're hanging out with Selena and her friends? It's hard to imagine you'd have much in common with them."

It was a fair enough assessment—outside of Nerosi, Finch doubted she really had much in common with Amber or Risa. Maybe it was because they hadn't had much of a chance to talk one on one, but last night the two of them and Selena had used their new group chat to complain about the current season of *The Bachelorette* for nearly an hour despite the fact they were all, presumably, in the same house at the time.

"I didn't really see it coming either," Finch agreed. "It's…a little overwhelming. I'm definitely the odd one out."

"I understand. Once upon a time, Simon and I tried to hang out with them, and being around Kyra for more than ten minutes kind of made me want to tear my hair out." She chuckled. "Sorry, that's a bit petty. But you know what I mean."

Finch nodded feverishly. "I definitely do."

"Maybe you and I should get dinner sometime this week," Sumera offered. "In town. There's a lovely place called Octavia's that a lot of the other girls like to go to for special occasions—we could go on Friday. Consider it my treat."

"That would be really nice." Finch smiled. "I think I'll get lunch with you tomorrow too, if that's okay. If I have to hear one more conversation about how kale smoothies actually can taste good if you use enough fruit, I'm going to lose it."

"Woof, my apologies." Sumera went to open her laptop up again. "Kudos to you for having the patience to put up with any of that. You must really like Selena."

Sumera resumed working on her paper, which was good, because that meant she didn't get the chance to see Finch blush.

twenty

Risa

I decided to ask the school librarian if she knows anything about local folklore

I assume, if what you said about that band is true, it's possible Nerosi has been here for some time

I lied and said I'm writing a research paper about local folklore and she offered to walk me through some primary sources if you're all around this afternoon whoa hold on since when do we read books

Amber

yah I'm still recovering from
as I lay dying tbh :/

Risa

Right, of course, I'd nearly forgotten
you two are illiterate. Rude of me.

god risa have some class

Finch

What time should we meet you at the library?

Risa

Right after our last classes?

Finch

Sounds good to me!

seriously tho im too pretty to read

Risa

You'll live.

That afternoon, Selena went from her final class to the library, her high ponytail swinging behind her. She wore a uniform sweater

over her collared shirt, as the October cold had fully settled in on
Ulalume over the course of the last few days. The leaves on the trees
around campus were almost entirely orange and yellow, scattering
across the damp grass that Selena cut across to get to the library.

She found Finch, Risa, and Amber already seated at a table in
the library. There was a warm mustiness that hung in the air from
the scent of old pages and ink. Selena took a moment to appreciate
the high ceilings and the massive windows that lined the walls—
she'd never been much of a book person, but there was something
comforting about being surrounded by them. She took a seat next
to Finch, who offered her a smile.

Not long after, a woman with dyed black hair and thick eyeliner
approached the table—it was easy to hear her coming based on the
sound of her combat boots on the creaky old floors. She pushed a
wooden cart full of books up to their table and flashed a smile at
them.

"One of you must be Risa," she guessed.

Risa nodded. "That's me. Are you Helena?"

The librarian nodded. "I am. I brought all of the sources I
could find related to folklore in our local history collection. Fun
topic for a paper—what class is this for?"

"It's more of a capstone project," Risa lied smoothly. Selena
was a little impressed, but then again, Risa was extremely good at
keeping a straight face. She'd once watched her jokingly convince
some girls at a party that her family money came from being
the sole caretakers of a cat island in Tokyo Bay, and they'd fully
believed her.

"Well, great choice regardless." Helena unloaded books onto
the table. She explained, "I actually did similar research when I

was around your age, so I brought a couple copies of documents I used back then."

"Would you mind walking us through some of the basics?" Selena asked. She pointed to the books. "These are great and all, but it would be nice to get a summary beforehand. Since I'm sure the primary sources are all…old, dense and boring."

Helena got a decent chuckle out of that. "Sure. I've got a student worker at the desk so I have a few minutes." She pulled up a chair and sat down. "Plus, I grew up here, so local legends have always been extra interesting for me."

Helena picked up an old leather-bound book that appeared to be fraying at the edges and explained, "I'd point you toward this book first. It's a firsthand account from Edmund Turner, Rainwater's founder, of how he discovered the island and decided to build a town here.

"Before Turner, Rainwater was uninhabited. A number of people tried to form settlements here but were unsuccessful because of the island's lack of natural resources. Despite being right on the ocean, there was always a dearth of sea life to catch, and plants never grew well in the soil.

"Not to mention the spooky stories, which is where the folklore comes in. Some of the early colonists told stories about strange creatures roaming the peninsula, animals that were just a little twisted. Things like two-headed snakes, rabbits with extra feet—"

"An eight-eyed stag?" Selena guessed.

Helena blinked. "Well—yes. I take it you've heard of it?"

The girls all nodded, Amber rubbing her bandaged arm and dropping her eyes to the floor.

"Then you understand why the peninsula had a reputation for being haunted by malevolent spirits. However, around the turn of the century, a group of men in the Massachusetts gentry decided they wanted to start their own town. Because no one else seemed to want to even bother with Rainwater, they decided to give it a shot."

"Why would a bunch of rich people from Massachusetts want to move here?" Selena asked. She considered her words and added, "I mean, not that we don't do that currently, but at least there's plumbing now."

Helena smiled. "Well, because around the turn of the century, there was an occult revival. Which is to say, people suddenly got interested in the sort of spooky stuff that's fairly passé these days—things like séance and mediums and secret societies. Edmund Turner was an occultist who was interested in starting a new community here where they all could practice their beliefs without the judging eye of the rest of society."

"Like…a cult?" Finch guessed.

Helena nodded. "Kinda like a cult, yes. Not quite Jonestown, but in that neighborhood. Turner gathered four of his closest friends, their families, plus a number of laborers and headed up here."

"So they chose Rainwater because it seemed haunted?" Amber asked, looking a bit pale.

"In a sense. See, Turner had actually scoped the place out first, and wound up having a near-death experience while he was on the island. When he got back to Boston, he told his wife that a strange creature had saved him, and it promised to help him if he came back and built a settlement."

Selena felt cold. "What…kind of creature?"

Helena shrugged. "Not sure, exactly. When Turner wrote about her, he referred to her as the Horned Queen. She appeared as a young woman with black eyes and a pair of bloody antlers atop her head. Some thought she was a ghost, others assumed she might be a spirit tied to the island itself."

Finch and Selena exchanged a look. Horned Queen was the term Victor had used too.

Helena continued, "While it isn't recorded quite as well as the rest of Rainwater's history, it's been surmised that Turner and the other founding families all began to worship the Horned Queen. And strangely enough, it seemed to work. There were more fish in the sea and game to catch. Not to mention the soil suddenly grew anything they planted in it. I have to assume Turner and the others took it as proof of the Horned Queen's power."

She set the old book down, swapping it out for a couple of sheets of paper that appeared to be photocopied out of a journal. She set them out in front of the girls.

"These are entries from Turner's private notes. If you're wondering how things turned out, these paint a pretty clear picture. While the town remained successful for the better part of five years, as time went on, Turner and the other heads of the founding families began to become reclusive. Even with new people moving in all the time and the economy thriving, it's apparent that Turner was a tortured man."

Selena picked up one of the pages in front of her. "So these are pages from his diary or whatever?"

"Yep, basically. Go ahead and read the top paragraph of that page out loud. Turner wrote it about a year after Rainwater's founding. It's pretty striking."

Everyone turned to look at her. Selena squinted at the page, studying the looped handwriting for a moment before clearing her throat.

"'*Flora's begun to worry about me. She tells me I grow paler by the day without the touch of the sun, as if my color wasn't stolen from me years ago now. She doesn't understand that what I've become is more than simply a man. I've been elevated by the Horned Queen, made something closer to a demigod. Our connection has given me access to a fraction of her power. If it weren't for the noise it makes within my mind, I suspect I could bring the entire world to its knees.*'"

Selena glanced up. "That's some cult leader shit if I've ever seen it."

Helena nodded. "As you can guess, Turner began to develop quite a case of megalomania. Some of his later journal entries detail plans to disband the council of founders, making him the sole leader of Rainwater. One of the methods he puts forth is to sacrifice one of them to the Horned Queen, who he said had promised him she would destroy the other founders in exchange for human body parts. He seemed to dismiss that though, knowing the town would never follow him if they discovered he had murdered one of their own."

"So he didn't kill anyone?" Finch asked.

Helena bit her lip. "Well, unfortunately the reason we have his notes is because he wound up throwing himself in the sea, and his wife found them while looking through his things. In that passage he mentions that he hears *noise* in his head whenever he believed he was accessing his…demigod powers, for lack of a better word. Near the end, his wife Flora said that he'd threatened to kill the Horned Queened to be free of his connection to her, but he couldn't stop complaining about hearing that same noise. Based on the sources we have, it seems he ultimately lost control of his actions, leading to his suicide."

"What happened to the other founders?" Risa asked.

"Many died or went missing not long after Turner. Two were stricken by a terrible disease with strange symptoms that wound up killing them, and the two others sleepwalked into the woods one night."

The girls exchanged looks—the only one who appeared unbothered was Amber, but that was because she'd clearly gotten bored and started scrolling through Instagram. At the realization that everyone else had gone pale, she put her phone down, mouthing the words, *Wait, what happened?* to Risa who just shook her head.

"Are there any pictures of Edmund Turner you have access to?" Finch asked after a moment.

"Oh! Yes, of course." Helen grabbed another book off the cart, this one much more recently published. She opened to the center, where there were a number of turn-of-the-century photographs of a couple of white men, all with mildly comical facial hair. She pointed to the man in the center—even without the sharp color one would expect in a photograph nowadays, it was clear he had pale white skin and hair. Just like Victor DeLuca.

Just like Finch.

"Does that seem like a good place to start?" Helena asked, closing the book with the photographs and handing it to Risa.

"I have a few more sources you can check out on the cart, but I should be getting back to the desk."

"Of course," Risa said, nodding numbly. "Thank you for your help."

"Any time," Helena said.

Just as she turned to step away, Finch blurted out, "Um—excuse me? Can I ask you a weird question?"

The librarian turned. "Depends on the weird question."

Finch winced. "Sorry, um—you said you grew up in Rainwater. Were you in high school around 2004?"

She nodded. "I was. I graduated from Rainwater High in 2005."

"Did you ever hear about a band called Killing Howard?" Finch asked.

Helena's eyes widened as a little smile began to form out of the initial shock. "Yeah, I did. A couple of my friends—Xavier and Theo—played in it. I used to go to all their shows when they were just getting popular. I thought it was the coolest thing ever. How do you know about them?"

Finch's eyes flickered to Selena before she lied, "I…found one of their songs online?"

"Oh, nice. I had no idea their stuff was available online. Here I am clinging to their old CD like it's going to somehow earn me money someday—"

"You have one of their old CDs?" Finch asked.

Selena almost wanted to elbow her for being overeager, but Helena nodded. "I've actually got it cataloged under local history, so you can borrow it, if you like."

"That would be amazing!" Finch said, eyes lighting up. "Thank you so much."

"You're welcome. I'll go grab that for you." Her eyes fell on the other girls. "Best of luck on your project. Let me know if you need any help with citations or anything."

She headed down the stairs.

─────────

That night, while Risa retreated into her room to look over the notes she'd taken in the library, Selena tried to work on her statistics homework. The only thing she got done was writing out some dirty jokes on her graphing calculator before Amber shuffled into the kitchen. She looked gray in the face, her expression drained.

"Do you know where the first aid kit is?" Amber asked.

"Under the kitchen sink." Selena turned off her calculator and stood, coming to Amber's side as she bent down to get it. The other girl had one hand holding the edge of the counter, and immediately it became clear that the wound on her arm had bled through the gauze that had been wrapped around it.

"You okay?" Selena asked, pointing to the arm. "That...doesn't look so good."

Amber shook her head. "It's been four days now, and it's still not healing." She set the first aid kit down on the counter before unwrapping her arm to reveal the wound—tiny black thorns had begun to sprout around it again, and Selena was immediately hit with a sickly sweet, rancid scent.

"I think it might be infected," Selena said, doing her best to breathe through her mouth.

Tears welled in Amber's eyes. "What am I supposed to do? Go to the doctor? How do I explain this?"

Selena pursed her lips. "Maybe there's no choice if it's not healing, especially if it's making you sick."

Amber sniffled. "I just...I'm so frustrated, Selena. Kyra convinced me to talk to Nerosi with her last night to ask for forgiveness and she said she can only heal it if she gets a set of eyes. Otherwise...it's gonna get worse."

"Worse?" Selena's eyes widened. "As in?"

"I don't know." Amber dabbed at her eyes. "But I'm really scared."

Selena put her hands on the other girl's shoulders. "Hey, it's okay. We'll figure it out, all right? I'm not gonna let anything happen to any of us."

Amber's lip began to quiver before she threw her arms around Selena. A little stunned, Selena stood there for a moment before wrapping her arms around Amber, feeling as her shoulders shook with a sob.

"Thank you," Amber said into Selena's shoulder. "That means a lot."

Selena nodded, then pulled away and pointed to the first aid kit. "It's not much, but maybe I can help you clean it out and re-bandage it?"

Amber nodded, drying the last of her tears. "Please."

And as Selena got to work, she forced herself not to let it show on her face as she wondered how they were possibly going to get out of this.

twenty-one

That night, as Selena was clicking through Netflix looking for something to fall asleep to, there was a knock at her door.

She groaned. *"What?"*

The door let out a soft creak, then Kyra stepped inside. She had on pajama shorts and a tank top. Her short red hair was pulled back in a ponytail, a few stray hairs framing her face. With her makeup off, her round face seemed deceptively soft, and it was enough to disarm Selena for a moment. The frown evaporated from her face.

Selena glanced at the clock, then at Kyra. "You know it's a school night, right?"

Her eyes fell to the floor. "I know. I just want to talk."

She sounded wounded. Her eyes were wide, and her lips parted slightly—Selena hadn't seen this side of her in quite some time.

Selena shut her laptop and pushed it aside. She gestured to

the end of the bed. After a second's hesitation, Kyra took a seat, crossed her legs, and bit her lip.

Selena's expression hardened. "You haven't come up here in a while."

Kyra tucked a lock of loose hair behind her ear. "I know. I wanted to apologize. Things have been…rocky, recently."

"Rocky?" Selena's eyebrows shot up and she nearly laughed. "That's putting it lightly. You've been making deals with a demon."

"Me?" Kyra's face flared red. "Don't be a hypocrite. You made a deal with her too, St. Clair. She told me *all* about it."

Selena cast her gaze the other way, knotting a hand in her hair. The back of her throat burned. She's spent the last couple nights doing nothing but beating herself up about it.

"I didn't *want* to. I had to. And so far—well, nothing bad came of it—"

"So you admit it." Kyra pointed a finger at her. "You know Nerosi isn't as bad as you keep insisting."

"That's not what I said." Selena slid out from under her sheets and crawled across the bed so she could sit on her knees in front of Kyra. She reached out and put a hand on the other girl's knee. "Look, I'm worried about you, okay? Once upon a time, you were my best friend here. I don't want you to get hurt."

Kyra's face fell. "Friend? *Just* your friend?"

They were quiet for a moment. Selena's hand left Kyra's knee, her expression falling. She noticed the constellation of freckles on Kyra's crossed arms, remembering how she used to trace shapes between them with her fingers.

"Kyra, I'm sorry. I don't want to play this game with you anymore. You hurt me too much for us to be more than friends."

"You're *sorry?*" Kyra's eyebrows bent inward as she scowled. "Look, I know things sucked last year. But we moved past it! For God's sake, you're the one who agreed to sleep with me after I apologized! Forgive me for thinking maybe there was something between us."

Selena flinched, but kept her voice even. "I was lonely, Kyra. And hurt. I accepted your apology because I was afraid to lose you. I think that's probably why I kept hooking up with you too. I thought that if I could just be your friend on the surface, but be closer in private, then maybe I could keep you around without the vulnerability of being in a real relationship."

Kyra shook her head, her face turning red. "So you admit it? You used me?"

Selena flinched. "I should have said no to you a long time ago. Which is why we need to end this. We're not good for each other as partners... or friends."

Now it was Kyra's turn to flinch.

"Is this because of Chamberlin?" Kyra snapped.

After a moment's pause, Selena nodded. "Sort of. She makes me want to be a better person. And ending the toxic mess I have with you is part of that."

Kyra got up, arms crossed and face ablaze. "So you'll sleep with me for months in secret because you're too scared to be in a relationship but now a depressed girl with the charisma of a wet cracker appears and you're ready to U-Haul with her?"

"You don't know anything about Finch." Selena put her hands on her hips, leveling a glare at Kyra. "Unlike you, she actually gives a shit about how I feel. And I…care about her. More than I've cared about anyone."

"Don't hold your breath." Kyra shook her head, stalking to the door. "Fine, then. Have fun with this unrequited love shtick—because this is as good as it's ever gonna get. A girl like that will never love you back." She clenched her teeth and whispered, so quietly Selena nearly didn't hear it, "Not like I do."

Kyra closed the door behind her.

———————

As soon as her last class let out early on Thursday afternoon, Selena took a quick detour through the swirling fall leaves and went to the ivy-covered math and science building. She waited outside classroom 204 for the bell to ring, the floor creaking under her as she shifted her weight back and forth. When it finally did and students began to file out of the classroom, Selena waited until Finch exited, then reached out and touched her arm.

Finch jumped, letting out a yelp while Selena laughed. "Sorry, did I scare you?"

"Oh!" Finch put a hand over her heart. She had half of her white hair up in a topknot today and her uniform tie was a little askew where it'd been hastily tucked into her sweater. "Maybe a little. I'm okay."

Selena grinned. Even just seeing her here, like this, with her too-big school uniform and a pencil still stuck behind her ear made Selena's chest ache with warmth.

"I wanted to see if you'd want to come hang out at my place," Selena asked. The two of them headed down the halls, past the old portraits on the walls, photographs of the various classes of girls who had attended Ulalume before them. "We could listen to that Killing Howard CD for clues."

Finch smiled, eyes glittering. "I'd love to. As long as your roommates are okay with it, of course."

"Risa and Amber like you a lot," Selena said. There was a beat before Selena added, "And Kyra can choke. So. I'm gonna say yes."

"Sounds good," Finch chuckled.

The two of them walked side by side to Annalee Lighthouse, close enough that their hands brushed a couple of times. Every brush of Finch's pinkie against her felt like an electric shock up Selena's arm, her face growing redder and redder each time it happened. She was grateful for the chill in the air to explain away her pink cheeks.

When they made it to the lighthouse, Selena led Finch up to the top floor, where the light had once been before the building had been converted into a living space. Miles of gray sky stretched out in front of them, a fluffy blanket that they could see through every angle of the room because of the walls of windows. Not far off, the sea crashed into the jagged cliffs, and a few boats bobbed in the choppy water in the harbor.

"Wow," Finch marveled, stepping up to the window and gazing out at Rainwater. "You really do have an incredible view from up here."

"Not bad, right?" Selena had snagged her laptop on the way up and she popped the CD into her external CD/DVD drive. It took a couple moments for the drive to boot up and read the disc, but soon the songs appeared in Selena's library, and she clicked the first one.

Selena sat down on a cushion and then patted one beside her. "Pull up a seat."

Finch sat leaned back against the window. Selena found herself sneaking a look at Finch as she closed her eyes. She instantly lost focus on the music, instead mapping the gentle upward curve of Finch's nose, the way she wrinkled her brow gently when she focused.

For a moment, Selena was overwhelmed by the urge to kiss her.

"*I've seen the color of space,*" Killing Howard sang, "*And I'll sink my fingers into the ripples of an Arctic sky to tear open the void just to keep you safe.*"

"Ripples of an Arctic sky—do you think they mean the aurora borealis?" Finch asked.

"Honestly I thought it was a sex thing."

Finch sputtered a laugh and gently whacked Selena on the shoulder. "No! Have you been listening at all? This whole song is about wishing you could protect someone you love but you know is doomed. It's very sad."

Selena bit her lip. "Sorry. Got a little distracted."

"Are you okay? You're acting sort of weird."

"What? No, I'm grine—fine! And great!" Finch narrowed her eyes and Selena winced, squeezing her eyes shut. "Sorry. Ignore me."

Finch raised an eyebrow but didn't push further. Selena forced herself to focus on the music instead of Finch, as much as it pained her. But soon she started to pick up on what Finch had been saying about the meaning of the song. Whoever had written it seemed to feel like they had some control over what was endangering the person they loved, but ultimately they feared they couldn't save them.

"Can I ask you kind of a weird question?" Selena asked after the song ended. After Finch nodded, she added, "I know you've said you have sort of a…connection with Nerosi in the way that Victor DeLuca and Edmund Turner did. In that journal, Turner talked about having a fraction of Nerosi's power. Do you think it's possible Victor did? And maybe you do too?"

Finch wrinkled her brow as she considered it.

"Maybe," she finally said. "Any time I try to focus on our connection—like when I hear Nerosi's thoughts—I lose touch with reality a little. It's really scary, honestly."

"Like the noise that Turner talked about in that journal?" Selena guessed.

Finch nodded. "I can see how that would drive someone mad. It makes it feel like you're lost inside your own head, and you can't control your body."

Selena considered this, drumming her fingers on her knee. She asked, "Have you ever heard of spotting?"

Finch shook her head.

"It's a thing dancers do while spinning so we don't get dizzy. You pick something that isn't moving to stare at so you have a point of focus to steady you. Maybe you just need something like that."

"I'm not sure staring at a wall will help me not lose my mind," Finch laughed.

"Not like that." Selena hesitated for a moment before reaching out and taking Finch's hand in hers. "Something physical, like this. So you have an anchor to hold you."

Finch looked down at their clasped hands and Selena's heart skipped. She squeezed softly, shifting so she wove her fingers through Selena's.

"What exactly do you want me to try?"

"Well, you've heard Nerosi's thoughts a couple of times, right? Maybe if you try to focus on your connection with her, you could get another look into her head. We might be able to predict her next move."

"Seems worth a try," Finch breathed.

"If you start feeling like you're losing control, just squeeze," Selena said. "I'll throw some water at you or something."

"Can't argue with that," Finch muttered through a smile. She closed her eyes. "Okay. Here we go."

For a moment, nothing happened. Selena held her breath as Finch exhaled through her nose, eyelids quivering softly as she focused. But then, the air in the room seemed to cool a bit, raising goose bumps on Selena's arms. Finch furrowed her brows, her free hand rising to press over her heart as if she could grab ahold of it.

She squeezed Selena's hand.

Selena squeezed back. "You're okay."

Finch nodded softly, squeezing her eyes shut tighter. The last remnants of color in her skin vanished, and when she opened her eyes, Selena was shocked to find they'd turned entirely black. They shone brightly in the afternoon light like polished obsidian, the room around her reflected back in them.

She squeezed Selena's hand.

Selena squeezed back, too breathless to speak.

The next moment, Finch blinked and gasped, eyes returning to normal. Selena jumped to grab her, but Finch shook her head, softly rubbing her forehead as she said, "I-I'm okay."

"Did it work?" Selena asked.

Finch nodded. "Y-Yeah. I only heard a couple things, but—it

sounds like she's getting impatient. I'm not sure about what, but…
whatever it is, she's starting to think we might need another
warning."

Selena's eyes widened. "You mean like the stag attacking
Amber?"

"I'm not sure. Maybe." Finch rubbed her temples. "I'm afraid if
I push too much, Nerosi might notice. That and…"

Selena's eyebrows rose. "Is everything okay?"

"I think so." Finch gestured to the air in front of her. "I have
this sort of…visual sense whenever I'm around something supernatural. It's these colors in the air I used to think were migraine
auras. When I tapped into my connection to Nerosi, the air started
radiating them like I've never seen before."

"Does that seem bad?" Selena asked.

Finch shrugged. "I don't think so. I guess it's just a little
disconcerting."

Selena considered this. "Do you think you could do it again?
Hear any more of Nerosi's thoughts, I mean?"

Finch took a breath, then nodded. "Yeah. Let's go again."

For the next hour, the two of them sat at the top of the lighthouse while Finch attempted to gain access to Nerosi's mind. Any
time the connection became too much, Finch would open her eyes
and catch her breath. All the while, Selena gripped tightly to her
hand, squeezing when she seemed to be getting lost. Soon, they
were pressed up against each other, their hands resting between
them on their thighs, fingers woven together. Finch didn't seem
to be gleaning much information from Nerosi other than that she
was very, very hungry for…something.

"It might take some time," Finch wondered aloud as the black faded from her eyes once again. "Before Nerosi actually plans to make a move. But if I keep listening, I bet I'll catch it."

Selena nodded. "Exactly. Plus, I think our spotting technique works."

Finch cracked a little smile. "You're not sick of holding my hand?"

Selena hadn't even realized she was still holding it. No part of her wanted to let go—in fact, what she really wanted to do was to pull Finch closer and kiss her for hours and hours, to lay here on the floor of this room and stare out at the sea together and listen to music and hold her close enough to feel her heart racing in her chest. She wanted to weave their fingers together and walk into town to get coffee and split a pastry at the café. She wanted to listen while Finch played a melody on the piano with that look on her face like nothing could ever bring her down.

Kyra's words came back to her like a slap in the face: *A girl like that will never love you back.*

Selena fell silent, expression darkening.

Just then, Finch's skirt pocket buzzed.

"Sorry." Finch took out her phone, opening it up. "Let me put this on…"

Her words cut off, her eyes widening. Softly, she mouthed a curse.

"Is everything okay?" Selena asked.

"Damn it," Finch breathed. She stood up, rushing to pick up her things from the floor and shove them in her little lavender backpack. "I'm so sorry, I just realized I'm running super late to meet Sumera for dinner. This was great, though. Maybe we can try again soon?"

"Y-Yeah." Selena's face fell. "Sure. Um—"

"Okay great—see you later, Selena!"

A moment later, she was rushing down the stairs, vanishing out of sight.

twenty-two

Finch burst into her dorm room to find Sumera sitting on the couch, arms crossed, wearing a sunny yellow hijab that directly clashed with the storm brewing in her darkened eyes.

"I'm sorry!" Finch immediately said before the door was even closed behind her. She kicked off her shoes in the doorway, hurriedly saying, "I-I know we had a reservation in town but I can change really fast and maybe we can still—"

"I canceled it," Sumera said smoothly. "We were going to be too late anyway."

Finch's face fell and her shoulders sagged. "Oh. Sumera, I'm so sorry, I got so distracted hanging out with Selena, and I didn't notice what time it was until I got your text."

Sumera exhaled a breath through her nose, closing her eyes. "Selena. Of course."

Finch swallowed thickly. "I promise I'll make it up to you. I'll buy both of our dinners next time."

Sumera pursed her lips but nodded. "Finch, it's fine. I know you didn't mean to. People forget things. And I know that this is a personal grudge, and it shouldn't feel this way, but I hate knowing it was because of Selena."

"But—why?"

Sumera frowned, rubbing the back of her neck. "It's just that…she and I have history, and it wasn't good. I never told you because I hate dredging up the past, but seeing you hang out with her made me so mad. Maybe a little jealous too."

Finch shook her head. "I don't understand."

Sumera bit her lip. "Maybe we can start by ordering dinner. Because this might take a minute."

Two orders of tom kha kai and Thai tea later, Sumera and Finch both changed into pajamas while Sumera finally explained her grudge.

"Selena used to be my best friend," Sumera started, crossing her long legs under her on the couch. "We met at orientation our first year. I thought she was funny, and I really liked hanging out with her and Simon after she introduced me to him. We played video games together, explored the peninsula on weekends, and got dinner at Octavia's all the time. We were pretty much inseparable.

"But then Selena met Kyra and Amber. Back then, Kyra was at the top of the social pecking order, and she took a shine to Selena immediately. Selena started hanging out with them more and I…got jealous, honestly. I still hung out with Simon, and Selena occasionally would still join us, but it wasn't the same. Come sophomore year, she stopped responding to invitations completely.

"The few times we did get together after that were…tense. Selena knew I was mad at her for ditching us, but she refused to apologize. Simon was willing to put up with it, but I wasn't.

"Plus, the more she hung out with them, the meaner she got. She stopped caring about the same stuff we used to, and she had this obsession with being cool and putting on this front. She started dressing differently, acting differently—it was like her whole personality changed for them. I resented her for it."

"But she's still friends with Simon," Finch pointed out, taking a sip of her Thai tea. "Why didn't he do anything?"

"He tried." Sumera shrugged, worrying at a loose string on her pajama pants. "But Selena didn't care. So he shut up about it and let her change so he could still be her friend, in secret, since he wasn't cool enough in Selena's eyes to tell her other friends about him. I didn't. She refused to realize her friendship with those girls was toxic, so I refused to hang around and watch her lose herself."

Finch let her words sink in. It all made sense—why Selena was so afraid to talk about her actual interests, why she seemed so different around Simon.

"I'm so sorry things ended like that," Finch finally said, meeting Sumera's gaze. "I…I don't want that to happen to us. Aside from Selena, you're my best friend here, Sumera."

"Aw. Finch." She put a hand over her heart. "That's sweet."

"I mean it." Finch set her mug down on the table. "Can I…tell you something else?"

"Oh." Sumera blinked. "Sure. What's up?"

Finch took a breath and, before she could lose her nerve, said, "I wanted you to know I'm a lesbian."

Sumera's eyebrows shot up. "Reall—you are?"

Finch giggled nervously. "Yep. Really."

"Did you know that when you got here?" Sumera asked. "Or is this new?"

Finch paled. "Are you mad I didn't tell you?"

"Of course not. I'm happy for you—that seems like a big deal to realize." Sumera stood up from the couch and held out her arms. "I apologize for everything. Can we hug?"

Finch met her in an embrace. "I'm sorry too. Friends?"

"Friends." Sumera pulled back and asked, "I must ask—are you hanging out with Selena because you fancy her?"

Without thinking, Finch blurted out, "I mean, it's not just that."

Sumera withheld a laugh while Finch clapped a hand over her mouth.

"Oh, darling." Sumera patted her cheek. "You're so pink. This explains a lot. I saw you walking with her earlier and you were staring up at her like she paints the stars in the sky every night."

"Please don't tell her," Finch begged, covering her face with her hands and shaking her head. "She can't know. She's so wildly out of my league, it's almost embarrassing."

Sumera scoffed. "I'm not so sure—she looked about as enraptured by you as you were by her. And trust me, I once listened to her talk about the worldbuilding of *Mass Effect* for two straight hours—she's not nearly as cool as you think she is."

Finch blinked. "You think…Selena could like me back?"

"Absolutely. In fact…" Sumera shook her head. "Okay, I might regret this, but Griffin Sergold is throwing a party for Halloween that Simon and I were planning on going to together. If the two of you wanted to grab food with us beforehand, you're welcome to."

"That would be amazing!" Finch threw her arms around Sumera again and into her shirt said, "You're the best, Sumera."

Sumera hugged her back.

———————

Selena got the text from Finch about going to Griffin's Halloween party with Simon and Sumera as her biology class started Friday morning. She was so distracted that she almost didn't hear the teacher rambling on about their new unit on anatomy, and the dissections they were going to do, including a worm, a starfish, a sheep heart—

"And," Mr. Fitzpatrick said, "Next Monday, we'll be taking apart a human eye, graciously donated to us by the local university. They know our standards are very high at Ulalume, and after hearing how many of you are intent on medical school, I'm happy to say each of my classes will have access to one."

Selena and Amber both perked up at the same time. Amber's hand flew up.

"Where are you going to store them?" she asked, tilting her head to the side. "Like, in the fridge?"

A few girls around them giggled, but Mr. Fitzpatrick quickly hushed them. "No, no—Amber, that's a good question. A representative from the college will be dropping them off in a special cooler for organ transport. The same kind they use for transplants."

"Cool," Amber said, lowering her hand.

Once the class resumed, Amber leaned over to Selena. "We have to get that cooler."

Selena nodded. "I'll text the girls."

twenty-three

Halloween arrived with a cold snap.

With the promise of potentially getting eyes to give Nerosi in exchange for healing Amber, Selena's head was far away from the situation at hand as she strolled toward Octavia's to meet Finch, Simon, and Sumera.

Downtown Rainwater was home to a variety of kitschy shops—diners, boutiques, and pawnshops were the most plentiful, but Selena also passed a few specific tourist traps that offered kayak rentals and whale-watching tours. A New Age shop boasting tarot readings and crystal healing made Selena roll her eyes as she passed.

Soon, Selena found herself in front of Octavia's, a 1950s-style bar and diner that overlooked the sea. There were vintage cars parked outside, freshly polished so their candy-colored exteriors caught the light even as the sun set into the sea. A massive blue

cursive sign out front had the restaurant's name, paired with a
neon depiction of a waitress holding a tray with a lobster on it.

Selena readjusted her costume—a purple dress and green
ascot—before pushing through the front doors.

Inside, the walls were decorated with old lobster fishing gear
and ship décor as well as newspaper clippings from Rainwater's
history. Most of the tables were full, and Selena eventually found
Simon, Sumera, and Finch seated at a booth in the back with a
small vase of flowers between them, the window to their right
showing the sea slamming against the cliffs.

"I'm just saying that Saitama's entire power is a satire, so
there's no point in comparing his strength to characters from other
non-satirical shōnen protagonists. The whole point of the series—"
Simon looked up, noticing Selena's arrival and said, "Oh, hey! You
made it! Great costume. Daphne from *Scooby-Doo*, right?"

Selena glanced down at her dress, straightened her red wig,
and said, "Yep. What exactly are you? The Phantom of the Opera?"

Simon was dressed in a full suit with a black and red cape
flowing from his shoulders, along with a top hat and a white mask.
"I'm Tuxedo Mask."

"I made him do it." Sumera leaned forward from her spot on the
other side of Simon, and immediately Selena understood what she
meant. She'd clearly spent a good amount of time making a hijabi
version of a Sailor Moon costume, with a long blue pleated skirt and
a fake black cat on her shoulder. "Did you two also plan this?"

That's when Selena looked up and realized Finch had on
a brown wig and thick square glasses. As the realization set in
on Selena, she had to laugh, because despite not coordinating it,
Finch had elected to go as Velma.

"Great minds, I guess." Selena slid into the booth beside Finch, putting her arms on the tabletop. "Been a while, Mer."

Sumera pursed her lips. "I guess it has."

A thick silence settled over the table. Selena could practically feel Finch tense beside her. After a moment, Selena realized that it was because Simon was desperately trying not to look at her, and it occurred to her that Simon never actually got an explanation for why Finch ran out on him a few weeks ago.

A waitress appeared. "Ready to order?"

Grateful for the chance to turn their attention elsewhere, they all ordered but as soon as she was gone, the silence was back, Sumera glaring at Selena while Simon and Finch did everything they could not to look at each other.

Selena's mind wandered to her first year at Ulalume when being here with Sumera would have been the highlight of her day. She, Simon, and Sumera used to all sit at this very booth for hours on end doing homework and shooting paper straw wrappers at each other from across the table and talking about whatever was on their minds. It felt so simple then.

"I'm sorry," Selena said without fully meaning to.

"What was that?" Sumera asked.

"I'm sorry." Selena took a breath to steady herself and restarted. "I was a really terrible friend to you." She looked at Simon. "To both of you. Honestly, I've been a bad friend to pretty much everyone I know up until recently. And I know the reason things are this way is because I prioritized social status over the two of you, which I never should have done. I apologize."

"This is a surprise," Sumera said, not with any amount of malice.

Selena shrugged. "Yeah, well. I'm trying to be a...better person. So there it is. You don't have to accept it, but I thought I'd offer an olive branch, at least."

"It's certainly a start," Sumera said, offering the tiniest hint of a smile.

"I'm also sorry." Everyone turned to Finch as she nervously gripped her skirt. "I'm sorry I never explained why I acted so strangely at your party, Simon. That was my first kiss and I wanted it to feel a certain way and it...didn't. I wasn't attracted to you at all."

"This doesn't really feel like an apology," Simon pointed out.

"It's an explanation. I ran away because I realized I didn't like kissing you. N-not because you're a bad kisser or anything it's just that I'm sort of, like, one hundred percent gay."

A beat of silence passed over them as the wires in Simon's brain tied together their loose ends.

"Oh." Simon's eyes widened and pointed to Selena and added, "Oh! That's why you wouldn't tell me back in Tunger! That makes so much sense." Back to Finch, he added, "Honestly, that does make me feel better. Apology accepted."

Finch smiled. "Thanks, Simon."

Not long after, their food arrived, and with the air at least somewhat cleared, it was much easier to keep the conversation going. Sumera talked about how the volleyball team was headed to the state championship and Simon said he'd almost finished up applying to all of the colleges he was interested in. Selena threatened to find an apartment for the two of them in Boston once they both got into their respective dream schools—Simon had been talking about going to Emerson for media arts since forever—and Sumera and Finch invited themselves to come stay if it happened.

And for a moment, surrounded by friends, Selena felt just a little bit better.

When the four of them arrived at Griffin's party an hour later, the house was already vibrating from the sound of the music inside.

The house, a two-floor gray home not far from downtown, was coated in toilet paper. Finch's heart raced as Simon broke away from their group to say hi to some Rainwater High guys drinking beer out front. She debated turning around and heading back to Ulalume, but Sumera put a hand on her shoulder.

"Listen," Sumera said. "If we get in there and it's totally awful, we can go watch *The Craft* back in Pergman as soon as the costume contest is over."

"You'll be fine," Selena added. "Nothing to be afraid of."

Finch bit her lip. It was almost as if Selena forgot how sideways the last party had gone for her. "Right. Just a party. Nothing to worry about."

They headed inside while Finch did her best not to hyperventilate.

Inside was packed with students from Rainwater High, though Finch recognized a few Ulalume girls' faces. Finch pressed herself to Selena only to realize shortly after that she'd missed Sumera excusing herself to grab apple cider, leaving the two of them alone.

"Come on," Selena said at her side, nudging her toward the hall. "This way."

The air was thick with sweat and peaty smoke, the lights casting a golden hue that hung around everyone's heads like halos. Music echoed in Finch's skull, making her wince.

The living room was a bit more sparsely occupied, as everyone in here appeared to be playing spin the bottle.

A golden-haired boy wearing an oversized Red Sox jersey and a dark beard painted on with eyeliner popped up and cried, "Selena!"

After a moment, Finch recognized Griffin Sergold. He swept Selena up in a hug as she laughed, a huge smile on her face.

She hugged him back. "How are you, Griffo?"

Involuntarily, Finch's hands tightened.

"Better now that you're here." His eyes fell on Finch. "Oh, hey. New girl from Ulalume. You wanna play?"

Finch's face flushed. "I, um—"

"Come on," Selena said, smiling. "It'll be fun."

Finch's stomach flipped as Selena took her hand and led her over to the circle. A few of them greeted Selena as she sat down, and one guy passed her a can of beer that she quickly cracked open and chugged without hesitation. Someone offered one to Finch, but she shook her head, her memory of the last time she drank still fresh.

"All right," Griffin said, grabbing the bottle of Jack Daniel's at the center of the circle and passing it to another boy. "Whoever it lands on gets seven minutes in heaven with whoever spun. Penalty for refusal is removing a piece of clothing."

Finch blanched.

For a few rounds, Finch sat in stock-still horror as the bottle landed on various people who either disappeared into adjacent rooms to make out or removed socks, wigs, or—in the case of one enthusiastic drunk boy—pants. Selena sat beside her cracking up every time it happened, seemingly unaware of the fact that Finch was desperately trying to become invisible.

A girl Finch vaguely recognized from Ulalume who was wearing a bald cap—Finch wasn't sure, but it seemed like she was dressed as Eleven from *Stranger Things*—got the bottle next and spun. It slowed, pointing at Finch.

Just as her pulse began to thrum, though, the bottle edged to the side, pointing to Selena.

Selena snorted. "Up to you, Flo."

The other girl turned red. Her eyes flickered to Finch, and immediately she flinched. While she hadn't exactly meant to, Finch realized she'd been shooting the other girl the most poisonous glare she could manage.

The girl shrugged off her blue jacket, and a few people booed her.

"What?" she countered. "I'm straight!"

"Straight-up coward's more like it," Selena laughed. She crawled forward and grabbed the bottle, then spun it.

The next few moments went in slow motion. The bottle spun, a few guys pretending to nudge it toward themselves while some of the girls giggled and leaned toward or away from it. Finch heard her heartbeat in her ears.

It slowed in front of her. She inhaled sharply.

But when it finally came to a stop, it wasn't on her.

Instead, it pointed directly at Griffin.

While Finch's heart tumbled into her stomach, a loud chorus of *oooh*s erupted from the group. Selena shot a sideways smile at Griffin, who stood, helping her up as well. He quickly slung an arm around her shoulders and asked, "My room?"

She rolled her eyes but smiled and nodded. "Sure."

And just like that, she was gone.

While someone else snatched the bottle and spun it, Finch stood, her whole body feeling numb. She stepped out of the circle, unnoticed, and wandered into the hall. Selena and Griffin had disappeared, and she didn't recognize anyone.

The back of her throat burned. The hazy smoke in the air made her eyes sting, and she felt sick to her stomach. Over and over, her mind replayed the image of Griffin pulling Selena into his arms, the big smile on her face. The two of them looked like exactly the kind of couple you'd see in a teen sitcom as a quarter-back and a cheerleader walking the halls hand in hand. The two of them made a whole lot more sense together than Finch and Selena ever would.

Not that Selena was interested in that, judging by how happy she'd looked to be swept up in his arms.

Finch finally found Sumera and Simon pouring themselves glasses of apple cider, Simon spiking his with Fireball.

Sumera said, "Hey! I was wondering where—"

"I'm gonna go home," Finch said, voice uneven. "I don't feel great."

Sumera's eyebrows shot up. "Oh. Okay. Do you want me to come with you?"

"No." Finch sniffled, wiping away a tear. "I'd rather be alone, but thank you."

Sumera and Simon both awkwardly said goodbye as she turned and headed for the door, keeping her head down.

She only fully started to cry when she was already out the front door and heading into the woods.

———

Griffin shut the door behind him while Selena went to sit down on his bed. It was comforting in a way—she'd slept over here a couple times when she was a sophomore and she and Griffin still got together often. They'd never actually had sex, but they had fallen asleep together, talking late into the night about their goals for the future when they finally got out of Rainwater.

"I haven't seen you much recently," Griffin started. "I've been meaning to text you. That guy from Simon's party still giving you trouble?"

Finch's image flashed in Selena's mind. "That's all water under the bridge now. Sweet of you to remember, though."

"'Course I remembered." Griffin smiled, then took a step closer to her. "So, you still got feelings for that guy?"

Selena bit her lip, then nodded. "I…yeah, I do. And she's a girl, actually."

"Oh, no way! That's great, Selena." He came and sat down next to her on the bed. "I guess that means you don't actually want to make out?"

Selena let out a peal of laughter. "Nope. I just didn't want to have to take my dress off since that's pretty much all I've got on. You won't tell anyone I cheated?"

Griffin dragged his pinched forefinger and thumb over his lips and pantomimed throwing away the key.

"You're a real one." Selena wrapped her arms around him and added, "I guess we've got six more minutes, huh? You wanna tell me how your college search is going?"

A big smile broke across Griffin's face, and for the next few minutes, he described, in detail, the personal essay that he wrote about not making it onto the lacrosse team his freshman year of high school and how the experience made him a better person. As soon as the seven minutes were up, they agreed to talk again soon, and Selena headed out into the hall.

A couple of people patted Griffin on the back as he came out of the room, mostly ignoring Selena as she scanned the party looking for Finch's brown wig. When she couldn't find her, she kept searching until she found Simon and Sumera chatting with a couple of people near the drinks table. Simon was taking a hit off a joint while Sumera waved the smoke away politely.

"Have you seen Finch?" Selena shouted over the music.

"She said she was sick," Simon said. He offered Selena the joint, which she held up a hand to refuse, mostly because of the absolutely venomous look Sumera shot at her.

"She looked like she was about to cry," Sumera said, raising her eyebrows. "You wouldn't happen to know why, would you?"

Selena's eyes widened. "Wait, really? We were playing spin the bottle and I only left for a minute, did someone say something to her?"

"You were playing spin—?" Sumera's eyes widened. "Are you serious? You don't understand *why* Finch might be sad if you were playing spin the bottle and left to kiss someone else?"

Selena blinked. "I mean, I didn't actually kiss him."

"Did she know that?"

Selena opened her mouth to say something but closed it immediately after, realization dawning on her. Of course Finch wouldn't know that. But it wasn't like she'd care about Selena kissing Griffin unless—

Oh.

Oh.

"I have to go," she said, already turning to run for the door.

Whatever Sumera's reaction was, Selena didn't see it. She was already outside, the wind whipping at her hair and nearly blowing off her ascot. She wove through a crowd of boys in coats doing a keg stand and ran toward Rainwater Road, heart racing in her chest.

Selena cursed to herself, jogging down the road. In the dark, she was barely able to see anything with the clouds covering the moon and the lack of streetlamps. Fog had rolled in, and it was hard to see much more than a few feet ahead of her. She was totally alone.

Until, ever so softly, she heard the sound of crying.

It was coming from the woods. Quickly, Selena turned, following the sound of it and picking her way over fallen trees and roots in the undergrowth. The deeper she went, the thicker the fog became. Goose bumps raised on her arms.

Nearby, a twig snapped.

A chill went up Selena's spine. "Finch?"

No one responded.

Selena wrapped her arms around herself, taking a hesitant step forward. This part of the road was close enough to the sea that she heard the crashing waves against the cliffside. The wind whistled through the trees, stirring up leaves.

The crying grew nearer, louder.

"Finch?" Selena called again. She cupped her hands around her mouth. "*Finch!*"

Softly, she heard, "Selena?"

She rushed forward just to be spit out of the fog and into a meadow of decaying flowers, bent at the stem and browning from the cold. It overlooked the ocean, and the chill of the sea air bit through Selena's dress and sank into her bones.

Finch, sitting up against a tree, wiped tears from her eyes.

"What are you doing here?" she asked.

"I came to find you. Sumera told me you ran off." Selena knelt down in front of her. "Is this because of Griffin? Because I—I didn't actually kiss him. We just talked."

Finch wouldn't look at her. "It doesn't matter."

"Yes, it does." Selena touched Finch's knee. "What's going on?"

Finch stared up at the blanket of clouds covering the sky, the moonlight barely piercing through. "It feels so...trivial to even bring up at a time like this. Who cares how I feel when..."

She looked to the side and trailed off as something seemed to catch her eye in the meadow. She wiped away her tears, gently cursing under her breath.

Selena asked, "What is it?"

Finch rose to her feet, tensing. "There's—something here. I can feel it."

"What kind of something?" Selena asked, the hair on the back of her neck standing to attention.

Finch turned fully toward the cliffs, her lips parted. "An Echo."

The next moment, a flickering image came into view in the foggy center of the meadow. He appeared almost translucent, as if he were made of fog himself.

"Victor," Finch breathed.

Victor rubbed his eyes in disbelief, shaking his head at the sight of her. He had dark circles under his eyes, and his hair appeared unwashed and greasy. As he stepped toward them, he did so with a slight limp, wincing as he put weight on the weak foot.

"You," he said, pointing at Finch. "You're the ghost."

She pointed to herself and asked, "You can see me?"

He nodded, stepping closer. Finch moved to draw back, but Victor was already reaching for her, eyes wide and hand shaking. Just as the hand was about to touch Finch's arm, it went straight through it.

Finch jumped back, shivering.

"Is Nerosi doing this?" Selena asked.

"I don't think so," Finch said. She studied Victor for a moment before asking, "Victor, what year is it?"

"2004," he answered without hesitation.

Selena started to mutter, "How…"

"Simon was saying that there are stories of the Echoes being almost…sentient. Like Rainwater reflects memories back and forth that are relevant to different people. So I think, maybe, Victor is seeing us in his time, and we're seeing him in ours. Kind of like…living ghosts."

"I've been seeing you ever since I died and came back," Victor said, almost accusatory. "Walking around Rainwater, on the Ulalume campus—you've been everywhere. Why would I see you? What do you have to do with me?"

"We're both connected to Nerosi," Finch said, hand unconsciously rubbing the spot over her heart. "And we need to figure out a way to get rid of her. She hurt one of our friends, and she keeps getting sicker. It's only a matter of time until she hurts us too."

Victor's breath hitched at the sound of her name. "She fooled you too?"

Selena felt a chill that had nothing to do with the temperature.

Victor nodded to himself. "My band has been giving Nerosi things for a couple of months. At first, it just seemed like weird but harmless requests, but now—" he winced "—everyone is dead. Everyone except me. And I don't think I'll last much longer."

"*Dead?*" Selene repeated. "What happened?"

Victor bit his lip, rubbing the side of his head. "Nerosi got in our heads, trying to force us to give her the body parts she wanted. She gave us nightmares so we couldn't sleep for days a-and made it seem like she was there in front of us even when we were alone. My girlfriend, Margo... It got so bad she thought the only way to make Nerosi go away was to take out her own eyes."

The image of Margo crying on her bed in Tunger came back to Selena, with the blood dripping down her cheeks from the empty sockets. She shivered.

"Margo bled out in the tunnels after she gave Nerosi her eyes," Victor explained, his voice wavering as tears filled his eyes. "I think Nerosi used her powers to get rid of the body. Then the stag got Theo and Xavier—there was nothing left of them to find. A few days ago, Sloan walked into the sea to make Nerosi leave her alone. And now Nerosi and I are in each other's heads all the time. Sometimes I don't know which thoughts are mine and which are hers. She won't let me go until I give her a heart."

"You can't give it to her," Finch breathed.

Victor nodded. "I know. If I'm right, what she has planned is far beyond the scope of killing teenagers. And if I give her that heart, she'll be able to do it."

"What do you think she's going to do?" Selena asked.

Victor, who had already been shivering slightly, began to shake.

His teeth chattered, and his arms wrapped around himself. "Right now, she can't leave that room in the tunnels. But she's using the body parts to build herself a physical form. Once she has a heart, she can go wherever she wants. And she's...hungry."

Selena's throat went dry. "For what?"

"Everything," Victor breathed. "She'll consume it all. The town, the island—whatever she can reach."

Selena nearly laughed at the absurdity of his statement. She'd never been this far out of her depth in her life, and it felt like a terrible cosmic joke that couldn't be true. "How the hell are we supposed to stop her from doing that?"

Victor was silent. He took a shaking breath while Finch bit her lip.

Finally, Victor said, "There was...one plan I came up with, once. When the connection between me and Nerosi is active, it forms these weird ripples. From what I understand, the ripples are places where the fabric of reality is thinned or warped. I think if I were able to focus enough, I could create a rift like the one I pulled Nerosi through in the first place and then...it's just a matter of forcing her inside."

"Have you ever made a rift before?" Selena asked.

Victor shook his head. "I've tried. But I start to lose touch, and I don't know if I'd be able to stay in control. Not when she's already got me spread so thin. Not when she's this powerful."

"If she has the power to consume an entire town..." Finch said, pupils blown and face white. "What exactly is she?"

The image of Victor began to flicker, and Selena cursed under her breath. He said something, but his voice sounded too far away, incomprehensible.

"Victor!" Finch cried, reaching for him. "Wait! What is she? You have to tell me!"

Victor's face went even whiter, his lips parted and quivering. His eyes darted from one girl to the other, and when his voice finally broke free of his throat, it was choked, like something else was trying to claw the words back in.

"Nerosi," Victor said, "is a god."

A moment later, he was gone.

twenty-four

"How the fuck are we supposed to get rid of a god?"

Back at Ulalume, Finch and Selena sat on the couch in Finch's suite. Finch's wig and glasses sat on the coffee table with Selena's green ascot. Finch had let Selena borrow some sweatpants for her goose bump–covered legs, but they were comically short on her.

They'd spent the rest of the walk back from the meadow in silence until they made it back to Finch's room, when Selena had started cursing a blue streak and Finch numbly made tea, watching the bubbles in the glass electric kettle while her mind raced. She had to focus on something mundane, normal—something that made it feel like she was still living in the real world and not a nightmare.

Finch sipped her tea. It was peppermint—the kind her mother used to make her when she was anxious as a child. "I guess this isn't the kind of thing we can find at the library, is it?"

"Not unless *The Complete Idiot's Guide to Killing Gods* came out recently," Selena muttered. She rubbed her face, careful to avoid smudging her makeup. "How do you feel about warping reality so bad you tear a hole in it and then shove a god through?"

Finch bit the inside of her cheek, remembering how it felt to tap into Nerosi's mind back in the lighthouse. While she'd been able to retain focus the last time with Selena's help, if she'd been alone, trying those things would have been impossible. The way the power tugged at her mind, threatening to break her—it was too much.

"I...I might be able to create a rift if I really focused." She shivered. "It's the *shoving her in* part I'm more worried about."

"I guess we should take it one step at a time." Selena was so distracted, she failed to notice the hallway door opening even as Finch tried to shush her. "First we focus on how to tap into your abilities enough to open a rift. Then we look for a way to push her through. But hey, once that's over with, we'll have avenged Killing Howard, ended this bizarre pact with Nerosi, and put this whole cult thing behind us, right? Easy enough."

A voice behind her said, "You're gonna *what?*"

Simon stood in the doorway, staring at her wide-eyed.

Finch cursed.

"What the hell are you doing here?" Selena asked.

Simon held up a key. "Sumera gave me her key so I could come in while she stopped to grab a few snacks from the vending machine? We were going to see if you two wanted to watch a movie, but clearly you have *much* bigger priorities."

The girls exchange a look. Neither dared say anything.

Simon managed to find his voice. "To clarify, maybe I was hallucinating just now, but did you say you're in a *cult*?"

"A cult? No," Finch lied, forcing a lopsided smile. "We're not—no. Definitely not."

Selena covered her face with her hands.

"Oh my god." Simon shook his head. "That's why you both came to me asking about Killing Howard and the stag. That's what the whole investigation was the whole time and you didn't even tell me you were in a cult!"

"I wouldn't call it a cult, exactly," Selena offered. When Simon's eyes widened, Selena quickly defended, "On a scale of one to ten, ten being the most cult-y and one being the least, it's maybe a six at best. It's not like we meet in a basement wearing robes to chant demands to our ancient god."

"Selena," Finch hissed.

"A six is still pretty cult-y," Simon said, his voice raising an octave. "Are you—you're not doing human sacrifices, are you?"

"No!" Selena argued. "Of course not."

But based on the way Finch's expression wavered and she bit back a frown, Simon's eyes looked like they were about to bug out of his head.

"We're *trying* not to do human sacrifices," Selena amended.

Simon blinked. "And here I was thinking you guys were hooking up, but I guess you were a little busy premeditating some murder for that. Unless of course you have a great explanation that I'm missing."

Finch's cheeks burned from the first part of Simon's statement while her stomach flopped at the second—how could they possibly explain this to him? It barely made sense to Finch, and she was living it, unlike Simon who had only seen the situation as a mystery to solve. Plus it felt, somehow, like it could put him at the risk of being collateral damage.

"How good are you at keeping secrets?" Finch asked, voice barely above a whisper.

Simon's eyebrows shot up.

Selena held out her hand, fingers closed in a fist except for the smallest one. "Simon, you have to pinkie swear you won't tell."

Simon stepped forward and swore without hesitation. "I *really* hope you aren't actually planning to kill anyone."

"Kill anyone?" Sumera appeared in the doorway behind him with an armful of snack food. "Did I miss something?"

"Nope!" Finch blurted out. She laughed sheepishly, rubbing the back of her neck. "We were telling Simon the plot of a…game. That we were playing."

"Yeah," Selena quickly agreed. She met Simon's eyes. "Remind me and I'll tell you the rest later. I can sum it up while I walk you to Rainwater Road."

Simon shot her a long look. Finally, though, he nodded and said. "Right. Looking forward to it."

———

Simon questioned Selena for a solid three hours, first on the walk to Rainwater Road and then more over FaceTime right after he got home. When she finally thought he was done, she got a notification not long after saying Simon had shared a document of additional questions with her to be filled out at her leisure.

But overall, he'd taken it well. Which was saying something, all things considered.

When Selena finally curled up in bed, she fell asleep for almost twelve hours. She spent Sunday trying to focus on finishing her assignments, but she couldn't stop thinking about how Victor had looked and sounded in the meadow. If her and Finch's plan didn't work, was that going to happen to them? Would Nerosi target them by tearing their minds apart from the inside, or send her stag to kill them?

Just how much time did they have before it was too late?

Selena was still thinking about it when she woke up Monday morning and made coffee. She opened the refrigerator door to grab creamer.

Instead, she found a Tupperware full of eyeballs.

The mug in her hand tumbled to the floor and shattered. Coffee flooded the tile.

Selena screamed.

"Jesus—cool it, St. Clair."

Selena spun. Kyra rose from the couch—she hadn't seen or heard the girl when she came downstairs. She wore one of her shorter uniform skirts, and the top three buttons of her blouse were undone. A black headband held back her short red waves.

Selena pointed into the fridge. "Are those—?"

Kyra nodded. "Got them this morning. A college boy came to drop them off nice and early—Mr. Fitzpatrick told me exactly when and where. I just asked nicely." She shrugged. "Easy."

The hot coffee soaked into Selena's sock, but she didn't move.

Kyra's self-satisfied smile seemed eerily sharp. "Something wrong, St. Clair?"

Kyra approached her, and her gait seemed…wrong. Too fast, too exact, like a prowling animal. Selena pressed herself to the counter, aware of how far she was from the knife block.

"Kyra?"

Both of them turned.

Amber stood in the hallway, her skin looking gray-tinged and dark circles shadowing her eyes. Her cheeks, too, were gaunt— she'd begun to lose weight the last few days, leaving her body looking bony and small beneath her uniform. The gauze around her arm was stained black from the strange fluid that kept leaking from the wound.

"Morning. I got your eyes." Kyra gestured to the refrigerator grandly. "Congrats. You may deposit them to Nerosi at your earliest convenience."

"*Wait.*" Even Selena was caught off guard by the desperation in her voice. She slid out from where Kyra had cornered her and went to Amber's side. "There's something both of you need to know first."

She went on, "Finch and I found out last night that Nerosi isn't some helpless spirit down there. The more we give to her, the more powerful she gets. And we've already given her too much."

Selena quickly explained what she and Finch had gathered over the last few days, about finding the Echo of Victor and him telling them about Nerosi's goal to create a physical body and escape the tunnels. How once they gave her the eyes, her new form would be nearly complete.

"You honestly trust some ghost you found in the woods?" Kyra rolled her eyes. "I knew you were gullible, but this is a new low."

"I'm not the one in this situation who's gullible," Selena shot back.

"Don't talk down to me," Kyra said darkly.

Selena took a breath through her nose. "Listen, I just want you to be aware of what we're dealing with. I can't stop you from talking to her, but beyond helping Amber…we have to stay away from her as much as we can while we figure out how to stop this."

There was a long pause before Kyra said, "Believe what you want, Selena. I don't care anymore. And also?" She shot a look at Amber. "You're welcome."

She headed for the door.

twenty-five

As Finch walked from music class to history the next morning, she got a text from Selena. Apparently, the eye sacrifice was over, and Amber's wound was finally beginning to heal. Finch darkened her screen and let out a breath, pausing in the hallway to stare up at the ceiling as that weight lifted off her shoulders.

She didn't have much more of a chance to celebrate, however, because she felt a tap on her shoulder the next moment.

Kyra loomed behind her.

"Do you have a minute?" she asked, nodding toward the girls' bathroom.

"I-I'm going to be late to class," Finch started to stammer.

Kyra's eyes narrowed. "Are you sure about that? Because I have a message from Nerosi that I suggest you listen to."

Finch's throat felt like it was about to close up, her breath short. Looking over her shoulder briefly, she bit the inside of her cheek before following Kyra into the bathroom.

The bell rang a few moments after the door swung closed behind them. With class starting, the stalls were all empty. Kyra pulled herself up onto one of the sinks, crossing her ankles primly while her polished Mary Janes glinted in the light. She leaned back on her hands, a sideways smile on her face.

"You look nervous," Kyra said, cocking her head to the side. "Are you scared, Chamberlin?"

Finch held her ground. "Not of you."

"Just everything else?" Kyra chuckled. "You're like one of those little toy dogs people put in their purses that can't stop shaking. No wonder Selena likes you."

Finch scowled. "What do you want from me, Kyra?"

"Well, since you've stopped coming to visit Nerosi yourself, she sent me to chat with you." Kyra leaned forward, putting her elbows on her thighs. "Now that she's gotten sacrifices from me, Risa, Selena, and Amber, you're the only one left. And she wants to offer you quite a deal."

Finch drew back. "Wait—she got a sacrifice from *Selena*?"

Kyra's thick, well-shaped eyebrows rose. "Did she not tell you that? Classic Selena. She loves to talk a big game and flake when it's most important. Maybe you haven't known her long enough to see that."

Finch opened her mouth to interrupt, but Kyra cut in, "She got hurt right before your little performance. She was so scared it would end her career she asked Nerosi to fix her up. She was spitting blood for a few days—but I guess that's expected when you let a god rip out your teeth, huh?"

Finch was stunned silent, and Kyra laughed like she'd told a joke, slapping her knee.

"I'm sure that'll give you something to chat with her about. But that doesn't have anything to do with the matter at hand." Kyra crossed her arms. "Nerosi and I have been talking about you a lot recently. How you summoned her and have that little connection to her. Without you, she wouldn't be here. But then again, without her, neither would you."

Finch took in a shaking breath. "What did she tell you?"

Kyra looked down to examine her nails, nonchalant. "That you drowned back in May. I must say, you look pretty good for a girl who's been dead for almost six months."

Ice began to creep up Finch's spine, and the color drained from her face. Her heart started to race. Nerosi had kept her alive. Saved her. Not out of the kindness of her heart, obviously, but Finch wouldn't be standing there if she were dead. It wasn't possible.

She whispered, "That's not true."

"Denial. That's cute." Kyra let out a sigh like she was talking to a petulant child. "You were underwater for half an hour, Chamberlin. It's a miracle the fish hadn't started eating you yet before Nerosi resurrected you."

Every part of Finch's mind grasped for an excuse to prove to Kyra she was wrong. But there was nothing—Finch's only memory before she clawed her way to the surface was inhaling water and everything going dark. How the agony of it had finally stopped.

She wasn't supposed to have crawled out of that river. If fate had had its way, she'd still be down there.

Or six feet underground.

"She also told me that you parents weren't so lucky." Kyra's eyes flickered up from her nails to meet Finch's gaze, hand curling back around so her palm faced inward. "It's terrible they had to die so soon. They would have been really proud of you."

Finch hadn't realized she'd started crying until she noticed the tears dripping from her chin. She wiped them away with her shirt sleeve, shaking her head.

"On that note," Kyra hopped off the sink, looming over Finch. "Nerosi wants to offer you a deal."

Finch sniffled. "What could she possibly give me?"

"Well—that's just it. She wants to give you your parents back."

Finch inhaled sharply. The inescapable emptiness that had lived in her chest since that day in May began to twinge. She placed a hand over her aching heart.

At the sight of her reaction, Kyra smiled and continued, "Now that she's nearly at her full strength, she can do things you couldn't even imagine. And she feels terrible about not being able to save them the first time, but now..." Kyra shrugged. "All she needs from you is a heart. In fact, she'd even take yours. That's a pretty good deal, right? Two lives for one? Maybe then you wouldn't be so haunted by the fact you're walking around holding hands with Selena while their waterlogged corpses are rotting in the ground."

Finch's shoulders began to shake. Kyra grinned down at her. Maybe it was just the light, but there was a sharpness to her teeth that Finch had never noticed before and a sallowness to her cheeks. Underneath the makeup, for a moment, Finch thought she could make out the sharp edges of her skull protruding from the skin.

Finch's teeth ground together. "And what's she offering you for this, huh? Are you acting like her little minion so you finally have an excuse to be the high school mean girl you always wanted to be? Or is there something in it for you?"

For a fraction of a second, Kyra's smile faltered.

Finch planted her feet firmly in the ground.

"I don't know what you mean," Kyra said, shaking her head. "I'm the most popular girl at Ulalume, my grades are perfect, everyone loves me—"

"That's not true though, is it?" Finch wiped away the last of her tears. "Some people may be bending over backward to suck up to you, but that's not what you want. You're like me, when it comes down to it. You feel like you're an outsider, you're everyone's second choice, and no matter how much Nerosi inflates your ego, she can't give you what you actually want, because even she can't force someone to genuinely care about you, can she?"

With each word, Kyra's smile faded, and the fire in her eyes flickered out. The color in her face drained, and she leaned back, shrinking back into herself. For the first time, Finch realized they were the same height.

But just as soon, Kyra's mouth bent into a scowl.

"Fine," she snapped. "Your loss. Your parents will stay dead, but that doesn't matter, because you'll be right behind them. You know why? Because Nerosi was going to give you and the others one last chance to make amends, but clearly, that's not gonna happen."

"I'd rather be dead than whatever you are to her," Finch told her.

"You're a little bitch," Kyra spat.

Finch smiled, revealing the dimples in her cheeks and crinkling the sides of her eyes.

"I learned from the best."

With that, she turned, throwing open the bathroom door and leaving Kyra gaping behind her.

Selena's eyes widened. "*You* told off *Kyra?*"

Finch nodded. "Yep. And then I walked down the hall to a different bathroom and had a panic attack."

Selena didn't know whether to laugh or make a pitying sound, so instead she did both.

The two of them had met under a lamppost by the edge of campus after Finch texted Selena what had happened with Kyra earlier. Kyra's threat—whether or not it had been empty—that Nerosi was gaining more power by the day only meant that shortened their timeline to get Finch's powers to a place where they had any chance of confronting the god.

The sun hung low in the sky, lighting the foamy sea with pink and blue hues. It had been the first sunny day that week, a brief whisper of warmth before New England winter closed another finger of its icy fist. Selena had watched Finch reenact the confrontation with Kyra all with her upper half drowning in a too-big denim jacket, looking much too adorable to have made anyone lash out at her.

"Is it weird I'm a little proud of you?" Selena asked.

"For having a panic attack?"

"For standing up to Kyra." Selena patted her on the back. "You've come a long way. Now, let's get going—I want to get to the training ground before it gets dark."

Finch's eyebrows shot up. "You said it was an...abandoned pool house?"

"Yep. This way, no risk of anyone walking in and questioning us about cults for three hours straight." Selena gestured to the road. "Shall we?"

The girls made it to the pool house as the last of the light began to fade. It was behind Rainwater High, the outside overgrown with vines, but the windows still intact. Signs warned people not to enter, but based on the graffiti that covered the inside and outside of the building, that hadn't stopped anyone. Finch slowed to tilt her head up at the greenhouse-like upper windows, coated in dead vines.

Selena tossed Finch a flashlight from her tote bag. "You're gonna want this."

"This place is inviting," she whispered, her voice stuck between dread and sarcasm. "Are you sure it's safe to—?"

But Selena was already headed toward the entrance—a lower window with a broken lock that she'd used many times before. She pressed her palms into the glass and shoved it inward, wincing at the rusty squeak it released. She swung her leg around the sill and looked over her shoulder at Finch.

"Come on," she said. "We're not going to open any rifts in reality by standing around."

She dropped inside, landing on the dusty floor. It was just as she remembered it—a huge greenhouse-like open space with the empty pool in the center. The inside of the pool was covered in graffiti, while the floor was littered with candles melted at the bottom so they stood upright on their own. Old blankets covered what had once been lounge chairs while plastic milk crates full of more candles, a few abandoned love notes, and empty bottles sat beside them.

Selena pulled a lighter from her backpack and lit some of the larger candles, hoping to illuminate the space more. Behind her, Finch yelped as she fell through the window, barely landing on her feet.

"What *is* this place?" Finch called out while Selena kept lighting candles. "Are people…living here?"

"'Course not. It's…kind of a hookup spot." Selena straightened up to examine the space now that there were enough lit candles to see around the room. "And nobody comes here on weekdays."

"You seem to know this place pretty well," Finch commented, shooting her a look, one eyebrow raised.

"I don't know—I think there's a sort of…dismal allure to it."

"It smells like old socks in here."

"Homey, right?" Selena gestured to a bed of pillows and a blanket resting in a pane of moonlight—she knew it was clean, mostly because she'd been the one who put them there for her and Kyra more recently than she'd like to admit. "Come on—let's get started."

As Finch reached inward to connect with the gripping sensation that had encircled her heart since she died, she did her best to envision the world in front of her as a curtain she could tear into.

Blood roared in her eardrums. Her vision darkened at the edges, a haze beginning to cover the scene in front of her. Her pulse sped up, and she felt that grip, like fingers digging into her heart, shudder.

The connection between her mind and body snapped. Each sense winked out, leaving her in the dark, lost.

The cold set in a moment later. Tendrils wrapped around her ankles and began to pull her down deeper.

Suddenly, she was back in the river. The headlights of her parents' car blazed as it hit the riverbed, her parents' blank, lightless eyes staring out through the windshield. They looked straight at her, hair floating like halos around their heads, skin alabaster as bubbles of air slid from their slackened mouths up their faces.

Finch screamed, voice turning to bubbles as she reached for them, kicking frantically.

She was so desperate to get to them that she nearly missed the squeeze against her hand.

Instantly, she regained a pinprick of vision, and the pool house came back into view through a narrow lens. Finch had just enough feeling in her hand to squeeze back.

She opened her eyes wider, vision flooding back all at once. The ripples in the air in front of her grew in size, pink and undulating. She used her free hand to reach out and touch one.

You want to be a god, little Finch? a voice whispered, so quiet it may not have been there at all. *Like me?*

The skin along Finch's arms twitched. She furrowed her brows, trying to grip the curtain of reality in front of her.

Until a cut suddenly opened up on the back of her hand, and an eyeball popped out from inside.

She felt it roll into focus and blink back at her.

Finch shrieked.

All at once, cuts began to slash open along her arms, like someone was dragging a hundred knives across her skin at once. Trickles of blood leaked from them as more eyes burst free from the wounds, rolling and blinking of their own accord. Finch felt one tear open on her cheek and she screamed. Another pushed free from the side of her neck, weeping blood.

"Stop!" Selena cried. "Finch, come back!"

At the sound of Selena's voice, Finch let go of the conduit between her and Nerosi, cutting off the flow of power all at once.

The eyes all twitched before vanishing into nothing.

Finch let go of Selena's hand, gasping for air. Her fingers scraped at her scalp as she dug them into her hair. Her chest felt ready to burst. Tears dripped from her chin, though she hadn't noticed when she'd started crying.

"You're okay," Selena insisted, moving to crouch in front of Finch. She put her hands on her shoulders and said, "Look at me, okay? I'm right here. Just breathe. It's not real."

Finch took a few more ragged breaths, squeezing her eyes shut for a moment before nodding. She slumped forward, and Selena caught her, holding her against her chest while Finch caught her breath, shaking her head.

"I pushed too hard," Finch whispered. "I-I let her in too much."

"But you stayed in control," Selena said, rubbing a hand gently against her back. "She's trying to scare you, all right? You were in control right until the end."

Finch pulled back, nodding and wiping away the wetness on her cheek. "That was awful."

"I've got you," Selena promised. "I'm not gonna let you go."

Finch nodded, sitting back and taking a breath.

"Okay," she whispered. She sniffled, but steeled her gaze. "Let's go again."

For another hour, Finch pushed the limit of her connection

with Nerosi, desperately trying to envision a rift tearing in the air in front of her. Only once did she begin to lose focus, and Selena was quick to snap her back, calling her name and drawing her back to reality.

Finch had been about to say they should call it a night when she noticed something hovering behind Selena's head.

It was shifting and shining in the air, barely the size of her hand. Finch leaned sideways until she could see all of it, the hues of pink and green rippling like a tiny fragment of aurora. It was small—barely a paper cut in the fabric of reality—but it was there, the darkness of the void barely visible behind it.

Finch inhaled. "Selena, I did it."

Selena blinked, then glanced over her shoulder. She nodded softly and looked back at Finch and said, "Listen, I can't see it, but I believe you."

"Seriously! It's there—I did it!"

Just as quick as she said it, the hole began to stitch itself up, but that didn't stop the feeling of euphoria that washed over her. She grinned, heart swelling as she punched at the air, throwing her arms up.

"I can't believe it worked!" Finch threw her arms around Selena, pulling her into a tight hug. Selena let out a tiny, gasping laugh while Finch loosened her grip so she could look Selena in the face as she said, "I think…maybe we have a chance."

At that moment, Finch became acutely aware of how small the distance between them was. Her heart raced. Her eyes flickered to Selena's lips and she blushed.

Something new ached in her chest. Not pain, like back in the bathroom with Kyra. This wasn't the clawing emptiness she was used to—no, it was an overwhelming desire to eliminate the gaps between her and Selena, to let the pieces of them fit together until it was the only thing Finch could feel.

She'd spent weeks now shoving down thoughts like that, telling herself it didn't matter how she felt—not when everything else was so dire. But now, she realized, she had no idea how much time she had left before this Nerosi nightmare hit its boiling point.

So why hold back?

Finch swallowed, every nerve in her body crackling with electricity. "Hey, Selena?"

"Hmm?"

"There's something you should know." Finch tried to swallow, but it felt like her throat was closing up. "Um. I've wanted to tell you for a while now, and I promise I won't be mad if you don't feel the same way but I…I really like you. As in, I have the most horrifically massive crush on you."

She winced. *Oh god.*

But then, Selena sputtered a laugh.

Finch's eyes went very round.

"I know," Selena said, pushing her hair back out of her face. "You're not exactly subtle, Finch. I was a little slow on the uptake, sure, but after Griffin's party… Well, there wasn't exactly a straight explanation for that one."

Finch turned vibrantly pink. "And you didn't say anything?"

Selena gestured around. "I dunno, I thought maybe bringing you to the most infamous hookup spot in Rainwater and lighting a thousand candles might get the message across."

"What message?" Finch asked.

"Jesus H. Christ." Selena said, leaning close to her. The world behind her fell away, leaving nothing but her eyes, bright and shining in the candlelight. "Come here. A little closer."

Finch leaned in, her eyes wide like twin moons in the dark. "Selena—"

Selena cut her off with a kiss.

Finch froze as a firework went off in her chest. The feeling sizzled from her heart out into her veins. Her pulse raced in a way it hadn't since she died, and for the first time since May, it was as if she were fully alive once again.

She let the tension release as she caught Selena's lip between hers and kissed back.

Selena reached for her, pulling Finch into her lap. Finch wrapped her legs around her while Selena ran a hand up Finch's neck, skin soft to the touch. If any doubt remained as to whether or not she was imagining what was between them, it was gone now, burned and vanished like flash paper. Selena's fingers wove through Finch's hair, scraping up more sparks as they moved. When she tightened her grip, Finch let out a soft hum against her lips.

Selena pulled away enough to press her forehead to Finch's, exhaling. Her eyelashes trembled against her still-closed eyes, and she nudged her nose against Finch's, a languid half-smile taking over her face.

"Does that clear things up for you?" Selena whispered, half-laughing. "No judgment, of course. If you're still confused, I can maybe make a PowerPoint breaking it down. Or Google Slides— whatever you prefer."

Finch shook her head, biting back a laugh. "Shut up and kiss me."

And she did, leaning forward until Finch lowered herself onto the bed of pillows. Selena pressed a line of kisses up her neck, the skin white with a blue tinge like skim milk. Her lips pressed warmth into her skin like tiny, shining stars.

And for a moment, they both let themselves bask in the glow.

The temperature dropped inside the pool house, but under their musty collection of blankets, Finch and Selena didn't notice. Selena nestled her face against Finch's throat, closing her eyes and breathing softly against her skin. In the past, whenever she'd been close to someone like Griffin or Kyra, there had always been a sense of haste, like she needed to get up and leave before they realized she'd been too vulnerable. But now, half asleep, she felt like she could stay forever listening to the sound of Finch's heartbeat.

She paused, waiting to hear it. After a long moment, it gave out a single thump before going quiet again.

Selena's face tightened. She reached out and took Finch's wrist, pressing two fingers into the network of blue veins beneath her skin.

Finch blinked her eyes open, furrowing her brows.

"I can barely feel your pulse," Selena whispered. "How is your heartbeat this...quiet?"

Finch paused for a moment, biting her lip. Her pale eyes shifted to look at her wrist, a tiny frown twitching into place. She exhaled, wincing.

Selena's eyes widened. "You're scaring me. What's wrong with you? You're not dying, are you? Finch, I can't deal with some *Fault in Our Stars* shit right now—"

"Not dying." Finch pursed her lips, the low candlelight casting flickering shadows across her face. "Dead. Died. Past tense."

"Excuse me?"

Her eyes were shining. "You know how Victor's mom told us that he died and woke up?"

"Oh, yeah." Selena paused. "That seemed a little—"

"I think that happened to me too."

Selena closed her mouth.

Finch said, "Back in May, after I visited Ulalume and met you for the first time. On the drive home, the eight-eyed stag appeared on the road while my dad was driving over a bridge. He swerved to avoid it and we crashed through the barrier into the river. The car sank and..." Finch released a shaking breath. "We drowned. We all drowned."

Silence grew between the two of them. Selena just looked at her, unable to find words large enough to confront a tragedy that huge. It was hard to find something to say about an unspeakable thing.

Selena took Finch in her arms and held her as tears dripped from her cheeks. They stayed like that for a long time, holding each other as candles began to extinguish, burned to the end of their wicks. They winked out like stars fading in the morning sky.

Finch curled her legs up to her chest, digging her fingers into her calves. "Nerosi sent the stag—I know it. She needed someone she could lure to summon her, so she killed me." She took a shaking breath in. "If I'd been alone—if I'd driven by myself like Victor—my parents would still be here."

"Finch." Selena wrapped herself around the other girl, as if she could shield her from her own thoughts. "You can't blame yourself. It was all her."

"I-I know. It's just—I always want to blame myself." Finch squeezed her eyes shut. "I was worried if I told you about the accident, I'd scare you away."

Selena pressed her fingers into Finch's cool skin and kissed her hair. "Thank you for telling me."

"Are you mad?"

"Of course not." Selena tilted Finch's face to her own with a gentle finger, staring into her pale gray eyes. She leaned forward and kissed her forehead, her thumb stroking her jaw. "Listen I...I've kept a couple of things secret too. So I get it."

Finch wiped away a tear. "What do you mean?"

Selena bit the inside of her cheek. "I made an exchange with Nerosi. Before our performance. I was so desperate because I got hurt and—"

"It's okay," Finch said. "You don't have to explain yourself to me. I get it—really, I do."

Selena began to say, "Are you su—?"

But just then, Finch's face went entirely blank. Selena said her name, and she didn't respond, instead staring at her like she wasn't even there. There was no light behind her eyes. Selena shot up, grabbing Finch's arms and digging her fingernails in.

"Finch?" she asked. She shook her. "Finch!"

A second later, Finch took a sputtering breath. She sat up and steadied herself against the ground, gasping for air. Selena hovered in front of her, hands held out but unsure of where to go.

"What just happened?" Selena demanded.

Finch went entirely white. "I saw something. I was in Nerosi's thoughts."

Selena's eyes widened. "What was it?"

"She asked Kyra to get her a heart," Finch said, wincing as she pressed her knuckles against her forehead. "And she agreed."

"She wouldn't," Selena breathed.

Finch shook her head, meeting her eyes.

"She would. And she's going to do it tonight."

twenty-six

"Risa says that Kyra left the lighthouse about ten minutes ago on foot," Selena explained as she and Finch jogged across the empty Rainwater High campus, the grass of the football field frosty beneath their feet. "So it looks like she's headed off campus. Did you get any indication from Nerosi where she could be going?"

Finch shook her head. "She told Nerosi she was going somewhere with... I think the phrase was *easy prey*? Where are people most vulnerable?"

"Um, a hospital?" Selena guessed. "Retirement home? Kyra wouldn't just rip out a random old or sick person's heart."

"So who would she kill? Is there anyone she doesn't like?"

"Aside from you?" Selena asked. Seeing the way Finch frowned at her, she corrected, "Sorry, too honest. I mean—she generally isn't a fan of most boys. Especially boys our age."

"You know a place with a whole lot of boys?"

"You know what's wild, the annual Rainwater Boy Festival is tonight." When Finch shot her a sharp look, Selena waved a hand. "Bad time for jokes, sorry. No, not really—"

She stopped. Finch skidded to a halt beside. Selena pulled out her phone and stared at the screen for a moment, blanching.

"Well, that answers that question—Amber says Kyra told her she's going to a party on Gibbs Beach." Selena cursed. "Shit, that's on the far end of the peninsula. And it's definitely gonna be full of stupid drunk boys."

"Is there a way we can cut her off?" Finch asked.

"Not unless we had a car," Selena muttered.

The two of them exchanged a look before, at the same time, they said, "Simon."

"I'll tell Risa and Amber to meet us at his place," Selena said, picking up the pace again as her fingers frantically flew across her screen. "If they leave now, we'll get there at the same time, and we can cut Kyra off before she gets to the party."

"Are you sure this is okay?" Finch asked. "I don't want to put him in danger."

Selena pressed her lips into a line. "It's gonna have to be. Come on."

The girls sprinted down the path toward Rainwater Road.

Fifteen minutes later, Simon's mom's Jeep flew off the road and directly onto Gibbs Beach. Finch had tried briefly to tap into her connection to Nerosi to see if she could catch any more of the god's thoughts, but when she tried, Selena caught sight of her eyes briefly flashing black before she had to stop and gasp for air—she didn't seem to be making a connection. At the same time, Risa, Amber, and Selena had kept an eye out for Kyra, but she hadn't shown up anywhere along the road or in the adjacent woods. Selena's stomach had twisted as she realized that could only mean one thing: Kyra had beat them to the beach.

The tires soared over the dunes as Risa and Amber yelped and held tight to the emergency handles above their heads. In the front seat, Selena narrowed her eyes as she scanned the beach for a head of red hair.

"We'll have to split up," Selena shouted over the thumping bass of Simon's go-to driving playlist, looking back at Finch and the others over her shoulder. "There's way too many people here for us to do this from the Jeep."

Simon hit the gas so they soared off another sand dune. "Noted!"

He slowed as the biggest crowd of people they'd seen came into view in the headlights. Even though the temperature had dropped substantially, that hadn't stopped most of Rainwater's teen population from showing up at this party. People in coats and hats floated around a bonfire, drinking out of Solo cups. Up against the rock spire, Finch caught sight of Griffin Sergold making out with a girl.

Finch pointed it out to Selena, who said, "Aw, that's nice. Glad to see he still hasn't figured out how to subtly finger someone in public."

Finch squeaked, "Subtly *wha*—"

"Simon, you should stay in the Jeep so we can get out of here quickly if need be, and you'll have some protection if Kyra finds you," Risa cut in. "Everyone else, text as soon as you see anything."

Simon cut the engine. "Great. Staying in the Jeep—very exciting. Makes me feel super useful."

"Do you want to get your heart ripped out?" Risa asked him.

Simon blinked. "Um. No?"

"Wonderful." Risa popped open her door. "Let's go."

The four girls hopped out of the Jeep—Selena whispering a quick *Sorry, buddy* to Simon as she did—and started across the wet sand in opposite directions. Selena's hair ruffled in the breeze, heavy and thick with the salt scent of the sea. She looked over her shoulder at the burning glow of the bonfire and the groups of Rainwater High kids dancing around it, cheering and laughing and whooping. Behind them, the shadow of the sea foamed at the mouth, hissing over the sand as it crept closer to their bouncing feet.

No red hair. No Kyra.

Selena cursed.

She began to jog around the perimeter of the beach, eyes darting left and right as she silently begged for Kyra to appear. As she went, she stopped a few people she knew from both Rainwater High and Ulalume to ask if they'd seen her, but it seemed no one had. She kept desperately checking her phone, hoping to see any sort of update from any of the girls, but there was nothing.

Finally, in a last-ditch effort, she stopped about twenty feet from the outskirts of the party and dialed Kyra's number.

Much to her surprise, after three rings, she picked up.

"Hello?" Kyra asked.

"Holy shit," Selena breathed, raking a hand back through her hair. "Kyra, where are you? And what are you doing?"

Kyra chuckled, and the sound of her laugh sent a pang through Selena's chest—she could still remember all the times she'd laughed like that last summer as they explored New York together, taking the Q to Coney Island and splitting ice cream on the beach. It was so familiar, but something about it sounded slightly…off.

"Turn around, St. Clair."

Selena spun, sea wind whipping her hair around her face. She pulled it back to find Kyra staring her down from across the beach, barely lit by the glow of a dying, lonely fire with no one else around it. Her red hair and coat stood out like a smear of blood against the cliffs. Another figure, golden-haired, had his back to her and was wandering toward the cliffs, where the opening of a small sea cave was visible.

"I don't exactly get what you see in Griffin," Kyra's voice crackled from the phone. "He kisses like a golden retriever. Maybe I'm doing all us girls a favor by taking care of him. He always seemed like a dick."

Any warmth evaporated from Selena's skin.

"Kyra, no, please—" Selena begged, taking one step, then another, then sprinting toward them. "No! Don't touch him! Don't you dare—"

The call dropped.

She watched Kyra drop the phone into her pocket before following him toward the sea cave.

"Griffin!" Selena screamed, voice instantly torn away by the wind. She scrambled over rocks, boots slipping and sliding over the slick moss on the surfaces. She struggled to stay steady as the sand sucked at her feet, threatening to swallow her whole. "*Griffin!*"

Something slammed into her side.

She hit the ground hard, rocks instantly cutting into her exposed skin and shooting pain through her ribs and hip. A shadow brought a hard, blunt edge down beside her head. She shrieked and rolled out the way before it could crack against her skull.

She scrambled to her feet as it charged again. In that half second, the flash of eight eyes glinted in the moonlight.

Selena dove out of the way, barely avoiding being gored on the stag's jagged antlers. Its nostrils flared, hot breath escaping in a puff of frost. A low growl rumbled in its throat as its lips pulled away from its teeth, revealing black gums and yellow, lupine teeth that were broken and sharp. Its hoof scraped the ground and it bowed its head to charge once again.

Selena's hand gripped a handful of earth and she launched it at the stag, a flurry of rocks and sand raining down on it. Disoriented, it let out a grunt, flailing its neck. Seeing an opening, she launched herself at the creature.

She got a hand on one antler as it swung to try and snap at her. Spittle flew from its jaws. Its teeth snapped down on open air, just missing her arm. With her full strength, still enhanced from Nerosi's gift, Selena clenched the antler prong and threw the stag down.

The tip of the antler broke off in her hand as the stag skidded across the sand with a yowl. In a flash, it was back on its feet. The muscles of its shoulders clenched and twitched beneath its thick hide as it locked eyes with her. It reared back, ready to charge.

Selena threw her arms out, unable to defend herself.

Just as the stag pushed off from the ground, however, a flash of blue hurdled into its side. The impact sent the stag flying, cutting off its howl. Its body hit the rocks with a sickening crack. A pair of headlights illuminated its body twitching as dark blood began to pool beneath it. One of the bones in its legs stuck out, pearly white, at a jagged angle while its chest quivered, ribs shattered.

Selena gasped as Simon met her eyes from the front seat of the Jeep.

A moment later, the stag stopped moving.

Simon threw open the door and hopped out. "Did I get it?"

"Holy fuck," Selena breathed. "Yeah, Simon, *you got it.*"

His eyes fell on the creature and he winced. "Is that the eight-eyed stag?"

Selena nodded. "*Was* the eight-eyed stag, yeah. Thanks for that."

"Five years straight of hunting for cryptids," Simon breathed, "and when I finally find one, I have to kill it."

"Shit," Selena breathed. She shoved the piece of antler she'd broken off into her jacket pocket, then pointed to the sea cave, "Come on—Kyra went that way with Griffin. We don't have much time."

The two of them hopped into the Jeep, Simon throwing it into reverse before hitting the gas. The tires bounced wildly over this rocky section of beach, and Selena had to brace herself against the door. Simon gritted his teeth, slamming his foot down harder on the pedal.

They skidded to a halt in front of the sea cave and Selena stumbled out, screaming Griffin's name. She pulled out the flashlight she'd used at the pool house and aimed the beam at the rocks in front of her. Nearly slipping more than once, she vaulted over them and into the mouth of the cave, screaming Kyra and Griffin's names.

Inside, the cave was completely silent save for the gentle drip of water from the ceiling. Selena's flashlight lit up the wet rocks and a matching set of tracks in the sand. She set off after them as Simon shouted her name behind her.

She ignored him, aiming her light down the passageway, looking for Kyra and Griffin's silhouettes as she pressed on deeper into the cave. She was so intent on looking for them in front of her that she failed to look down until her boot connected with something soft that let out a faint *crack* under her weight.

Selena froze. Not breathing, she took half a step back. She moved her flashlight from the wall slowly to the ground. At first, she thought she'd found a piece of bleached driftwood until it became apparent its shape was too rounded at the edges.

Selena let out a piercing scream.

"Selena!" Simon cried out behind her. "Where are you?"

But Selena couldn't stop screaming. Not when Griffin Sergold's wide, blue eyes were staring back at her, lightless and dull. His jaw hung open so his white teeth winked at Selena like tiny pearls, tongue visible behind them. There was a lipstick stain on his neck, which hung limply at a sharp angle. His golden hair clumped in wet ropes where it dipped into the pool of blood forming beneath him. It leaked out from his chest, where the ribs had been snapped open like a maw to reveal his unmoving lungs and the empty space between them. An empty space that seemed much, much too big.

Because Griffin, dead at Selena's feet, was missing his heart.

twenty-seven

Finch was the last one to get to the sea cave.

Risa stood stock-still in the mouth of the cave while Amber retched in the corner. Finch jogged past them just to skid to a halt as she found what they were looking at.

Selena was on her knees, cradling Griffin's head in her lap as she sobbed. She tucked his hair behind his ears, his blood staining her fingers. Simon was at her side, hand on her shoulder as they shook, racked by sobs.

Finch inhaled, the smell of coppery blood clouding her thoughts.

"Selena, we have to go," Simon said. "We have to get back to Ulalume before that heart gets put to use."

"How could she do this?" Selena sobbed, tears dripping down her cheeks. "H-How...?"

"Selena, we can't help him now," Finch said. She knelt down

beside her, trying not to look directly at the corpse in her lap. "But we can still save everyone else. We just have to go *right now*."

Selena whimpered. "I can't leave him here."

Finch met her eyes. "We don't have a choice. We have to stop Kyra." She straightened, holding out her hand. "Come on."

Selena's eyes shimmered, cheeks blotchy and red. She mouthed Kyra's name, and her frown shifted into a snarl. She gently let Griffin's head go, then reached out a bloody hand to grip Finch's.

"When we find her," Selena growled, "I'm gonna rip her apart."

———————

Simon gunned it all the way to Ulalume, even as rain furiously battered against the Jeep. His wipers flailed, and the pelting raindrops looked like golden needles as they cut through the headlight beams. The girls held onto the emergency bars while Selena slumped in the front seat.

"What if there are other people down in the tunnels?" Amber asked as Simon's Jeep finally entered the Ulalume grounds, bouncing over the cobblestone road toward the dorms.

"I think Sumera's friends with pretty much everyone who goes down there regularly," Simon said. He threw the Jeep into park outside Pergman Hall, then pulled out his phone. "I'll tell her to spread the word not to go down there. Lie that there's a gas leak."

"Are you sure you want Sumera involved?" Selena asked, still numb. The last thing they needed was to bring anyone else into this nightmare.

"Maybe we can convince her to guard some of the entrances," Simon added, ignoring Selena's comment. "I will too. That's our best bet."

"Simon," Selena started again. "I—"

"I know that puts us in danger," Simon quickly cut in, "but if there's something I can do to stop some ancient god from swallowing up my home, then I'm gonna do it. It's worth the risk to me."

"Selena," Risa said, "we have to go. We don't have time."

"Right." Selena put a hand on Simon's shoulder. "Don't you dare fucking die."

He nodded. "Right back at you."

The girls descended into the tunnels, grateful to see them cleared out. Simon had been right to let Sumera know—as one of the unofficial queens of the tunnels, her word was law, and if she said not to go down, people didn't.

They dropped down from the Pergman entrance to the passageways, the air unusually damp and cold, eerily similar to the biting chill of the sea cave. Finch stood at Selena's side while Amber and Risa stuck together behind them. The only sound was the hum of electricity in the air and their quickened breathing.

Selena felt something slip into her hand and looked down to find Finch clutching it tightly in hers.

Risa pointed to the floor. "There—blood. She's been here."

"How is she moving so quickly?" Selena muttered under her breath.

"She's the closest to Nerosi," Amber whispered. "Maybe she got…extra gifts."

A shudder ran through each of them at once.

They plunged deeper into Ulalume's concrete labyrinth. The pipes above them hissed, louder and louder like they'd all begun to boil. The graffiti on the walls appeared brighter than usual, the paint practically glowing. The heavy air clung to them as they went deeper and deeper in.

Selena spotted a discarded piece of metal pipe on the floor and picked it up, brandishing it.

Finch glanced up at her, eyes wide.

"Kyra has the ability to make anyone do what she wants just by saying it." Selena let go of Finch's hand and smacked the pipe against her palm. "So I'm gonna break her jaw before she can."

"How could she do this?" Amber whispered, gesturing to another spatter of wet blood on the floor. "Kyra's never been… nice, exactly. But I never thought she could do something like this."

Selena opened her mouth, but trailed off as she saw a shadow pass over Finch's face.

"I'm not sure it's the same Kyra anymore," Finch said, eyes falling to the floor. "She's been talking to Nerosi nonstop for months now. When you want something as much as she does, sometimes you overlook the red flags. Having someone like Nerosi in your head… I don't know if she could have said no."

"You'd know plenty about that, wouldn't you?"

The girls flipped around. But the tunnels were empty.

"You all heard that, right?" Selena whispered.

Risa nodded, tensing. "Got any more pipes you want to pass along?"

The tunnels fell quiet. Selena's hands tightened on the end of her pipe as she stepped in front of Finch. Risa cracked her knuckles while Amber grabbed Risa's arm and pressed herself against her, trembling. Seconds ticked by slowly as they waited for an ambush.

"We have to keep going," Risa said. "She's just taunting us."

"All right," Selena took a step back. "Watch your backs. You never know—"

Something writhed in the corner of Selena's vision.

She swung around, pipe slashing at darkness. For a moment, she thought she'd imagined it as her makeshift weapon cut through nothing but air.

But then, with a shriek, something hit the floor.

"Amber!" Risa cried.

"Help!"

Selena spun in time to see Amber reaching out for them as something yanked her by the ankles into the darkness. She clawed at the concrete, the edges of her nails snapping off. Her screams ricocheted off the walls in a cacophony that echoed back and forth like it was a hundred voices at once.

The last thing they saw before she vanished completely was an oily tentacle lashing over her mouth, silencing her.

"Amber!" Risa screamed again. Without pause, she took off down the hall, arms pumping and sneakers slamming against the concrete.

"Wait!" Selena cried. "Risa!"

Something soft and fleshy shot out and connected with Selena's head with a smack. She stumbled, catching herself on the wall while Finch screamed. Stars skittered across her vision.

She blinked sight back into her eyes to find Kyra standing over her, grinning.

Or, at least, what used to be Kyra.

This girl's hair sparked, lifting at the ends of its own accord. Her face was waxy-pale and damp like she had a fever, and sweat soaked her shirt, torn and stained with rusty brown and black fluid.

Greasy black streaks smeared across her exposed skin, leaking droplets down her face and over her parted lips so it stained the spaces between her teeth. Her eyes glowed yellow, and her sharpened teeth curved into a wicked smile. Worse, at the center of her chest, a nest of tentacles writhed like snakes, twisting in on themselves and sloughing off more of the viscous black oil. One of them was wrapped around Finch's neck, lifting her into the air as she choked.

Lifting her hand, Kyra sunk her fingers into Griffin's soft, bloody heart.

She wheezed a laugh, black spittle dribbling from her teeth. "Hey, St. Clair. You're going to want to see this."

twenty-eight

Kyra dragged them, screaming, back to the room where everything began.

The floor still bore stains from Selena's sacrifice, but the ash had been refreshed so the lines were clear and dark against the dirt. The candles' flames burned dark purple. Overlapping circles, triangles, and stars—a strange geometry in and of itself—glowed like embers on the walls and around the antler altar.

The creature Selena had grown to know too well stood in the center of the room, waiting.

To Kyra, Nerosi said, "You've taken well to your new gift."

Kyra's stained lips split into a maniacal smile, and she laughed once, ropes of black saliva flicking from her teeth. Her grip tightened around the other girls, and Selena struggled to breathe with it constricting her chest. The tentacles were sticky, the texture something like slime-covered velvet over rock-hard, squeezing muscle. Something viscous squelched against Selena's ear as the tentacle flexed, and bile crept up her throat.

"You were right," Kyra said, her voice rising to an almost child-ish, gleeful pitch. "Fearsome is so much more useful than pretty."

"Kyra," Selena choked, trying to wriggle her arm free from the other girl's grasp. She still had the pipe in her hand, and if she could move enough, she could use it. "Open your eyes! She's using you!"

"Oh, like you used me?" Kyra said. She held the heart up to Selena's face, her pointer finger slipping into the vena cava with a squish that pushed clotted blood free. Finch gagged at Selena's side. "At least now I receive as much as I give."

Selena's eyes rolled all the way back into her head while Amber's eyes widened. "What does that mean?"

"Don't worry about it," Risa choked.

"Enough," Nerosi growled. One of the scars on her arm opened up and a slithering, snakelike tendril reached out for her. "The heart, Kyra."

"Don't!" Selena struggled hard at Kyra's grip. She met her eyes, sparking and dangerous as they were, and saw all the times they'd leaned on each other, done each other's hair, or kissed in secret behind school buildings.

"Kyra, listen." She was close to being able to turn her wrist—as revolting as the slime was, it allowed for a bit of give. She just needed to stall. "You're better than this. I know you better than anyone, and the Kyra I know would never put people in danger like this."

Kyra hesitated, the tentacles in her chest twisting slower. She was quiet.

"Come on," Selena begged. "Think about it, will you? You can choose to save everyone in Rainwater if you get rid of that heart. You don't have to be the bad guy."

"The heart," Nerosi said again. "Now."

The hesitation that had come over Kyra broke away. The tentacle holding Selena shot backward, pressing her against the wall with a yelp.

"Screw you, Selena," she snarled, moving to hand over the heart to Nerosi. "You did this to me."

Whether or not that was true, Selena had managed to free her wrist.

She stabbed the pipe deep into Kyra's tentacle.

Kyra screamed, and the heart dropped to the floor. The tentacle loosened, and Selena slipped free, landing on her feet. She leaped across the room, but another tentacle lashed out and sent her flying against the wall. Her body connected with a sickening crack and her vision turned red.

"Kyra, no!" Risa shouted. "Don't be stupid about this! You'll kill everyone you care about!"

"I don't want to die!" Amber sobbed.

"Please," Finch begged. "Don't let her control you."

Selena lifted her head, vision clearing.

Kyra was looking at her. She had the heart back in her hand, dusty with ash. Her mouth pulled into a grin.

Kyra handed the heart to Nerosi.

And she swallowed it whole.

Finch screamed, but the sound was lost to chaos exploding before her.

Nerosi's body lost the last of its translucence as a wicked smile cracked across her pale face. The air around her began to shimmer violently as reality warped and distorted. A stabbing pain shot through Finch's brain and she let out a scream.

All at once, every single scar on Nerosi's body opened up and wriggling flesh burst forth, slick with liquid and writhing as it took shape. She was now the size of a bus, with four clusters of tentacles that served as her legs. Her torso and neck were vaguely deerlike, the long neck leading up to a head with five faces with thick snouts full of wolf-like teeth. She had bony antlers atop her head, fresh velvet supplying them with ichor.

This is what the others had meant when they called her the Horned Queen.

At first glance, Nerosi's skin seemed to gurgle and seethe, but Finch soon realized the monster was instead coated in half-formed human faces and limbs that pressed against the skin as if fighting to tear free before descending into its guts once more. Eyes popped open randomly across the entire creature, whether they were on the neck or inside one of the mouths. Its bones protruded, the spine vertebrae exposed and curving into sharp, serrated points.

The god let out a low, rumbling laugh.

Selena screamed, "Run!"

In her shock, Kyra had lost her grip on the other girls, and they tore free of her grasp. The four of them bolted.

"What do we do?!" Amber screamed as they raced down the dirt corridor toward the regular tunnels. Behind them, Nerosi's five snouts cracked open and she let out a multitone shriek that made the girls clap their hands over their ears.

"Keep running!" Risa cried.

They crossed over the threshold between the natural and concrete tunnels. Their footsteps echoed through the corridor while the ground shook beneath them.

"Finch," Selena gasped, "You need to open that rift before she gets out of the tunnels."

Her eyes rounded. "N-Now? B-But I can't—"

Selena looked over her shoulder, cursing under her breath. "You're gonna have to."

Finch looked back to find Kyra stepping out of the altar room, Nerosi's gruesome form spilling out after her. Both sets of their tentacles lashed, smiles open and hungry.

"You keep going." Selena told the others, clenching her jaw. "I'll hold them off once they get through the door."

Finch shook her head, eyes wild. "Selena, you can't—"

"Focus on your powers," Selena said, brandishing her pipe. "I'll be right behind you."

Risa grabbed Finch's wrist before she could say another word and dragged her away.

The three of them sprinted, hearing distant screeches behind them. Finch kept checking over her shoulder, waiting for Selena to appear, but she didn't. Risa kept her hand locked around Finch's wrist as she dragged her forward, never letting her slow down, even as the ground trembled beneath their feet and the lights flickered wildly overhead.

The girls burst into a wider section of the tunnels, a huge room that made Finch go cold. Standing in front of the ladder to the surface was Simon, ready to stop anyone from descending.

"Simon!" Finch shrieked, acute panic hitting her at the sight of him. Voice choked as images of Nerosi tearing him apart filled her mind, she cried, "Run!"

"Where's Selena?" he demanded.

"Behind us," Risa said. She spun, digging her nails into Finch's arm until she looked at her. Risa's eyebrows were bent, gaze sharp enough to cut. "What did Selena mean by powers? What can you do?"

"I-I—" Finch stammered, glancing between them. "I can—sort of—maybe open a rift to the void. I might be able to stop Nerosi but I've never—I don't think I can do it, not when she's like this—"

"Do you want Simon to die?" Risa asked her, eyes never breaking contact with hers. "Amber? Me? Selena? Because it sounds like unless you do something, that's what's going to happen!"

"Come on, Finch," Amber begged. "Just try."

Finch glanced up at Simon. He nodded, urging her on, while looking like he might throw up at any moment.

"O-Okay." Finch nodded to herself and bit her lip. She'd never done this without Selena nearby to ground her. Images of her consciousness trapped in the vision of her parents' death flashed back to her, but she shook her head to ward it away. She took a breath.

"Okay. I'll try."

While the other girls escaped down the hallway, Kyra barreled toward Selena, mouth open and jaw unnaturally distorted so that additional hooked teeth burst free from her blackened gums. Behind her, Nerosi lumbered forward with impressive speed. The smell of decay grew stronger and stronger the closer she got—her new body seemed to be rapidly decomposing. It was a terrible sort of sweet, like fruit left to rot in the sun.

Selena tightened her grip around her pipe, then slid sideways.

She smashed the pipe down on a hissing valve that instantly snapped free. Boiling water shot out and steam burst into the air. Nerosi let out a disoriented snarl while Kyra screeched. The water scalded Kyra's face and neck, leaving them a violent shade of red.

One of Kyra's tentacles shot out wildly, grabbing for Selena, but she was faster. She took a running swing at another valve that skittered to the floor, flooding the concrete with another hissing stream of hot water.

"Sorry, thought you might need a shower," Selena taunted, throwing her arms up at her sides. "Because frankly, you smell like shit."

Another tentacle shot for her, but the steam in the air acted as a smoke screen, letting Selena step out of the way and vanish into the mist. Kyra cried out, higher and more piercing than before. Selena ground her teeth, wincing at the sound.

She spun, sneakers splashing through the puddles on the floor, and sprinted in the other direction.

The monsters trailed behind her, the scent of boiled meat mixing with the rotting stink in the air. Selena used her pipe to snap every valve she saw, leaving columns of water shooting out behind her, hissing and spitting. At one point, she thought she heard Kyra howling her name, but it was lost to the sound of water slamming into the ground.

Selena kept running until the large entrance room that led up to Pergman came into view. Risa and Amber stood on either side of Finch, whose head hung, her hair in front of her face. Simon wasn't far away, staring wide-eyed as Finch's outstretched hand twitched and grabbed at the air in jerky starts and stops.

"Selena!" Amber cried at the sight of her. She sounded breathless. "You—you have to help! I-I don't think Finch's powers are—"

Before she could finish, a shadow vaulted over Selena's head. Kyra landed between the two of them, the tentacles in her chest fanned out like a twisted chrysanthemum in bloom. Simon yelped and swore colorfully.

"You dragged him into all this?" Kyra said, extra teeth gnashing. "You are a terrible friend."

Selena's heart sputtered. Kyra had already killed Griffin—there was nothing stopping her from getting to Simon.

That is, until Risa spun, drawing something from her purse. "Quiet, Kyra."

The next moment, she aimed a can of mace and a lighter at Kyra, the aerosol catching fire and bathing her tentacles in flame. Kyra screeched, stumbling back as the fire licked up the writhing mass toward her face. She hit the floor, screaming, skin sizzling, the smoke smelling unsettlingly like burnt bacon.

From behind them, another unearthly cry shook the floor. The sound sent cracks shooting up the concrete walls.

Nerosi had arrived.

The creature squeezed halfway through the door, neck twisting in quick, cracking succession as her heads surveyed the room. The stink was enough to make Selena dizzy, desperation clawing at her to get out to fresh air before it choked her.

"Finch!" Selena called. "You have to do it now!"

Slowly, Finch raised her head, hair falling back away from her face. Selena's breath caught as she realized there was a faint rippling aura surrounding her, and her entire body was shaking. Her eyes were jet-black.

"Kill them," Kyra spat.

But Nerosi wasn't moving. Her faces all focused on Finch. While Finch's hand trembled in the air, the warped color around her grew brighter. Aside from Finch's shaking, they both appeared to be fully paralyzed.

Kyra let out a snarl, dragging herself to her feet.

"Fine," she growled. "I'll just do it myself."

She attacked.

———————

Finch stood in total darkness.

The tunnels had vanished behind her, and even the sight of Nerosi's true form wasn't enough to ground Finch in reality as she desperately opened the conduit between the two of them. Instantly, she'd felt Nerosi's power begin to flow into her chest, the grip around her heart growing tighter. When she practiced with Selena, she would draw the power to her more gradually but now, panic speeding her pulse to a crescendo, she'd drawn it all toward her at once.

And now, she was drowning.

From the darkness sprang visions of a place that looked like an alien planet in a science-fiction movie. The dry, chalky ground cracked like chapped lips, while gnarled blue-green trees twisted out between the fissures. Lakes of shadow cut between the trees before her, roiling like the sea. Figures moved in the woods, screams echoing off unseen walls. Long purple grass sprouted from the stumps of trees, and flowers with icy-blue veins pulsed like they had a heartbeat.

"Do you like my home?"

Finch spun. Nerosi, in the humanoid form she'd first met her in, stood behind her. She had her hands folded in front of her, long white hair swept over one shoulder.

"What is this place?" Finch demanded.

"I told you—it's where I come from." Nerosi reached out and ran her hand along the knotted bark of one of the trees. "Beautiful, isn't it?"

Finch gritted her teeth. She squared her shoulders, fists clenching at her sides. This was the monster that had ripped her life away from her. Part of her feared the heat with which her rage burned within her, but another—most of her, in fact—welcomed it.

"Why are you doing this?" Finch asked. "That's the only thing I don't understand. What do you get out of all this needless death? Is it power?"

Nerosi didn't offer any sort of reaction. "How are you to understand the intentions of a god?"

She turned, meeting Finch's eyes. For the first time, Finch didn't wince away at the sight of them, but took them in fully for the first time. She noticed that they weren't just black mirrors—no, instead there were tiny pinpricks of light inside, and the longer Finch stared, she realized it wasn't even mere stars. No, contained within each shining orb was the form of an entire galaxy, vast in a way that stole Finch's breath from her chest.

A cold horror washed over her at once.

This creature was no mere monster. She was something much, much larger than that.

"You see them?" Nerosi asked, unblinking. "The worlds I've consumed? Your tiny town means nothing to me. I want it *all*."

She pointed to a scar on her arm and it opened to reveal another of the black orbs, star clusters trapped within like a mosquito in amber. "Nothing else will sate my hunger."

Finch's head spun, unable to wrap around what she was saying. There was no way this creature could absorb entire realities and store them beneath the skin—right? It was impossible, the scale of it unthinkable.

"I have to thank you, though." Nerosi's hand passed over the scar so it stitched closed over the orb. "I never would have been able to enter your reality without you. When I brought you back, I anchored myself within you. The way that realities stitch together—it's quite difficult to pass between them once you've gotten lost in the void around them. But you made it possible for me to manifest that small part of myself down in the tunnels. Thank you for that."

Finch shook her head, feeling sick to her stomach. "Why me?"

"Oh, Finch." Nerosi pressed a hand to her chest. "Because of that little heart of yours. How strongly it wants—I guess I saw a bit of myself in you. We share a longing—that ache you can't escape. Granted, your goals were much smaller than mine, but still. We're one and the same."

"If I'm so insignificant, why are you wasting your time on me?" Finch asked. "And on my friends? Why don't you tear apart this world and swallow it like you did with the others?"

Nerosi chuckled, not unpleasantly. "Oh, I intend to. It's just that I need all my power to do so, and I'm missing a piece."

She reached out a hand, pointing to Finch's chest. "The tiny little spark I loaned you to keep you alive. I'm afraid I need it back."

Finch clapped a hand over her heart, taking a step back.

Nerosi held up her hands. "It will be much easier if you give up, Finch. I can't take something that isn't willingly given. But then, if you resist, I have ways to force you to give it back, and you won't like them."

Finch's fingers clutched at her chest, lips drawing back from her teeth in a snarl.

"*Never.*"

"Pity." Nerosi squared her shoulders and took a breath. Two new mouths cracked open in her cheeks, and three voices at once said, "Goodbye, Finch Chamberlin."

The fist around her heart closed.

twenty-nine

Selena looked up long enough from fighting Kyra to see Finch tilt her head back and scream.

Nerosi let out a shriek as well that made the girls clap their hands over their ears. She began to sway, tentacles writhing as Finch dropped to her knees, clawing at the sides of her head.

In the moment of distraction, Selena ran to Finch's side. She slid onto her knees in front of her. She reached out, grabbing Finch's hands and squeezing them so hard the bones inside cracked.

"Finch," Selena said as the other girl's muscles writhed and twitched, seemingly of their own accord. "Finch, listen to me. You have to keep fighting her. If you can't open the rift, we're going to die here. But I know you can, you just have to—"

One of Kyra's tentacles shot out from nowhere, wrapping around Selena before wrenching her out of Finch's grasp. Kyra launched her across the room.

Selena flew head over heels into the wall. Red bursts danced across her vision. Her body slumped to the floor and a tinny screech filled her ears.

Kyra cackled. She had burns all over her face and neck—the skin cracked and splitting, blisters bubbling up in swaths.

Distracted by Selena, Kyra didn't see Amber come at her with a pocketknife. The blade flashed before Amber sliced it across Kyra's face, a spatter of black fluid spraying out and drenching Amber.

"That's for calling me an idiot," Amber snarled.

But Kyra was fast—a flying tentacle caught Amber around the throat, lifting her from the ground. Her legs bicycled as she struggled against Kyra's grip. Slime and hungry suckers squelched against Amber's neck.

"No!" Risa screamed. She ran and jumped for the tentacle holding Amber, clawing at it. Skin tore off in her hands like wet tissue paper.

Kyra flung them both back. Selena heard bone crack as they hit the floor.

A shock of pain splintered through Selena's nerves when she tried to get up. She smelled her own blood, sharp as copper against the lingering smell of raw sewage and catfish and moldy peaches. Nearby, Simon screamed. Selena willed herself to get up, but her limbs shook. *Am I going into shock?*

Weakness began to overtake her, blotting out her thoughts.

If she hits me again, Selena realized, *that's it.*

I'll die.

She tried once more to stand, but collapsed. Before her, the creature that had once been Kyra bore down on her. It would be impossible to escape her now.

Selena shut her eyes, tears sliding free. Finch's face shimmered in her mind's eye, gentle and kind and forgiving as always. Selena sputtered a sob. "I'm sorry."

She braced herself for the killing blow.

Finch's consciousness began to unravel.

The vision of Nerosi's home twisted and fell away, replaced by the inky darkness of the void. Nerosi's attack manifested in a feeling like hooks stabbing into the folds of Finch's mind and pulling it in different directions. She screamed, pain the only thing her mind could focus on.

The hand around her heart tugged. Nerosi's voice boomed in Finch's head: *Give up and it will stop.*

The words sounded foreign through the sensation of tearing and boiling that had bloomed within every nerve. She was both on fire and very cold, her mind losing its ability to distinguish between the pain in her mind and in her body—if, in fact, she still had one. She'd lost feeling in her physical body long ago.

She was nothing, no one but searing agony incarnate. There was no Finch, no girl with white hair and a slow heart. All she knew was this.

Until, gently, she felt a single sensation that wasn't pain.

It was a soft grip, holding her hands. It was such a shock that Finch's eyes focused, her real ones, and for a moment Nerosi's true form and its swaying tentacles and hungry mouths stared down at her.

And in front of them, Selena.

Her hair was a tangled mess, blood leaking from her nose and staining her hands. She sat on her knees, warm hands gripping Finch's. She had cuts and bruises up and down her pale arms, staining her skin like inkblots. Her clothes were torn, and her green eyes shone brightly.

For a moment, Finch couldn't hear her. She fought the roar of agony in her mind enough to focus in and catch as Selena said, "I know you can beat her."

A tentacle snatched her away in a blur.

Finch couldn't find her voice to speak, but her lips spelled Selena's name. Before her, Nerosi took a lumbering step forward, all of her eyes boring down at her. The sight of them and the rippling distortion in the air was nearly enough to drag her mind back into darkness.

Instead, she staggered to her feet.

"Are you finished?" Nerosi asked, her voice coming from all four snouts and from within Finch's mind, creating a discordant growl.

Finch held out a hand, once again opening the conduit between them. The shift was so sudden that Nerosi's eyes widened, seeming to realize what was happening.

Finch let out a cry as a floodgate opened between them, and she tore open the air in front of her.

A noise between a wail and a war cry shook the room.

Selena forced open her eyes.

A blinding light filled the room, so bright it left spots in Selena's vision. When they finally faded away, what she saw in the middle of the room made her heart skip a beat.

Standing at the center of the room was Finch, radiating an aura so bright it was almost like staring into the sun. In front of her, slashing through the air, was a rift of darkness like she had torn through the skin of reality to reveal the emptiness inside.

Selena gasped.

The rift yawned wider, and a wind seemed to whip up from within. At first Selena thought it was swirling around the room, but as Nerosi let out a guttural cry, she realized the rift was pulling Nerosi toward it like a black hole. The god's tentacles lashed out for something to grab on to.

Unfortunately, all they found was Finch.

Finch didn't react as she was torn from the spot she'd anchored herself to. Nerosi began to squeeze her, tentacles tight around her neck.

Finch silently choked. The rift behind her instantly began to flicker, stitching closed at the edges.

"No!" Selena cried.

She sprang up, shot with adrenaline all over again. Even as her muscles screamed in protest and her vision swam, she ran full-tilt toward Nerosi. She bent her knees and launched herself onto the monster's back.

A human face embedded in Nerosi's flesh beneath Selena shrieked. Nerosi reared back to shake her off, head smashing into the ceiling as she did. Concrete rained down. Selena sunk her fingers into yet another one of the faces, even as its gaping maw bit at her skin. A tentacle whipped around to pry her off, but she jumped and tore into another part of the god's corporeal form before it could reach her.

As Selena dug her fingers into the god's skin, she realized she'd landed on her rib cage. A big swath of flesh was gone, revealing the pearly bones beneath.

And Griffin's beating, human heart in her chest.

Selena knew what she had to do.

Hanging on with one hand, she plunged a hand into her jacket pocket, withdrawing the object inside. It was a jagged piece of curved antler—the one she'd snapped off the eight-eyed stag.

With a vengeful cry, Selena drove the antler into Nerosi's heart.

Black ichor and blood spurted against Selena as Nerosi shrieked in pain. She jerked, the force enough to send Selena and Finch both tumbling to the floor. Selena hit the concrete, pain shooting through her bones and up her nerves.

Finch gasped for breath beside her, hand on her bruised throat. Above her, the god continued to shriek. The rift had nearly closed, little more than a tiny scar in the air now.

"Finch," Selena said, dragging herself to the other girl's side. "You have to open it again."

Finch looked up at her. Her eyes were shining with tears and the skin around her throat was an angry red. There were hollows beneath her eyes and bruises all over her body. Blood leaked out of the corner of her mouth, staining her pale lips.

Selena tightened her fingers around Finch's. "You can do this."

Finch met Selena's eyes once more, gripped her hand, and nodded. She held out a hand toward the closing rift.

Reality in front of them began to warp once again as Finch channeled her power. Selena felt it radiating through her fingers. The air rippled and then tore, the rift extending even taller than it had been before. Finch's eyes went black as she stared into it, brow furrowing in concentration.

Nerosi let out another scream as the void dragged her inside. Her tentacles desperately grabbed at the edge of the rift, catching the sides of it. Each of her snouts snarled, snapping at the air.

"No!"

From the corner of her eye, Selena saw Kyra struggling to stand. Dragging herself half with her arms and half with her tentacles, she crawled toward the rift, reaching for Nerosi.

Finch's fingers twitched as the edges of the rift closed and Nerosi was jerked farther inside. Only a few tentacles remained on the outside, clinging to the ragged edges of the tear in reality. She let out another inhuman scream as her grip loosened.

Selena opened her mouth to cry out, but Kyra was already in front of the rift, reaching out for Nerosi.

All at once, Nerosi lashed out a tentacle to grab Kyra and lost her grip on the rift. Kyra screamed as she was wrenched from the concrete. Her hand barely caught the edge of the rift as the void tried to suck her inside.

"Kyra!" Selena screamed. She moved to stand, but Finch gripped her hand tighter. The other girl's eyes were black, and her expression was entirely blank, but the message was clear enough.

If Selena let go, Finch would be unmoored.

Her gaze fell on Kyra once more. Kyra, who had been her best friend. The same friend who used to take selfies with her on city streets, dress her in designer clothes to go out for the evening, who ran her fingers through her hair and told her she was the prettiest girl she'd ever seen.

But this was also the Kyra who had outed her purely out of spite. Who hadn't hesitated to step on her friends to get ahead. And who had fallen so far as to rip out Griffin's heart with her own two hands.

No matter how much she still wanted to, despite everything, Selena couldn't save Kyra from herself.

"I'm sorry," Selena whispered.

Kyra's face barely had time to curl into a snarl before her fingers slipped.

She and Nerosi tumbled backward into the dark.

The edges of the rift shimmered before it closed and vanished.

For a moment, all was quiet. Finch's eyes flickered back to normal, and she gasped for breath. Her skin was slick with sweat and blood and ichor.

Finch's eyes met Selena's. "Did it work?"

Tears filled Selena's eyes. She threw herself at Finch, hugging her so hard it cracked something in her back. Finch slowly wrapped her arms around Selena, pressing her face into her neck.

"Yes," she said, failing to hold back a sob. "Yes, it worked. We did it. We won."

"Oh." Finch let out a weak laugh. "Who'd've thought?"

All Selena could do was cry, which was unfortunate because that meant when Finch kissed her the next second, all of her tears rubbed off on her. Selena laughed and sobbed all at once. Then, she kissed her back.

Because, if for only that moment, they were safe.

And they were free.

epilogue
[three months later]

Winter fell on the Ulalume campus with a heavy blanket of snow that lined the cobblestone paths, covered the tops of the curved lampposts, and hung icicles at the edge of the buildings' Gothic-style roofs. The temperature refused to rise above freezing most days, even when the sun was shining brightly overhead.

Nine months after her death, Finch stared out at the campus with a small smile on her face. She was curled up in a bay window in the common area in Pergman Hall, nursing a cup of tea while she stared at the snow falling outside—they'd already gotten almost a foot that week, but it was tapering off. Yesterday Finch had woken up just in time for Selena to drag her to the all-school snowball fight being waged on the quad.

Steam curled from the mug and against her cheeks. The window at her side fogged up, and Finch drew a smile on it with her fingertip.

Sumera, joining her on the bench, asked, "Is it too strong? I always make it too strong."

Finch shook her head. "No. I like your strong chai."

Sumera smiled at her. While she hadn't been forced to witness the horror of that day in November, she'd felt the fallout of it as much as everyone else. She'd been there when they heard word the coroner had declared Griffin's death the result of an animal attack, effectively shoving it under the rug. She'd also attended the funeral at Rainwater High with Finch, Selena, Risa, and Amber. And on the nights when Finch couldn't sleep because of nightmares, she'd stay up and watch movies with her until they both fell asleep on the couch.

Finch couldn't thank her enough for that.

"I like your hair, by the way," Sumera said, pulling her knees up to her chest.

Finch smiled, reaching up so her fingers brushed the newly shaved sides of her undercut. She hadn't told anyone she was getting it—it was more for herself. These days, every time she looked in the mirror and saw her white hair and pale skin, she sometimes had a hard time seeing herself behind them. The sight of her hair as it had grown out had begun to conjure images of the monster in the tunnels, with her long white locks and jagged smile.

So she'd gotten it cut—and dyed it back to her natural, chestnut brown shade. It felt like reclaiming a part of herself she hadn't realized she'd been missing.

"It's very gay," Finch laughed.

"Indeed." Sumera grinned. "It suits you. And Selena's going to absolutely lose it when she sees you."

Finch's chest filled with warmth at the sound of her

girlfriend's name. With Nerosi gone, they'd finally been able to do the things normal couples were supposed to: go out to movies together, kiss in the hall between classes, and take trips into the city to go shopping and take pictures at the beach. Last week, they'd even accidentally mistimed when Sumera was getting back from volleyball and got caught in a compromising situation on the couch in the dorm room. Luckily, Sumera was putting a lot more effort into restoring her friendship with Selena, so she let it go pretty quickly.

Just then, Finch's phone buzzed, and as her eyes scanned the message, she hopped to her feet. "Selena heard back from the Boston Conservatory."

Sumera's eyebrows shot up. "Did she get in?"

"She's waiting for me to get there before she opens the email." Finch stuffed her phone in her pocket and quickly finished her chai, setting the mug down on a coffee table. "Sorry, I have to go, but let's plan on watching that documentary together later."

"The one about the Isabella Stewart Gardner heist?" Sumera clarified. She smiled. "Count on it."

Finch waved goodbye before heading toward Annalee Lighthouse.

Selena sat in front of her laptop, nervously tapping her foot as she waited for Finch to arrive. Simon sat on one side of her while her moms tried to angle their iPad so both of them were on-screen and could see Selena. Roxane and Simon were chatting about his recent acceptance to Emerson College and planning how they might spend Thanksgiving together in the fall. Selena's other mom, Zinnia, had her arm around Roxane and kept gently reminding Selena to breathe.

"I'm here!" Finch called as she stepped through the front door, quickly kicking off her snow boots and running to join Selena on the couch.

Selena glanced at her, then immediately did a double take. "Holy shit, your hair."

Finch blushed. "Is that a good *holy shit* or—"

"You look so cute!" Selena reached out and rubbed the shaved sides, almost forgetting for a moment how wildly anxious she was. "How could you not warn me about this? Finch, my moms are here."

Roxane and Zinnia St. Clair waved from the iPad. Roxane said, "It looks lovely, Finch."

Finch managed a weak smile. She had met Selena's moms a couple times now, and Selena was convinced that Roxane might like her more than her own daughter based purely on the fact that Finch always did her own dishes and didn't drink milk straight out of the carton.

Finch offered a quiet thank you to Roxane while Selena cut in and said, "Okay, no more stalling. I'm going to do it."

Finch slid her hand into Selena's. "Good luck."

With a shaking hand, she went to the student portal and tapped on the decision letter.

The first word she spotted at the top, in big letters, was CONGRATULATIONS.

Selena jumped to her feet. "I got in!"

Simon, her moms, and Finch all shouted at once. Simon threw his arms around her while Finch leaned in to give her a kiss on the

cheek. Selena turned and swept her up in her arms, spinning her
around and shrieking with joy.

"You earned it," Finch said as soon as Selena finally put her
down. "More than anyone."

"Fuck yeah I did!" Selena slapped a high five with Simon and
told her moms, "When I come down to see you this weekend, we're
going to Citrus & Salt, and I'm stealing some of your margaritas."

While Zinnia nodded and grinned, Roxane, stone-faced, said,
"Absolutely not, Selena Rose. And watch your mouth."

"I was talking to my cool mom," Selena jeered. She winked at
Zinnia, who winked back.

"You're both invited as well," Zinnia said to Simon and Finch.
"Mocktails all around."

The five of them chatted for a few more minutes before Selena
ended the call, bidding them goodbye and promising to talk more
soon about weekend Amtrak tickets.

Around then, the front door opened, and Risa and Amber
stepped inside, kicking off their snow boots. Amber was laughing
at something Risa had said.

"Guys, I got into the conservatory!" Selena cried.

Amber threw up her arms and then launched herself at Selena
for a hug while Risa nodded and congratulated her as well. Amber
started talking about how she was waiting to hear back from
Boston University while Risa added that, since she had recently
gotten into MIT, she'd only be a few miles away from Selena in
Cambridge.

Selena threw an arm around Finch. "Once you get into the
music program at Berklee, Boston's not gonna know what hit it."

Finch smiled. "Yeah! It'll be nice to have all of us around."

All of us.

Selena's smile faltered. Not for the first time, Selena found herself staring at the closed door at the edge of the hallway.

Kyra's parents had shown up a few weeks after she "disappeared" to look through her things. Local police had already combed through it and come to a familiar conclusion: because her phone, purse, and coat were all missing, Kyra was probably a runaway.

Now that she was gone, her parents had collected her things and brought them back to New York. The room was empty. Sometimes at night, Selena would go inside and sit on the floor, just to see if she could still sense some piece of her inside.

"Selena?" Finch asked. "Is everything okay?"

"Oh! Yeah, sorry. Got distracted thinking about everything I'll have to show you in Boston." Selena put on a smile. "Listen, let's get out of here. There's a massive celebratory chocolate shake at Octavia's with my name on it."

Later that night after a truly baffling amount of dairy and french fries, Selena brought Finch up to her room, shutting the door behind them.

They laid down, side by side, on Selena's bed, their legs woven together and Selena's thumb gently running over the angle of Finch's chin. The night outside was bitter cold, but here, underneath Selena's floral-print bedspread, Finch felt as warm as she possibly could. The sea outside hummed in her ear, along with the soft sound of Selena's breath through her nose.

"Selena? Can I ask you something?" When she nodded, Finch

went on, "Earlier, before we went to Octavia's...what were you thinking about? It seemed like something was bugging you."

Selena bit her lip. She hadn't talked much with Finch about Kyra since that night in the tunnels. In fact, she hadn't talked to anyone about it. It felt like too much of a burden to put on someone else.

Still, if she trusted anyone in this world, it was Finch.

"I was thinking about Kyra. And how I didn't try to save her when everything happened." Selena closed her eyes. "I know that I probably couldn't have done anything but...even after everything, I still care about her. Not in the way she wanted me to, obviously. But I still wish I could have done something."

Finch reached out, sliding her fingers into Selena's. "I know how you feel. I still feel guilty for what happened to my parents sometimes. But you can't blame yourself."

Selena nodded to herself. "I guess the past is in the past. It's just hard sometimes to wrap my head around the fact that she's gone." She lowered her voice. "And that...Nerosi is too."

Finch went quiet. She reached up, pressing a hand to her chest.

"She's gone, Finch," Selena repeated. "Really."

Finch nodded. "I know, I know. It's just...the piece of her that brought me back—it's still in there. As long as I'm alive, she's going to be with me, even if it's only this little bit."

"Hey." Selena gently kissed the crown of her head. "If somewhere, somehow, Nerosi ever tried to hurt you again? I'll be there. We got through it together, and if anything else happens, we'll get through that too."

Finch's eyes shimmered for a moment before she tilted her head up to press her lips to Selena's, knotting her fingers into her hair and holding her tightly against her. Selena caught her bottom lip between hers and kissed back harder, her fingers finding the skin on Finch's back and scraping softly against it. Finch felt Selena's heartbeat, sure and strong, just like her.

Finch pulled back, pressing her forehead against Selena's. "I love you, Selena."

The other girl's eyes flashed open. "You what?"

The second she said it, Finch clapped a hand over her mouth. She hadn't meant to say that out loud.

"Um—" she flushed. "Oh my god. No—um, I'm so sorry, that was way too sudden. I didn't mean to—"

"You seriously did not just blurt that out." Selena was already laughing, tugging Finch closer to her and smiling wider than Finch had ever seen. She kissed her on the mouth, then all over her face, hands all over her at once as she laughed through each kiss. "I cannot believe you sometimes. You're absolutely impossible."

But then, she said, "I love you too."

Finch's entire body flooded with warmth.

Whatever the future might bring, whatever darkness might be lurking around the corner, she'd always have this.

[acknowledgments]

The problem with taking ten years to write a book is that it feels like there are a million people I need to thank and only so many I can include, so if you've impacted the creation of this book in any way whatsoever, know that I am eternally grateful.

To my badass agent, Erica Bauman: your unwavering support and faith in me—even when I'm freaking out over the phone about whatever my publishing anxiety du jour is or just chattering about my cat nonstop—will never go unnoticed. I am incredibly lucky to have you in my corner.

To my editor, Annie Berger, who decided to give this deeply weird, creepy, and queer book a chance: you shaped this story into something beyond what I ever thought it could be. You and the entire team at Sourcebooks made what felt like an impossible dream come true—a simple thank-you isn't nearly enough to sum up my gratitude, but it will have to do.

Speaking of the team at Sourcebooks: to Cassie Gutman, Stephanie Cohen Perez, Nicole Hower, Kerri Resnick, Beth Oleniczak, Madison Nankervis, Jenny Lopez, and everyone else who had a hand in making this book what is, a million times thank you. Your work behind the scenes is very much appreciated.

To my critique partners, Ally Larcom and Alex Moore: you've read this book SO MANY TIMES it's not even funny. In Alex's case, you've read a new version of it every other year since we were, like, fifteen? DAMN. Thank you both for your feedback, and more importantly, for your friendship.

To my early readers Jenny, Alice, and the wonderful students of Dan Weaver's Book Editing course at Emerson College: thank you for putting this story in perspective and offering so many clever ideas to make it better.

To my friends, Courtney, Kim, Rachel, Abby, and Kathryn—thank you for not only living in the same apartment as me at various times over the last few years, but also being there for me when I needed help with everything from plot tweaks to author photos. And to Claire, Erin, Rose, Ronna, Elizabeth, Simone, Forrest, and Ally (once again) for getting me through quarantine. I'm blessed to have such talented, fun people in my life who support me as much as you all.

Thank you to my brother, Colin, for always making me laugh, my sister, Kasidy, for being the legit coolest person I know, and my nephew, Vincente, for having the creative wit that only a kid can have. And to my parents, Scott and Karen, who have always supported me in this wild journey. I'm sorry for killing off Finch's parents—I promise I'll treat the parents better in the next book. Maybe.

Finally, to all the educators, librarians, booksellers, and readers who I've been lucky enough to have in my life: your love and support is what makes all this worth it. For that, thank you.

[about the author]

Kayla Cottingham is a YA author and librarian. Originally from Salt Lake City, Utah, Kayla lives in Boston, where she loves to go hiking in the woods, pet any and all dogs, and play RPGs. She is passionate about connecting young people with books featuring diverse voices so they can see themselves and their communities represented on the page. *My Dearest Darkest* is her debut novel.

FIREreads

#getbooklit

Your hub for the hottest young adult books!

Visit us online and sign up for our
newsletter at FIREreads.com

 @sourcebooksfire

 sourcebooksfire

 firereads.tumblr.com